THE COMPANY OF FIENDS

Tempting Monsters, Book Two

KATHRYN MOON

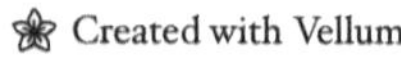 Created with Vellum

FOREWORD AND CONTENT INFORMATION

Thank you so much for returning to the Tempting Monsters universe! For a complete list of content information *please* check out kathrynmoon.com/books but here are some pertinent details!

This is a why choose monster romance with mature themes and includes mf, mmf, mmfmmmm, and mm content. (These abbreviations make me cackle to pronounce.)

Sexy Stuff Includes (all consensual): D/s master/pet dynamics, pain/pleasure play (extreme heightened sensation, no physical damage)

Content Warnings Include: murder (off page discussion and on page action), violence (strangulation, gore, magical spoilery violence, all in scenes of action and conflict), past family emotional trauma

Note on golems: Prior to this publication I discovered that my use of the term 'golem' in A Lady of Rooksgrave Manor was inaccurate and insensitive. I'm no longer going to be using it in reference to any of the lovely marble statue men like Booker, they'll simply be called what they are, which is enchanted statues. My apologies to have caused any offense by my wrongful use of a beautiful piece of Jewish mythology!

CONTENTS

PROLOGUE

There was something about the theater that reminded me of a church. Or what I imagined of them. Pa had never taken me inside one. I think he was afraid of me being struck down by the Lord's might. We'd passed by their open doors on Sunday mornings, bells ringing above our heads and the busy conversation floating out from the pews inside, Pa's grip tight around my wrist, dragging me through the busy streets of London.

Now I stood alone in the empty center aisle, rows and rows of red velvet seats at my sides—stained and worn cushions waiting for their patrons—and gazed up at the barren stage. Even my breaths echoed in that hollowness, the cavern of air ahead of me, unlit and unoccupied until this evening. The sounds of the company backstage—the laughing and crashing and calls of orders—were as much a blur as the many voices of prayer from those churches years ago. There was even a vast organ taking up the wall to the right of the stage, although I imagined it wasn't chorales and hymns it would deliver to audiences.

Forgive me, Pa, I thought, walking slowly forward and staring at the dark floorboards, scuffed and marked with chalk. *I think this is the only place left for me.*

"Hello."

I startled in place, searching the seats around me, the doors, and the stage, until I finally caught a giant shadow shrouded in the darkness behind the barely parted curtains.

"I... I'm here to speak with Mr. Reddy," I stuttered out, shuffling closer, my eyes on the shadow.

Was it enormous because he was up on the stage, towering over me, even from so far away, or—

The figure stepped forward into the dim light, and even though I'd promised myself I wouldn't, a gasp escaped my lips. It, he, was one of *them*—a monster. He was giant, after all, not just an illusion from the stage, with three vivid green eyes studying me from above, a long dark tail trailing behind him on the ground, and several arms visible, the lowest pair crossed over his stomach.

Pa had hidden me from this world as much as he was able, and the only monsters I'd ever met had come to our tiny flat disguised as humans. In truth, Pa had hidden me from humans too.

"You'll be the new girl," the man on the stage said, his two symmetrical eyes squinting, the one centered above growing wider, all fixed to me.

"Y-yes," I said, nodding, my hands wringing at my back.

He nodded and pointed to my left, an entirely new arm revealed at his back, six in total. "There's a set of stairs up to the stage from there. It's the easiest route if you come through the theater. But no one does. You'll learn your way around eventually."

I sighed and hurried through the aisles of seats to the hollow, black left doorway. His voice was melodic and low, carrying from the floorboards up to the walkways and rafters, a comforting contrast to my first understanding of the difference between myself and a monster. I fumbled my way up the short dark flight of stairs, my breath hitching as I looked up to find him nearby again.

He was even more enormous up close, my head barely reaching the center of his chest, those green eyes glowing down at me. He stepped back, holding out a hand, and when I focused there, I could almost pretend he was normal, although there was a glimpse of iridescence on his skin just under his cuff.

"Nireas. I play the organ here during the shows," he said.

What are you? I wanted to ask. But I bit my tongue and raised my eyes again to meet his, forcing myself not to gape or flinch or gasp. "Hazel Nix."

His top eye blinked first, and then the lower two, and I found myself smiling up at him. His hand was cool and large around mine. I followed the lead of the gentle tug as he drew me out onto the stage and then around the curtains hanging solemnly like columns.

"Fire in a theater is dangerous, and we don't like to overwork the pixies," Nireas said, leading me through, a strange new universe suddenly expanding around me in smears of shadow. He added, "You get used to the dark."

I'd never imagined what a backstage might look like, a theater was about what was in front of the audience, but this was huge and black and cavernous, a maze of rope pulleys and cupboards and strange furniture waiting for the right scene. Above me there was a whoosh of air, a black mass passing by.

"She new?" a voice over our heads called.

Nireas grunted in answer before turning his head in my direction. "What theater did you belong to before?"

"I didn't."

He hummed, a soothing note that echoed as we turned a corner and entered a wide open space full of clutter and props and backdrops. "House?"

"House?" I repeated.

"Did you work in one of the houses?"

Realizing his meaning, I blushed. "No. This will be my first job."

His steps paused as we reached a long staircase leading down into the belly of the building. "How did you find out about the company?"

There was light coming from below, just enough to make out the long angles of his face, and probably enough for him to see my gaze shy away. "It was recommended to me," I said, which answered nothing.

This time, it was Nireas's third eye which narrowed, but he walked down the stairs, drawing me with him, the voices below growing louder with every step.

The halls were even more narrow down here and crowded

with racks of clothing and tables of strange objects, so that Nireas had to walk sideways and I crowded close to his hip to avoid bumping anything out of place. Doorways were covered with curtains while girls and more monsters gathered in tiny rooms or chatted in doorways. The sound of laughter and grunts was barely muffled behind one half-shut curtain, and my eyes bounced quickly away from another, the view of pink flesh and traveling hands now imprinted in my vision, like I could still see the three bodies tangled together while I focused hard on the black fabric of Nireas's jacket.

"Here at the end of the hall," he said. "You'll find meals off to the right when it's long hours."

"Thank you." My voice was thin, and I realized I'd been holding my breath, trying to see everything at once, and half-terrified at what I did find.

He stopped and stepped in front of the final door of the hall, head tipped down. I looked up and found his lips turned down, brow slightly furrowed. It made me feel like a little girl in front of my father again, a disappointment and a problem to solve.

"Don't go exploring alone until...until you know what you'll find," Nireas said.

I frowned at the riddle, but he turned away from me again, knocking on the door.

"What?" a sharp male voice snapped from inside.

"New girl," Nireas said, shooting another frown over his shoulder.

"Send her in."

The door swung open, and my eyes fell to the floor after one brief glance. There was a feminine gasp, but this time, it was from the woman splayed out on a cluttered desk, her blouse hanging open to reveal bouncing breasts as the older man bucked forward between her hips.

This is what you came here for, I reminded myself. *You knew. Don't balk or they'll send you away.*

I forced my gaze up again and found everyone staring back at me. Nireas slipped away, his long dark tail dragging behind him, flicking and bumping against the heel of my boot once. Inside the office, the man carried on, his focus dropping back down to the woman on the desk. He was just shy of middle-aged, with grey in his hair and beard and crow's feet at the corners of his eyes, and his belly was round as he slapped into her thighs, grunting with renewed effort.

The woman squealed behind sealed lips, her eyes widening on mine and something...playful in her stare, like she knew how ridiculous the scene was. She was pretty, as far as I could tell with her head staring at me upside-down, and her thighs bracketed around the broad waist of the man. Her long dark brown hair was braided, and its tail thumped against the desk in time with their coupling, drumming faster until the man bellowed, hands gripping her breasts as he crumpled forward.

"Ungh. Good girl, Myra," he breathed, releasing one breast to pat it gently before pushing himself back up.

His brow was sparkling with sweat now, and he fell back into his chair with another exhausted heave of breath, hands fumbling his pants up but not bothering to tie them shut.

Myra, the woman, sat up on the desk and laughed lightly, pulling her blouse up to her shoulders but not buttoning it. "Gimme your hanky, you louse, I know you have one on you."

Mr. Reddy snorted and drew a scrap of fabric from his pocket, passing it to her. I let my eyes drift away as she stood, reaching to wipe between her legs as her skirt fell around her.

"You're the girl Mr. Douthwaite sent," Mr. Reddy said, leaning around Myra's soft frame to squint at me.

I nodded and braved his gaze, knowing my face was flaming but determined to learn to be as casual about such a scene as everyone in this theater appeared to be. "Hazel Nix."

He nodded slowly, glancing at Myra. "Out," he said to her.

"I'm on my way, aren't I?" she answered, laughing.

"Faster then, hussy," he said, lips quirking slightly at her.

She turned to me and rolled her eyes, tossing back the scrap of fabric he'd offered her. It landed with a wet slap on his lap, and he growled as she ran for the door, breasts still hanging between the open flaps of her blouse.

"Shut the door," he said to me.

Mrs. Elliston, who'd come to clean our flat every other Wednesday, had once told me it was God's gift to women that

He didn't let men's desires rise again when they'd just been satisfied, otherwise women would never get a chance to learn that our feet were for standing. I took it as a small reassurance now that I was alone with the man.

I turned and pushed the door shut, the hinges creaking as it closed with a small click.

"Douthwaite told me about you," Mr. Reddy said.

I turned to face him. His eyes were a bright green, and as his head tipped, I noticed the slight point to his ears. He looked human, but not quite.

I dipped my head. "He said he would."

"You could pass," he suggested.

I pressed my lips together and shook my head slowly. "Not for...not for long."

Mr. Reddy leaned forward. "So...what is it? Witch blood? Elf with clipped ears? Or was your father a werewolf and you get a little rowdy on full moons?"

What are you? I wanted to say. I had sworn to Pa to never tell anyone, not unless it would help me hide. But that's what Mr. Douthwaite said I would do here—hide where I was safe.

"My mother was a nymph," I said. "She left me at my father's door."

Mr. Reddy nodded slowly and hummed. "Flighty little creatures. Very commitment averse. Incredible fucks."

My jaw clenched.

"Easy to hide too. Show me your ears."

I turned my head and pulled my hair away from my ears. "The scars aren't easy to see."

"Good. There's only so many places in the world for people like us, Miss Nix," Mr. Reddy said, arms crossing over his chest and resting on his stomach. "I have my position because I fought for it and because I don't make a show of myself. Our audience pays to see humans, you understand?"

I nodded quickly.

His answering smile was grim. "But a little nymph blood suits this theater. You know what to do?"

This was the hard sell, I knew. But I wouldn't be able to fool him, I could tell that much about Mr. Reddy. "Only a little," I admitted. I'd bedded two young men, entirely in preparation to arrive here. Both experiences were short events. I'd already learned more about sex while walking through the underbelly of the theater.

Mr. Reddy shrugged. "The girls would get jealous if you got featured right away anyways. You'll get your practice, and you'll start slow. But be careful backstage. We're not used to innocents in these halls."

That explained Nireas's puzzling warning. I drew in a slow breath and glanced down at my lap, trying to hold onto my courage.

"I'll tell Myra to keep an eye on you," Mr. Reddy said, and I was surprised by the gentleness in his tone. It must've shown on my face because he gave me another one of those solemn smiles. "I know what you walked in on, but girls only come to my office when they want something. If that something is a day off or a good part, we talk. If it's a quick fuck, they hop on the desk. It's up to them. You understand?"

I nodded again, my nerves and worry settling. The truth was, those two brief experiences of sex had taught me only one thing —I wanted more. I wasn't even sure why. I hadn't moaned or giggled like the women here at the theater. I hadn't sweat and rutted like Mr. Reddy. I'd liked being touched. I'd liked the wonder on the young men's faces. No one had ever looked at me that way before, awed and thrilled, like I was *exactly* what they'd hoped for.

"You'll find your way here, Miss Nix," Mr. Reddy said with a nod. "Just play your roles like the rest of us."

Eight Years Later...

I.

SETTING THE STAGE

My hands slapped against the floor and I let out a long cry, bracing against the brutal thrusts of the demon, Eston, kneeling behind me. His hands were scorching on my hips, his rhythm steady and mechanical.

Just a rough and constant in and out.

He was a simple sort of partner, leaving most of the work up to me to howl and hiss and moan, and if I wanted to finish with him, I had to help myself.

Some days, it was easier just to pretend. After eight years with the theater, those days were growing more frequent.

The sharp horns and thorns of Eston's body jabbed at my ass as he rutted, and I paused in my cries of supposed pleasure for a moment to listen to the sound of the music. Nireas was playing and pedaling at the organ on stage right, the music growing faster and louder, every note sustained. Nearly to the crescendo then.

I yanked my own head backwards, Eston's grip on my hair going loose until he caught up with the gesture.

"You almost there?" I hissed, under the cacophony of coupling on the stage.

"Almost, almost," Eston whispered, nodding in time with his repetitive thrusts.

Which meant no, he wasn't close enough, and he would mess up the timing of the scene. Again. Poor Eston was shit at catching our cues. But he was an exceptional visual of a demon, so pretty even the monsters took notice, all midnight blue and opal shining horns.

I huffed and let my head fall forward, bearing my weight on one palm to reach beneath. My teeth grit as I found a grip on his enormous, heavy sac, the heat burning my palm as I squeezed.

I joined Eston in shouting, his bellow in earnest pleasure and mine in frustrated effort. But in the busy mess of the stage scene —one with so many amorous pairings to appreciate at once—I was sure no one in the audience would notice the difference.

Eston came at a high peak with a flurry of boisterous notes from the organ music, joining the stage in the frenzy of voices and pleasure. His heat lashed and licked inside of me, and a brief flurry of the pleasure I'd been faking swirled through me, drawing out a genuine, soft moan as I dropped down to one elbow and rested my forehead against the cool stage floorboards.

Applause roared and I turned my head, able to catch a brief glimpse of the audience standing and clapping, or embracing and rutting in their seats. My lips curled up at the sight of the joyous, beaming faces pressed together, watching us, adoring us. Those faces, those stares, the cries for more...the audience was why I was still here after all these years. Then the curtain swung shut, and I let out a long sigh.

Eston hissed, nudging inside of me again, more gently, before falling back on his heels. "Thanks, Hazel."

I waved a hand, giving myself a moment of rest, my ass and hips and cunt still stinging from working with Eston. It would heal soon, thanks to my mother's blood, which was why I was always the choice to pair with Eston.

Eston, and any of the especially "challenging" guest act monsters the theater hosted. The monsters who came to us, eager to demonstrate their prowess to others, or to sample all the theater might cheerfully offer them.

I sat up slowly, wincing and stretching, turning to find Eston had already risen and was joining the others.

"Gentlemen, ain't they?" Beth quipped, groaning as she rose and brushing back fire red strands of sweaty hair from her face. She'd been paired with one of the weres, and I could see the faint scratch marks on her hips.

"Ladies, hurry it up," Billy, our hobgoblin stage manager, snapped, sticking his head out from the wings and glaring at us stragglers through thick round glasses.

I bit my tongue as I stood, body aching, and hurried to stage left as a handmade wooden Grecian temple rolled out from stage right's wings.

"You on in the next act, Haze?" Beth asked.

"Still waiting to find out," I answered with a roll of my eyes, twisting and slipping past Johnny, a werebear stagehand, his thick fur brushing over my sore ass. Myra and Reddy tended to juggle girls in and out of scenes right until the last second, and I was often one they would toss in when another girl was too worn out to do the work.

Beth grinned. "I've got a short easy one coming up at the end. Wait for me and we'll walk home together?"

I used to always stay until curtain call, watching each scene from the wings. These days, I liked to slip back home at the first chance. But it was late already, and walking back with Beth would be safer than going alone. We lived in the same neighborhood and always made it nearly to my block together.

"Sure," I agreed as we rushed down the stairs with the others to the dressing rooms, a cascade of naked flesh, all grubby and bruised.

The dressing room hall reeked of sex every night of a show, full of sweaty bodies and us girls with our thighs pressed tight together until we had a chance to clean up. But it would be right and fresh by morning again. Ever since Myra had bullied Mr. Reddy into giving her the position of manager, the backstage of the theater had become a tidy, clean, and almost cozy place. Myra was sweeter to the theater pixies than Reddy had ever been, and they worked tirelessly for the cakes and honey milk she had us girls put out for them.

I squeezed past the others, too used to this routine to care when a clawed hand patted at my breast or a tail slipped between my legs to tease. They were friendly gestures from familiar monsters, nothing more. No one followed me into my small but private dressing room, a space barely wide enough to be considered more than a closet, but one of the few that wasn't shared and wasn't for a guest-starring monster.

But I was not alone as I ducked under the curtain.

"Hello, nut," Ronan greeted.

I blinked, my eyes adjusting to the warm candlelight from the short stubs burning by my mirror. Ronan was seated at the edge of my pilfered chaise—one he had helped me drag through the alleys and down into the narrow hall, the scuffs of running into walls invisible against the rough wear the chaise had already seen from previous owners. It was pressed to the back of the room, a perfect but tight fit.

My lips twitched at the sight of him, all charm and smirk, his great black leathery wings tucked carefully behind him, rust-red skin shining wickedly in the firelight. I'd learned not to get attached to many people in the theater—a bittersweet lesson ingrained in me by years of repetition. Monsters came and went. Girls grew tired of the work. Only Mr. Reddy, Myra, and a few others like Nireas had been here as long as I had now. Ronan had arrived three years ago, a new imp to replace the one who'd just left us, and I'd done my best to ignore his enthusiasm and energy. He would grow weary like the rest of them, and then he would leave.

But Ronan was infectious.

"Shouldn't you be on curtains for the rest of tonight?" I asked.

"Look," Ronan said, tapping his booted foot against a bucket on the floor. "I brought you snow."

My eyes widened and I ran forward, Ronan's grin growing wide. The bucket was filled to the brim with fresh, white snow, barely even melted, and I let out a soft sigh at the sight. We wouldn't have much more this year, and it was the best cure for a rough fuck.

"Ohhh, Ro!"

"I knew you were paired with Eston," Ronan said. "Turn around."

As it turned out, it was good to have a friend at the theater. I squealed as Ronan lifted a handful of snow and pressed it gently to one of the welts on my ass from Eston, but the squeal turned quickly into a moan of relief.

"I've got the curtains covered for the rest of the night. No rush," Ronan said, a hint of an offer in the words.

"Hmm, keep scooping," I answered, flashing him a smile over my shoulder, surprised I could still blush at the fix of his coal spark stare on my ass.

He laughed, drawing up another handful and resting it against my left cheek, sliding the hand on the right lower and closer to my inner thigh. Icy water slid down the back of my legs, cooling the flush of heat from Eston's mechanical-like fucking and being on stage.

"They ought to give someone else a turn with him," Ronan muttered. "The other girls would make Reddy give him better instructions."

I shuffled in place, widening my stance, and whimpered as Ronan let the remaining wintery handful—now mostly melted—slide over my sore sex. "Eston is what he is. I don't mind."

"An empty-headed, over-decorated, low-level demon?" Ronan suggested.

I snorted and shrugged. He wasn't wrong. "He's there to make the stage prettier."

"That's *your* job, nut," Ronan corrected, and I bit my lip as his numbing fingers stroked my sex, soothing and teasing me all at once.

"My job is to make him look like the world's best fuck, and to make sure he comes at the musical cue," I said.

Ronan's other hand slid up to my hip, drawing me back a few steps until I could feel his warm breath on my now chilly ass. "Did you at least get off this time?" he asked, and I was sure he already knew the answer.

"Keep scooping," I said, not ashamed to sound a little breathy.

Aside from being handsome and helpful, one of Ronan's other best qualities was that he really was a *very* good lover. I tried to keep my sexual interactions to the stage or the occasional dazzled patron monster. I had enough of the work to do under the spotlight without adding a backstage tryst in the mix.

When Ronan arrived, he'd seemed to be like all the other new recruits—an intolerable flirt. He'd been easy enough to ignore after five years of seductive visitors who always left, but then he went and made me come three times in our first scene on stage together. That kind of talent was hard to only sample once.

"Are you leaving early?" Ronan asked, streaking snow up and down my chafed inner thighs as I squirmed and bit back the high sounds in my throat.

"Beth asked me to stay and Myra mentioned a scene swap," I breathed, my hips rocking to brush myself against Ronan's knuckles.

"You work too hard."

I huffed. "On my back, Ro."

"Come on. We both know what it takes to organize a simultaneous orgasm," Ronan teased.

It's always shockingly easy with you, I thought, but I only released a soft sound of relief as he slid those cold fingers inside of me, pumping out some of Eston's release.

My eyes were falling shut, ready to let Ronan manage what Eston had absolutely failed in, when I caught the slight twitch of my dressing room curtain. I stiffened and Ronan's touch paused as Myra drew the curtain to the side, barely offering a reaction to the sight of the imp's hand between my legs.

"Scene swap?" I asked, blinking.

"Not tonight, honey. But stick around? There's a gentleman who'd like to meet you. A patron," she said, eyebrows bouncing up.

"Oh!" Ronan's fingers were drawing free of me, and I was thinking of Beth and of my bed in my flat, and the thought of sleeping in tomorrow morning. But meeting a patron was part of the work here at the theater too, and a part I often enjoyed. I nodded, and Myra's smile widened. "Sure."

"He's a regular," Myra said. "Never asked about any of the girls before." I nodded again, and she mimicked me. "I'll bring him by later."

"What kind?" Ronan asked for me.

"None of your business," Myra snapped at him. She was soft for us humans, but almost always stern with the monsters. He huffed a laugh against my back, and I hiccuped a gasp as his fingers dipped back inside of me. "An orc," Myra said to me. "Most well-dressed one I've ever seen too. Very fine."

"Very good grunters, I hear," Ronan muttered at my back, and I swatted his hand as Myra vanished.

"Don't let her hear you," I hissed at him.

"Does she really think you don't do enough for the theater as it is?" Ronan asked.

"What we do with patrons is up to us," I recited, and Ronan huffed. "It *is*. I've been coy with plenty and they've still bought season passes. Most of them would like to be guest acts but are just too shy for the stage. They want to feel special."

"No such thing as a shy orc," Ronan said, and he scooped up a fresh handful of snow, laughing as he pressed it to my sex and I screeched behind my teeth, the frigid ice shooting right into my veins and drawing out a shiver.

"Bastard!"

"Mmm, it's true," Ronan murmured, leaning in and licking gently over one of my bruises as the snow melted against me. I wasn't sure if he meant to defend his statement about orcs or affirm that he was a bastard, and as he rubbed against my nearly numb clit, drawing back sensation, I didn't really care.

"Maybe I will fuck the orc," I said, shrugging. "Well-dressed means moneyed."

Ronan nipped at my ass, frozen fingers plunging inside of me and drawing out a rough gasp from my throat.

"Moneyed might mean he wants a little human pet in a pretty apartment," I continued, breaths ragged as Ronan's touch fucked me smoothly, warming quickly in the heat between us, cool water and demon's cum splashing out against my thighs. "I've been thinking about retiring."

Ronan paused, and his hand on my hip tightened. "Have you?"

Had I? Only in the sense that it seemed inevitable, what all the other girls did when they left.

"It's been eight years," I said. "I should've started looking for someone ages ago."

"Why leave?" Ronan's touch was gentling, focusing more on

my clit, a lovely warm contrast to the chill still lingering. "You could be like Myra."

I snorted. Myra had her position because she was all but married to Mr. Reddy and she well and truly had his cock on a leash. She'd scoop my eyes out before she let me follow in her footsteps.

"Moneyed might just mean he wants to pay for a scene with you," Ronan said. "Just one more guest monster rutting under the spotlight, thinking that fucking you in front of the audience means his cock is worth more than theirs."

I frowned at the truth in the words. Brave patrons *did* pay to be featured. And usually they were about as good at the work as someone like Eston. I rose to my tiptoes, arousal skittering away again. Ronan's arm wrapped around my waist, drawing me back to lean against his shoulder, his legs bracketing mine, pressing them closed so his hand was tightly fastened against my sex.

"At least let me get you off before you meet the tosser," Ronan said, words slightly muffled as he sucked a kiss against my back.

It was tempting. Ronan was the only man I'd ever met who would genuinely enjoy finishing a girl and taking nothing for himself. Oh, he might *try* and talk you into sucking him off or taking a ride, but he was always cheerful, even when you refused. And there was a kind of power in being able to say no without any consequence, not even a cold shoulder.

His thumb was on my clit, fingers searching gently inside of me, warm mouth dragging up and down my spine with little fiery flicks of his tongue. It did feel good, a sweet contrast with the faint aches remaining from Eston. But I was tired. I'd been in two scenes already tonight, and now had a patron to meet before I would see my bed. And Ronan picking over the issue just made all my irritation linger.

I reached down, setting my hand over his, and started to pull away. He leaned back, his expression calm but uncharacteristically somber. "Not tonight," I said.

And Ronan was my friend for a reason. He turned his hand beneath mine, grasping it gently and drawing it to his lips to kiss the backs of my fingers. His other hand pet the inside of my thighs, not gripping, as I stepped away.

"Fair enough, Hazelnut," he said, standing. He leaned back and snatched up my robe draped over the back of the chaise, holding it open for me to slide into.

"Thank you for the snow," I said softly.

"Anytime in winter," he answered lightly.

I turned to face him, tilting my head back a little to study him. His smile was easy, no sign of offense, maybe just a hint of disappointment in those firelit eyes of his. I rose to my toes and Ronan ducked, meeting me in an easy kiss, familiar and delicious all at once. He tasted a little like butter and spice, I'd always thought, something that warmed on my tongue and was always pleasant to return to.

"Sorry for teasing," he rasped out, nose nudging mine, hands warm on my hips. And curled into him like this, with that spice on my tongue and his whisper in my ear, I could almost change my mind.

Better not to, I decided.

"You can make it up to me next time," I said, pecking at his lips once more, resisting the itch in my fingers to comb through those thick, inky black strands of his.

"Next time it is," Ronan said with a nod, bumping his forehead against mine. His long, curling horns caught a glint of the candlelight as he ducked his head to catch my eye. "You *do* deserve more than the theater, Hazel. But don't settle for the first poncy monster who offers."

Some days, I hoped Ronan would move on from the company sooner rather than later. He wouldn't stay, I knew that much, but the longer he lingered, the easier he was to grow attached to. He didn't have deep pockets—he was only an imp— and from my experience, he was too pretty to trust with a heart. But I did like him, perhaps a little too much.

"Go manage the curtains," I said, drawing away and wrapping the robe around me. "I'm catching a nap before I consider any offers, poncy or otherwise."

2.

A GENTLEMAN ORC'S DISGUISE

"Hazel," a voice hissed, and I sat up with a start, blinking in the weary light of my dressing room.

My candles were close to sputtering out, and Myra was standing over me, eyebrows bouncing and hands on her hips.

"There's someone here," she said, and I stared stupidly back at her. "To see you!"

Right! The *patron*. The orc.

I scrambled up, glancing down and flicking my robe back to rights. I looked up over Myra's head—she was a tiny woman, and I'd always been taller than most—to see the large figure waiting in the doorway.

He *was* a fine dresser, one of the best I'd ever seen backstage at the theater, in a beautifully tailored black jacket that accentuated the obvious bulk of the man beneath. He wasn't strictly speaking handsome—orcs usually weren't—but his hair shone red in my dim little doorway and his eyes were a bright golden yellow, fixed to me. His features were big and a little bulky, like him, right down to the shining white tusks that framed his full upper lip.

"Sorry," I whispered to Myra.

She rolled her eyes and stepped back. "Hazel, this is Hunter. Hunter, this is one of our very best actresses, Hazel Nix."

He bowed, which was almost laughable down here in our shabby dressing rooms, and I managed an awkward curtsey.

"It's too crowded for me to join you, of course," Myra said with a wave and a laugh. "I'll leave you to your conversation."

There would be one of the stagehands in the hall for me to shout if I needed, but I watched this massive man hover in the doorway, stepping out of Myra's way as she exited, and knew I wouldn't have trouble. A pushy patron would've been on the chaise by now, patting the cushion or his lap and waiting for me to join him. This orc, Hunter, remained in place, the curtain parted and resting against his shoulder.

"Come in before the whole hallway tries to join us," I teased.

Hunter's head turned to glance down the length of the hallway, the noise at full volume, which meant I'd slept through curtain call. I enjoyed a brief glimpse of his face in profile—a very strong nose and a promising mouth—and then he stepped in, the curtain shutting and its spell-woven fabric dulling the sound.

"We should not have woken you," he said, bowing slightly again and making my lips twitch with the slow and formal tone of his deep voice. "My apologies."

"If you didn't, no one would have, and I hate to sleep down here when everyone's gone. An empty theater just feels like a skeleton," I said. He'd only just stepped inside, no farther. Not at all pushy. He would take *coaxing* to flirt with. I turned and flounced down onto the chaise, aware my robe would flash skin for him to admire, and this time, I was the one patting the cushion. "Myra says you come to the theater often."

Hunter nodded, walking slowly forward, holding my stare well past my own ability to gaze back. "For two months now. I'd heard of the theater, of course, but I didn't expect to find the performances more than idle entertainment."

He didn't sit, and the power of his natural frame was only slightly lessened by his gentle speech.

"Your performances, in particular, are my favorite," Hunter said, ducking his head and offering relief from those bright eyes. Now that it was gone, I was determined to draw it back again.

I twisted, drawing out a slow smile on my lips as the robe slipped down on one side, revealing my leg. "What, *in particular,* about my performances makes them your favorite?"

I'd met plenty of orcs at the theater, and to my knowledge, they were a lusty, boisterous, eager species. Especially when it came to fucking. I didn't know many that would need such a strong invitation to touch a woman, let alone to *flirt* with one. And while Hunter's eyes fastened to my bared thigh, the yellow light within them blazing, his hands fisted at his side and he didn't move an inch.

"I hope it is not...untoward of me," he said, the words slow and careful like he was reciting them, those eyes finally raising to mine. "But it was your attention to your partners."

My lips were parted, prepared to continue teasing him, but his answer wiped all my wit away. I'd expected a comment about my body or the sounds I made, or something about how passionate I was or what big cock I could take. Not this.

"You take great care to watch them, to move with them. More than anyone else in the theater," Hunter said, with such incredible sincerity that I was at a loss for words.

It's my job, I thought, but Reddy and Myra liked us to keep up a certain illusion that we were all here for the fun of it, not the money. It wouldn't be half as fun for our audience if they knew all the work that went into staging a grand, mixed-species orgy.

"I've made you uncomfortable," Hunter said softly, stepping back and dropping his stare again.

"No!" I rushed, leaning forward and snatching his wrist, almost amused by the way he stiffened in my weak grip, stumbled forward at my leading. Didn't he know what a marvelous beast he was? How had an orc become so...domesticated, like a nervous human rather than a monster? I bent until I knew he could see my smile, trying to coax him closer with tiny tugs. "No, not uncomfortable. Flattered, sir. I'm very *flattered* by your words."

Hunter's tusks dug into his upper lip as he smiled, and I rose up from the chaise, holding him in place by that tiny anchor of my hand on his wrist. I stepped forward, and he huffed softly before taking a deep breath. I was tired and still sore, but this orc was so charmingly *earnest* that I thought I might suffer a longer night for his sake.

"You are very kind," I said, pressing myself to his hip and

watching the throat in front of me bob with a hard swallow. I was taller than any of the other girls, and still, this orc towered over me. I lifted my free hand and rested it on his chest, leaning in and arching to stare up at him. "And I'm glad you asked to meet me."

Hunter clenched his jaw, and for the first time, I saw a hint of the hunger and power I'd expected from him, a brilliant spotlight focused on me from those lamp yellow eyes. His wrist twisted in my grip, and I braced myself for him to pounce, to tackle me back to the chaise, relieved to find my own excitement at the prospect.

"Haze, are you ready to walk—Oh!"

Hunter all but leapt backwards and away from me, graceful even as he bumped into my dressing table, rattling the rusty mirror against the wall. Beth stood in the doorway, trying to fight her laughter, hand raised in apology.

"I'll go," she said quickly. "I'm so—"

"It's fine," I said at the same moment Hunter spoke. "I should be leaving."

"No!" Beth and I cried out together.

"I'm leaving, you're staying," Beth said to him.

"It really is fine, please don't go," I pressed, shuffling forward, only to have Hunter skittishly dart out of my reach and for the doorway.

"I've kept you too long," Hunter said, offering me a bow, even as he backed away. Over his shoulder, Beth still hovered in the doorway, mouthing an apology to me.

"You will come back," I said, the words firm. Hunter stood straight, eyes wide, and I folded my arms over my stomach. "You'll come to the theater again. To see me."

It was almost an order, but it did the trick. He bowed again, smiling. "I will."

I nodded and relaxed as he ducked out the door, sighing as Beth stepped inside.

"Jumpy, isn't he?" Beth said. "Bet if he'd already had his cock in you, he wouldn't have been so eager to run."

I shrugged and turned away, hiding my frown and searching the room for a proper dress to walk home in.

"Remember that time Myra brought you a troll at intermission?" Beth asked, giggling.

I snorted and winced. "Mm, she learned not to do that again."

Beth laughed. "He practically took up this whole room! Made all the walls rattle and rutted you right through to curtain call."

"And then she put us on stage together the next week," I recalled, laughing a little. I'd been sore for days after, but the troll had a dry sense of humor, and he'd whispered naughty poetry in my ear all through the second act while fucking me through a series of orgasms that left my voice hoarse. I shot Beth a wicked grin as I tore off my robe. "He was *great* fun."

&

STEPNEY GREEN WAS DECEPTIVELY quiet in the late hours. Beth and I knew the best routes to avoid passing pubs where men who had too much to drink would linger in doorways, or the roads of the infamous East End where we might be mistaken for available bawds—ladies searching for quick clients. But the fastest route home from the underground station to Wellesley Street required a walk through Stepney Green park.

"Do you want me to walk with you?" Beth asked as we neared the edge of the green.

I considered it. Most nights, the park was quiet and still, or the neighborhood was jolly, excited but safe. But not *all* nights. Some nights, the desperation of the East End came wearing the faces of anxious thieves, those whose hunger allowed them to think of no other way but to take what they lacked. Other nights, the faces were those of men who took what they wanted because they knew they could not be stopped.

But those men could be found in parks and alleys and backstage at theaters, and I suspected many fine and grand rooms too. Jamaica Street was as dangerous as the quiet park, and a longer walk home.

"I'll be all right," I said. Beth never needed to walk the whole way through with me anyway. I stepped onto the grass and gave her a wave. "You get home, and I'll see you tomorrow."

"If you're sure," she called back, already turning and marching for the corner.

Stepney Green Park was three blocks deep, and there was a point when I reached the center and the city around me vanished, all the lamps blocked by trees and buildings. I should've been frightened, should've been afraid of how vulnerable I was in the darkness. I should've walked faster, rushed toward the corner of Wellesley Street where the lamps flickered dully, but the block was full of quiet families stuffed to the rafters of their flats.

My steps slowed in the dark, the wet grass soaking through the gaps in my old boots. The hem of my dress whispered against the ground, and an owl greeted me with a gentle cry from the trees. I closed my eyes and moved steadily forward, the air cool and damp, forcing myself to block out the sounds of hackney taxis and pubs and arguments bleeding through drafty windows. Here, in the center of Stepney Green Park I could almost *forget* that I was in London, or at least that was what I liked to pretend. I had never left London, barely left Stepney, but there was a part of me that knew what the whistle of wet grass and rush of wings and scream of a captured rabbit all meant. Home had always been here in London, and yet home had never been here, not for part of me.

My mother's blood, I thought, breathing deeply.

But it wasn't earth and trees and little whiffs of city smoke in my nose. My steps froze and my eyes opened at the stench of tobacco, sweat, and beer. The man in front of me was a shadow, hidden from the moon by the strength of one of the lovely oaks in the green, but my eyes were adjusting quickly.

"Purse," he said, his arm raising in the thin sliver of light just enough to catch it on a large dull blade—dull, but dangerous all the same.

I pulled my purse out of my pocket quickly, tossing it in his direction. It hit the ground just behind him, and it was obvious from the soft slap of fabric in the grass that there was barely anything for him to take. He grunted but didn't turn his back to me, only stepped backwards, knife still extended in my direction.

"I don't have anything else," I said, holding my hands out in front of me.

It was the truth—I always took a hackney right to my door on the nights we were paid—but the man let out a snarl, rising up with my nearly empty bag of coins and lunging for me. I stiffened and flinched at the huff of rancid breath in my face, but held as still as I could.

"Get on your hands and knees," the man rasped, stuffing my money away and then yanking on my arm, bringing it to his crotch. "If you don't have more coin, you can make yourself useful another way."

Except he wasn't even remotely hard, even as he forced my hand into rubbing at him.

"Let me go," I said, my words even. A warning.

He released my hand and then slapped me sharply on the cheek, a pounding heat rising on the spot. It would bruise, but only for an hour or two. I would heal by the morning.

"On the *ground*," he hissed.

But the quiet words were interrupted by a low growl from behind me. Both the thief's and my own eyebrows shot up at the sound, and I could only blink before a small man in an elegant long coat and gleaming top hat was barreling into the thief. He dragged the larger man away from me and over to the broad trunk of a tree with far more strength than I would've expected from such a small-statured man. A large white glove gripped the thief's throat, squeezing tightly, drawing out garbled notes of panic.

"Creatures like you don't deserve to live," the strange little man said, in a voice that was deep and snarling. "My people would not suffer you. But as murder is not welcome here, I will at least ensure one thing."

I gasped as the thief was dropped, only to have his hands snapped up. There was a shocking *crunch* that echoed around us, and then a high, wailing scream from the thief.

"Run," the little man growled.

And in spite of his freshly broken hands, the thief darted away, his head down and voice strangled with pain as he ran directly from us toward the safety of Jamaica Street.

I gaped at the figure in front of me, petite and entirely at odds with the ferocious tone and actions I'd just witnessed. There was a furrow of displeasure on the otherwise incredibly average and middle-aged face in front of me as he watched my attacker depart.

"Sir, I—I don't know—"

"My apologies, Miss Nix, for my violence," the little man said, and my jaw dropped again.

Now, without the growls and snarls, as calm seemed to come over him, I recognized that voice. One of the large white gloves reached up and up and up—I blinked at the confusion of space—and then lifted the top hat from his head, revealing white tusks and yellow eyes.

"Hunter," I said in a gust of breath, my hand rising to rest over my racing heart. "What on *earth* are you doing out here?"

He bowed, and that too was familiar, until the hat returned to his head and he was once again a petite and unremarkable little human man. I'd seen such illusions used before, but this one was especially good and so shockingly at odds with his appearance—another mark of this orc's wealth.

"Forgive me for my presumption, but when I realized that you and your friend were traveling through the city on your own, I was concerned for your safety. Rightly so, I'm afraid," he said.

The surprise of the past five minutes had left my tongue loose, and I nearly corrected him. I was capable of protecting myself, most especially here on the green, although it wasn't necessarily worth the risk of exposure.

"However, I think I must now insist that you allow me to walk you to your door," Hunter continued, releasing a heavy breath. "No further. I intend no imposition. Only your safety, Miss Nix."

"Hazel." I shook myself from the confused stupor of the moment. "Please, call me Hazel."

He bowed again, and I huffed out a nervous laugh as I walked forward to meet him. *He followed you!* an anxious voice warned. And he might nearly have seen proof of my secret if he hadn't stepped in.

Hunter held out his arm for me to take, and I had to look

away to make sense of the fact that an arm that appeared so low below mine required me to reach up slightly to hold onto.

Did I have any reason to fear this orc? He'd left so hurriedly at the theater, in spite of my obvious invitation. And he *had* stepped in on my behalf. But to follow me home...

"Thank you for your help," I said, to cover my spinning thoughts.

"I saw your friend to the corner, but I wish now I'd remained with you," Hunter said, and I leaned forward to see the illusion's lips turning down with his frown.

"I'm fine," I said, squeezing his arm and admiring the bulk of him with my hands, even if I couldn't enjoy it with my eyes. "You were perfectly in time."

"Your purse—"

"Only pennies lost," I said, continuing with a tease. "Did you change your mind after you left my dressing room?"

We were nearing the road, and it was enough light to see a blush on the funny little man's face that I hadn't caught on Hunter's own skin yet.

"It's wrong of me, I know, but I had no intention of alerting you to my presence if it were not for the immediate danger of the—" Hunter's words stuttered as I leaned into his side, finding his shoulder with my temple. There was a little traffic on Stepney Way, and we paused to let it pass.

"I suppose I will have to be grateful to my attacker for forcing you into the light then," I said softly, and Hunter stiffened.

"Miss Nix, that man—"

"He made sure we didn't part so easily. I didn't *want* you to leave earlier, you know," I said. I was looking down at the small man's face, and I wondered what it must look like to Hunter.

He was quiet as we crossed the road to Wellesley Street together.

"You weren't afraid," Hunter said, and this time, it was my turn to go silent. He frowned again. "Because you are used to such attacks?"

"Thefts, yes," I said. "I have two more purses at home. I make them myself now from old fabric scraps so I don't waste money losing money." His frown grew deeper. There were no lamps on Wellesley near my flat and no sign of anyone outside, and I wanted to pull the hat from his head and stare up into his face again, watch those yellow eyes narrow or light up with every word.

"At the theater, we learn a great many things. And many of those are...for our scenes. But Mr. Reddy and Myra also make sure we know how to escape the grasp of much stronger bodies. How to protect ourselves," I said.

"I would rather you not be put in danger," Hunter muttered.

"This is my door," I said, pulling him to a stop.

Hunter gaped at my little brick building, frowning up at the lamplit windows on the first floor.

"First story is mine," I said, not quite sure why I was sharing.

Most of the girls from the theater lived in a women's only boarding house with lenient hours, and a few like Beth shared flats with some of the East End whores, who wouldn't wonder why we weren't back until after midnight. As far as I knew, I was the only one who lived alone, and I kept that fact to myself to avoid a sudden influx of roommates.

"I should leave you to get your rest," Hunter said, reaching that deceptively large white gloved hand of his up to my cheek, thumb grazing over a tender spot that made me flinch. I'd forgotten the slap already, but he growled at the spot.

"You could come in," I found myself saying. "I could...make us tea."

"You've had a long night, Miss Nix—"

"Hazel."

"—and I should leave you to your rest," Hunter rumbled in that amusingly short illusion of his.

As frustrating as I found his refusal, there was also something delightful about it. I wanted to drag him inside and throw him down into my bed. I also wanted to preen at the rare chivalry and consideration.

As he raised my hand to his lips, I decided to compromise. There was a dark alcove between my building and the one just before it, and Hunter only grunted as I pulled him into the shadows where we wouldn't be seen. I pulled his hat off his head as I pushed him into the dark, grinning at the obvious strike of surprise on his features, eyes brilliant and fixed to my face. I had to grab his collar and tug him down an inch or so, even as I rose to my toes, but he moved so easily at my command.

Kissing an orc was simultaneously straightforward and an interesting puzzle. The tusks were less complicated than you might first guess. Orcs' mouths were broad and their lips were full. Hunter made the puzzle even easier, freezing at the first brush of my mouth against his, sighing and just barely parting his lips for me to wrap my own around the top plush cushion and press softly.

"Goodnight, Hunter," I murmured, blinking open my eyes to find his wide and staring.

I kissed him again, and this time, he responded. A low and quiet groan vibrated against my mouth, and a strong arm banded across my back, drawing me roughly to his chest. I cupped his broad jaw in my hands, impressed with the silky-smooth texture of his careful beard, and arched as he took a hungry lick of my lips and a full press of his mouth to mine. His coat was too thick to know for certain how affected he was, but he held me still against him for a long time, only shifting the kiss slightly, a little whisper of a slow exhale warming my cheeks.

He lifted his head and stared down at me as I smiled.

"Goodnight, Miss Nix," he said, blinking slowly. "I will see you at the theater again soon."

He took his hat from my hands, stepping away and lifting it onto his head, vanishing back into his human disguise. I thought even the dowdy little man looked more vivid now after the kiss.

"Inside, Miss Nix, so I know that you are safe."

It was my turn to blush, and I hurried past him, up the stairs to my door, aware of his stare with every step.

3.

SECRET AUDIENCES

"**A**nd bend forward now. Face down and ass up, ladies," Myra called, pacing the floorboards downstage.

The two newest girls tittered at her order, but the rest of us slid into the familiar stretch, backs arched and arms extended in front of us. I took slow deep breaths as the last of the aches and kinks from the night before loosened.

"Press up, lower your hips, extend your neck and head as high as you can. Tits up, girls!"

More titters and a brief scoff from Evie on my right. I glanced at her just in time to catch the roll of her eyes.

"They'll get used to it," I whispered.

She nodded, and we both turned our heads in deep neck stretches. "Have you seen Beth?" she whispered back.

"Only last night," I answered, taking the opportunity to scan the stage as I turned my head in the opposite direction.

"Think she'll make curtain?" Evie asked.

Beth was our least reliable actress, mostly when it came to rehearsals, but she'd missed performances every so often, usually when some charmer out of a pub had caught her attention for a few days. She was sweet and fell in love too easily, but the theater couldn't afford to cut girls loose. All the humans who worked in the company were charmed with secret-keeping, tongue-tying magic, but even a spell could unravel with enough time. No, once you joined the theater, you stayed until you found a nice monster to settle down with, to make sure you kept your lips sealed about the other world that existed right behind humans' backs. So

Beth's absences were forgiven, so long as she came back within a few days.

"She usually does," I said. "Give it till tea."

"On your backs now, girls, spread those legs for your partners, wide as you can!" Myra called, and we all rolled on our blankets, legs parting in the air. "Bend your knees, we want nice open hips. No cramping mid-fuck tonight because the show won't stop for you to stretch!"

"I'll get stuck on the spanking scene if she doesn't show up," Evie hissed.

"Better start drinking water now," I said, shrugging.

We all had to pick up the slack sometimes. The show must go on and all that.

&

AFTER TEA and with a good pile of mending done for the day, the truth became obvious.

"She's not coming," Alexa said, holding up a velvet corset around her middle and studying herself in the mirror. "I guarantee she was face-down, ass-up in a gent's bed till dawn."

Us girls—and occasionally our male and human compatriot, Hugh—gathered together in the hall where the light was best, between tea and curtain call, tidying and teasing one another, enjoying each other's company before the halls were swarmed with the monsters we worked with.

"She has three scenes tonight!" Margaret squeaked out. She was one of our new recruits and had made an impressive sampling of all the stagehands in her first few weeks. She was kind to all the monsters and enthusiastic, and if she didn't fall in love, she'd last a long time in the company.

"We swap scenes all the time, it'll be all right," I assured her.

"But who's going to tell Myra?" Evie asked.

I stared hard at the slipper in my hand, but the slow prick of every stare in the hall turning in my direction was impossible to ignore.

"You know them best, Haze," Alexa said, sweetening her

voice and leaning in to drop her head on my shoulder. "And besides, you'll be the one who takes the silks act."

Beth was small and light and absurdly brave. She and Ronan had arranged an erotic aerial act that mainly relied on Ronan's strength and Beth's flexibility, but it looked elegant and skilled to the untrained eye. I was far too tall to replace Beth, but none of the other girls would trust Ronan with their safety in the middle of sex while twenty feet off the ground.

"Evie will be stuck on spanking," Alexa continued, brushing long dark brown locks over her shoulder and twisting them as she thought. "Christine and Isabella's nights are already stacked, so they're out."

The other two new recruits nodded eagerly. Between them and Margaret, Margaret was the best. Christine took the monsters in stride, but she balked at the more risque scenes. I thought Isabella might settle down as quickly as she could with the most innocuous monster she could find, since she wrinkled her nose at any with unusual features.

"Margie is looking fresh today, I'm sure she can take two in the mid-show frenzy," Alexa settled on with a shrug.

"Two...two *cocks?*" Margaret whispered, brown eyes growing huge. "At once?"

"One in the mouth," Evie suggested lazily.

I shared a smirk with Alexa as Margaret's mouth stretched open, as if she was testing the idea already, and Christine giggled nervously.

"Myra'll take it better if you go with the plan already sorted," Alexa said, nudging my shoulder and turning to stare at me with pleading grey-blue eyes. "She talks to you like a partner. She talks to the rest of us like we're children underfoot."

"Speak for yourself," Evie scoffed, pinning up her dark curls.

"The longer you stay and the less problems you cause, the more Reddy and Myra like you," I said, for the new girls' sake.

"And Hazel is their favorite because she can fuck anyone and always shows up to work on time and never falls in love with guests," Evie added.

I pressed my lips together and slid off the table I'd been perched on. I hadn't fallen in love with any of the guests, that was true, although I'd been tempted a few times. But guest monsters left, and stagehands could never resist the chance to try out an excited new girl. It didn't take long here in the company before I was slow to warm to new men, at least off the stage. Some girls, playful and charming ones like Alexa, found a regular or two and seemed to fall in love as easily as stepping onto the center stage in that warm spotlight.

"Is it bad if we like the guests?" Christine asked.

"We *all* like the guests," Alexa said.

"We just don't like them *too* much," Evie said as I walked down the hall to Reddy's office. "Guest acts usually like to try and fuck every girl they can while they're here. You can't get jealous, and you can't make a stink if you fancy one and they're paired with someone else for a scene."

"And even if they tell you they want you to leave the theater to be with them, don't believe it until the carriage is at the door and they're asking where your bags are," Alexa agreed.

I stopped and knocked at the familiar door, turning my head and leaning in to listen. It wasn't quite as common to catch Mr. Reddy and Myra in the act as it had been when I'd first arrived at the theater, but it was still a fairly regular thing. They weren't a subtle couple.

"I thought you told that creep to bugger off," Myra snapped from inside.

"He's not the sort of man I can say no to every time, Missy. This was the easiest compromise."

"For you, maybe! Not for the girls," Myra hissed.

I shouldn't have been snooping. Fights between the couple were so common, they never even bothered to keep the door closed. Now they were hissing and whispering, and curiosity itched through me. What secrets did they have to keep from the rest of us?

"Hazel can handle it," Reddy said softly, almost lost beneath the chatter from the girls behind me. I straightened, and any reservations I had for spying vanished.

"Oh, can she? You always say that! You work that girl to the bone every night as it is, Red."

"Myra—"

"No. Listen to me. She's getting tired. And rightly so. I'm going to find her a nice man who will set her up in a lovely house and worship her all day long. Preferably with his mouth."

I rested my forehead against the doorjamb gently, a warm rush of gratitude for Myra rising up in me.

"So long as you find him for her *after* we get through this," Reddy said with a sigh.

"Oh, Reddy. I hope you know what you're doing," Myra said, sounding equally as weary.

"If I don't, I know you'll tell me, love."

There was a muffled sort of shifting from within and I waited, trying to decipher everything I'd heard. Had Reddy agreed to allow a guest to join the company that Myra objected to? One he would pair with me? Resentment and acceptance seemed to slide in place inside of me at the same time. I *would* be the best choice of all the girls if Reddy and Myra had concerns, and I would be fine. Better me than them.

After the scrape of a chair, and before the couple had time to get too amorous, I knocked on the door.

"Who is it?" Reddy barked.

"Hazel."

"Come in, lovey," Myra called.

A few years back, Myra had asked Mr. Reddy for a desk of her own in his office, and it had been a chilly atmosphere for three weeks in the theater before he'd finally agreed. I opened the door and stepped up to the small but tidy desk in the near left corner of the room, Reddy's great old behemoth scooted back in the opposite direction.

"Has Beth arrived?" Myra asked as I entered.

Neither she nor Reddy showed any signs of their discussion, and if I hadn't known they'd just been talking about me, I wouldn't have guessed.

"She hasn't. We've got Evie taking her spanking, Margaret's getting advice on entertaining two cocks for the group mid-show act, and I'll run the silks with Ronan."

Reddy chuckled from his desk but didn't look up from the notebook he was scribbling in, and Myra blinked at me for a moment before sighing. She smiled, and I wondered if I was imagining the hint of sadness in her gaze.

"Thank you, Hazel. You have it in hand, as usual," Myra said.

"She always does," Reddy echoed, and Myra flinched before turning away from me, nodding.

"Good girl, and tell Alexa to take your chase scene. You deserve an easy night for once," Myra said.

Reddy looked up from his desk, staring at Myra's back, but he said nothing and I slipped out, shutting the door behind me again.

❦

THE REAL TRICK to The Company of Fiends' aerial act wasn't strength or knowing how to wrap the long stream of silk correctly around your body. As far as I knew, Mr. Reddy had seen a proper aerial act at a carnival once, and decided to throw it into the theater's rotation. After all, how hard could the work be when you had actors who could fly?

No, the most important part of our version of silks was trusting Ronan Fuchs.

Trusting an imp was always a risk. Ronan might be struck by a spontaneous impulse to drop me at any moment, just to make the audience gasp and me scream. He had a flair for that kind of drama. It was what made the act so good. But an imp's mischief wasn't cruel, especially not Ronan's. He would always catch his partner.

Still, I held onto his horns like my life depended on it as he held me upside-down, the silk and his hands wrapped around my waist as his long black tongue licked me from ass to clit.

I gasped and writhed, eyes wide in the blinding glare of the spotlight as he thrust that tongue inside of me, growling against my sex. We were spinning slowly with the gentle force of one of Ronan's wings flapping. I tried to remember all the notes for the scene—keep your body extended, point your toes, make a pretty picture with your legs around his back—but Ronan knew my responses too well to let me focus on the work. My toes were pointed because they were starting to curl, and my back was arched because of the sparkling blade of an orgasm now racing through me.

I gasped and whimpered as Ronan rumbled, pleased with me or with himself. I didn't care. He lapped at me as I shivered, my legs starting to slip from their coil around him. He pulled away, sliding me against his chest until we were nose to nose, his cock bumping against my now slippery sex.

"You don't taste like orc cum," he said through a bared-teeth smile—our usual way of communicating with one another on stage.

I gasped at the words, afraid I might suddenly burst into laughter on stage, and before Ronan could thrust into me, I reached down and loosened the spiral of the silk around my waist. I spun in the air, and after a bark of surprise and a great gasp from the audience, Ronan was diving after me, a graceful hurtle toward the stage floor.

He caught me by the swirling tail of rich blue fabric, snagging it in his grip and then catching me by the waist. Below, the audience roared with delight, clapping as Ronan flew us up to safety.

"Daring," he said. He untwisted the silk from around my waist, creating a cradle for me to sit in, and then tossed the loose end of silk up to the rafters, where it was caught by another imp and tied off.

"He was a very shy orc," I answered through my broad smile as Ronan's hands braced my back. I stretched out, my stomach tightening to hold me straight as Ronan hovered over me.

"A shy orc?" he asked. "Never heard of such a thing."

"I think he might be here tonight," I said, studying the audience but unable to make out any faces clearly through the glare of light pointed at us. It was a magic trick we knew—stare blindly out into that light, and plenty of the monsters in the seats would think I was looking at them.

"Legs," Ronan said.

My legs stretched around him and I reached up, grabbing onto either side of the silk cradle. Ronan winked at me, a playful warning, and then flapped his wings as he drew me close, turning us in a sudden somersault through the air while thrusting his hips and sinking his cock inside of me.

I let out a broken cry that turned to laughter as we swung forward toward the audience, flipping and swaying. Beth was tiny and graceful and used to the act, so she and Ronan made something dramatic and pretty out of it. Ronan and *I*, on the other hand, couldn't help but *play* when we were together, too good of friends to resist a laugh in the middle of a scene.

It didn't matter. The audience cheered as we swayed in the air, Ronan's rocking pace slow and wonderfully deep, using his wings to steer us so we spun in one direction and unraveled twice as fast in the other. I relaxed, let my shoulders and head hang, leaving the control in Ronan's capable hands as he fucked me and flew, swinging us back and forth, spinning and turning. At the corner of the stage, Nireas watched us, his fingers moving over the keys and pedals, making a melody out of our movements.

"Do you like him?" Ronan whispered. I blinked and almost stiffened, forcing myself to stay relaxed, elegant for the audience. "The orc patron."

Oh. I hadn't told anyone about Hunter following me home and rescuing me, and talking through my teeth in the middle of a sex scene wasn't the time to do so. "He seems sweet. A good kisser."

Ronan apparently didn't have anything to say to that, and I tested out my strength, rocking to meet him, the tempo of Nireas's music increasing slightly.

Ronan hunched over me, pressed his chest to mine, and ground himself against my clit until my breath started to catch.

"You thought I meant *him*," he whispered in my ear, his gaze gesturing down to the organ. "Our musical giant."

Gegenees, I corrected, but only to myself. Nireas was a kind of giant, I supposed, but his was an old Greek race.

"He's watching you," Ronan continued.

"He's watching us," I answered, gasping as his hips bucked roughly into mine, the silks shivering in my grip. "For timing."

"No, nut. He's watching *you*. He doesn't give a fuck about anyone's timing. Doesn't watch Beth," Ronan hissed my ear, nuzzling against my jaw to hide his speech from the audience.

Nireas *was* watching, his dark gaze holding mine as he played.

"He watches you in every scene, watches you in rehearsal, backstage."

"Stop," I whispered.

"Have you fucked him?" Ronan asked.

"No."

Nireas only did one scene for the theater, aside from playing music, and I'd never been offered the part. I suspected it was an intentional slight from Nireas, just another piece of a puzzle that formed eight years of him avoiding me like the plague, but I didn't want to say so.

"I bet he's big. That's your type," Ronan rumbled in my ear, and his hips slapped against me, drawing out a high cry from my lips and an echoing note from the organ. "Should I fly you down there right now? Thrust your pretty wet cunt in his face and—"

"Stop," I hissed, releasing the silks to grab onto the base of Ronan's wings, where they were especially sensitive.

He shouted, arching and taking those dangerous whispers away from my ear. I squeezed at the roots of his wings, and his thrusts grew urgent. He released my back, letting me dangle from the silks around my ass, his cock sinking deeper. The audience cheered as we both groaned, as what was meant to be elegant and slow became rough and clumsy and determined, almost animal.

And damnit, but Ronan was right—Nireas's stare was palpable, a fold of concentration or worry on his brow as he watched Ronan bucking into me. Worse, I'd known. I'd always known Nireas watched.

Watched but never touched, although his stare was almost enough. It caressed over my breasts, skimmed over my lips, and tugged on the roots of my hair, written out in melody as he played and studied me.

"He wants you, and he won't touch you," Ronan hissed down at me.

I started to shake, my hands slipping from Ronan's back.

"Ronan, please," I whimpered.

"Show him, Hazel. Show him what he refuses to have." Ronan used the silks and the rough beat of his wings as leverage, crashing us together.

My arms fell back, legs spread but dangling, and the sound of the audience was washed beneath the storm coming from the organ music as I hung in an arch, body tensing and all but breaking with the force of my finish. But I couldn't close my eyes.

Not while Nireas was watching.

4.
A LAMPPOST FOR A SPOTLIGHT

I froze as the curtain to my dressing room twitched, wondering if I would slap Ronan when he walked in, or drag him to the chaise and ride his cock until he was in too much agony to torture me with his stupid chatter.

But it wasn't Ronan at all who so tentatively pushed the fabric aside. Of course not. The imp would've barged in without an invitation.

"Hello, Miss Nix, might I—"

"Hunter!" I cried, darting forward and dragging the gentleman orc inside the room with me. One boundary Ronan would leave alone was interrupting a patron's visit, if only because Myra would prick holes in his wings if she caught him.

Hunter's eyes widened as I yanked on his arm, but he stumbled into the narrow room and the curtain slid shut behind him. I'd replaced my candle from the night before, and Hunter's shadow crawled high up the brick wall to the ceiling.

"I was hoping you'd be here tonight," I said, aware of my own blush as I thought of Ronan's teasing.

Hunter gaped at me briefly, so obviously surprised by the declaration he seemed to forget to speak. I leaned in, ready to whisper in his ear that I'd searched the audience for him, see how he responded to the flirtation, when the words tumbled from him.

"I thought I might offer the use of my carriage to you this evening, and to your friend of course," he said, the latter part added in a quick afterthought.

"Will you be in the carriage?" I asked, grinning.

He blinked at me, and his gaze slid to my shoulder where my robe was hanging loose. "I'm happy to walk, so you and the other young woman might have—"

I laughed and let my hands stroke up Hunter's arms, admiring the muscle I found hidden under all that fabric. He stiffened under my touch and as I stepped forward to lean into him, his hands hovered at our sides.

"You mistake me, sir. I was *hoping* you'd join me at my door again," I said. Hunter's smile was genuine but nervous, and I released him from my teasing. "Beth didn't show up to the theater today, so it will just be me and I'm done for the night. Sit there and I'll change and we can leave right away."

"Is she unwell?" Hunter asked as he took a seat on the chaise, and I was surprised by the real concern in his tone.

I watched a reflection of him in my mirror as I shed the robe, that sharp hunger appearing on his features again as he watched me pretend to hunt through piles of mending to find a dress.

"She's unreliable. Probably found one of her lovers on the way home and was too tired to come into work today," I said, shrugging and then bending to rummage under a stool, glancing through my lashes to watch Hunter's black claws dig into the knees of his trousers, gaze fixed to my ass.

"You—" His voice came out a growl, and he cleared his throat before speaking again. "You often miss your final bow."

It wasn't a question. Hunter had been watching for me these past couple months.

I stood again, feigning a gasp as I spotted my dress draped over the rickety chair in front of my mirror. "I do," I said, debating whether or not to tell him that after eight years, a curtain call was starting to feel like an unnecessary chore. It was easier to be cleaning up and getting ready to leave, than swarming up and down the stairs with the rest of the company.

"You don't care as much for the applause as the others," he said.

It was my turn to pause in surprise, and I hid the reaction under the skirt of my dress, wrestling my way through the bodice. "I suppose...an audience will clap at the end of a show no matter what," I said, straightening the waist of the dress around me as I thought. "Even if they only enjoyed themselves a little bit. I prefer the reactions that come during a scene—the gasps or the cheers, even the laughs. Those are honest, rather than queued, and...they're for *me*."

It was more than I meant to say, my own quiet obsession with my audience's adoration. My need for their stares on me, their approval, a craving and hunger buried so deeply in me, it seemed to clench with every beat of my heart. I cleared my throat and shook my head, drawing in an uneven breath. "How many buttons shall we fasten, hmm?"

I turned in front of Hunter, offering him my unbuttoned dress. The chaise creaked, and Hunter's body was warm at my back. My breath hitched at the first gentle scratch of his claws on my lower spine.

"We could even leave them undone if you like," I said, reaching to pull my hair over my shoulder.

The waist of my dress grew snug as he fastened the buttons into place. "I think you try to tease me, Miss Nix."

I couldn't help my grin as I turned my head, charmed by the furrow of concentration on his green brow. "It's only teasing if I don't mean it, sir."

ॐ

HUNTER'S CARRIAGE was warm and cozy, and he ignored my invitation to sit at my side, so I rested my head against the cushioned side and watched London pass out the dark window. He wasn't wearing his charmed disguise—the carriage was also spelled for his privacy—and seemed content to stare at me without making any other advances.

I knew Myra was hoping this orc might be the "nice man" to take care of me in my not-quite-old-age, and while I was sure there were signs of interest, Hunter was proving to be a bit of a puzzle. I'd never heard of an orc who only liked to *watch*, but perhaps this was the case. If only I knew how to ask.

"Have you always lived in London?" I asked as we bumped

along the paved roads, murky fog from the sewers rolling and fluttering around the wheels of the carriage.

"No, my kind come from the woods far north of here," he said, finally turning to stare out the window, frowning at the city around us. "Like the trolls. And you?"

We were rounding Stepney Green Park and turning onto Jamaica Street, and I studied the familiar shops and public houses. "My father had a farm in Somerset, but I don't remember it. I've lived here nearly all my life."

"And your father, did he return?"

"He died," I said absently, noticing a crowd of figures halfway down the block that we were slowly approaching.

"I'm sorry for your loss, and so young—"

"Hunter," I said, not mentioning that I was older than I looked, sitting forward and reaching for the door of the carriage as I realized where the crowd was gathered. "This is Beth's apartment, can we stop?"

Hunter didn't hesitate from rapping against the roof of the carriage, and I gathered up my skirt and jumped out the moment the driver appeared to open the door. The crowd was dense, but it was mainly made of black uniforms with gleaming buttons and badges—police, all hovering and bustling in and out of Beth's door. I walked slowly forward, eyeing the windows of the building—expecting a fire—and then the door where the men darted in and out.

It wasn't until Hunter caught up to my side, draping his coat over my shoulders and stopping me with a hand on my stomach, that I noticed the mound of white on the ground, surrounded by the boots of police officers. It was placed beneath the bright glow of a street lamp, the flame turned up high for their work, and it shone even in the shadow of the crowd.

I gasped as one of the men reached down, pulling back the bright white of the sheet to reveal an even more brilliant glow of fiery orange-red hair.

"No." The word gusted out of me in a breath, my eyes growing wide.

That was Beth's hair, three shades brighter than my own and wonderfully glossy. There was a flash of a photographer's camera, and I whimpered as the sheet was flicked back up over the head of the body on the ground. My hands covered my mouth, and I searched that crowd as if one of the faces of the men swarming Beth might offer an answer. My eyes snagged on another pair, too far away to see the color, but an undeniably sharp gaze in a beautifully handsome face. The man was dressed in a suit rather than a uniform, with a heavy black coat draped over his shoulders and a bowler hat tipped back on his head. He had high cheekbones cut down the side of his face like daggers and a perfect pair of bow lips, which only slightly distracted from his very obvious narrow-eyed stare now fixed to me.

"Miss Nix, I think it would be best if we left the scene," Hunter murmured in my ear.

I startled as I remembered him, finding the small human man at my side rather than the broad and protective orc, and nodded dumbly. I couldn't focus enough to find the striking man in the crowd again, and then Hunter was turning me in place, guiding me back to the carriage and lifting me inside.

He didn't wait for my invitation now, squeezing onto the seat at my side and reaching for my hands. His touch was scorching around my fingers, and I gasped again as we lurched into motion.

"We all...just thought she'd missed a day," I said, my head whipping to stare out the window as we passed the crowd.

There! There was the man again, glaring at our carriage, eyes flicking rapidly, clearly unable to see in through Hunter's protective spells.

"Did it happen tonight?" I wondered aloud.

"I will make inquiries, Miss Nix," Hunter said.

I blinked and turned back to him, the passing street lamps rolling the shadows back and forth over his human disguise in an eerie effect.

"You will?"

"I have connections within the monster community, of course. But my disguise also is well seated with the humans, including the police," Hunter explained. "Would you prefer to return to the theater?"

I opened my mouth to say *yes*. Someone would need to tell Myra and Reddy. There was a chain hanging from Hunter's pocket, and he didn't stop me as I pulled it free, flicking open the round watch and frowning at the time.

"No. No, we can't. No one but the stagehands who board there will still be there," I said. Ronan would be there, but he wouldn't know what to do in this situation.

The carriage turned, and I realized how quickly we were driving now as I tipped forward into Hunter's chest. But he was warm and he smelled like the earth of a garden, vividly alive in summer, and I dropped the pocket watch in favor of gathering his jacket and vest in my fists. His arms wrapped around my back as I sank into his frame.

"We are nearly to your home, Miss Nix. It will be all right. I'll walk inside with you."

"Stay. Stay with me, please," I whispered, wincing at the crack in my words. When Hunter didn't respond, I arched and tilted my head back enough to look at him, frustrated by the false face staring back at me. "If it won't trouble you...if no one is waiting for you..."

Perhaps he had a mate, and a human girl was simply an object of attraction to him. That happened sometimes.

But Hunter's warm hand reached to my cheek and his thumb stroked my jaw and down over the pulse of my throat. "I have no one waiting for me, little one. Are you sure?"

My laugh was ragged, the shock of seeing my friend on the ground surrounded by police leaving me stiff and awkward and cold in my own skin. "Sure? I've all but begged you to bed me, Hunter."

His brow furrowed and he nodded once. "If there is some sense of obligation, or if you wish to please your employer, you needn't worry. I will come to the theater, support its work, regardless of any—"

"Hunter!"

The carriage jerked to a stop and Hunter stretched around me, opening the door and hurrying to step down, his hand held out to help me down. I swallowed my objection to his statement.

"Come with me, please. I don't want to be alone," I said, stepping down and gripping his hand in mine. He followed calmly, already determined to search my apartment.

Beth is dead. She was in the street.

I knew our neighborhood wasn't safe, but I'd lived here all my life. Some of the villains on Jamaica Street had watched me grow up. I'd always had a sense that I was protected here, but was that really true?

I marched forward with Hunter's hand held tightly, unlocking the front door and ignoring the dark entrance hall and the sense that there might be an unfamiliar shadow lurking in a corner.

Hunter took careful steps behind me, disguising his size and weight with a predator's grace, although not even a light step would muffle the creaks on some of the floorboards. It didn't matter. There was no nosy matron in this house to raise a riot for my virtue, and the other residents were used to my late arrivals. I knew what they must think of me, but the truth wasn't so far removed from the rumor, and I didn't care so long as I wasn't bothered.

My flat was cold as I opened the door, and Hunter immediately prowled through the sitting room and into the kitchen, pulling off his hat at last. I busied myself with turning all the latches, locking the world out, and locking this orc inside with me.

Door hinges and floorboards complained as Hunter searched the rooms, as if he might find the culprit here in *my* home. I shuddered at the thought, recalled the shadows of men cast over the drape of white on the ground, and stared at the empty narrow fireplace in front of me.

Hunter's approach was less urgent on his way back to me, steps light and quiet. "I apologize for—"

I spun in place and rushed toward him, cutting off the silly speech as I crashed into his chest. "You'll stay the night?"

I regretted leaving the theater early and wished briefly that it was Ronan now wrapping his arms around my back. He wouldn't be so hesitant to squeeze me tight against his chest, and for all his pot-stirring and teasing, he was familiar. Safe.

But Hunter was warm, and his grip grew more secure and confident as the seconds passed, and he'd protected me the night before in the park, and even now, making sure my flat was safe.

I'd never brought Ronan home with me, and if I hadn't left with Hunter, perhaps I would've walked alone tonight and seen Beth on the sidewalk and—

Hunter twisted, and his left arm scooped me up from behind my knees, carrying me through the kitchen. My father's old bed was still tucked into the corner, close enough to the stove to keep him warm in the winters, partly because I'd never found the time after joining the theater to move it out, and partly because it was the familiar landscape of my home. Hunter didn't stop. He'd found my small bedroom in his searching, and he carried me there now.

"I will light us a fire," he said, setting me down on my narrow bed.

I clutched my hands in his coat, finding his gaze almost glowing down at me in the dark room. "We don't need one."

He held still as I undid the buttons of his jacket, pushing it back on his shoulders.

"Miss Nix, that's not necessary—"

"You don't sleep in your dinner jacket normally, do you?" I asked, trying to keep the words light but only hearing a hollow quality in my own voice.

Hunter huffed and remained still as the jacket slipped down his arms. I pulled it free and carried it to a small chair in the corner where my nightgown was waiting, resting it over the seat.

"Light the candle?" I asked, reaching for my nightgown and button hook.

Hunter puttered behind me as I changed my dress, and when I turned, I found him watching me, still nearly fully dressed.

"You should sleep, Miss Nix."

"Hazel," I corrected, eyes narrowing at him as I crossed and reached for his vest.

He didn't stop me from undressing him this time, but his lips were curved slightly downwards at the corners outside his tusks. "You're distressed," he said. "And cold."

Both were true, and I glanced down to find that the chill had my nipples peaked and clearly visible through my nightgown.

"You've just discovered a terrible tragedy," Hunter added.

"I don't want to think about it," I said quickly, hurrying to speak before he could correct me. "If I think about it, I'll need answers. Shall I run out into the street, back to those policemen, to ask?"

I shoved open Hunter's white dress shirt and gaped at the sudden reveal of a number of scars, deep and light, fresh and old. Battle wounds? He was so full of strange contrasts.

Large hands and gentle black claws lifted my face up to his. How old was Hunter? There was something ageless in that deep yellow stare of his, but he looked almost as though he might be even younger than me.

"I don't wish you to regret any deed between us," he said.

It was sweet and a little baffling, and I was in no mood to be circumspect. His shirt whispered off his shoulders and to the floor, and I was surprised that a man who took such care with his appearance didn't seem to mind all his fine things landing on my dusty old worn floorboards.

"Do you regret our kiss?" I asked.

"I could never," he said, the words warm and rough. His skin was warm and soft, and he didn't seem self-conscious as I ran my fingertips over an old scar, although he stiffened when I grazed them down over berry-dark nipples where I found twin bolts of gold pierced through, two beads shining on either side. My wandering hands traveled to densely carved muscles and then to the buttons of his waistband.

He reached to stop me, and I arched an eyebrow. "Do you sleep in your nicely pressed pants too?"

"I ought to tonight," Hunter growled, and the sound was making up for the chill of the room.

He didn't stop me as I pulled the buttons free, holding his gaze, glancing up to admire the play of candlelight over those deep red braids drawn back from his broad face. I didn't tease him any further, not even sure myself what my aim was. Hunter was a stranger, and yet not, our interactions far beyond any I'd had with a theater patron before. Beth was dead. The thought made my breath short and my head spin, and I stepped back as Hunter finished removing his pants and shoes, pulling his feet free.

I'd just managed to control my wild expression as he stood

straight again, and my eyes snagged on the glitter of gold that suddenly appeared in front of me. There were two more beads at the base of Hunter's cock, larger than the ones on either side of his nipples, and brightly polished. Another four winked at me from the head of his cock, almost like the points of a compass.

"They are...traditional with my—" Hunter's throat cleared, and a large hand reached to cover himself.

I shook myself from my staring and realized Hunter was shifting away, his cheeks a darker, muddier shade than before. "They're beautiful," I blurted out. "Are there more?"

I stepped forward and he flinched, backing up almost into my bedside drawers. "I know they can be shocking."

I knew one thing in all my time at the theater—never laugh at a cock. And it wasn't the cock I wanted to laugh at, it was beautiful and perfectly long and thick, but the enormous and skittish orc who was suddenly shy at revealing his elaborately decorated member.

"I've seen some before," I said, neglecting to mention I'd happily ridden pierced cocks for both work and pleasure. I stepped forward, and this time, Hunter didn't move. "May I?"

I reached out, and his hands lowered. He cleared his throat as I reached for him, shoulders high, but his cock jumped happily as I stroked down the ample length.

There was more gold below—a twin line of beads bolted through the underside of his length, which I'd seen before on other men—and then a few surprise additions around his shockingly heavy sac.

"They're beautiful," I said again, trailing my fingers over the ladder of beads to the four points at the head. Fluid gathered at his tip, weeping into my palm as I rolled one of the piercings. "These go all the way through."

"Yes," Hunter rasped. His shoulders had dropped, and his chest was heaving. "You're very kind," he said softly.

He didn't reach to guide my hand into a grip like any other man would, simply stood frozen as I examined him. I reached out to the large beads at his base. They were close together, and I suspected they would rub at my clit with a good seat on the orc's cock. He would be fun to lick. To fuck.

"They're about status, right?" I asked, and he perked up.

"For warriors. For our strength," he said.

Which explained the copious scars. "I've never seen so many before," I said, smiling up at him.

His cheeks were still dark, but he looked less ashamed of himself at last. I wrapped the hand he'd been leaking precum into around his length and pumped, watching his eyelids grow heavy and his lips part on a pant with one stroke. I reached down with the other to explore the piercings there too, and he stopped me with a grip on each wrist.

"You must rest, Miss—"

I cut him off. "Don't you dare say Nix." I squeezed the cock and balls in my hands, and he grunted, thrusting briefly before pulling me away.

"Miss Hazel," he said, voice rough but firm and lips twitching.

I sighed. There was only so far it was right to push, and I'd probably already stepped over that line. I twisted my hands in his, let him feel his own sticky arousal in my palm, and pushed him to the bed. He was obedient, although his eyes were narrowed with suspicion.

"We won't fit side by side," I said. "And I want your warmth. Lie down."

I turned to blow out the candle as Hunter pulled back the covers of the bed, its frame groaning slightly with his weight. I would've groaned too, although not as a complaint. I found him rigid and awkward on the mattress as I climbed in, but he adjusted himself for me as I worked my way to lying almost on top of him. His cock was half-hard against my hip, and my own sex pulsed slightly with the urge to grind into his hip as I settled, but he was the right height to nestle my cheek into his shoulder.

He drew the blankets up over us with his knee, and his arms circled my back, his hands resting just above my ass. "All will be well, little one," Hunter murmured, brushing his beard against the top of my head. "I will guard your safety tonight."

5.

STRANGE BEDFELLOWS

I tried to sleep, I really did. But all there was to think about was Beth on the ground, her hair bright as a copper farthing, and the long dark legs of policemen surrounding her.

And I was sure Hunter tried to sleep too, but his cock remained stiff against the skirt of my nightgown, a little fluid beading through to kiss my hip.

Goose bumps laced my back where Hunter wasn't touching, and my cunt was hot where I was pressed to his thick thigh. I knew what I wanted, and I was ashamed of myself. I hadn't cried for Beth, hadn't screamed in horror, and now all I could think of was her dead body lying on the sidewalk in Jamaica Street and the cock pressed to my hip. I hadn't thought of Beth while I'd touched Hunter, examined him, and when his nails dug briefly into my ass before retreating, I forgot her again.

I *wanted* to forget. I wanted to sleep.

I wanted...

I took in a heavy breath, my lips parted against Hunter's skin, the taste of green roots and fresh rain teasing my tongue. I shifted, trying to find a position where his hot skin wouldn't press so firmly against me, and my breasts scraped against his chest as I shifted. His cock twitched and Hunter bucked, and now he was there against the inside of my thigh, those gold beads on his cockhead warming the crease of my hip.

I wanted to fuck and pretend nothing was wrong, to push away the shock and the questions and the fear.

My tongue flicked out to wet my lips and found his skin first. Salty and surprisingly sweet, richer and muskier than his fresh scent, his flavor created a sudden craving on my tongue. Hunter's breath hitched, and those black claws scratched lower into the soft flesh of my ass.

We were frozen, suspended in the quiet of the room and the beats of time between our uneven breaths. Hunter would retreat. He'd proven as much already. There was something cautious and shy in his answers and refusals. I was aware of how absurd I was being, throwing myself at an orc who always tucked my hands away. I should've let him leave, or sleep in the kitchen on my father's bed if he wanted to make sure I was safe. I knew there was interest, but interest didn't necessarily mean intention.

And then his claws dragged back up, gathering a fistful of my ass and nightgown as his hips arched and rubbed against me. Rather than releasing the moan in my throat, I opened my mouth and latched onto the skin of his neck, my hands sliding up to grasp his shoulders. I sucked on his flesh, and it was like drinking down a summer I'd never known, the heart of a bursting garden on my tongue.

Hunter gasped and his hips stilled, but his hands flew up to my head, claws digging into my hair and scratching at my roots. I replaced the motion he'd abandoned, rolling and twisting myself on top of him, scratching the skin under my fingernails, digging my teeth into his skin.

"Ferocious little one," he gasped, bucking again.

Quit resisting, I wanted to say, but I refused to give up this taste of him. I shifted, finding a new spot on his collarbone and sliding myself to sit astride him properly. He was darker here, more like bitter pine needles, and I lapped and sucked greedily, lifting my hips once and drawing my nightgown out of the way.

We both gasped as our flesh kissed, the ladder of piercings on the underside of his cock now pressed to my sex. His hands returned to my ass as I started to ride the spot unabashedly, and I sighed and returned to my feast of skin as he pressed me closer at last. Those little gold beads felt like heaven on my swollen and needy sex, and I ground myself down, movements rough and clumsy.

This wasn't a scene, and while I should've been charming and playful with Hunter, like I would with any other patron, seeing to him more than to myself, this strange and dark moment made me selfish.

Hunter's growl was low as he started to move with me, and I was making his cock glossy and slippery along the bottom. I could've chased to my finish like that with his pretty gold taking care of me, but I wanted more.

Hunter's hands gripped me, tried to hold me in place for a moment, but he let me rise up on my knees, and I watched his eyes widen in the dark as I reached between us, guiding the head of him to my opening.

"Miss Nix—"

I might've waited, but then he used that absurd formal name. I glared down at him in defiance and sank onto his cock. I gasped at the curious little press of the beads at my opening, and Hunter's eyes fell shut on a moan. Then his hands were gripping tight again, and suddenly, we were crashing together.

I bit down on the cry in my throat as Hunter filled me, yanking me down as he thrusted up, and he let out one loud groan before I reached out to slap my hand over his mouth, his tusks an interesting bite against my palm.

"Neighbors," I whispered, rising up and shivering at the drag of him inside of me.

Hunter nodded, licking my palm and humming more softly, some of that raw excitement from a moment ago fading. I wanted it back. The shy and chivalrous orc was sweet and charming, but I wanted the warrior who had earned his scars and piercings, who'd taken me in one unapologetic thrust.

It was harder to do it without his help, but I relaxed my thighs and dropped myself heavily down onto his lap, nearly breaking my own silence as the beads at his base stroked either side of my clit roughly. I whimpered, rubbing and grinding myself in place, still close to the edge, and this time, it was Hunter who grew impatient.

He sat up and lifted me to his tip before immediately pulling me down again. We both dove forward, lips colliding, and while we managed to muffle our voices in a stroking, licking, fucking kiss, there was no quieting the bed, the thump of uneven legs on the floor, and the groan of old boards. I didn't care. I didn't even really care about the neighbors. I just didn't want Hunter being a gentleman. Not when I could have him fuck me with this simple brutality instead.

He grunted as our hips slapped together, and his claws scratched at the back of my neck as he used his grip there to haul us together, stealing my breath with every full pump of him inside of me. I wanted to cry every time he drew free, wanted to pin him down to use those beads for my own pleasure, wanted to sit and just feel the weight and power of him inside of me.

His kiss was still full of the flavor of summer, tongue sharp and long, tickling the back of my throat until I grunted and then retreating. I knew orcs had long tongues, had enjoyed a fair few, and I chased it in the kiss, found it before it vanished and sucked on the tip. Hunter's claws scratched deeper, his arms circling me and pinning me tight to his chest.

He was staying buried now, rocking with short but heavy thrusts, keeping my clit near those teasing beads, and I forgot to stay quiet. The cool surface of the wall kissed my back and my thighs stretched open as Hunter pinned me there, fucking me with quick hard snaps of his hips, holding me still by my neck and ass. I clung to him, thrilled with this new man in my arms, with the wild pound of our hearts together.

He snarled into the kiss and pulled away as I whined. "Come," he ordered, the word almost cruel as his hand circled to the front of my throat. He leaned back and looked down at where we were joined, pressing hard to the spot and rolling his hips so perfectly that I let out a strangely animal sound. His cock was rocking inside of me, the piercing at his base rubbing at either side of my clit.

"Come for me now, little one," he growled as I started to clench and flutter on his length.

I shuddered and obeyed, although it wasn't a choice but a simple matter of fact. I couldn't breathe with the grip on my throat, and it was just one less thing to think about. Vivid lights flashed in my eyes, illuminating Hunter's snarling expression and electric gaze on mine. There was a shocking splash of fluid between us and then a sudden flood of air as my back hit the mattress.

Hunter was on top of me, growling and rutting, my knees pushed to my chest and spread wide. My head tapped against the wall three times, and then his hand was there, either protecting me or holding me still so he could strike harder, deeper. We were sideways, I realized, Hunter's feet braced on the floor and his chest holding me down with all his strength and weight.

This is him, I realized. This was the orc Hunter hid behind fine clothes and human manners. He was exquisite. I stretched my knees farther aside, and he licked a stripe up my throat and right into my ear. His tempo was growing uneven, breaths almost panicked, and I reached over to stroke softly at his back.

"Yes, orc," I whispered in his ear, kissing the lobe and nibbling up to the sensitive tip. "*Yes.*"

He gasped and stiffened, and then thrust almost cruelly against me, filling me with hot cum at every punishing strike. It seeped out between us, thick and warm and smelling of summer, and I came again with a surprising shudder that made Hunter howl into the mattress by my hair.

"Forgive me," he rasped, stealing my breath with his weight, nudging his hips more gently to mine, still spurting in small bursts. "Forgive me, little one."

I opened my mouth to tell him the truth. I owed him as much forgiveness and this was *everything* I'd wanted from him, but his lips found mine first with a deep and pleading kiss that seemed to show no sign of ending. Long after my breath was stolen and my head was dizzy and my body limp, Hunter moved us back to lying down, his cock still buried deep inside of me.

THE CHAIN SCRAPED against the uneven floor, the ghostly voice of my father speaking through the metal clanks and scratches.

"You'll leave me."

"I won't, Pa."

"You will. Like her. Like your kind."

The words dragged down my back, made the tops of my ears throb and burn and itch. I carried the scorching bowl of broth in my outstretched hands, the chain hissing behind me with every step, cuff biting into my ankle.

"Don't leave me, Hazel." He was such a small figure on the bed in the corner, withering away, eyes huge and somehow empty too. I had the auburn hair I remembered from his youth, but now his was all grey and yellow.

"I won't leave, Pa," I repeated, my lips raw with the words.

"You will."

"I don't." The words snapped out, and the metal on my ankle scratched and tore at my flesh. I crumbled to the edge of the bed, and my father retreated into the wall at his back at my nearness. I never left, some hazy, wakeful part of my thought. You said I would, and I never did.

"You will."

"I can't, Pa." Tears were scratches of flames down my cheeks, and the spoon in my fingers burned my skin as I raised it to his lips. "Where would I go?"

❧

I KNEW IMMEDIATELY upon waking that I was alone, not as though I might be able to *lose* Hunter in my tiny bedroom. I huddled under my blankets, peeking out from the sheet to find morning dim and bleeding hazily through my window. I reached down to my ankle, half expecting to find torn flesh, the joint still aching. But my skin was unmarred and the pain vanished as I touched the spot. Because I'd never really been chained. Not with anything so simple as metal cuffs and links. The dream had been a blurry mix of memory and nightmare.

I passed a hand over my hip next and found a few raised scratches from Hunter's claws, evidence of what had passed in the middle of the night. There was more evidence between my thighs, and I winced as I shifted and the mess grew obvious. The air was warmer than I'd expected as I pushed the covers back, the soft crackle and pop from the kitchen revealing that Hunter had lit a fire in the stove. My nightgown was wadded up around my waist, and I shifted slowly. I wasn't sore, but there was a pleasant sense of *use* in my body.

I stood on wobbling legs. Last night had been the first time in weeks that I'd had sex just because I'd wanted to. But that only reminded me of *why* I'd wanted to.

Beth.

I hissed as I washed myself with a small cloth and cold water from the day before, and then hurried to dress. Myra and Reddy would be back at the theater by the time I arrived. They needed to know what had happened.

Aside from the fire in the stove, which looked as though it had been burning for a few hours, there were no signs of Hunter's presence. Part of me wanted to take the time to think of the orc—had I offended him in the night, would he return to the theater even after we'd had sex, or move on to a different girl —but I had put off my real concern long enough.

I dressed in a rush, grabbing the last apple from the counter and damping down the fire in the stove. It would be cold when I returned later tonight, but I was used to this flat feeling more like a grave than a home. My eyes avoided the bed in the corner, the familiar nightmare too fresh in my thoughts.

The theater took up all my time now. At first, it had been a relief to have the freedom to leave the flat and wander the city, to not only care night and day for my father. Lately though, home was just the place I took a few hours each night to rest. The privacy was wonderful compared to backstage, but there was a downside I was reluctantly discovering.

Loneliness.

I ignored it for the moment, wrapping myself in a shawl and hurrying out the door.

I liked early morning in my neighborhood. The drunks had gone to bed or been rounded up, and the familiar faces I'd grown up with appeared, throwing open shop doors or leaving their stoops to go to work.

"Morning, Miss Nix, lovely as always," John Winsor, the butcher at the corner of Jamaica Street, called to me.

John was portly and sweet, and getting nearly old enough to turn his shop over to his son-in-law. When I was a little girl, he'd been a young man just taking the reins from his own father. As he stared at me and smiled, nodded as I waved, I wondered if he noticed it. Was it time for me to leave? Did John realize how old he'd grown and how young I still looked? Did he count the years in his head and question why a woman who was surely now a spinster, never mind also probably a whore, was still in her first bloom of youth?

Pa had wanted us to leave the neighborhood even before he'd died, but he'd been too weak to force the issue. A decade later, and I was pushing my luck.

I certainly was as I walked slowly down the block, approaching the door of Beth's apartment building. They'd cleared her body away by now, of course, but there was a police officer exiting the front door, whose glance I avoided, and a few more speaking with locals around the block. I wrapped my shawl tighter around my shoulders and hurried my steps to the corner.

"Hazel! There she is."

I flinched, but it was too late to change course as Louisa Wadham stepped forward into my path, a basket over her arm filled with bread so fresh it steamed in the cool air, and a familiar figure at her side.

"Hazel, you knew the...girl, didn't you?"

I ignored Louisa, blinking into the crisp pale blue stare of the officer I'd locked eyes with the night before. He was clearer, although the brim of his hat still seemed to obscure the expression on his face. He had sharp features and pale skin, almost like vampires, but he glowed and stood comfortably in daylight. His clothes were tidy and crisp, but showed signs of age and wear.

I opened my mouth to deny my familiarity with Beth, or even the idea I might know what they were discussing, but Louisa spoke before I could.

"The pair of them walk home together from...wherever they are at night," Louisa said meaningfully.

Louisa and I had played together a few times when I was a girl, when my father was working and I could sneak out of the flat to explore the neighborhood. But Louisa had grown up, married the owner of one of the pubs on the street, and her hair was starting to turn grey around the edges. She stared at me with suspicion now.

"Miss..." the man said, those eerie blue eyes narrowing at me.

"Nix. Beth and I worked at the theater together," I said, marching forward. "I need to go there now. They don't know what's happened."

"They're interviewing the neighborhood!" Louisa squawked, but the officer just jogged to keep up with me.

"Miss Nix, I'm Detective Sergeant Piper. You were there last night." His voice was cool and heavy, almost comforting and dangerous at the same time.

"I was on my way home."

"In a carriage. You didn't wait for Miss O'Mahony?"

I chewed on my lip, steps slowing as my head raced. DS Piper was tall, and he cast a shadow over me as we walked. I wanted to help Beth, but Beth was dead, so what help could there really be? And Hunter had promised to investigate the matter. If I cooperated with London detectives, I might put the theater at risk, rather than offer any justice for Beth's death.

I glanced at the detective out of the corner of my eye and found him searching the street as we walked.

"She didn't come to work yesterday," I said, deciding the information was safe and important enough to their case to be worth saying.

"You don't travel to work together?" he asked.

I scrunched my nose, wishing I'd bitten my tongue and found a way to shake him off. I knew what Louisa and probably the rest of the neighborhood would lead the detectives to believe. We were whores. We wandered London looking for work at night.

"Beth isn't very reliable. And it's safe during the day. We only walked home together, and not always. No one realized anything was wrong just because she missed a show," I said.

"Does she walk home alone when you take a carriage?"

I shot a glare at the detective, wondering what he was really asking for in the question, my head too busy with ideas. "What does that have to do with anything?" I snapped.

He only blinked at me, and a ray of sunlight cut through the clouds to strike his eyes, revealing an almost silver cast to the color. "Anything could be relevant."

"Beth and I walked together the night before. I cut through the park so I left her...here, actually," I said, pausing and staring at the edge of the park. "Do you know when she died?"

"Did you see anyone when you walked through the park that night?" he asked, ignoring my question.

I opened my mouth, thinking of the thief, of Hunter, trying to imagine every possible consequence for anything I might say. The man who'd tried to attack me had left with broken hands. There was no way he could've hurt Beth after what Hunter had done. And Hunter...

Hunter had left me at my door with a kiss.

He'd offered to escort Beth home last night, seemed concerned by her absence. But the memory of his hand on my throat, stealing my breath as he fucked me with a selfish intensity, floated into my thoughts. I'd craved the violence that had exploded between us the night before, but it twisted strangely in my thoughts now.

"No," I said, abrupt and strong before shaking my head clear again and looking at DS Piper. "No, I was alone in the park."

His impassive expression didn't so much as twitch, but suspicion radiated from that stare. And I couldn't blame him. I'd hesitated too long. I knew too much, and I couldn't decide what could be spoken and what had to remain a secret.

"What theater is it that you ladies...act at?" he asked, stumbling over the words.

"The Bawdy Row," I said, resisting the urge to sigh at the first lie I was prepared with. "Tiny place down an alley in Covent Gardens. Not *much* of a theater, but I'm sure the neighborhood already gave you plenty of their thoughts on that."

His lips pressed flat, and it only drew attention to how full they really were and the fine cut of his jaw as it clenched. He was uncannily handsome, and it set me on edge, my head flitting from thoughts of Hunter to the sight of Beth's body.

"How did she die?" I asked.

"I can't answer questions about an ongoing investigation,

Miss Nix. However, I may need to speak with you again. Is there an address for you?"

I gave up the address reluctantly, adding, "I'm rarely home." He scribbled the words down in his notebook, and all I could see was Hunter's grimace, gaze glowing down at me. "Was she strangled?"

DS Piper blinked at his notebook, glancing up with narrowed eyes. "Amongst other things," he said, and then his jaw ticked, aware of his own slip.

I was aware of mine too, asking a question too close to a truth. Ice raced through me, and as I skirted back I nearly ran into someone else. DS Piper remained in place.

"I have to go. I have to... The theater needs to know," I said.

"We'll speak again, Miss Nix," that low and solemn voice called.

6.

A NEW ACT

"Dead," Mr. Reddy repeated.

"I saw her," I whispered.

Myra gasped and twisted to press her face into Reddy's chest, his arm tightening around her shoulders.

"What do you know?" he asked, frowning at me.

"Red," Myra hissed, leaning back to glare at him.

"Almost nothing," I said, my arms flapping uselessly at my side. "The detective wouldn't tell me anything." *Aside from that she was strangled...and more.*

"And what did you tell him?" Reddy pressed.

"Almost nothing," I repeated firmly. "That I saw her when we parted ways near our apartments. That she wasn't at the theater yesterday. No," I said when his mouth opened. "I told him the Bawdy Row."

Mr. Reddy's shoulders relaxed slightly, head nodding slowly. "Good girl."

"Hunter...Hunter was with me last night. He said he would make inquiries," I said, debating over saying more. But my trip to the theater had made my suspicions against the orc seem absurd. I'd practically forced myself onto him before he'd revealed any aggression. And why would he harm Beth? She probably would've been as happily eager to bed him as I was.

Mr. Reddy grunted. "I'll speak with him. But...more than likely, our Beth made her own bed."

Myra let out a strange sound, something between a growl and a sob, and Mr. Reddy petted a massive hand down the back of her head, revealing a rare tenderness as he kissed the crown of her head gently.

"What will you tell the others?" I asked.

"The truth," Reddy answered with a huffing sigh. "As far as we know, her death isn't connected to the theater. This is just a... great loss to our family." I liked him a little more for the gentle crack of his voice in the words.

"We should cancel shows," Myra murmured.

I caught the wince of Mr. Reddy's expression. He felt the loss of Beth, but he would feel it even more strongly if it hurt his pockets. I cleared my throat before he could refuse.

"We could dedicate a scene to her. No bawd, just..."

"Memoriam," Reddy said, the word heavy on his tongue.

Myra sighed and leaned back in the circle of his arms. "That would be lovely. Sweet. She deserves that from us."

Mr. Reddy gave his lover a solemn smile and a soft kiss, before nodding gratefully at me. "It should be you to go and tell the others," Mr. Reddy said, and I thought at first he was speaking to me until he cocked Myra's chin up with a thick finger and smiled gently down at her. "You're the right one. The kids look up to you. And I need a word with our Hazel."

I could just barely see the corner of Myra's frown as she stared back at him, but she nodded eventually. I wasn't worried until Myra turned, offering me a brittle smile.

"Thank you, lovey," Myra said, rounding Reddy's desk and patting my arms as she headed for the door. "I'm glad it was you who told us."

The voices of stagehands and actors rushed in as she opened the door, the cheerful notes and teasing and laughter such a jarring contrast to the hush of our conversation. Mr. Reddy watched Myra right until the moment the door snapped shut, then sagged into his chair with a *whoosh* of breath.

"We'll know more when we learn how she died. Her injuries," Mr. Reddy said.

And again, I should've told him what I did know, that she was strangled, but my tongue wouldn't form the words.

"This is a sorry business," he whispered, and I wondered if he meant Beth or the theater. His eyes flicked up at me, and his frown deepened. "Thank you." I nodded, and he pointed to the chair in front of the desk. "Sit."

The sound of the chair's feet scratching against the floor reminded me of the chain in my dreams of my father, and I winced and sank down slowly, aware of the fading ache of my body.

"We have a guest act arriving today," Mr. Reddy said.

"Is that why you didn't want to cancel shows?" I asked.

His lips twisted and his eyes narrowed. Years ago, when I first arrived, that expression would've terrified me, but Mr. Reddy was mostly bluster, and I was aware of a kind of respect we had for one another.

"I cancel shows, and everyone loses wages. I cancel shows, and our theater appears unreliable, our patrons wonder when we might close our doors to them again," Mr. Reddy said. "They won't feel our loss if they can't walk through the doors. No, you have the right of it. Make them weep with us. Make them remember Bethie by her absence under that spotlight. We are nothing if we aren't being watched by that audience, Nix."

My hands clenched in my lap, gripping fiercely around the fabric of my dress as I stared back at Mr. Reddy. The words unsettled me, but only because they rang with truth. No part of my life felt as vivid as when I was on stage. At least until last night.

"And the guest act?" I asked, thinking of the conversation I'd overheard between Reddy and Myra. Had that only been the day before?

"He's a demon. Folks call him the Gemini," Reddy said with a roll of his eyes and a shrug. His jaw ground briefly, and then he returned my stare. "He's not a good match for the other girls, Nix. Not...safe."

I'd been partnered with plenty of monsters that Reddy knew wouldn't work well with other girls. Some were too big. Some too rough. He'd never told me they weren't *safe*.

"Why?" I asked.

"He deals in pain," Reddy said flatly, watching me. "And pleasure, if I'm told correctly."

My eyes widened slightly, the words having a strange effect on me. "What do you mean? Plenty of—"

"I mean he's going to hurt you, Hazel," Reddy said. "I don't know how, but I do know that. It was all I could find out."

I licked my lips and found myself unable to look away from Mr. Reddy. "You're not talking about flogging or stockades."

He shook his head slowly.

There was plenty of pain measured out in the theater. Most of our scenes involved some element of acting terrified or as if our deeds were against our will. But it was *measured*. Mr. Reddy didn't want us truly hurt, not if it meant we couldn't go on stage the next night and do it all over again.

"You'll be safe. That's all I can promise," Mr. Reddy said, and I heard the strain, saw the fold of his brow and the nervous tap of his fingers.

He didn't like this. He didn't *want* this act for me, or for anyone else. *Hazel can handle it*, he had said to Myra.

Could I?

Maybe at one point. A year or two ago, even. Myra was right —I was tired. And now with Beth in my mind, I was a little frightened too.

"You mean I'll survive," I said.

Mr. Reddy's lips pressed flat and white, and that apology on his face was buried under a hard determination. "Don't be dramatic. You're the only one I can ask. Maybe, if I swap Alexa and Evie every other night."

A rough laugh escaped me and my head shook, eyes tearing off of the older man and drifting around the room. Reddy knew full well I wouldn't want my friends hurt. Hunter's snarl was in my vision again, the clamp of his hand around my throat, the burn and weight of his body on mine.

"Who knows. Maybe I'll enjoy myself," I murmured.

Mr. Reddy's shoulders sagged. "You might," he said weakly, thinking I'd surrendered in the conversation.

Maybe I had. I knew that if Reddy thought I was the only option, I couldn't let him put the other girls through the act.

"When does he arrive?" I asked.

"Today. You won't rehearse. Not yet, at least. Not if you don't want to." Mr. Reddy fumbled over his words, and I realized he really was worried. Maybe not *for* me, but that I might have refused.

I *could* refuse. I could leave the theater. I had a little money saved. It wouldn't be the nice man and the great house Myra wanted for me, but I might find my way to a decent life.

I closed my eyes, and all I could see was a brilliant spotlight glowing down on me like a sun in a black sky, warming my cheeks. The rushing hush of a crowd breathing, waiting, *needing* me pounded in my ears. I opened my eyes, and there was Mr. Reddy again, in his dark office, watching me with a sympathetic frown on his lips, knowing I wouldn't refuse. I wouldn't leave.

"All right. I'll do it," I said.

His gusting breath of relief reminded me of the sound of dirt being shoveled down into a grave.

"ARE YOU OKAY?"

I stiffened briefly as Ronan floated down with a beat of his wings into the seat next to me. On stage, a cluster of the company quietly discussed a memorial scene for Beth, but I'd stepped away, my head too full to talk.

A warm arm stretched over my shoulder, and I twitched with an impulse to pull away. It faded quickly and I sat up, Ronan's eyes widening as I moved only to sit myself down in his lap.

"Not particularly," I whispered, twisting and bundling myself against Ronan's warm chest.

His arms wrapped around me, and then his wings too, shielding me in a lovely dark cocoon. "'Course you're not. Stupid question."

It was quiet inside of Ronan's embrace, our breaths echoing together against the thick membrane of his wings.

"I took the orc home with me," I whispered, not sure why I was confessing.

Ronan's nose sniffed against my hair. "I know. I...I don't want to tease you if—"

"No, don't coddle me," I said quickly.

Ronan was quiet again, and then he shifted, holding me a little tighter as his voice grew light. "Did you enjoy yourself?"

I opened my mouth and shut it again.

"Fuck. You saw Beth. I'm sorry, nut, I'm buggering this all—"

"Hazel?"

Ronan and I both stiffened briefly at Myra's call.

"Has anyone seen Hazel?"

It was the slightly high, nervous squeak that made me curious, and Ronan's wings parted, breaking our bubble and revealing the theater. He was frowning at me, a line of worry between his eyes, and I pressed my finger over the spot briefly before turning and standing up.

"Here," I said, finding Myra stage right by the curtains, a tall figure at her side.

"Who's that?" Ronan muttered, rising at my back, his hand on my hip.

"New act," I answered in a whisper.

He was striking, with broad and gently twisting horns, and his body wasn't spiky and bright like Eston, but it also wasn't correctly proportioned to be mistaken for human, limbs a little too long. His eyes reflected the faint stage lights we were using, and his body moved in disjointed jerks and twitches. But when his chin lifted, there was an elegance to him, an uncanny beauty and faintly violet shifting glow under velvety bronze skin.

"This is Constantine," Myra said, inching away from the new arrival as I approached the stage, aware of Ronan following me.

The crowd of the company stared up at Constantine. Even Nireas, who so often existed just slightly separate from the rest of us, sat on his bench in front of his organ and studied the demon.

"This is Hazel," Myra said, and her eyes didn't raise above his chest. "She'll be your partner for your scenes."

Constantine's clothing was an interesting mix of textures and fabrics. Demons often had a confused sense of fashion, and his was more cluttered and disjointed than usual, with contrasting colors layered on top of one another, a long tunic hanging almost to his knees underneath a short jacket.

He bowed, and those eerie animal eyes remained fastened to

me as I approached, glinting and glowing, never blinking. I stiffened, trying to suppress an involuntary shiver at the predatory interest in that stare. I wasn't sure if it was the abrupt motions of his body or the uninterrupted focus, but his gaze didn't feel like the sexual energy I was used to.

He rose slowly as I neared and then rushed forward to the edge of the stage, making one of the girls in the far corner gasp with the sudden snap of movement. I froze briefly, and Ronan's hand landed warmly on my lower back—a reminder that I was in a room full of friends, not alone with this disconcerting stranger.

I took a slow breath and when I reached the stage, Constantine bent, long arms reaching down and slender but strong hands wrapping around my waist. There was a charge of energy rushing through me at his touch, but he lifted me from the floor and onto the stage with no effort. Up close, his bone structure was even more unusual, cheekbones too high and jaw too broad. His grip was firm but not painful around my waist, and yet it was as if he'd fastened me in place by fierce pins and I would be unable to move on my own again until released.

"You're a pretty creature," Constantine said, and the words were carefully spoken and somehow didn't fit together.

"Thank you, sir," I answered, but I couldn't find my usual charm as those metallic eyes flicked over me.

I'd had sex with any number of unusual monsters during my time at the theater, some quite impossible to imagine the act with, but none had unsettled me like this demon. I wished Mr. Reddy hadn't warned me, but even so, I think I would've been nervous in Constantine's presence.

"There's no rehearsal today," Ronan said, and there was a beat of his wings as he leapt up to the stage, brushing my hair and pulling Constantine's gaze away.

But the demon's hands remained around my waist, and when I tried to move, they were as secure as an iron gate.

"Just making the introduction," Myra said, a little more easy and flippant now that Constantine's focus had been claimed by me. "But you're right—we start rehearsals tomorrow. Beth's act and...and Mr. Constantine will be the only new additions. I'll start the rest of the casting now."

"Come on, Hazelnut, let's plan Beth's bit," Ronan said, and out of the corner of my eye his outstretched hand hovered, waiting for Constantine to release me.

Over the tall demon's shoulder, I saw Nireas standing from his bench, all three eyes narrowed and glaring at us.

"I should like to speak to you, creature," Constantine said, his voice almost a whisper.

"Her name is Hazel," Nireas snapped.

Creature. Between the word and Constantine's focus, a little bubble of panic rose up in my throat. Did he *know?* Mr. Reddy wouldn't have told, surely. He relied on my disguise, on the human girl monsters paid to watch. And yet...

"Yes," I said, nodding and reaching trembling hands down to those immovable fingers.

His grip loosened immediately, and I released a breath I hadn't been holding, a wavering smile rising up to my lips.

"I'll show you your dressing room," I offered. "We can talk there."

A boot stepped forward at my side, and I shot Ronan a warning glance, my smile still fixed in place. His jaw was tight and his eyes were fixed to Constantine, but he didn't move as I led the demon back to the wings, ignoring the tall shadow of Nireas out of the corner of my other eye.

"She always gets the tricky ones, don't she?" one of the girls whispered on the stage.

"Can't say I mind this time," someone else answered.

"Did you travel far to join the company?" I asked, raising my voice over their whispers, not that I thought it would do much against a demon's hearing.

"Not very," Constantine said, his eyes still glittering in the dark. Not glowing like Hunter's or Ronan's, but catching every stray trace of light and reflecting it like a mirror, I realized.

"Are you nervous to be on stage?"

"No."

I licked my lips. He wasn't chatty, was he? There were only so many of my usual questions I could think to ask, when he seemed so disinclined to speaking.

But I would try again. "Why...why are you called the Gemini?"

"I will show you," he said. The stairs down were almost too narrow, but he held me fast to his side, our hips and shoulders rubbing as we stepped.

Why did you call me "creature"? I wanted to ask, but I was too afraid of the answer.

Everyone was together upstairs, except perhaps Mr. Reddy, so the hall was unnaturally quiet as I walked Constantine down to the dressing room reserved for guest acts. It was at the opposite end of the hallway as my own small room, and I was slightly relieved not to be taking him into my own space.

"We always tidy up for new guest acts," I said, reaching the doorway. It was one of the few rooms with an actual door rather than a charmed curtain, and I pushed it open.

The room was spacious, although we occasionally had to house guest acts elsewhere if they couldn't manage the stairs or were too large to accommodate backstage, but Constantine was one of the more innocuous monsters we'd hosted.

Still, it gave me chills as he shut the door behind us.

There was a lamp burning in the far corner, and two candles lit on a side table by the door, the warring light twisting our shadows on every wall. We stood facing a comfortably sized bed. I knew Mr. Reddy provided lodging for guest acts that needed it outside of the theater, but I was also very well familiar with why there was a bed in a dressing room. Guest acts were often popular with those of us who worked permanently at the theater. I wondered briefly how many would brave the room while Constantine was here.

"Turn around." There was an echo in his words.

Or so I thought until I turned, gasping slightly and blinking at the sight before me. I thought at first the candlelight was playing tricks on me, or my eyes were, as Constantine flickered and blurred. It was as if I was staring at a photograph where the subject had moved before the image was captured. Suddenly, there were two faces, turning in opposite directions on one neck, one red and one blue. Except neither of the faces were Constantine's.

Not all of it, at least.

I stumbled back as two faces became two figures, equally tall but unevenly matched. One was a deep, rich blue, those metallic eyes matching the shimmer of his skin, but his nose led to a disconcerting blank place where the mouth should've been. On the other figure, those glinting eyes were missing, but full lips remained on vibrant red skin. The strange collection of clothes also seemed to have been dispersed between the two figures, the red figure dressed in soft, draping fabrics, the blue one in sharply tailored wool.

"Gemini," I whispered.

"He is Con," the red lips spoke. "I am Antin."

I let out a huff of breath but trapped it in my chest before it might turn into a laugh, my eyes bouncing between the pair of them. The longer I looked, the more differences I saw. Con's body was slimmer, but carved with tight muscle, his hands larger, those eyes boring deep into me. Antin was broader, like a shield, and his lips curled up gently. I wanted to inch closer to him, let him wrap me in those long arms and soft fabrics, safely away from the apparent danger of his other half.

"The act is...the pair of you," I said, glancing down at their hips and blushing slightly.

A pair was fine. I could handle two cocks.

Con's shoulders were hunching, his body tensing, and I fought the urge to dart around Antin and run for the door. He *was* the predator preparing to hunt, and I had no illusions that I was not the prey.

Antin shrugged, but his hand lifted and rested on Con's shoulder, and Con's eyes flicked to his, the ferocity fading slightly. "Do you like pain, sweet creature?"

I swallowed, staring between the pair of them, thinking of Hunter's strength the night before. "A little," I breathed, stepping back again, making Con's gaze snap back to me, his body freezing in place once more.

"The act will be more than a little pain," Antin mused, head tipping. "But I will be there with you."

I wasn't sure what that meant, but I was growing curious. Con looked as though he wanted to devour me, but it was Antin whose sweet and full mouth held my attention, and he was still holding Con with a simple, gentle touch. As edgy and tense as the blue demon looked, he wasn't fighting his other half, but waiting. For permission?

"Show me," I whispered.

Antin's hand lifted and Con's silver stare sharpened to a blade as he stepped forward, one hand reaching out to me. A weaker, cowardly part of me stepped back, and the bed hit the back of my legs. Con paused immediately, glaring at me, and I licked my lips, trying to laugh away my own nerves.

"Will I... Will it hurt for long?" I asked, glancing at Antin.

"Only as long as he touches you," Antin said.

I steeled myself with a deep breath, and nodded. *Temporary. Temporary will be all right*, I told myself. I looked back to Con, to that cold stare.

"It's better for you to know now," Antin murmured.

"Yes. Touch me," I said to Con.

His hand snapped out, and I understood immediately, my body crumpling backward to the bed, my vision flashing white.

My god.

The *pain*.

7.

THE GEMINI

It was a sudden current, outshining every point of reference I had. Hotter than the burning iron handle of a pan I'd grabbed bare-handed, deeper than the broken bone of my arm when I'd fallen from a ladder, sharper than the claws of a dragon that had raked down my back in accidental passion. I couldn't scream because I couldn't breathe.

Surely no one could survive this pain. This was a hell of a thousand knives and the strike of lightning, and yet there was nothing to feel at all because it was too strong.

And then a hand brushed down my cheek, cool and gentle, and the room landed all around me, Antin's ruby face above me, bare brow furrowed. I gasped, trembling between two simple touches—one excruciating, and one just blissful enough to cut through the blinding agony. I opened my mouth to scream, and that gentle hand covered my lips.

"No, sweet creature," Antin whispered.

Con's hand stroked up the back of my jerking, kicking leg, and I let out a high whine, the world flashing white again as he tapped against the back of my knee.

"Settle, it's all right," Antin said, bending. His lips pressed to my forehead, another hand brushing over my shoulder, sliding beneath the collar of my dress, and I understood.

Antin's touch was divine—my head dizzy and my thoughts soft as he kissed the spot—but when he drew away, the torture of Con's touch and the pleasure of Antin's gift found a balance again. I moaned into Antin's hand and blinked in a daze as he smiled at me.

"We will start gently with you," he said.

A tear slipped out of the corner of my eye at the words, in devastation and gratitude. If this was gentle, I would not conquer *rough*. Con's single touch at the back of my knee rendered me both weak and vibrating with the need to escape. It was one long resonance of stabbing versus the sweet and velvety-soft waves of relief Antin provided. But Antin touched me twice for Con's single point of contact. They were being merciful.

Antin's hand on my chest was moving my dress down my shoulders and his lips grazed my cheek, drawing a shudder through my body, my back arching into the careful pass of his fingers, aware of what they promised. Con's hand drifted up beneath my skirt, grazing the insides of my thigh, and my eyes widened as an unexpected and potent arousal pooled in my cunt. The shock of the initial pain was transforming from a stab to a heavy pound, a profane ache that I associated with the frenzied height of fucking.

"More?" Antin asked.

My gaze flicked down to where Con sat between my thighs, kneeling on the floor at the foot of the bed. His gaze was a warning, his body tense and trembling, and I wasn't sure if he was restraining himself from the urge to destroy me or preparing to fling himself away at my request. I jerked my head in a single nod. There was a sudden smirk in Con's stare and that still hand swiped up, barely grazing my sex.

I screamed behind Antin's hand on my mouth at the sudden bolt of electric torment throbbing through my cunt, hips kicking and breath snapping through my chest with every one of those brushing touches. Then Antin ducked down again, hand moving away and lips just barely landing against mine, and the pain fused with an ecstasy so sweet it made me sob into the kiss.

I came, weeping and shaking on the bed, my arms reaching up to cling to Antin. I found his skin under the swathes of fabric and moaned at the sudden rush of delirious pleasure, and then cried out into his lips as a long digit pressed up inside of me, violent only in the sensations it drew out of me.

This was horrible and it was a gift, and it was only a kiss and one finger pumping carefully into me. I was terrified, and I *needed* to know more.

"More," I gasped against Antin's lips.

Instead they both tore away from me at the same moment. The whine in my throat was broken, pathetic, and I swiped at the tears blurring my eyes with a rough slap against my cheeks.

But the Gemini wasn't leaving me.

Con stood from the floor, and I watched with wide eyes as he pulled a leather belt free from his trousers.

"For your screams," Antin said, sliding off the bed and meeting his other half by my spread legs.

He took the belt from Con and leaned over me. It was folded in half, and I stared between the two men and the leather warily.

"Unless you would rather it was Con's hand covering your mouth," Antin said.

I opened my mouth immediately, and Antin smiled. The leather was thick and pliable as Antin placed it between my teeth. It wasn't the first time I'd had leather in my mouth, but it was the first time I shook and shivered as I bit down, the flavor heady and musky and unpleasant.

I yelped as Con moved to the bed, barely touching me as he yanked down my dress, exposing my breasts to the cool air of the room. I stared up and his animal eyes were on mine, impossible to escape, a wild excitement in his gaze.

Antin knelt between my thighs, and unlike Con, he had no reservations about touching me fully as he pushed my skirt up to my waist. His hands on my thighs set off a sudden explosion of bliss inside me, and my hips lifted from the bed, arching toward him, my eyes fluttering shut as I moaned around the leather, ignoring the taste in favor of having something to *suck*.

I was at the edge of coming when fingers dove into my hair, scratching against my scalp. The deep, dense wave of simple pleasure was split with the momentary knife stab of pain from Con's touch, and my scream was strangled. But Antin had two hands for Con's one on me, and I was learning quickly that the pain was just a lightning rod of sensation that added to the pleasure, that my body adjusted and transformed it into something glorious.

Antin's hands pushed at my shaking thighs, and my face was hot, eyes open and fastened to Con's stare as I came with a gush, exposed and pinned between their demonic powers and strength.

"Beautiful," Antin murmured.

Eston came suddenly to mind, pretty and clumsy and simple, and I let out a crazed giggle, comparing him to Constantine. This was power, horrible and beautiful, unlike any belonging to the demons I'd met before. I was writhing between their hands and already aware of a dangerous truth.

I wanted more.

I swallowed my cry as I stretched and leaned into Con's hand at the top of my head, my whole body tensing as the cut of pain grew sharp again. But I held my eyes open and watched his own widen in surprise. He glanced up toward Antin and then back down to me.

Antin's hand landed on mine, and I gasped, toes curling at the decadent lick of sweetness, aware of how firmly he held me down. Con reached for the other, and I tried to force myself to relax, but my muscles refused and I thrashed as his fingers tangled with mine, drumming slashes of agony rushing through me to meet Antin's opposing pleasure. They clashed in my chest, my heartbeat stuttering before finding its rhythm again.

"She is..." Antin whispered.

Con only lunged forward, arching over me, and I screamed in expectation as his cheek landed on my breast. He nuzzled the spot briefly, and I thought my lungs might collapse. Then a slick, hot tongue stroked up my sex, and I sucked in a sudden breath.

My toes pressed to the floor for leverage as I pushed into their faces, their hands pinning me in place, a torrent of conflicting sensations snapping and stroking through every muscle, every bone, licking and biting over every nerve. They were the gentlest touches I'd ever been granted at the theater, feather-soft, and yet they blinded my vision and transformed my body into a jerking, thrashing, foreign creature.

These weren't orgasms, they were deaths and rebirths, teased and tickled out of me, more the result of the crashing aches and sweeping soothes. I shuddered and rocked into Antin's sweet lips, while my shaking hand pushed Con's touch to my breast. He leaned back, found my stare again, and watched me as he pinched my nipple gently.

I screamed, saw only light, expected my heart to stop and my body to cleave in two, even as I flooded Antin's tongue with my release.

I tried to spread my legs even farther apart, to tear myself open for them to fill me, but I was entirely boneless now. Con's almost playful pinch and release of my nipple was spiking pain through me, my body twitching with each press, light flashing like the booms of cannon fire.

"Enough," Antin murmured, drawing away.

But Con continued. Without Antin, the pain stole my breath again. And yet it was right too, simpler than the pleasure, grounding.

"Enough, Con," Antin repeated, but the words were spoken so gently.

I whined, not capable of more, and Con stroked my other breast. Shockingly, I felt another flutter of my cunt on nothing, the pain a strange stimulus.

Suddenly, all touch was torn away. There was no sense of the bed beneath me, and I was blind, or my eyes were shut on the vivid light. I heard a whisper of a voice, but it was buried beneath the echoing pound of my blood in my veins and the sudden gusts of my breath.

And then those were lost too, and the bright prism of light behind my eyes faded, then I fell into nothing.

A COOL TOUCH ROUSED ME, drifting down from my cheek to my throat. I hummed, the taste of leather still on my tongue, and turned my face into a soft pillow—too soft to be my own. My body was still throbbing slightly, but not with pain, just awareness, like the volume of sensation had been raised.

"Wake up, Nix," a low voice called, both unfamiliar and yet...

I stiffened briefly, my arms curled against my chest, and shifted on the mattress. My dress was righted, and I opened my eyes to find myself lying on my side in Constantine's dressing room. But it wasn't Constantine at my side. A heavy, spiked black tail was swishing in agitation against the floor, kicking up dust one of the girls had missed during cleaning.

I turned my head slightly to find three eyes on me, their corners creased with worry. Nireas.

"We—they've been looking for you. The Gemini left hours ago."

I curled in on myself, still lost in the empty place Con and Antin had brought me to, and Nireas's hand passing down my side barely registered as the shocking event it really was. How long had it been since he'd touched me?

"Did he hurt you?" The words were rough.

I let out a muffled laugh and Nireas's fingers gripped at my waist, too tight for a moment, and then pulled away completely.

Yes, Con had hurt me. Changed me, even. I shook my head against the pillow and licked my lips, surprised to find some of Antin's sweetness still remaining.

"No," I whispered. Yes. But I had no complaint. Only a strange and concerning new craving.

"Nix."

"Her name is Hazel," I murmured, repeating what he'd snapped at Constantine just hours ago.

There was a huff of irritated breath, and then Nireas froze as I sat up suddenly, facing him. He had two hands braced against the bed on either side of me, one against my waist, and another hovering in the air between us. I suspected his other two hands remained clasped behind his back, where he often hid them.

His eyes were wide and his lips were parted, a peek of the beautiful iridescence of his skin just below the buttons of his collar.

"He didn't hurt me," I said, and Nireas blinked, wiping away his surprise. "It's going to be quite a scene, though. Better to know a little of what I'm in for before rehearsals."

Nireas's expression hardened at my words and his lips

opened, but my head was still dizzy with Constantine and his nearness was only making that worse.

"Who was looking for me?" I asked, before he could speak.

"I was."

Nireas stiffened and drew back, a sudden rush of cool air surrounding me and replacing his warmth. His gaze dropped down and mine drifted to Ronan, standing in the doorway, wings tucked and gaze glowing.

"Everyone's heading home. I'd like to walk with you," Ronan said, glancing between Nireas and me.

There's nothing to see, I told myself. "You don't have to—"

"Don't be a pest and argue, nut," Ronan said, smiling, but with a hard edge to the words. "We'll all feel better if we know you make it home safe."

Nireas cleared his throat, and two of his eyes stared at the wall behind my head, but the third at the center was still fixed to me. "He's right."

I sighed and nodded. Beth had been killed. Mr. Reddy certainly couldn't risk the same thing happening to me. I scooted back on the bed, and Nireas stood abruptly, hurrying for the door without another word. I kept my eyes down as I slid off the mattress and headed to Ronan, but he caught me in the middle of the room, and there was no teasing as he searched my face and neck.

"You're all right?"

"I'm *fine*," I said. It was harder now to believe how much pain I'd been in, how shockingly ecstatic every touch from Antin had been, like all the sensation they'd thrust into me had just evaporated. My thighs were a little sore, probably from tensing, but otherwise, I was...practically untouched. "He splits into two men, did you know that?"

Ronan blinked at me, the tension in his wings relaxing as they folded tighter to his back. "He gives the other girls the shivers."

He gave me the shivers too, but now I was anticipating them with something a little too much like excitement. I opened my mouth to tell Ronan about the difference between the pair, how careful Con had been to keep his touches balanced with Antin's, how the mind-numbing pain had crashed and blended into the body-melting pleasure to create something higher and grander than either. But Ronan's brow was still furrowed, and he was still searching my skin for bruises or wounds.

I stepped into his chest, just catching the bounce of his brows as I wrapped my arms around his middle and tucked my face into his throat. "I'm fine, Ronan. Really. It's just another act. Reddy knows what he's doing."

"That's what I'm afraid of," Ronan growled in my ear before pressing a rough kiss to my temple. "All right, nut. Let's get you home."

8.

A WICKED SPEECH

I was aware of the stares of the neighborhood as Ronan and I walked together, aware of the policemen at the corners of the streets, and the one ambling through the green as we cut through. The sun was high enough in the sky to cut over the tops of buildings, and the park was missing the stillness I was so fond of.

"You make a handsome human," I whispered to Ronan as I caught a young woman on another man's arm gaping at my escort.

Ronan's coat was large and ill-fitted, but it was charmed to disguise him, the heft of his wings vanishing, his horns glimmering away, and his skin turning from vibrant rust red to a weathered tan. He still had his lovely black hair, all glossy on the top of his head, and sharp cheekbones beneath almost golden-brown eyes. Plush lips smirked at my compliment, and his eyes flicked to me.

"Starting to prefer the other side, hm?"

You don't belong. Not with my kind. Not with your mother's, the old memory of my father hissed. *If they only knew what you were, they'd never share their smiles with you.*

"I like you as yourself," I murmured back, my arm squeezing briefly around his. "But now I wonder if perhaps Mr. Reddy should consider a theater where humans come to admire monsters."

Ronan huffed and rolled his eyes, but they flicked around the park to see the women who watched him, his shoulders straightening and his stride smoothing into a prowl.

"You're a rare breed, Hazelnut," Ronan said, and my heartbeat stuttered until he added, "A human who takes our kind without any illusions."

I snorted. "The theater uses plenty of illusions."

"I don't mean on stage," Ronan whispered, head turned and lips close to my ear. His breath was still hot and smoky, and it rushed down the side of my throat. "Do you know, Beth once asked me to tie my tail back."

I blinked and turned, our noses almost bumping. "What?"

"For the scene. She didn't like it touching her. I even suggested once that in one of our trick falls I catch her by my tail. She gagged," Ronan said, chin tipping up in defiance.

"I...I didn't know," I said, frowning and trying to recall any instance of Beth complaining about any of her partners. And we had, all the girls did occasionally, although it was usually about scratches or not getting off. Never our partner's features or abilities. Reddy wouldn't have allowed it from us, surely.

"Reddy overworks you, and the girls know he'll do it. If they refuse an act, you'll be there to pick it up," Ronan said grimly.

"Everyone seems to have an awful lot of opinions about this lately, usually without discussing it with me," I muttered as we stepped back onto the sidewalk. I leaned past Ronan to check the road for traffic, waiting for an ice cart to pass before tugging him across the street with me.

"What is it about being cared for that sets your teeth so on edge, nut?" Ronan laughed.

I rolled my eyes and ignored the question as we turned the corner to my street. There was a familiar black carriage waiting on the road in front of my house, and Ronan and I both slowed at the sight.

"Has he been here all day?" Ronan asked.

I shook my head. "He left in the night." I ignored Ronan's puff of annoyance and stared at Hunter's carriage.

I hadn't been planning on inviting Ronan inside with me. We had the boundary of the theater to provide sense to our...friendship, and I wasn't sure what it would mean to stretch that boundary, especially to a place so personal. Now, with the reappearance of Hunter, I was tempted to change my mind, to keep Hunter out and let Ronan in. It was contrary and would only add to the confusion I carried lately.

"I think I need to speak with him. He might have information about Beth," I reasoned.

Ronan grunted.

"He was sweet last night, Ro," I whispered.

"Oh, was it his sweetness I was smelling on you today?" Ronan bit out.

I ground my teeth, but there were a few familiar faces on the street and I didn't want to make a scene. Or at least not more of one than poor fallen Hazel Nix on the arm of one man only to be passed off to another.

"It was my climbing onto his cock like I was in heat that you smelled, as a matter of fact," I hissed back.

Ronan's eyes grew huge and he jerked, and I regretted my words instantly. Until suddenly his lips were twitching and snorting laughter escaped. I released my own sigh of laughter and shook my head.

"Fair enough, nut," Ronan said, grinning and lifting my knuckles to his lips, a wicked glint in his gaze out of the corner of his eyes. "Go enjoy the orc. I'll see you at rehearsals tomorrow."

I sighed and squeezed his hand before he released me, turning on his heel and heading back the way we'd come. Ahead of me, the carriage door opened, the diminutive disguise of Hunter stepping down. He waited for me on the sidewalk, his head bowed and covered by the brim of the top hat.

"You came back," I greeted softly.

"I can't stay, I shouldn't come in—"

"Please," I said, wincing at the small bland human in front of me. "Please, I'd like...to *see* you."

He had watery blue eyes, so lifelike, and they blinked at me as the little human figure seemed to swell and grow slightly taller. "Very well, Miss Nix."

I led Hunter inside and barely had the door shut before I was tearing the hat off his head. Hunter—handsome, broad, tall Hunter—stiffened as I collapsed against his chest.

"I hate that stupid hat," I muttered, frowning as his arms remained hanging at his side. I leaned away slightly and looked up. It was the first time I was seeing Hunter in daylight, and the color of his skin was softer, the lines of his face gentler. "I think you should get a disguise that looks more like *you*."

His lips were parted, eyes wide, and since he seemed unable to find anything to say in response, I rose to my toes, arching into him.

Pathetic, I thought. Had I forced him into sex the night before? Was I demanding this kiss now?

But he groaned as my lips met his, arms wrapping tightly around me and mouth slanting. His tongue was hot and rich as it stroked my own, and I shuddered as his claws dug through my skirt to grip my ass.

"I can't stay," he said again, tearing his lips away, eyes a little wild now. And in spite of his words, his grip on me tightened, pressing me hard to his hips. "I only came to...to apologize for my treatment of you last night."

"Your treatment?" I repeated.

"I was too rough—"

"You were wonderful."

Hunter blinked at me and his hands loosened in surprise, but he didn't retreat. I had room now, so I stroked one hand down from his chest to his crotch, finding the *very* generous cock slightly hard already.

"Your cock was wonderful," I said, and Hunter's black tongue flicked over his bottom lip. "I loved how you *fucked* me."

"I should not have...have held your throat," he murmured, eyelids growing heavy as I stroked him through his pants. His breaths were ragged as I tightened my grip. "You are too fragile, too precious. I shamed myself."

"You made me come so hard," I teased, grinning, leaning in and kissing his chin. His eyes rolled back and he bucked into my hand, and I resisted the urge to laugh. "Hunter, look at my throat now."

His face was torn and folded, as if I was torturing him, and his eyes were on the ceiling when he opened them again. I stretched my neck, still stroking and squeezing him through his pants, and his gaze dropped to my throat, black tongue flicking again.

"I'm fine. You didn't hurt me," I said softly, and his breath shuddered out in a gust. "You took care of me when I was frightened, and you made me feel *so* good when I needed you."

I debated telling him that he could be rougher, but he was sagging into the door, hips rolling into my grip on his cock, stiff and jumping against my palm.

"Fuck me again, Hunter," I breathed against his lips.

I'd been almost reluctant to see him minutes ago, but the moment he was in front of me, smelling like summer and apologizing for such a perfect experience, disinterest crumbled. Myra was right—I could make something with this orc. He just needed encouragement.

"Please," I whispered, sliding my hand up to the fastening of his pants.

"I have to go," Hunter growled.

I flinched and drew back, but Hunter didn't release me. One hand on my ass slid up to my back, drawing me close, and his head turned, cheek nuzzling against my brow with a little scratch from one tusk.

"I've been called away, little one," he said.

Called away, or is he leaving so I don't trick him into bed with me again?

"I left in the night, embarrassed by my actions," he continued, kissing my forehead. "It was as ignoble as my roughness—"

"Hunter," I said, objecting and trying to escape his grasp.

"Or so I thought. I shouldn't have left. And I don't want to repeat the deed now." He kissed my forehead slowly and loosened his arms.

I debated between tearing away and remaining. "Where do you have to go?"

"North. I made a promise to a friend to lend my help and—"

I sighed and leaned back, staring up at him with a weary smile. "And you're too good not to keep your promise."

His answering smile was tight. "Believe me when I say that

the temptation to rut you over the back of that chair, to hear your whimpers as I stuff you with my cock, to *feast* on your full cunt until you rinse my tongue with your release, is *very* challenging to refuse."

I arched an eyebrow at the orc in front of me. "Sir, that is a very wicked speech."

"Don't tease, little one," he rumbled.

"I liked it," I said, patting his chest. He sighed, and his head thumped softly against my door. "When do you return?" I asked.

"I refuse to miss one of your performances," he said, turning thoughtful. "I came to offer my apology—hush, listen—and to offer the use of one of my carriages for your safety."

One of my... He wasn't trying to impress me with the boast.

"That isn't necessary, I'll be fine," I said, sharing a genuine smile with him to soften the refusal.

It didn't work. He frowned back at me, head shaking. "You can't convince me your neighborhood is safe, Miss Nix."

"Hazel," I snapped, adding more gently, "Or little one. I like that too."

Hunter blushed, and I wondered if he was even aware of the pet name he'd granted me.

"I'll be escorted home by someone from the theater," I said. "Save your carriages for when you'll be in them with me."

His eyes narrowed slightly, and I wondered if he would object, prefer I use his carriage than have one of the stagehands take me home at night.

Instead the hand on my back lifted to cup my throat. "You meant it?" he asked softly. "You enjoyed last night?"

"I meant it."

"And you...will allow me to repeat the attentions?"

A bright giggle at the formality of the question burst from my lips, and Hunter's cheeks darkened further. "You make it sound like you've walked me around the park or brought me flowers like a lady's suitor," I teased. Hunter blinked and looked away, and I found I hated when his eyes weren't on me, so I pushed, "I'd let you fuck me right here, on the floor, right now, if you weren't so determined to leave."

Hunter's cock jerked against my hip, and his growl vibrated against my chest as I grinned at him.

"If I had time to savor you, I would show you exactly how eager I am to obey," Hunter snarled, dropping his forehead against mine. "But I need many hours, not a few brief minutes, little one."

Brief but delicious, I thought, but I decided not to torture my poor orc any further. I found his lips with mine, rewarded with the rumbling remnants of his growl and the gentle, thorough stroke of his tongue.

"Until curtain call, Miss Nix," he said as he pulled away, the glitter of his eyes giving away his intention to rile me.

"Don't wait for the curtain," I said, tipping my chin up. "I'll be waiting for you backstage."

9.

SUSPECTS AND STAGING

I paused on the threshold of my home the next morning, staring down the steps at the round black brim of the detective's hat. He looked up as the door clicked shut behind me, a flicker of surprise brightening his features, and I was struck again by how handsome he was. My tastes had shifted away from humans' softer features since I'd started working at the theaters, but DS Piper was undeniably striking. Beautiful, even.

"Miss Nix."

"Detective Sergeant," I greeted with a dip of my head.

This isn't good. He shouldn't want to speak to me again.

"How well do you know Miss O'Mahony's roommates?"

Confusion sent me hurrying down the stairs. "Her roommates? I knew... I knew she had roommates, but I'd never met them."

"You weren't friends."

"We're...we were friends at the theater. I liked Beth," I said softly, turning away from the detective. Let him follow me through the park again, I decided. "But we only walked home together in the evening."

"From the Bawdy Row?" he asked, the sharp tone of his question raising alarms in my head.

"Yes."

"Did you know what Miss O'Mahony's roommates did for a living?"

"You think they had something to do with her death?" I

looked at him, but he only stared back, that pale blue stare promising to not answer any of my questions. "She never said."

"But you guessed," he said.

"I guessed as much as anyone in the neighborhood guessed about Beth, and me too," I said, shrugging through the lie. Beth had told us how relieved she was to find work off the street, unlike the girls she lived with. "I never met them."

"So you wouldn't recognize them if you saw them?"

I slowed, searching for clues in his questions and on the cool, impassive stone of his face. "I wouldn't."

"And they don't work at the Bawdy Row?" he asked, almost mocking.

I glared at him, afraid with every step that I was walking into an unseen trap he'd already laid for me. "They don't."

"And how long have you worked there?"

"Eight years."

"And what have you been doing in the four months since it closed?"

Fuck.

I was mindlessly marching forward, gaze focused on the tall trees of the park across the way, as if they might provide me sanctuary from this interview. Would I need to stay at the theater, avoid coming back to the flat where this detective might find and interview me? That was if he even let me make it to work today without hauling me into a cell.

A bright honk startled me out of my thoughts at the same moment a strong arm banded around my waist, yanking me into a wall of a chest and out of the way of a galloping cart rushing down the road.

I caught my breath, aware I was being held against DS Piper, that his breath was rustling the back of my hair, that we were frozen with his arm squeezing a little tighter around me rather than letting go.

"Tell me the name of your pimp."

Mr. Reddy, I thought dizzily, but I yanked myself away from the man, spinning to face him.

"I don't have one. Neither did Beth."

"You don't work at the Bawdy Row. I assume you never did,"

he answered back sharply. We stared at one another for a long moment, and I tried not to study the dazzling cut of his jaw. His eyes flicked out around us before he grabbed me by the elbow, hauling me across the road to the peaceful shade of the park. His head ducked close to mine, and his hand on my elbow was too tight to pull away. "I don't care what you do, but I'm trying to find out what happened to your friend. You want that, or you wouldn't keep asking questions."

"Can't you see I'm asking questions because I don't *know?*" I hissed.

"You know something!"

"Nothing to do with her death!"

His lips pressed flat, the needles of silver in his stare blazing bright as a newly minted crown. He glanced around us and released my arm at last, marching forward into the park. I debated circling back to my flat, but he was walking in the direction I needed to go to get to the theater. He paused and looked back over his shoulder, raising his eyebrow expectantly. Ronan had once offered to teach me to punch, and I wished in that moment I'd learned the skill.

I followed, and he waited until I reached his shoulder before speaking again.

"Her roommates have vanished."

"Because there are police swarming the neighborhood," I said, shrugging.

"Maybe," he said with a nod. "Mostly likely. Or perhaps they know something and are being kept quiet."

I chewed over that as we walked. "I know it seems like the most obvious answer, but Beth *wasn't* a prostitute." *Not in that way*, I allowed privately. "She didn't have a pimp. We...really do work at a theater."

"Which one?"

I shook my head and shrugged. "Are you going to arrest me? I won't tell you. I *can't*."

DS Piper's pretty eyes narrowed and his jaw ticked. "You expect me to believe you work for a theater you can't talk about, and it would have absolutely nothing to do with her murder?"

I'd talked myself into a hole, and if I dug any further, I would lead the London police straight to the company, Myra and Mr. Reddy and all the monsters. I slowed to a stop, and DS Piper matched me.

"I won't talk anymore," I said.

"And if I say yes, you're arrested?" he asked, voice lowering, and he leaned in.

I shrugged again.

His eyes narrowed. "Will you be safer in a cell?"

I laughed, rough and uncomfortable. "Not remotely."

"If someone is threatening—"

"They're *not*," I said, my hands reaching for the detective's before thinking better of it and crossing my arms in front of my chest. "Enough. Enough, I'm not saying any more."

Would Mr. Reddy try to find me if I didn't come in for rehearsals? Would he force Constantine on one of the other girls? Ronan would worry. And Hunter... Hunter wouldn't be back for days.

DS Piper stared at me, eyes scanning back and forth over my face. I forced myself to keep looking back, pretending it might persuade him to listen.

"We would've had her time of death wrong if you hadn't told us she hadn't come to work," he said. Unsure how to answer, I remained silent, and he remained watching me. "In a theater that doesn't exist," he added in a mutter.

I pressed my lips flat, and his frown carved attractive lines over his forehead. He was older, although there was no silver in his hair to match his eyes.

Quit mooning over him!

"Do you promise to find me if you learn anything relevant?" he asked suddenly.

I blinked, and my mouth opened to answer *yes* immediately, knowing it was the key to being allowed to leave now. I stopped myself to think. Lying would be easy. Mr. Reddy and Hunter were trying to discover what had happened to Beth, and maybe they would do so before the police. But would they care if Beth had been killed by a human lover, or would Mr. Reddy only want to ensure his investment in the rest of us girls was secure? I didn't like to think so, but I wasn't sure.

"I will," I said finally. "I swear."

For some reason, that only made DS Piper frown even harder. "I usually know when someone lies to me," he said. "With you...I can't tell."

I wasn't sure if I should be relieved or not, so I said nothing.

"I'm not arresting you," he said on a sigh, turning to the side. He lifted his hat from his head, and I found my eyes catching on his ear as his hand reached up to drive long fingers through thick dark hair. Rounded, with a little wrinkle at the top from an old scar. I blinked at the spot, and then his hat was back on.

Humans had them too sometimes. The doctor had thought the pointed tips of my ears were just a familiar deformity, one that small farm communities might become suspicious of if it weren't corrected.

A coincidence, I told myself, although my heartbeat was racing through my veins.

He turned back to me, and my stare whipped to the ground, the edge of the park in sight.

DS Piper stepped closer, and his voice dropped low and so quiet I almost had to lean in. "You're one of the only leads we have," he said. "As far as anyone in the neighborhood knows, you and Miss O'Mahony's roommates were the only people who knew her. You're not going to be let off the case records until we have something better to follow."

His voice was gentler, but it didn't make the words any less of a threat. I was their only suspect, or their only lead. Unless Beth's roommates turned up or I gave them something useful to follow, I would remain the focus.

I couldn't provide myself an alibi without bringing Hunter into the mix, and Mr. Reddy and Myra would both have my head if I put one of their patrons in the line of police scrutiny.

"I don't know what to do," I whispered.

"Think," DS Piper answered, equally quiet. "And hope we find those women."

Rehearsal for Beth's scene was quiet, clumsy, and full of the sound of gentle sniffles. Alexa only made it through half of "In the Sweet By and By" before her voice strangled. Nireas played somberly on till the last note.

"I think that's enough for today," Myra said softly from the foot of the stage.

And still we stood, wooden and quiet on our marks.

Mr. Reddy leaned forward in the front row, eyeing the lot of us with that critical squint of his, but his lips only pressed flat. Whatever notes he had for the scene, he would save for another day.

"No one is going to want to watch this," a dull voice called from the other side of the stage.

I blinked and searched the shocked expressions. Ronan landed from the rafters with a thump, and his glare shot in one clear direction. Ah, Eston.

"What?" Myra gasped, hands clasped over her chest.

There was a moment of silence as Mr. Reddy stood slowly from his seat, gazing up at our demon cast member. "I said no one is going to want to watch this," Eston said more firmly, raising his horned chin and catching the dimmed half-lights pointed toward the stage. "There's no sex."

"That's not what this is about!" Alexa cried out, her hands fisting at her sides.

"Go to her," I whispered to Samson, the beautiful, onyx enchanted statue in our company.

I'd caught Alexa, Samson, and our vampire Leon together in Leon's dressing room on more than one occasion, but Samson often watched Alexa from the wings with a stoic kind of longing. I wasn't sure he'd realized yet how happy the girl and the vampire were to include him. He stomped steadily to her side, that massive muscled arm wrapping around her shoulders. She leaned in gratefully, and I found myself smiling.

"Sex is what this theater is about," Eston answered, crossing his arms over his chest, and not even glancing once at the rest of us. "We ought to make a scene out of her death—"

"Eston!" Ronan barked.

"—make it somber if you like, but this is boring. The audience will walk out," Eston continued with a shrug.

"He hasn't had a decent idea since the dark ages," one of the were-bears behind me muttered, and I heard Margaret's high giggle.

Based on Eston's flashing glare in our direction, so did he.

"Eston, do I pay you to think?" Mr. Reddy asked suddenly from the floor.

"You pay me to fuck," Eston said, stepping forward.

"No," Mr. Reddy said, shaking his head. "No. I pay you to step onto the mark you're told to, to put your cock where you're told to, to come when you're told to, and to walk back off that stage when you're told to. And if you didn't shine quite so bright and look so pretty under our pixie lights, I wouldn't even do that. So keep polishing your horns and following your stage cues, and shut your mouth until you're told to open it."

I folded my lips between my teeth and looked down at the floor. I'd been on the receiving end of one of Mr. Reddy's directorial dressing downs in the past, and I felt a stab of sympathy for Eston, in spite of his horrible suggestion. The rest of the stage didn't quite manage to restrain their titters. Eston wasn't a favorite, but he'd been with us for a few years now. I understood what it was like to assume, after such a length of time, that I held a special kind of value to the Company of Fiends. And to be swiftly disabused of the notion.

Mr. Reddy must've shot the others one of his patented stares, something between violence and minor irritation, because the laughter faded abruptly.

"You heard the Missy. Enough of that run today. Off stage. Last scene, Hazel and the Gemini."

I stiffened, but I'd known the moment was coming. In all honesty, I'd been thinking of it for most of the past day. My eyes searched the seats in front of the stage as the rest of the company drifted to the wings, some of them trickling back down into the audience to watch. I found Constantine toward the back of the theater, rising and already watching me as he approached.

It was normal for the company to watch each other rehearse.

Rehearsals had more to do with staging and checking lighting cues—a spotlight from directly above on a large monster bent over a woman would ruin the view for the audience—than they did with any intimate moments between partners. Still, I found myself wishing Mr. Reddy might send the rest of the cast away for this. Constantine's effect on me made it impossible to maintain any control. The second he touched me, I would be reduced to sensation, howling and physical, totally at his mercy. It shocked me how ready I was to repeat the minutes from the day before, to surrender all thought and sense to this stranger again.

I didn't want witnesses. I didn't want Ronan or Mr. Reddy or Nireas or anyone to see me helpless under Constantine's hands. It wasn't the pain I was afraid of. It was the exposure.

Which was why it made no sense for me to be struck with sudden disappointment at Constantine's announcement.

"I won't touch her until we perform for an audience."

I blinked, still frozen in place. So did the rest of the cast, only half of them in their seats. Mr. Reddy stared squarely back at Constantine, apparently less disconcerted by his presence than the rest of us. The pair of them stood on the floor in front of center stage, Myra sliding away to sit down in Reddy's abandoned seat.

"How exactly do you propose rehearsing until then, without touching her?" Mr. Reddy asked, but he restrained his tone with Constantine in a way he certainly hadn't bothered with Eston.

"I will instruct her on what to expect, as well as your stagehands," Constantine said, smooth and unaffected. He bowed his head in a jerk to Mr. Reddy after a pause. "I will take your own thoughts into consideration, of course. But it is better for her if I restrain myself in the meantime. And ours will be a...spontaneous demonstration."

A visiting ghoul had once suggested to Mr. Reddy that he would be most entertaining if allowed to improvise his performance—as he often *improvised* visiting the dressing rooms of the rest of the company—and Mr. Reddy had dressed him down in front of the company for over an hour, culminating in a broken bench and a torn curtain.

"I see," Mr. Reddy bit out. "So glad to be taken into consideration."

But he bowed and gestured for Constantine to step on stage.

Constantine did so, his unusually long legs allowing him to rise in one impossible step. "We will need a bench," he said, and it was only because we had all been stupefied into silence that we were able to hear him. "Or a platform. Something I can display her on."

I shivered as he approached, and he stopped in center stage, a slender hand lifting and beckoning me closer. My body tripped forward as if Constantine had forged some invisible chain to hook inside of me yesterday and I'd been unaware of it until now.

"Something comfortable," he added with an eerie tip of his head.

"What kind of music do you want?" Nireas asked, and I found myself able to tear my gaze away from Constantine for the first time in minutes at the sound of his voice.

Constantine circled me slowly and I watched the floor, watched the shadows bend and duplicate. The audience gasped, and I knew he'd split into his two figures. I itched to twist and look at them again, half wondering if I'd made up the image of Con and Antin and the insanity of their touch.

"No music," Antin said, stepping forward. His hand was extended towards me and I straightened, stretching my neck as if I might coax him into touching me, even as Con's shadow loomed at my other side. "She will be our music. Her cries and screams. You can do that for us, can't you, sweet creature?"

I swallowed hard, thought of tipping into him. It would only take a few inches for his fingertips to brush my throat. I would shatter on the spot at that bliss, in front of the whole company. And I was *sure* Con would punish me.

"Yes," I gasped out, some remembered burn of the day before rushing up to flood my cheeks.

Antin nodded, and I wished for the trap door I was standing on to suddenly break open and swallow me.

"We will begin like this," he said, voice gentle. "She should be dressed. Something fine. Jewels too, for us to remove."

I shuddered, my eyes closing to those slow and soft words. Every touch the instruction promised would be agony or ecstasy, depending on whose hands were used. And until the performance, I wouldn't know which.

Worse, I didn't care. I was eager for both.

10.

A ONE-WAY BRIDGE

"You're avoiding everyone," Ronan said, sliding through the curtain of my dressing room a few days later. He stopped in the entrance, staring at me where I was curled up on my chaise, my hands crossed over my stomach.

He was right too—I'd been leaving before dawn in the morning to avoid the police still drifting around the neighborhood and keeping to myself at the theater when I wasn't needed for rehearsals.

"You're nervous about the performance tomorrow," he guessed, frowning.

"Come here," I said, shifting in my spot and stretching out one arm to him.

He let me ignore his words for a moment, crossing the small room and sliding over me so his wings weren't crushed. I set my hands on his hips and he settled his weight on top of me, reassuring and heavy, careful too. With my only scene dedicated to Constantine, who maintained his course of not touching me, and Hunter out of town, it'd been a rare stretch of days since I'd had sex, and I was surprised by the immediate clench of need that rose from Ronan's weight and his familiar smell.

"What are you doing?" Ronan asked with a laugh as I wiggled beneath him, pulling my skirt up to my waist.

"What do you think?" I teased, bumping my nose against his and stealing a quick kiss.

He watched me, wings shrouding us, as I settled beneath him, wrapping my thighs around his hips.

"Are you in the mood?" I asked when he didn't move.

Ronan's smile was slow, but there was something restrained in his eyes. "I'm always in the mood for you, nut."

I smiled, arching and rubbing myself up against him, but when he didn't move at all I stopped. "But?"

His grin locked and then fell apart, even as his arms circled my back, holding me in a lovely bend that pressed our hips together. "But I'm worried about you, and I think you know that and are trying to distract me."

I rolled my eyes and Ronan huffed out a breath, head dipping and his lips stroking my jaw near my ear as he whispered, "Hell, Hazel, I'm tempted to let you. It's been weeks."

I opened my mouth to say it hadn't—we'd just had sex on the silks together—and then realized he knew as well as I did that it was different like this, just us alone in my dressing room for the fun of it.

"You don't need to worry, Ro," I answered, rubbing my cheek against his curling horn, sliding a hand up to ruffle his hair and then grip one of his longer twisting horns. He groaned at the touch, bucked against my hips, but then sat up slightly.

"He watches you," he said.

I pressed my lips together and shrugged. "I'm his partner. And anyways...you all watch us, don't you?"

"No, he *only* watches *you*," Ronan said, frowning.

"You said that about Nireas," I hissed, my thighs loosening their grip on him.

Ronan pulled away, sitting up and bringing me with him, and I couldn't decide if I was relieved not to be pinned under him for this conversation or annoyed that he was pushing it on me at all.

"That's different. Nireas and I, we've been here for years. And I mean, you know as well as I do that I didn't start out constant—"

"Constant?" I squawked.

Ronan scowled. "When's the last time you caught me fooling around with any of the other girls, Hazel? You haven't, because I'm not interested. I haven't been interested. Just like Nireas isn't interested."

"Nireas isn't interested in *me*," I said, trying to rise from the chaise, but Ronan still had his arms around me.

"He is, whether he's too stubborn to show it or not. And this...this new demon isn't looking at a single other member of the company, nut. He's *staring* at you. Any time you're near enough to be seen," Ronan whispered, eyes wide. "Tell me he doesn't frighten you."

"He doesn't..." I stalled and sighed. "He *does* a little, although maybe not in the way that you mean." I waved my hand between us at Ronan's frown and pushed against his grip on me until I was able to scoot back a few inches. "He's unusual. I *am* nervous about the performance tomorrow night. But I'm not frightened. And I don't need you trying to *make* me scared."

Ronan sat up, shock and frustration striking like lightning on his face. "I'm not!"

"Then why *this,* Ronan?" I asked, throwing my hands up. "Yes, I'm avoiding everyone. Not because of him or tomorrow. Just...things are complicated." It was a weak excuse, but I didn't want to tell Ronan that what really disturbed me about Constantine was how I couldn't seem to wait for the moment we finally were on stage together. Or that what was bothering me was the words of Detective Sergeant Piper.

Ronan pulled back, finally releasing his arms. "Things are complicated and you can't tell me why?"

"I don't want to," I snapped.

His face twitched away from me, almost as if I'd slapped him, and my hands clenched in my lap.

"I care about you, Hazel," he said, the words flat for such a tender admission.

"I know you do," I answered, sighing, trying to relax, about to reach for him.

"Do you *want* me to?"

No, I thought immediately. And then, almost just as quickly, *Of course I do.*

"Yes," I said softly, and Ronan didn't pull away when I reached for his hand. "But I want you to listen to me too, not just...decide you've sorted out who or what I should be afraid of—"

"Even Myra is afraid of him," Ronan said, and then stopped abruptly at my warning expression, my lips flat and eyes hard. But only for a second. "What happened when you were alone with him, nut?"

I growled and threw Ronan's hand back in his lap, rising from the chaise. "You're not listening."

"You're not saying anything! You never say anything!"

"What good would it do when you already seem to *know* everything?" I shouted, marching for the door.

The chaise creaked and Ronan's boots hit the floor, but his grip was gentle on my elbow as he reached for me, easy to tear myself free from.

"Hazel!"

I spun in place, fighting the urge to lash out and thump my fist against Ronan's chest, but he stumbled back from the force of my glare alone. "He made me come, Ro. A *shocking* number of times, actually. He made me lose my goddamned mind with a single touch," I spat out. Ronan's eyes widened, mouth gaping open. "And I can't *wait* for him to do it again. I'm going to scream so loud, and I hope Mr. Reddy has the charms in place because I think all of London might hear me when that demon absolutely *masters* me in front of everyone."

Ronan's shock faded and shuttered behind a handsome mask at my words. I wasn't sure if he was jealous or offended or if he simply didn't believe me. I wanted to believe I didn't care.

"I hope you enjoy the show," I said softly, and his eyes flashed, but he didn't stop me from turning around again and walking out of my dressing room. "I know you love to watch."

Conversation bubbled from the far hall that led to the canteen, and I realized it must've been a mealtime. My so-called "rehearsal" would take place soon, although at this point, I knew as much as Constantine was willing to share with any of us. Con and Antin would undress me, touch me, fuck me. Theoretically, I would survive the experience.

I considered briefly storming down to his dressing room, demanding another demonstration of what tomorrow night would feel like. Would it be Con's cock fucking me, or Antin's? Would they balance their touches like they had before? But I heard Ronan call my name again and decided that farther would be better. I darted up the stairs to backstage, slipping through a collection of scenery facades and around to the stage left wing.

Giggles sounded from the stage, and a low growl.

"Ohh...Goliath." A soft squeal followed the sigh, and the rather obvious clue of wet slurping.

I smirked and shook my head, glancing behind me briefly to be sure Ronan wasn't following before I tiptoed slowly forward. Goliath, a lovely yeti member of the company, liked playing with the girls on stage, and it sounded as though he'd finally sweet-talked Margaret into a tryst.

"Mooooree," she moaned, voice high. "No, no, finish me first. Just keep—Yes!"

Good girl, I thought. *Don't let them skip a good finish.*

I considered my options. Goliath wouldn't care if I waited in the wings until they were done—he could probably already smell me—but I wanted some fresh air, the fight with Ronan still simmering in my veins.

I paused near the curtain, fairly certain Goliath could keep Margaret distracted while I made my escape. His pale, shaggy bulk blocked me from view, Margaret's ankles over his shoulders. I caught the swing of his familiar, heavy cock, already dripping cool arousal onto the stage.

Margaret came with a scream, and Goliath didn't give her another second, lunging forward and thrusting inside of her with a roar that shook the walls of the theater. So hard, I was sure I caught sight of movement at the far corner of the seats.

My heart leapt into my throat as a figure skirted toward the center entrance, stopping again. It could've been anyone, of course—I couldn't see clearly from this far—but no one from the company would be skulking at the back of the theater, rushing for the doors. Goliath and Margaret were groaning and moaning, bodies clapping together, and I darted through the dark short set of stairs that would lead to the seats, hunching down and running for the back of the room.

And when I reached the back, saw the outline of a bowler hat and the long broad silhouette of the man hiding at the back of the theater, my heart stopped altogether.

Detective Sergeant Piper's eyes were wide, but it wasn't the rutting private performance of Goliath and Margaret he was staring at. It was me.

I glanced back at the stage to be sure the couple was too absorbed in one another to notice us, and then charged for the detective. He didn't fight me as I caught his sleeve, dragging him into the dark stairwell.

"Miss Nix—"

"What the *fuck* are you doing here?" I hissed, one hand on his sleeve and another at the collar of his coat, pulling him backwards to the exit doors, out of sight of the stage. "How did you find—"

"I followed you."

I stopped abruptly. Margaret and Goliath were a noisy pair, and DS Piper's eyes flicked in their direction before his face flamed with color and he shook himself.

My hand snapped out, cracking against his cheek with sudden vengeance. I wasn't sure if it was leftover rage from Ronan or anger with myself for not realizing the potential danger presented by the detective.

His eyes widened and red bloomed on his cheek, his hat tipping sideways to reveal the curious wrinkle at the top of his ear again.

Followed. I'd allowed myself to be followed. Allowed a human detective to find the...

I gaped at DS Piper as he blinked and stared back at me, no sign of anger on his features.

"What are you?" I asked.

His brow furrowed at that and he leaned back, dropping his voice. "What am I?! What was that...that beast on stage?"

I took a moment to study him. The fine features, the clipped ears, and yes... It was here in the dark stairwell—an almost imperceptible *glow* to his eyes and skin.

"A yeti," I said softly. He blinked, jaw working and head slowly shaking. "Tell me how you got in."

"What is this place?" he asked, ignoring me.

"A theater," I answered, tempted to smile as he gaped back, a slow calm rushing over me with understanding. I turned my head as I realized that Goliath and Margaret were shouting their way to completion. "Come."

I took ahold of DS Piper's arm again and tugged him through the dark, heading for a side exit before anyone found us.

"Wait—" Piper gasped out, trying to slow our progress.

"Detective Sergeant, the only humans allowed in this theater are the ones getting fucked," I snapped back.

His feet stumbled eagerly along with mine after that.

"Humans," he whispered, following my lead. "Humans, as opposed to..."

I reached ahead of me with my free hand, found the door with fumbling fingers, and threw it open.

"Monsters," I said, turning back to watch DS Piper flinch at the sudden light, ducking his head before whipping it back up to stare at me.

I pulled him out of the building and let the door shut behind us. The theater was surrounded by warehouses of storage and a few empty buildings that Mr. Reddy had purchased just to give us shelter from passersby. There was no one outside to see us, and the sounds of the city were muffled through layers of brick buildings.

"Did you open the front door yourself?" I asked.

DS Piper was pale, his eyes constantly traveling around us, as if he was searching for another monster like Goliath to suddenly appear around a corner.

"How can this exist?" he breathed. "How can..."

Does he know? I wondered. Had his ears been clipped as a child too? Did he believe he was human?

"Did you open the—"

"Yes, of course I did!" he barked suddenly, stiffening and swelling in his heavy jacket, reminding me that I'd dragged us both out in late spring, and I was only wearing a thin dress. He shook himself, a shaking hand lifting to cover his eyes. "Monsters."

"Vampires, werewolves, demons," I said.

And perhaps I was being a fool. Perhaps I would have to drag the detective back inside and hand him over to Mr. Reddy until they found a witch to erase his memory. But I'd seen new girls marveling over the truth of theater, stating how impossible it was.

"And fae?" he asked.

Fae. He *knew*. He knew they existed, I was sure of it now.

"Not lately," I said, and DS Piper twitched. "We had an Unseelie fellow a few years ago, Jacobi, with the finest, most delicate wings I'd ever seen in my life."

Piper was breathing heavily, sucking in huge lungfuls of air and gusting them out just as quickly, eyes still darting, mind most certainly racing in panic.

"Did they take your wings too?" I asked, reaching a hand up to brush my fingers over the top of his ear. He stiffened in front of me, lips parted, but his breaths stopped altogether as he stared back at me in horror. I smiled carefully. "No human walks into the theater unaccompanied or without an invitation to work. We have all sorts of charms in place to keep them out, to keep the theater *safe* and secret. What are you? A quarter fae?"

I thought he might not answer, that he might even run from me. Then his tongue peeked out, wetting his lips before he spoke.

"Half," he whispered.

I nodded, relaxing slightly.

"They couldn't cut my wings, so I keep them hidden," he added, searching my face with that terrified stare.

I winced for him. "I imagine that isn't comfortable."

He released a shuddering breath, stumbling backwards and hitting the wall of the building. His legs were shaking. "I had... had no idea..."

"That there was more," I finished for him, nodding along as he blinked at me. "A whole world. Right under our noses. Or, more correctly, out of the corner of our eyes."

"A yeti," he said, sounding the word out with a frown.

"A mountain race from the east," I explained. "Although Goliath was born here in England, I believe."

"And...and this theater..."

"It's like a bridge," I said, reciting words I'd once heard from Mr. Reddy. "A connection between the two worlds. I don't know why exactly, but humans fascinate monsters. A forbidden fruit, I suppose. My neighborhood isn't so wrong about Beth and I. We are...a kind of whore, in truth. But we only work here at this theater."

He frowned at that, looking at the door.

"Detective Sergeant, regardless of why you can walk through those doors, *don't*," I said sternly, catching his attention again. "You live as a human. You pass for one. You work with them. If you step into that theater again, you'll be walking in from the wrong world. This isn't a place you can snoop without consequences. The theater protects its own, humans and monsters alike. There's nothing for you to learn here that you can take back to your superiors."

He reached up, pulling the hat from his head, and I couldn't help but glance at those ears. I didn't remember getting mine clipped, if it had hurt or if I'd cried, and I imagined sometimes what I might look like now with the pointed tips. More like my mother?

"And what if the theater has something to do with why she was killed?" he asked, standing straight again.

"No one who works here would ever hurt Beth," I said, wanting to speak of Myra or Mr. Reddy, but knowing I'd already risked enough.

"And what about your audience members?" he asked. "Can you vouch for them too?"

I wrapped my arms around myself and thought over his words. "If you're right, then I hope for my sake you find the killer soon," I said, and he drew in a sharp breath before I continued. "But you can't investigate here. Not if you want to keep walking in the world you live in. If you cross the bridge, you won't find the road behind you if you turn back."

The hat returned to his head and his fingernails scratched over the stubble on his cheeks as he glared down at the ground.

"You should leave before someone comes looking for me," I said.

That shocked him out of his stillness, gaze flicking to the door we'd exited from and through the alley.

"Humans really can't find this place?" he asked.

"None ever have on their own," I said, shrugging. "Be honest with yourself. Do you really want to report this back to your inspector? Would he believe you? Or would you just make that world you're hiding in look a little too closely at you?"

"I understand, Miss Nix," DS Piper snarled, hands clenching at his side. He started marching toward the end of the alley, but he paused halfway, his back to me and head turned just enough to see the strong lines of his profile. "If you want your friend's death to find justice, you'd better hope her killer was human. The police can't solve a crime we can't investigate."

I didn't answer, waiting and watching until he turned the corner, away from the theater marquee and back toward the bland and predictable streets of London.

I pulled the door open and hurried back inside. Rehearsals would've started up again, and while I wasn't needed until the last scene, my absence altogether might've been noticed, especially if Ronan was still looking for me.

But it wasn't Ronan who looked relieved as I wove through the aisles to join the others.

"There you are, lovey!" Myra called under her breath, jumping up from the edge of the stage, a pile of boxes wrapped in glossy black paper stacked in her arms. Behind her, Alexa squirmed on a table set for a feast, posing and stretching to check lighting marks, a few stagehands play acting at taking bites, standing in for her collection of vampire scene partners who were still dead to the world in the basement.

"Hazel," Ronan whispered, rising from a seat at the edge of the aisle, his hand extended for me.

I dodged around his stretching wing and reaching hand. "Myra needs me."

"Where were—

"These came for us during lunch," Myra said, almost vibrating with joy as she bounced on her toes, her grip on the boxes firm. "Your costume for your scene. Come downstairs with me. We'll see if it needs tweaking."

"Out of the way, Missy," Mr. Reddy hissed, trying to watch the stage. "No, that light on her cunny needs to be brighter! Brighter, I said!"

I ducked out of Mr. Reddy's way and followed Myra back to

the wings. "I thought I was wearing the pink gown for the scene?"

"Oh, that old rag? We've used that dress for years now. No! You need something fine, the Gemini said. And jewels, remember?"

The only "jewels" the theater had were a few paste necklaces, all of which had gems missing, and one tarnished tiara.

"Mr. Reddy let you buy a new gown?" I asked.

"Pfft, I didn't even bother asking. No, these came from a patron," Myra said, turning just enough to let me see the sly smile on her lips as she scampered down the stairs to the dressing rooms. "I mentioned we needed something new for your scene, and he offered to help."

I thought of what DS Piper had said, that Beth's killer might have been a member of our audience, and I had to grab onto the railing to help myself down the stairs, my head spinning dizzily.

I'd told him too much, broken promises to Mr. Reddy about keeping the theater secret. And why? Because I'd known DS Piper was mixed blood, like me? It wasn't enough. What if I'd just guaranteed a station of policemen arriving on the theater's doorsteps? I opened my lips to whisper the words to Myra, all but having to chase her speedy steps through the hall, but then we reached the curtain of my dressing room.

A sudden waft of fresh, sweet fragrance floated to me as Myra flicked the curtain aside and stepped into my room. I followed after her, swallowing my confession and stopping still at the massive, overflowing vase of flowers on my dressing room table. The arrangement was so large it covered my entire mirror, and it was made up of sweet pink rose buds, bright narcissus, blooming branches, and drooping ferns.

"Yes. He sent that too," Myra said, words bubbling giddily. "With a card."

I spotted the card as soon as she mentioned it, the corner tucked under the vase—a lovely copper jug, with filigree and a sloping handle.

"You can read it after, come and see what he chose!" Myra urged.

But the little white card called to me more than any promise of a gown or jewels, as did the heavy, lush arrangement in the vase, as if someone had gathered an entire conservatory together to send me flowers. Myra huffed behind me as I pulled the card loose.

We've walked a park together once, but you were right in my neglect of flowers, little one.

- A lady's suitor

I blushed at the words on the heavy paper, so simple and polite. It was the most gentlemanly note I'd ever received from any patron.

"Hunter," I murmured.

"He likes you," Myra said softly. "I like him for you."

I pressed my lips together, leaning down and taking a long inhale of the bouquet. There were branches of juniper and pine in the mix too, and all together it smelled like springtime, a little bite of winter just clinging to the edges like frost. I liked Hunter too, but I couldn't shake the feeling he had a version of me in his head that I wouldn't be able to live up to.

"Let's see the dress then, I suppose."

"You sound as though you think it will be made of briars," Myra laughed, moving to my chaise. "Light all the candles and open the curtain."

Paper ripped in eager hisses, Myra's patience at an end, as I brightened the room as much as I was able, joining her on the cushions as she opened the first box. Deep, emerald green silk rested on powder pink tissue paper, and even in all her eagerness, Myra's fingers hesitated over the fabric.

"I'm afraid to touch it," she whispered with a soft giggle.

I found myself suddenly eager, lifting the bodice from the box and gasping as it almost slipped through my fingers, the fabric cool and as smooth as water.

"There's no boning," I said.

"And no bustle," she murmured. "Not fashionable, but *oh*, it is fine, isn't it?"

I stood, the soft draped shoulders of the dress in my hands, my eyes on the delicate embroidery of blossoming branches wrapping under the bust and around the hips.

"Monsters don't care about fashion, do they?" I said, smiling.

"Mm, not when a dress like that will reveal every bit of your lovely figure," Myra agreed with a firm nod. "Clever orc. And he's added stockings. The Gemini will appreciate that."

I shivered at the thought of Con's touch tracing down my legs as he removed the sheer delicate stockings, with briars and buds around my upper thighs. Usually, the company presented more urgent and carnal scenes, dresses torn away from girl's bodies rather than carefully removed.

I glanced down as Myra gasped and realized that while I'd been mooning over the dress, and the idea of Con and Antin removing it from my body, she'd opened the boxes of jewelry.

"Oh, well, this is curious," Myra said, tipping the necklace back and forth on its velvet bed.

"It's beautiful," I said, marveling at the brass branches that curled and the pink glittering petals and emerald enamel leaves.

"I suspect the Gemini was thinking something...a little more traditional," Myra mused. "These are very pretty, of course."

I suspected Myra herself might've been more in favor of large diamonds or rubies, or at least very good imitations of them, but I liked the necklace that looked like a wreath of glittering flowers. Orcs and nymphs had their homes and privacy in nature, and Hunter might not have known my origins, but he'd tied us together in his taste.

"Then the Gemini should've brought his own jewels. I'm wearing these," I said.

Myra flashed a bright smile up at me. "Smart girl. Please that orc, rather than the demon. He's the one that's going to make a difference for you, I'm sure of it."

I wanted her to be right. I almost even believed it. But I wondered if I was really what was best for Hunter. I liked him, and perhaps Myra was right and I even *needed* him, needed an escape from the company. But I hated to think of him as my meal ticket. He was too good for that.

"Try it on, lovey," Myra murmured, reaching up to squeeze my arm. "We need to be sure it fits you."

Would being Hunter's human mistress fit me? Or would it be like the theater, where I answered to one man's needs and ignored my own, ignored half of myself? Hunter wanted the human girl, a fine lady to fit the image of the gentleman he cultivated for himself. I was neither of those things. I didn't even know truly what I was, had never been offered the freedom to explore it. How could I find a place in the world for myself when I was always half in hiding?

II.

UNMADE, REBORN

onan spun slowly, silks wrapped around the roots of his own wings, our faces uplifted to him as he cradled a lost figure in open empty arms.

The audience was hushed, and I resisted searching the crowd for a hint of tusks or a flash of green skin. Alexa's voice cracked with feeling as Ronan flipped, freeing his trapped wings, claws grabbing onto the fabric as he swooped above. He was performing the act without Beth, as if she were still there. Wax dripped over the edge of the candle I held, running down the side and cooling with a harsh kiss against my fingers. I bit my lip at the burn easing on my hand and the sting rising in my eyes.

Behind me, Samson hummed along with Alexa, low and a little tuneless, and his hand squeezed my shoulder in support.

The only person I was truly close with in the theater was Ronan, and I kept even him at arm's length. It would've been a lie to call Beth a sister to me, or even to say we were cut from the same cloth. But we'd belonged here together, caught in the same small web of an in-between world. People left the theater all the time, so often I'd grown cautious of connection, but this was like Beth had been stolen from us. And worse, she'd been hurt. Not just stolen from the theater, but from her own life.

I held my breath, resisted my own tears, and tried to hush my thoughts as Ronan twisted and curled and spun slowly down to the floor with the last notes from Alexa. One by one, candles flickered out in our hands, wicks pinched between licked fingers, the warm glow of the stage fading into pure dark and silence.

Pixies brought up the lights at the floor just enough for the audience to watch the red curtains swing shut. For a moment, I thought perhaps Eston was right—no one would care for our goodbye to Beth. Monsters didn't come to *care* about the humans in the company, but to covet them. My eyes fell shut, and a moment later a steady, simple applause pounded from the other side of the curtain. There were no cheers or whistles and shouts like there might be for a scene, but we stood together on the dark of the stage for several minutes, and the sound only grew and held. Not enthusiastic, but respectful, carrying on like a heartbeat up to the rafters.

"Come on now, everyone," Frank, one of our were-bear stage-hands called, ushering us back to the wings. "We've got to set up the next scene. Get downstairs and get ready."

Samson was waiting for Alexa and Leon, and I wasn't sure if Ronan was the first person or the last person I wanted to speak to at the moment, so I turned and hurried away, weaving through bodies on our way downstairs.

I flicked back the curtain to my dressing room, inhaling a deep breath of the sweetened air from my bouquet, before I remembered the promise I'd grabbed from Hunter before he left.

And there he was, sitting on my chaise with his hat in his hands, resting on a bouncing knee. He straightened as I entered, opened his mouth to speak as I crossed to him, huffed a laugh as I knocked his hat to the floor.

"That one was new," he said.

"I don't care," I answered, taking the hat's place on his knee and wrapping my arms around his shoulders.

Hunter groaned as I tipped my head and slanted my lips over his, sucking hungrily and teasing the seam of his mouth with my tongue. His arms wrapped around my waist and tightened, pressing my chest to his, dark claws snagging in the loose cotton. His tongue met mine, and I twisted on his lap, climbed closer, surprised with my own *need* for this man.

I moaned his name as his mouth traveled down to my jaw, and one of Hunter's hands slid down to squeeze my ass, to press my core over his crotch.

"I didn't dare hope for such a welcome," he mumbled into my throat.

"You should have," I said, wrestling far enough back to hunch, to peck at his mouth as I spoke. "You should've hoped for more."

Hunter watched me with that same rapt confusion as I reached between us, my hands unable to make up their mind about what fussy, fine article of his clothing ought to be removed first. I was tempted to seek immediate access to his cock, but I missed the smooth, thick texture of his skin too and wanted it warming my own.

"There is something," he said, reaching out and catching my hands.

I struggled briefly, smiling at him, but he held fast until I settled. "Which is?"

"To taste you."

I blushed at the offer, or was it a demand? "To taste me where, sir?" I teased.

"Your cunt, little one," Hunter said solemnly and with his own rising color in his cheeks. "Would you allow me that? One taste?"

"Only one?" I blurted out, frowning.

He blinked at me. "You would allow me more?"

"I sometimes wonder if we aren't speaking entirely different languages," I said, tapping my fingers along his chest where I could reach. Hunter's brow furrowed in confusion, and I dipped my head, pressing my lips to his for a moment and then drawing away. "What if I wanted you to make a feast of my cunt? Show me your tongue, sir."

Hunter's eyes widened and his lips parted, and in his surprise, he was unable to stop me from reaching up and pulling his jaw farther down. I arched an eyebrow, and his tongue stretched out, revealing its full length and dark color. Orcs had beautifully long tongues, twice as long and strong and flexible as a human's.

"What if I asked you to fuck me with that tongue?" I asked, watching Hunter's eyes as I leaned close again, stroking the tip of my own tongue up the center of his, the vibration of his growl rising at the touch.

"Would you ask those things?" Hunter rasped, eyelids growing heavy.

I wanted to laugh. It took twice as much talking to get a little fucking from Hunter, but his lack of assumption was sweet, and when I did succeed, he was well worth the wait.

"Feast on my cunt, Hunter. Fuck me with your tongue," I said softly.

His growl was something like a purr, and he leaned in, breathing deeply at my throat, his hips lifting and pressing into me, allowing me to feel his arousal.

"Tonight?"

"Why wait?" I asked, growing a little breathless, working myself against him, my chemise thin enough to offer me friction as we moved together.

"You have a performance tonight, little one," Hunter said, tipping his head back. The yellow of his gaze was just a bright, thin glow, black pupils blown with obvious interest. "One I intend to watch."

I restrained my flinch at the thought of Hunter watching me with Constantine. The orc could barely imagine me offering my permission for him to lick my cunt. I couldn't imagine what he might think of what was to come. Which settled me a little.

"Not for an hour, at least," I said. Hunter grinned and I sighed, remembering. "But you want several hours."

"I do," he said, nodding, patting my ass. "Perhaps even just for licking, now that I know you have no objections."

I snorted and then blinked as I realized he was being serious. "Where did you go this week? Or if you can't tell me, did it go well?"

Hunter hummed, and then he was turning and sliding to lean back on the chaise, carrying me with him until I was draped on top of him like a blanket.

"I was once a member of a house that...offered pleasure partners to monsters," Hunter said.

Oh. I tucked my chin to hide my expression. So he'd gone back to the house? When he could've been here...

"I ended my membership, but I have a great deal of respect for the madame of the house. She was kind and did her best to..." Hunter frowned and I relaxed, realizing this wasn't a liaison he'd attended. He huffed, in his own thoughts, and dismissed them with a shrug. "The house is facing some danger at the moment. I don't intend to be a member there again, but I couldn't refuse a request for help."

"And did it go well?" I asked.

"It remains unresolved. I may have to return. But I've made my terms simple," Hunter said, flashing me a smile. "I must be able to attend the theater's performances."

I forced my own smile into place. He was offering me a compliment, certainly, but it meant that whatever our connection was, it revolved around the theater.

"They're lucky to have your help," I said, brushing a kiss over his cheek. "And perhaps you might lend me your help too?"

"Of course," Hunter said, starting to sit up, face falling into a solemn frown.

"Good. After all, you ought to be able to admire me in the costume you paid for," I teased.

Understanding passed brightly over Hunter's features as I slipped away from him. "You're testing my strength to resist you again, aren't you, little one?"

"Whatever could you mean, sir?" I asked, grinning as I pulled my thin gown up over my head until I stood naked in front of Hunter, praised only by the vivid glow of his gaze as he drank me in.

❧

"ARE YOU READY?"

I startled at the low whisper in my ear, the tall shadow suddenly appearing out of the corner of my eye.

On stage, Evie was doing what Mr. Reddy called our "juggling act," where one human took on an increasing number of monstrous cocks. Evie was the best at multitasking, and she'd gotten the act up to six with the use of her feet. Impressive, indeed, although by the end, the audience could barely make her out in the tangle of limbs.

The music Nireas chose for the scene always made me laugh,

jaunty and bouncing, like something you might hear cranked out in Piccadilly accompanied by puppets. Personally, I thought it was a shame the witty finale was always buried beneath the roars of satisfaction from the monsters surrounding Evie.

"How could I be?" I whispered back to Constantine.

Goliath started to grunt in warning—a cue to Evie, the other monsters, and even Nireas that the finish was coming. Quite literally.

"I barely know what's about to happen," I said.

"You know enough," Constantine answered. "Do you really think you could follow cues and scripts once I started to touch you?"

There was something almost playful in the words, and I turned my head to look at him. He was still eerie, those metallic eyes bouncing back the stage lights, his body moving in one jerk after another, but I'd grown used to those features this week. We'd been close during rehearsal and he'd spoken softly. He hadn't touched me again, and sometimes I was grateful, and other moments I hated the waiting.

"I suppose not," I said. "Do *you* know what you're going to do?"

"I'm going to touch you, undress you," he said, inching closer, close enough to share hints of rough spice and carmelly sugar on his skin, his breath an almost imperceptible temperature as it stroked over my shoulder. "Fuck you. I will hurt you and soothe you."

"It doesn't sound like much of a show, if all they'll see is you touching me and me screaming," I admitted.

Constantine smiled, and somehow, it made his features fit together better. My shoulders relaxed and I tipped my chin up.

"Perhaps," he said, head dipping abruptly in acknowledgement. "I am less concerned with the audience's response than I am with our own."

I wasn't sure if I was part of the "our," or if he only meant his two halves.

On stage, the septuple came to a collective, bellowing finish, and the audience laughed and clapped and cheered—a few of the more lusty members joining the act in their completion, from what I could see. The lights dimmed slowly and the curtains closed, and the stagehands hurried to pull the cluster apart, Frank lifting Evie up off the cocks she was seated on and cradling her limp and giggling body back to the wings.

From the other end of the stage, two were-bears carried out the bench Constantine had requested. It was Mr. Reddy's design, built especially for versatility and offering a good view to our audience. When Constantine had declared it "grubby" in Wednesday's rehearsal, I'd thought Mr. Reddy would lose his temper with Constantine at last, but whoever the demon was, he had some shocking kind of power over our director and producer. So the bench had been reupholstered in a deep, cherry-purple velvet.

"Go," Billy hissed at Constantine and me.

I hurried forward, searching the floor for my mark in front of the bench, surprised to find my body bubbling with nerves. I hadn't been nervous to appear on stage for years now. Sometimes, I felt almost like a piece of machinery, just a pretty cog in a clock, making the theater tick along. Evie had said I was Reddy's favorite because I showed up and could fuck anyone, but it was more than that. I could act, as much as any of our scenes needed me to. I followed cues, always found my mark. I knew every act, every job, as well as I knew the work I did myself. And with all of that knowledge, all of that experience, the nerves had softened and faded away. Maybe the excitement had too.

It was back now. I stopped in front of the bench, the glimmer of stage lights just barely visible through the seam of the curtain, and bounced briefly on my toes, the silk stockings slippery against the floor. Hunter had sent me an elegant pair of shoes, but Constantine and Reddy both dismissed them. The curtain twitched, and Nireas's last notes went still. There would be no more music for the rest of the show. It was only me and Constantine now.

I caught one deep breath, steeling myself, and then the curtains parted and a bright, warm spotlight found me. I lifted my chin high, shifting just slightly in place, allowing the spotlight to glitter on the jewelry Hunter had gifted us, at my ears and wrists and throat.

The audience was silent as they watched me, waiting. In this gown, fabric kissing and stroking over my form, and with these bright gems glittering on me, I was not the helpless human creature Mr. Reddy's audience paid to see. I was pristine. Hunter had taken great care backstage in brushing out my hair until it was glossy, and Myra had proven herself to be a much defter hairdresser than I'd realized, twisting my long auburn locks up into something worthy of a princess.

Suddenly, I understood. Constantine would destroy this version of me, unravel me in front of everyone. But he'd given me this moment, this brief, haughty dignity where I was beautiful and untouchable, an impossible object for any of the monsters in the audience to ever hope to possess.

I stared down my nose at the front row, watched blurry faces frown, bodies shift in discomfort, knowing that any moment, I would be sent toppling from the pedestal the finery provided.

The audience's focus on me distracted from Constantine in the shadows, and their sudden bouncing gazes on either side of me was my only warning.

"Now," a soft voice whispered in my ear.

I didn't feel Con's fingertips at the lobe of my right ear, but a scream tore out of me at the sudden, brilliant slicing that stroked down my throat and up into my skull. The audience gasped as I arched in place, hands flailing out in front me. I was on the tips of my toes, about to lose control of my legs, when as quickly as he had struck, Con's touch vanished, just a sweet burn left licking the right side of my head. I stumbled in place, hands clutching air, and my scream died in my throat, my breath catching.

A silvery-blue hand held the earring I'd been wearing, and I turned to meet Con's eyes. There was no sympathy in his gaze, but no glee either.

Antin took my other ear, and this time my knees really did wobble, a heavy roll of pleasure dripping down from my head right into my cunt. My eyes fell shut, and my lips fell open on a moan. Antin's hand was gone again as swiftly as Con's, but the pulsing in my core remained, thrumming heat and need through me, eager dampness growing on my sex.

I tried to straighten, to find my mark on the floor, my eyes blinking dizzily at the audience, but Con was fast. Lightning cracked up and down my spine, but I didn't have time to scream before it was gone again. My whole body trembled in the wake of the attack. The clasp of the necklace was open, and it slid cooly down my chest as I sobbed for air.

My legs were liquid already, and it was Antin who caught me as I fell forward. I gasped, and his own breath hitched in my ear as I wrapped my arms around his shoulder, clinging to the sensation rushing through me, as if he could be both wave and anchor.

"Show them your face, sweet creature," Antin whispered, his voice strained as his power stroked between my legs, over my skin, all by the grip of his hands on my arms trying to steady me.

My face was pressed to his shoulder, the contact amplifying every color in the room as I turned my head, rocked in his arms with the pulse of pleasure, and stared out at the audience. I cried out, stiffening with the snaps of pain as Con undid the buttons down the back of my dress, sagging as those sharp bites forced the first tide of an orgasm to wash over me, a bright, wordless cry echoing up to the mezzanine.

Antin freed himself from my grasp, pushing me gently away and leaving me to slide down to my knees. My palms clapped against the floorboards of the stage, arms shaking. My dress was open, sliding down from my shoulders to expose my breasts. I lifted my chin slowly, facing the audience on my knees, panting for air and shuddering through aftershocks. I arched my spine hard, and the spotlight shone down on me, a soft murmur of study rising from the quiet mass in front of the stage.

"Very good," Antin murmured, and I shivered, wanting to turn and lean into the words. "Beautiful. Stand for us, sweet creature."

I let out a gusting laugh as Con's gleaming, elegant hand appeared in my periphery. I sat back on my heels, wetting my lips, and turned to look at Antin. There was sympathy in his smile, his head tipped down to face me, as if he had the eyes to see my hesitance.

My hand trembled as it lifted from the floor, and I couldn't watch the moment my fingers landed in Con's palm. My body stiffened at the slam of contact, the beating drum of pain. Con was strong, hauling me up from the floor, but he couldn't force my legs to work while I writhed in the onslaught of his touch.

Antin stepped forward, his hands stroking down my sides, drawing the gown down my waist, over my hips, and I fell back into Con's chest, sobbing and shaking, screaming when I could catch my breath.

"Beautiful," Antin murmured. "Such a good girl for us. There now."

His hand petted between my legs as the silk dripped down to the floor, and the audience gasped with me as I howled and thrashed and came against his fingers, my legs spreading wide to invite more.

They lifted me between them, and I twisted in their hold, my body entirely free of any thought, wholly consumed by the crash of agony and ecstasy meeting inside of me.

Like flying, I managed, a wisp of a thought, before I was released, draped over the velvet bench, my back bowed and limbs splayed to expose myself for the audience's view.

"Breathe," Antin whispered in my ear, his cheek brushing against mine and forcing me to gasp, to breathe again, to recall my own mind and body. "That's it. You're doing so well."

"Please," I whispered, not sure what I was begging for.

"It's a relief, isn't it?" Antin asked, kneeling behind my head. I tried to stretch, to reach his skin, wanting a taste of him. "To be released from your own head?"

Con was so gentle, but there was no escaping the scratch and burn of his touch as he dragged down one stocking from my thigh. My leg kicked, and I yelled curses as I tried to regain control of my own muscles.

"Don't fight. You won't hurt him," Antin said, and he bent his head, brushing a kiss over my forehead, a confusing current stretching between his lips and Con's knuckle stroking the sole of my foot.

"Kiss," I whined, reaching back for Antin. His lips, so full and rosy, stretched in a smile even as he skirted out of reach.

Con's grip was more direct on the next stocking, and I screamed and thrashed and bucked through the torment, forgetting my need for Antin until I was limp and gasping and the pair of them both stood out of reach.

"You're bare to us now, sweet creature," Antin said, and it wasn't a whisper for my ear, but a declaration to the entire room.

I was sweating, boneless, stretched and arranged to bare everything, hundreds of eyes staring back at me through the shadows and the blinding spotlight.

"What do you want?" Antin asked.

There'd been no discussion of this in rehearsal, no prompt for me to follow. No script to provide me with the words. The audience held its breath, waiting for my response.

"The truth, sweet creature," Antin said, and I believed him.

Mr. Reddy would write this scene with me moaning and begging, or screaming and trying to escape. And what would he, or even Antin, say if I pleaded for respite, crawled on my shaking limbs back to the wings, retreated from the stares? I knew what I would say as Hazel, the practiced, obedient, professional actress of the Company of Fiends.

But that woman was still standing center stage in finery and jewels. I had no cue, and my answer to the question was unwritten.

"Touch me," I said softly.

I pressed my feet to the bracing boards at either side of the bench, arched my back even deeper, pressing my breasts into the open air in invitation, and tipped my head back to find Antin. He was upside-down in my vision, smiling gently as he walked slowly closer. I lifted my head up and sucked in a breath at Con's slow approach, the intent metallic stare fixed to my cunt.

Antin's knees thumped softly on the cushion behind my head, and I sighed and shivered as he grazed my jaw and throat.

"I want to be erased," I breathed, blinking up at him.

"Never," Antin murmured back. "But you can be remade."

He bent as I stretched, and our lips met in a simple press that created a frenzy inside of me. Con's hips brushed the inside of my thighs, a duller pounding pain, and then his cock stroked against the lips of my sex. Both men gripped me, Antin stealing my hands in his, Con's wrapping around my hips, pinning me in the whirlwind of their touches, blotting out the room, my thoughts.

Con's deep plunge inside of me was the blade cutting me free of the edges of my own skin, Antin's teasing tongue licking at my lips the breeze that swept me loose in the air. I moved, rocked and writhed, because they were two opposing forces battering me between them.

Antin's kisses drifted to my throat, behind my ear, and his hands guided mine to my breasts.

"Share it all with them," Antin whispered. "Breathe, sweet creature."

I breathed so I could scream and cry and babble pleading nonsense. Con's touch was careful, but his fucking was ruthless, steady and rough, deep and electric. Antin grew gentle, grazing, and it threw their balance in Con's favor, my voice hoarse with howls and whines.

Explosive color burst inside of me, in my vision, and I was vaguely aware of my own mess of arousal slipping down my thighs, slicking Con's hips in their rocking. I clutched at Antin's wrists as he pinched and plucked my nipples, long pulses of heady pleasure meeting the bone-rattling shock of Con's driving thrusts.

"You are exquisite," Antin praised in my ear. "Our pretty gift. See how unruly you make him."

I let out a ragged moan, my throat already hoarse from shouting, and Antin lifted my head for me so I could watch Con. His head was thrown back, chest heaving, the silvery blue of his horns shimmering under the spotlight, sweat glittering on the carved planes of his chest, more like armor than muscle. He dropped his chin and that bright, dangerous gaze met mine, flashing and stealing my breath with its focus.

Con leaned forward, and Antin traced patterns on my breasts as I panted for air I couldn't catch. The knife's edge gaze held mine as Con bent forward, lowering his face to my breasts, Antin's touch retreating to my throat, my pulse drumming so hard, I thought the whole room must be booming with my heartbeat.

Con's nose traced gently between my breasts, his body

churning on top of me, hips working in a hypnotizing circular pattern that stroked inside of me.

And if there was pain, it was blurred now. I'd been carved open, gutted, rinsed clean, a pure vessel to be filled. Pain *was* pleasure, a shock, a kiss, and a pound, the gentle stroke of a hand up and down my thigh.

"Closer," I whispered.

Antin was gone and Con stretched above me, his hands wrapping my legs around his back. My skin crackled everywhere we touched, my blood sizzling in my veins, and still I rolled myself into him, found his horns in my grip, and screamed my determination to drive this demon into the same hurricane of need I was drowning in.

He had no lips to kiss me with, but he stroked his face against my skin, somehow sweeter and more desperate than Antin's tender presses.

I'd forgotten the audience, forgotten the stage, and in the final moment I forgot Con too. I came with a scream, with an explosion I was certain would shatter my own bones, with my nails raking down Con's back, trying to escape the crash of destruction.

Cool hands bit into my hips and heat like fire filled my core, fuel to the storm burning through me. The world was an avalanche of noise and color, bursting and decaying, and the only concrete thing I understood was *relief*—relief so deep and heavy, it was in my marrow. In all the chaos, there was a void of quiet, and I sank into the place eagerly, leaving the past few hours and weeks and years behind me.

Con ripped himself away, and reality was stark and cold.

The avalanche was applause, loud and boisterous in my ear, and I flinched away from the noise. There were bright spots in my vision from too long in the spotlight, and I managed to drape a heavy arm over my face to block out the glare, but the colors remained in the shadows of my eyelids. I shivered, and traces of unnameable sensation raced through me.

Strong arms gathered me up from the bench, drawing me to a warm frame, and I knew by the spice it was Constantine. He had never touched me in his unified form, and I wasn't sure if it was how overwhelmed I already was, but Con's spectacular pain had vanished, leaving only the mundane ache of tired limbs. Antin's gift evaporated too, leaving only the familiar sexual throb after release.

Darkness rushed in and my arm slipped loose, hanging down, tired and tense. I tucked my face into the bare chest at my side and tried to find my way back to that heavenly moment where I'd lost all sense.

12.

AN ORC OF MEANS

I sighed at the gentle scratch of claws through my hair.

"I should like to take her to my home this evening, tend to her. Do you believe she might object?"

"Oh, sir, why would any young woman object to such a generous offer? And believe me, she'll be bright and cheerful and so pleased to see you just as soon as she wakes," Myra trilled.

Hunter huffed and stroked his claws down my scalp again, to the back of my neck.

"If you're certain," Hunter said.

My eyelids were heavy, and they lifted with reluctance, just in time to watch Hunter pass Myra a tidy fold of paper. It vanished into Myra's skirt before I could make sense of the conversation.

"Should I call for your carriage?" Myra asked as my eyes fell shut again. "I can direct your driver to the back so you don't have to fuss with the crowds in the lobby."

Hunter grunted in agreement, continuing the soothing brush through my hair. I took stock of myself as Myra bustled with swishing skirts out of my dressing room. There was a sort of numb buzz in my sex and a soft ache in my breasts, and my whole body felt *tight*, like my muscles had been twisted just a bit. My mouth was dry, my throat itchy, and I rolled to my back with a slight whimper.

Hunter's thigh was under my head, his face upside-down above mine as I blinked my eyes open again. A thumb stroked down my jaw and over my throat, feeling my hard swallow.

"Can you sit up?" Hunter asked. "I have water and wine for you to choose from."

I fought to sit up and groaned at the resistance of muscles in my stomach. Hunter interrupted my effort, gently managing the job for me. I glanced down and found myself in the simple white chemise I'd been wearing in the first act, its ties still loose, and decided it was probably Hunter who had dressed me.

"Water," I said.

He brought the glass of water to my lips first, and I searched the room, relaxing as I found the green gown draped carefully over a chair. The water was icy and wonderful, and I reached up to wrap my hands around Hunter's. I gulped until the glass was close to empty and pulled away with a gasp of air.

"Thank you," I said, squeezing around his wrist.

He was difficult to read in the dark of my dressing room, but his hand twisted in mine, tangling our fingers.

"You're taking me to your home?" I asked.

His eyebrows rose. "You heard? Yes, unless you'd prefer to return to your own."

I bit my lips, wincing as I shifted on the chaise, my feet dropping heavily to the floor. I was sore, mostly from straining and stretching, but there was still some lingering sensation in my sex, and it made me hesitate.

"I have a very large bath," Hunter said, catching my eye. "And a very soft bed. And a great many oils that warriors use to soothe their bodies after battle. I believe you went to battle tonight, little one."

I held my breath as he leaned in, tensed as his lips touched my forehead, and then released a long sigh. This was Hunter, and while it would be a lie to say his touch did nothing to me, I'd forgotten the difference between the stunning power of Constantine and the normal, soothing pleasure of a kiss on the forehead. I pressed into Hunter's lips and pulled away at the same time as him. My lips were smiling, while his were turned down.

"That performance was not what I'd expected," Hunter said, eyes reading my face back and forth.

"I'm all right," I whispered, my voice not up to much more.

"You will be, with more care," Hunter agreed, pausing to stare at me a moment longer before asking, "Did you enjoy that scene?"

I took in a long breath and felt for the second time this night that I was missing my script. Did Hunter want me to say no? Was he disturbed by what Constantine and I had done, and did he want to believe that I needed rescuing from the deed? But Myra wasn't here to tell me how to please the patron, and I'd been honest with Hunter so far. I didn't want that to change.

"Yes," I said. "I did enjoy it."

"This is the truth?" Hunter asked, eyes narrowing slightly.

"It is." I was too tired to press the point, my voice too weak to elaborate.

Hunter nodded and steadied me against the back of the chaise as he stood. "I'll have honey water made for you. You'll need it if you're to have any voice by the end of Sunday."

I blushed as he turned his back to me, and he retrieved his hat from my table, on the other side of the bouquet he'd sent.

"I'll dress you in a moment," Hunter said, "But first, what do you think?"

He put the hat on his head, and I gasped as he smiled, tusks suddenly vanishing. His skin warmed and his eyes darkened too, and the tip to his ears was missing, but otherwise, the face staring back at me was entirely Hunter's, right down to his thick red beard and sharp cheekbones.

"You'll prefer the hat on now," he said, glancing down at the floor.

"No!" I said immediately, shaking my head as he looked up at me again. "But I certainly prefer this to the last one."

HUNTER'S HOME was in a nice neighborhood, one that had been more fashionable a few decades before but was still quietly respectable. The home was large, with a stable and a coach house, and an almost hollow quality to it as we stepped inside.

"An acquaintance recommended the house to me, and I was

able to keep most of the furnishings in the auction," Hunter said, watching me.

My legs were still wobbly, and I was overly aware of the uneven hem of my skirt, probably dragging in dust from the streets of my neighborhood onto the elaborately cut marble tile.

"It's very beautiful," I said.

"It's very large," Hunter murmured, looking around the space with a slight frown.

A gargoyle in a butler's black uniform waited by a winged staircase, granite skin polished smooth and expression blank. "Everything you requested is waiting upstairs for you, Master Hunter," the gargoyle said with a low bow.

Master Hunter, I mused, lips twitching, as Hunter guided me to the stairs.

I wanted to break away, go snooping through the house. I'd only been to a patron's home once in all my years at the theater, for a performance at a private party, and we'd been brought in through the service entrance and the house elf servants had kept a close eye on us. But Hunter's arm was wrapped around my back, and my body was tired. The promise of his bath, or even simply the bed, was tempting enough to miss a tour of the home. Still, on our route upstairs, I noted the empty places on a wall where the mark of a lost painting remained.

"What do you *do*?" I asked Hunter as he led me down a hall still missing its carpet.

"A bit of everything. I speculate, invest. I own a few companies now. A railroad line on the Continent," Hunter said, shrugging.

My eyes widened at the list. "And how does an orc come to find himself in such a...human line of work?"

"I was a warrior," Hunter said, and I nodded. "There were prizes for my victories, both battles and sport. I thought I might be able to fight my way to tribe leader. And then, years ago, my tribe had a guest. The Red Wolf of Ireland visited us, paid his respects to our leader as he traveled through our territory. He was...wild, yes, but refined too. He told me stories of the world I hadn't ever dared to explore."

"The human world," I said, and Hunter nodded.

"I wanted to conquer your world too," Hunter said, flashing me a youthful grin. He stopped in front of a door, opening it, and I caught my breath at the sudden revelation of candlelight, bright polished tile, and fragrant steam.

I stepped inside and Hunter followed, the door clicking shut behind us. His tub *was* large, as big as the platform we used on stage sometimes, and built up out of the floor almost as high as my waist.

"I took my gold, found my disguise, and Conall—the Red Wolf—helped me establish myself here in London. It's not a warrior's honor, and I haven't found my victory yet, but I enjoy the challenge this world poses."

I listened as I studied the room. Hunter either had an innate sense of romance, or his butler did, because the room was warm with the flickering glow of candles and there were bowls of floating blooms at every corner of the tub.

"What challenge does London pose for you?" I asked, smiling at Hunter over my shoulder.

"Human manners are very different than orc," Hunter said, shrugging off his coat and crossing to me, reaching for the buttons of my dress immediately. "Courting a pleasure partner. Defeating a business foe. There is much more subtlety."

"You don't have to do everything the human way," I said, admiring the strong, stern expression on his face as he unbuttoned my dress. "You're more of a gentleman than any human I've met."

Hunter didn't answer, his strong hands pushing my dress off my shoulders. I pulled my arms free of the sleeves and leaned back against his chest, forcing his arms to circle around me.

"I think you've spent too long in the theater," Hunter growled in my ear.

My eyebrows rose at that, and I twisted to look at him as he tugged the dress down over my hips. "What do you mean?"

"You accomodate what's asked of you," Hunter said, shrugging slightly and keeping his head ducked to avoid my gaze.

Irritation bubbled in my chest, and I stepped away from Hunter, pulling the chemise up over my head on my own. "You're talking about tonight?"

Hunter nodded. "In part."

I snorted and rolled my eyes, but Hunter caught my hand as I approached the massive tub, helping me balance as I stepped inside. The water was milky and just hot enough for a pleasant sting against my skin. I sank in with a sigh. It'd been ages since I'd gone to the trouble of filling an entire tub for myself, and I'd never had one this size to enjoy. Sitting down, the water reached all the way up to my chin, and I turned, watching Hunter undress.

I suspected the other "part" he meant referred to my eagerness with him, and it made me want to thunk his head against a wall, as if that might hammer in the notion that I craved his wild hunger and rough passion.

"I was nervous about the act at first," I said, and Hunter looked up, his shirt half-unbuttoned, fingers pausing for a moment. "Mr. Reddy only told me that it would hurt. But it's more than that. My only role in that scene is to respond, and the pain..."

"It does hurt, then?" Hunter asked, frowning, chest bare and pants parted just enough for me to see the piercing at the root of his cock glinting in the candlelight.

I nodded. "Very much. So much so that everything else disappears. It's freeing."

Hunter's dark claws were out on his flexing fingers, feet shucking off the legs of his pants, eyes cast down and brow furrowed. He was considering my words, and I marked the difference between Hunter's long pauses of quiet thought versus my argument with Ronan. Was it easier for Hunter to listen to me because we were still learning each other?

Not that there isn't plenty I've kept from Ronan too, I thought.

"Do you hurt now?" Hunter asked as I watched his strong thighs stretch, his cock hanging heavy and dark sac tucked behind.

"I'm no more sore than I usually am after a show," I said, keeping my place in the center of the tub so that Hunter's body rubbed against mine as he joined me. "I'll be fine again by morning."

Hunter nodded, sinking down in front of me, smiling as my hands wandered over his ass and back. "I'll make sure of it."

&

"MM... HUNTER?" I mumbled, facedown in the most decadent pile of pillows I'd ever imagined. I groaned as strong fingers stroked up the back of my thigh to my ass, pulling and digging into neglected muscles.

"You are very tight," Hunter noted.

I let out a giggle, and his treatment paused. "That's not the way men usually say that. Where did you learn this?"

"All warriors do. We have to take care of our bodies in order to fight well. We learn these skills and assist one another."

His hands slid back down to my calf, and I smiled into the cushions at the thought of dozens of naked, greased-up orc warriors like Hunter all giving one another massages. What a vision!

"What happened to your threats of licking me for hours?" I mumbled before gasping sharply as he gripped my foot, thumbs digging into the soles, and I squealed and gripped at the pillows under my hands.

"If you are still awake when I'm finished, I may follow through," Hunter said.

I grinned into the pillows, certain of my own triumph. But Hunter must've known better than I, or he was determined to continue the slow and exquisitely thorough massage until I was asleep. Either way, by the time he was rolling me onto my back, my eyelids were too heavy to lift.

13.

UNKEPT
WOMAN

I woke up feeling reborn. Had I ever been so comfortable in my life? So loose and well-rested? I stretched and blinked at the ease of the movement, wondering if I'd grown three inches after Hunter's massage.

The sun was bright, muted through sheer blue curtains, and Hunter was missing from the bed. I'd rolled over in the night once, and I recalled the way we'd been tangled together and how he'd settled me into his side with a kiss at the crown of my head. I turned to the spot now and found the dent of his head still in the pillow, the sheets rumpled.

Very nice sheets. Extremely smooth and cool. And a mattress without any lumps.

I'd never given Myra's determination to find us humans wealthy monsters much thought, but the appeal was clear now.

But I doubt very many monsters know how to massage as well as Hunter, I thought with a grin. I might grow very spoiled very quickly if I did manage to steal a life with him for myself.

For now...I needed to find out what time it was, and hopefully find Hunter in order to offer proper thanks for the night before. Preferably with my mouth. Or his, if he insisted.

I giggled at how new my body felt as I sat up, how bright the morning was, how pretty Hunter's bedroom was—clean walls and dark wood furniture, with soft blues and gold fabrics. I twisted in place and finally spotted the white note resting on the table at the other side of the bed.

My body stretched across the mattress and I hummed, the

luxury of the sheets almost erotic against my skin so used to cheap, rough cotton. I flipped open the note, smiling at Hunter's familiar, somewhat clumsy script. But my smile faded quickly.

I've been called away again, little one. I'm not sure how long my absence will be this time. My house and carriage are at your disposal.

- H

The light in the room dimmed, the sun caught behind a sudden cloud, and I flicked the note back onto the table, sitting up and searching the finery around me for a clock. Nearly eleven, and I was in Mayfair, far from the theater, let alone Stepney Green. And there, hanging from the door of a wardrobe, was an elegant blue satin day dress with puffed sleeves. My own more simple and old-fashioned dress was folded tidily atop my chemise on a chair by the wardrobe, and I rose and hurried there, ignoring the cool air on my bare body.

Hunter was generous, and *kind*. But he wasn't here, and I wasn't his mistress or his wife or whatever Myra made us into. Not yet, at least. I was still just an actress at the Company of Fiends, and I wasn't about to dress otherwise.

Gentlemen are often occupied with business, I reminded myself, but it didn't feel like a consolation. More like a warning.

I dressed in a hurry and slipped out of the bedroom, pausing in the hall for a moment to recall the way back downstairs. It occurred to me that my opportunity for snooping was now more available than ever, but the prospect was less appealing with Hunter gone. I moved quickly and quietly to the stairs, and then paused at the top of the landing, seeing the gargoyle butler waiting for me at the bottom.

"Breakfast has been laid out for you, madame," he said, an arm stretched out toward a set of double doors.

My stomach clenched at the thought. If Hunter's table was half as nice as his bath or bed, I would find the best meal of my life waiting for me. And for some unknown reason, that hurt too. I didn't want to eat alone, snoop alone, live here in this huge and lovely and unfamiliar house alone, while Hunter was away on some unknown mission.

"I have to go, actually," I said, walking down.

The gargoyle nodded once, undisturbed by the idea of a wasted meal. "I'll call for the carriage."

"No. No," I said shaking my head. "I...have errands to run. I will find my own way."

He nodded again, a little slower. "Then the carriage will be waiting for you at the theater tonight."

I huffed and shook my head. "No, please. I don't know what your...your master told you, but never mind all of it. I will not be using the house or carriage in his absence."

This gargoyle was an exceptionally good butler, because there wasn't even a flinch of response in his face as he stared back at me and nodded a final time.

"Very well, madame."

I nodded too, shoulders drooping even as I lifted my chin high, heading for the door. And in spite of his heavy, slow gait, the gargoyle managed to reach the door first, pulling it open for me.

It was warm out, and the sun was escaping the cloud that had briefly trapped it. A dozen stares turned in my direction, and I suddenly remembered I was in *Mayfair* in the middle of the day. Perhaps it would've been better to simply borrow the dress Hunter had left for me, if only so I wouldn't draw so much attention in my shabby dress, exiting out the front door of the fine house in the middle of the block.

I tipped my chin down to my chest and hurried on my way, ignoring the sound of the door clicking shut at my back.

I WAS GASPING FOR BREATH, body swamped in thunderous ecstasy, rocking into Antin's body on top of mine, Con's fingers just barely brushing through my hair, sprinkling in shocks and stabs to cut through the drowning.

"Beautiful," Antin breathed, lips grazing over mine as his rolling rhythm started to break and snap. "You are all that was promised, sweet creature."

I was too far gone to care, and even the spotlights were blinking behind swarms of darkness.

Antin groaned in my ear, draping heavily on top of me, every thought racing away as I sank into a terrifyingly sweet abyss.

It softened suddenly, and I seemed to rise to the surface again, the weight resting on me still dense but not so powerful. Con's touch was gone, and I opened my eyes to find Constantine's completed features, so handsome and close to my own. He turned his head and his mouth found mine, firm and needful, strong hands coming to circle my face.

I clenched in a final fluttering orgasm around his length, and he shuddered and hissed into the kiss, pulling away with me lifted in his arms. I hid my face in his shoulder again, but I was more alert than the night before.

Antin had taken the lead tonight, his overwhelming gift of pleasure somehow more exposing and dangerous than Con's pain.

"Will every time be different?" I whispered as the audience cheered us off the stage.

"Would you like it to be?" Constantine asked, cold and clipped.

I didn't answer, and Constantine continued on his path through the wing, back to the stairs that led down to the dressing rooms.

"We shouldn't miss curtain call," I said, even though it was a habit of mine and Mr. Reddy never really cared.

"You can't stand," Constantine said. "And the crowd is too loud."

I lifted my head at that, resting my chin on his shoulder. "Then my screams must be awful for you."

"If we were alone, I would gag you," Constantine said, but his lips twitched and I had the wildest feeling he might be joking.

"Why not have Con fuck me while I suck Antin?" I suggested.

We were halfway down the stairs, and Constantine showed no other sign of surprise but the sudden jerk of his foot missing a step, immediately corrected, his arms tightening around me.

"That would be...a good show," he said slowly. "You're much more alert this time. Pleasure agrees with you, sweet creature."

Nymph, I thought, but held back.

"Do they... Do you feel what the other feels?" I asked.

Constantine frowned and shook his head. "No, but some sense is shared. I know where I am and what I am thinking, from either side."

Which explained why Antin's movements were always so sure even though he couldn't see, and why he seemed to speak for Con sometimes.

Constantine turned briefly toward my dressing room and then paused, glancing down at me. "Do you have other clever ideas?"

"I might," I said.

He turned and headed for his own dressing room. "The imp chased me out of your room last night. Were you sore?"

I frowned at the thought of Ronan interfering in any way. "A bit. A...friend gave me a massage."

Constantine nodded. I hadn't been back in his dressing room since the day he'd arrived, and a little thread of nerves hit me as he settled me on the bed and went to close the door. We were both completely naked, and Constantine's movements were more fluid out of clothing, his elegantly elongated body moving confidently throughout the space.

He had the impression of a human form, but the details were too perfect, an uncanny finish on his frame. He paused, looking back at me, and I realized I'd been caught examining him.

"Why did you ask for a guest act?"

My legs were slightly parted, my body propped up on my elbows, so similar to the first time when he'd licked and barely touched me and sent me unraveling. I thought about crossing my legs, covering myself with a sheet, but Constantine's stare was too fixed, like any motion on my part might cause him to leap into action.

"I didn't," he said, stepping forward.

I frowned. "What do you mean?"

"I am here upon request." Another step.

Was that a clench of interest from my cunt, or a remaining flutter of the many orgasms I'd had on stage?

I'd assumed the conversation I'd overheard between Reddy and Myra about a man who couldn't be refused had to do with

Constantine. So either he was lying, or Reddy had some other fate in store for me.

"Roll over," Constantine said. One more step, and his feet would bump against mine.

I turned slowly, my stomach sore from clenching, my body nearly as weak as it had been the night before. My spine prickled and I stared up at the wall, where Constantine's shadow loomed up to the ceiling.

"Crawl up the bed."

I swallowed, trying to think of another question, as if it could erase this growing sense that I was helpless, alone in the room with this demon. Still, my knee slid up onto the bed, body wobbling as I lifted myself up, crawling slowly forward to the top of the bed.

"Spread your knees and lean down," Constantine said.

My breath hitched, and my arms gave out eagerly. Constantine's pillows smelled clean, untouched, and I knew without asking that no one but myself had laid in this bed since he arrived. I sucked in another deep breath as the mattress dipped by my feet. For almost a minute I waited, until a tingle of warmth and awareness melted over my ass and exposed sex.

"You smell like me," Constantine whispered, and his breath was close, tickling over my pussy, his own release leaking out of me as I clenched again, this time certainly in interest.

"You can...you can fuck me," I said into the pillows, lifting my head just enough to be heard. "If you want to."

I wanted him to, which was insane after this evening's performance. Con and Antin were powerful with a single touch, merciless and consuming. But Constantine, complete and entire, cast a different kind of spell. His touch had no unusual effect on me, but *he* did. I wanted to be as much under the control of his will as I was Con and Antin's touch.

Long fingers wrapped around either of my thighs, and I braced myself for his tongue or his cock, panting into the pillows, embarrassingly eager to be unmade again.

With a yank of his hands, I was flat on my belly, eyes wide on the empty wall. And then long fingers dug almost bruisingly into the backs of my thighs, a sterner and more determined version of Hunter's treatment the night before.

"In time, perhaps," Constantine said.

I groaned as he dragged his thumb down a long muscle, my whole body tensing and releasing with his grip.

14.

THE IMP'S NEST

nother bone-melting massage, another heavy sleep, I thought as a gentle hand stroked down my back.

I knew almost at once that the touch wasn't from Constantine and bolted upright.

Ronan's hand retreated, head dipping. "Sorry. I should've let you sleep."

"He's gone?" I asked.

Ronan frowned and nodded. "Are you... Did he..." He huffed out a breath and shook his head. "I'm trying not to be a prat."

A laugh escaped me, and I didn't have the heart to fight it. "I'm fine. He just...took care of me. We talked a little. I fell asleep."

Ronan nodded again and we fell into an awkward silence, so rare for us it made my stomach churn.

"What time is it?" I asked.

"After two."

I winced. "I suppose I'm staying here for the night." Two nights out of my own home would make the neighborhood stir with new chatter.

"Do you... Are you staying in *here*, or would you come up to my room with me?" Ronan asked, blinking and pressing his lips flat.

He's nervous, I realized, some of my own anxiety slipping away.

"Your room," I said with a firm nod. I'd been missing Ronan. Watching him from the stage during Beth's act had made my heart hurt, and our cold silence was all wrong, just one more uncomfortable weight on my shoulders.

Ronan's smile flashed bright, and he lifted up my robe from his lap. "Brought this for you."

A few of the stagehands and monster actors stayed in the theater or Mr. Reddy's buildings next door. Our pay wasn't great, and some monsters couldn't afford the disguise charms to keep their homes safe.

But in Ronan's case, I suspected he just liked the room he'd managed to grab upon arrival, and I didn't blame him.

My hand slipped into his as we tiptoed through the hall and back up the stairs to the theater.

"I wonder where he came from, don't you?" I whispered, thinking of Constantine vanishing while I was asleep. "Usually, the rare ones stay here."

"I saw him leave. He has a black carriage," Ronan said, flashing me a wicked grin. "But I didn't get the address...this time."

We stepped out onto the empty stage, the darkness of the theater exceptional at this time of night. I could see decently, able to make out some of the shadows of the first row, but I knew Ronan's vision was even better than mine.

"Ready?" he asked, and there was no reason but reverence for us to whisper alone in the dark like this.

I stepped closer, wrapping my arms around his shoulders, his own twisting around my waist. His tail even coiled around my ankle, more affectionate than useful. "Ready," I said.

Ronan's wings beat once, bringing us up to our toes, and then again in earnest, and we were flying. With a few strong flaps we were up past the rafters of the theater, into the open space, and then Ronan twisted and veered left, flying into the hollow loft space above the theater. At the far end of the broad room, a round window faced the street, the moonlight shining through and meeting a solitary candle.

Ronan landed with a few quick steps, but he didn't set me down and I didn't fight for him to release me. He carried me over to the large mattress he kept on the floor, surrounded by old velvet stage curtains and woolen blankets, a bird's nest of a bed, and one I was familiar with. It was cold up here in the loft, but Ronan ran hot, and I clung to him as he knelt.

"I'm sorry for picking the fight," Ronan said, settling at my side with one of his legs pressed between mine, his wings rising to cover us and keep out some of the cold. The moon and candle glowed through the skin of his wings, cool and hot, lighting up his earnest expression in tandem.

"You can't protect me from the work we do here, Ro," I whispered.

He frowned. "I'm not sure that's true, but I understand you don't want protection," he said, adding before I could argue, "And that...in the case of this demon, you don't need it."

"He's less scary the more time I spend with him," I allowed.

"Your scene is *intense*, and none of the other girls envy you this time," Ronan said, staring down at me. "But even I can tell you're enjoying yourself."

I snorted and Ronan grinned back at me. His hair was falling loose of his usual sweep, and I tugged him closer, snuggling into his warmth until he had to wrap an arm around my hips.

"How is the orc?" Ronan asked.

I blinked up at him, cupped his jaw in my hand. "Do you really want to talk about him?"

Ronan's smile was faint. "I just want to be ready for the day you leave, nut."

I stared down between us and thought of Hunter missing from his house when I woke up, of his tender touches and heart-felt refusals.

"Historically, I'm not the one who leaves," I murmured. I stroked my hand down Ronan's strong throat, over his chest, found his hips and guided his weight to lying fully between my thighs. His stare was warm on my face as I reached between us to untie my robe and pull it open.

"Whatcha doing, nut?" Ronan asked, even as he pressed our stomachs together.

"What does it feel like?" I asked, searching around his hips for the tie of his pants.

"Like you're changing the subject," Ronan murmured, pushing up on his arms just enough for me to reach my goal. My fingers paused on the tie, gazing up at him and waiting. His smile was slow, but there was the slightest wince at the corners of his eyes, so I stared at his mouth again. "But I like this subject better, and I'm not about to repeat my previous mistake so soon."

I found myself sighing as Ronan's hand guided mine, helping me loosen his waistband and push the fabric down his hips. I hadn't realized how much the recent refusals from Hunter and even Constantine had irritated my pride until I was struck by the sudden relief of Ronan's acceptance. His cock bumped against my sex, and Ronan groaned as his head ducked and his lips found mine. He was familiar, friendly, and whether I liked it or not, he knew me well.

Knew I liked my lips nibbled and the closeness of his nose brushing mine, our breaths mingling. Ronan knew every inch of me, and all my responses, and the urge to teach him more struck me suddenly. To tell him all my secrets, my greatest secret.

"I've missed you, nut," Ronan rasped against my lips, his cock stroking against me with a gentle rocking of his hips. "Missed having you like this."

I wrapped my hands around his face, then drew his mouth to mine in a greedy press and suck, silencing his words and the words that fought to rise to my tongue. Ronan's fingers dug into my back, scratched down to my ass, and tipped my hips to his. I stretched my legs wider and his tail found my ankle, twining around and around, squeezing my calf affectionately.

"I missed you too," I admitted in the smallest whisper.

Either he didn't hear me or he knew me well enough in this way too, my own resistance to connection. I craved the contact of familiar skin against mine, even as I rejected my own need. But fighting with Ronan had left me with a constant, faint queasiness and a weight on my chest for days. Now that it was gone, I was almost drowsy with ease.

Could I tell him? Would Ronan care what I was? I wondered, but my body jerked with an immediate, trained warning.

And then the head of Ronan's cock nudged against the lips of my pussy, slippery and hot, and I gasped into his kiss, his tongue stroking in. My arms circled his back as he went back to just rubbing himself against me, slicking himself on my pussy. I found the roots of his wings, tender and muscular, and Ronan's groan vibrated against my tongue as I gripped them in my fists. He bucked unevenly against me and pulled away from the kiss with a huffing laugh.

"Trying to rush me, Hazelnut?" he asked, his grin bright even in the shadow of his wings.

I ran my hands up the strong, leathery spines at the top of his wings and watched his eyes flutter shut, his breath panting out of damp lips.

"I could get you off, make you rush, just by petting your wings," I answered, eager to move my thoughts in a safer direction.

His tongue flicked out against his lips as I stroked down the fragile membrane, a full-body shiver racing through him, and a hot dribble of precum stinging against my clit.

"*You* could," he rasped.

There was a compliment I wasn't ready to hear in that, so instead, I smiled and trailed my fingertips playfully back to his wing roots. "We should suggest the act to Reddy."

"Don't talk about Reddy right now," Ronan laughed.

"Hmm? Why? Don't the mutton chops just make you— Ugghn!" I arched as Ronan thrust in to the hilt with one rough stroke.

"Fuck," Ronan sighed out, his back arched and head tipped down to stare at me, flames licking in those dark eyes. "Fuck, Hazel, your cunt is the stuff of dreams."

Still breathless from his thrust, I let out a giggle at the praise.

Ronan arched an eyebrow, drawing out and then slamming in again in another toe-curling, breath-stealing movement. "Wet," he said as I shouted and scratched my nails into his back. "Hot," he added, pulling out and driving in again, my back sliding against the velvet on the bed with the force. "Strangling my cock."

"Ronan!" I gasped out as he thrust again, my eyes slamming shut.

"Shh, I have you." Ronan softened on top of me, his forehead resting against mine as he started a slower but equally deep rhythm.

I whined, my feet scrabbling against the bed. He knew this too, this perfect tilt and stroke that touched the tenderest nerves inside of me. The coil of his tail on my leg squeezed and then lifted my foot from the bed, pulling it under his wing and pressing it high and wide, stretching me open for his taking.

Ronan pushed up again, and I twisted my face to the pillow, knowing exactly what he was doing now.

"Pretty tits," he whispered, reaching between us to tweak at a nipple and make me squeak with the lovely pull that echoed down to my cunt. "Such sweet nipples, just begging for touch."

"Ronan, please," I whispered, the praise drawing a hot flush over me.

He bent, holding one breast in his grip, and I braced myself. His lips fastened around my nipple and his hips stopped, cock pressing up inside of me as he took a deep, sucking draw from my breast. I arched and shouted, grabbing at his horns to hold him in place, riding his still cock with anxious, desperate jerks of my hips. Ronan sucked and bit gently as I grew frenzied beneath him, but as the shuddering peak rose inside of me and I started to quiver on his length, he moved his hand to the center of my chest and pressed me flat back to the bed, mouth leaving me before I could reach my finish.

"Asshole," I panted, but I laughed with him as he grinned.

"You're going to come so hard you can't breathe, and you know it," Ronan answered.

And then he repeated the whole process on my other breast, until my knuckles were white and the first licks of an orgasm were racing through me and I was *sure* he would misjudge when to stop.

He sat up suddenly, wings flapping in excitement as I snarled in frustration and thumped my hands in the pillows above my head.

"That was a close one," Ronan said, triumph in that stupidly handsome face of his.

"Fuck you," I spat out.

He only laughed, his hands stroking up and down my sides,

petting my body into a simmering state where the orgasm was close but not near enough to take for myself.

"You know what else I like?" he asked.

"We could be fucking right now," I muttered.

"I like this view," he said, and then he rose up to his knees, pulling my hips up with him so that I could see the picture of him between my legs, his cock stretching my sex around his dark length. And in spite of his teasing, I couldn't take my eyes off of us, especially not as Ronan pulled slowly out, an almost embarrassingly slick sheen covering his cock.

"Ronan, please," I whimpered, shivering as he pushed gently back in, circling his hips up and making my breath catch and my cunt clench.

"You look so pretty with me inside of you," Ronan said, his gaze coals in shadow, staring down at me as he fucked me so slowly I wanted to scream. "You turn all pink with need when you want to be fucked, and it covers you head-to-toe once you have a cock in you."

I growled and covered my face with my arm, and Ronan lunged forward, my body thrashing at the sudden rough plunge. He held my hip up in one hand and tore my arm from my face, gripping my chin in his hand.

"No," he snarled, brow furrowed. "You don't get to hide from me, Hazel. I want to watch you come apart on my cock. Hear you beg. And I'm going to fuck you until you can't speak or think or move. All night, asleep or awake. You're mine tonight."

I gasped at the threat, at the sudden flutter of my cunt on his rigid length inside of me, and whined.

"Please," I whimpered.

"Please what?" Ronan asked, grinning.

I wet my lips, and Ronan waited. "Please don't stop," I whispered.

He kissed me once, bruising and simple, and then sat up, swatting one breast, a stinging crack to the spot, before reaching to my pussy.

"I like this sweet little clit too," Ronan said, the snap of his hips making me squirm and grasp uselessly at the pillows, my breath short and rapid, my finish so close I could feel my muscles tense and brace. "Like the way it looks just pinched between my fingers like this—"

I howled as he squeezed my clit, and then my breath froze in my chest and I couldn't make a sound as the pleasure struck, hard and quick, snapping through me. Ronan growled, stroking inside of me even as I clamped down so hard it was like I was trying to push him out.

I reached for him and Ronan fell into me, my arms wrapping around his back and his face tucking into my throat, nibbling and kissing there.

"Don't stop," I panted, still shaking and fluttering.

"You know I keep my promises," Ronan rasped, kissing my lobe, slowing his motion on top of me to give us both a moment to breathe. "I won't be finished with you until dawn."

15.

LITTLE SECRETS

Ronan kept his promise and I felt the proof of it the next day, groaning as I rolled over, the sound echoing slightly under the cover of his wing. His warm frame followed mine, curving against my back, and I sighed, snuggling back into him.

Voices carried up from the stage far below, and I tried to muffle the sound against a pillow, turning over again and hiding my face against Ronan's chest. His arm circled my back, a soft kiss brushing over the top of my head.

"Can I hide up here today?" I whispered.

Ronan cleared his throat, squeezing me briefly. "Only if you want the entire theater in a panic."

Because of Beth. Of course.

"You can hide up here for another hour...maybe," Ronan said, twisting to look out the window. "We're already late."

And I was never late.

I sighed and wiggled away from Ronan's warmth, wincing as his wing lifted for me, cold air rushing in. I sat up, and then grimaced as I glanced down.

"My robe." My robe was filthy, forgotten beneath us for the entire night, and Ronan was smirking as if he was proud of the fact.

A small part of me allowed that he did deserve some credit for the mess he'd made of me during the night. Later, after some tea and food and stretches, I might even admit to him that was by far his best fuck to date, if only for sheer and spectacular stamina. For now...

"I have a few things you should be able to put on, at least until we get downstairs," Ronan said, stretching in the bed with the sun gleaming on his stunning red skin and his muscles flexing.

Between Antin and Ronan, I'd orgasmed so many times the night before that my eyes ought to have been permanently crossed, so *why* was I looking at this imp like he was breakfast?

"I'm hungry," I said, trying not to glance at his cock. "Thank god I don't have to rehearse. I'm going right back to sleep after I eat."

Ronan's smile grew even more smug, if that were possible, and he sat up, rolling out of the bed and to his feet. I admired the way the sun struck his rounded ass and wrapped my arms around my knees, resting my chin on top. I smiled as he bent over and debated teasing him with a whistle of appreciation. His balls looked like hanging cherries from this angle.

He stood up again, turning and holding out a white shirt and a pair of trousers, lips twisted in a puzzling frown. "I can always fly down and pull something from your dressing room, if you'd rather."

I shook my head, standing up and crossing to him to take the shirt, pulling it over my head. "This will do. It's not as though we haven't all seen each other naked anyway." I paused, watching Ronan slide into the trousers, his smile huge. "What?"

"What, what?"

"What are you grinning about?" I asked, laughing.

He shrugged. "It'll annoy you."

"Tell me anyways," I said.

He rolled his eyes and stepped forward, large hands cupping my ass and drawing me to press against him. "Forgive me for enjoying the idea of flying you down, in *my* shirt, full of *my* cum, after having you in *my* bed all night." He shrugged and pressed a quick pecking kiss to my lips before that bright grin returned.

"That does annoy me," I said, a little too breathless for such a simple kiss.

"I warned you," Ronan said lightly. "Now hold tight and cross your ankles."

I tucked my face into his throat, noting that Ronan still smelled of sex and something sweeter than usual, and then Ronan lifted me off my toes and ran for the edge of the loft.

The moment of suspension, floating in his hold in the open air, always made my heart swoop in my chest, and I gasped against Ronan's skin, eyes unable to resist opening, seeing the floor of the stage so far below us. His wings hitched us briefly upward before he twisted and we started to spiral down to the floor, the voices below clearing and rising, a little bright note of surprise from a girl, and the stamp of feet hurrying out of our way.

But it wasn't one of the other girls who greeted us as Ronan's wings beat us down into a steady landing. Nireas stormed forward, eyes wide and the shimmer around his throat almost ghostly pale.

"There you are!"

Ronan jogged back a few steps at Nireas's approach, and the giant halted abruptly, the lower set of his arms crossing over his chest.

"Here we are," Ronan said. "Where's the fire?"

"You're late," Nireas muttered, two eyes flicking down and the third still fixed to my face.

"How late?" I asked.

"Not just you," Evie chimed in from the edge of the seat, her hands twisting her lap. "Margaret hasn't arrived yet either. But you're here now, so maybe..."

"It doesn't change anything," Nireas said, shaking his head. "Margaret is still missing."

"She's not missing, she's just..." Evie protested, but her voice trailed off to quiet.

"Late, like Beth was late," Nireas snapped.

"Stop it," I hissed up at Nireas, his gaze sudden and fierce on mine. "Don't work everyone up. Margaret is still new, and she's...young."

"Mr. Reddy sent a few hands out to her neighborhood," Evie

said, and her hands started to twist again in her lap. "So hopefully..."

"You need to eat," Ronan said, rubbing a hand up and down my back.

"Your guest act isn't here yet either," Evie said slowly. "But I suppose no one minds."

I frowned at that, and Ronan's arm slid over my shoulder, pulling just a little to guide me toward the wings.

"Maybe it's not even a coincidence," Nireas muttered, still staring at me. "He left after she did, after all."

I opened my mouth to argue, to defend Constantine perhaps, but what did I know? I'd fallen asleep in his room. I looked to Ronan, but he was just glaring back at Nireas.

"Wouldn't surprise me," Evie answered softly.

I let Ronan's grip guide me, my head shaking slightly.

"We're just shaken up," Ronan whispered to me. "From Beth. It's just talking."

"I know," I said quietly. But the talking I'd just heard sounded like accusations, and of what? Margaret was late, that was all. That was all. It had to be.

"There's going to be more talking in the canteen," Ronan huffed. "How about I grab us food and we eat in your room? Or back up in the loft?"

"My room," I said. "I want to wash a little, and dress. You owe me a new robe."

Ronan only snorted in answer, and his hand squeezed mine as we reached my dressing room before he pulled away to head to the canteen on his own.

I took long, deep breaths as I stepped into my room, finding my way to the candle near the door and lighting it in the dark.

My bouquet from Hunter was starting to droop, but it still made the room smell wonderful, and I wondered if I could find a way to string the branches up and hang them from the ceiling to preserve them. Certainly at home, but it would be nice here too.

I lit my small room up and was in the middle of stripping out of Ronan's shirt, ready to change into my own spare dress, when I heard the curtain shift behind me.

"That was quick. There must not have been a line," I said.

The answering grunt—a little choked—had me spinning in place. Nireas was ducking into my room, still slightly bent, his stare on my hips and waist, sliding up to my breasts as I turned. And even when his eyes rose up to mine, he didn't stop staring, just tracked his gaze slowly back down again.

"What do you need?" I asked, ignoring the effect his study had on my body, refusing to shy away from it either.

I'd meant what I'd said to Ronan. We'd all seen every inch of each other dozens, if not hundreds, of times, possibly even a thousand times when it came to Nireas. At least, he'd seen me. I'd never gotten much of a good look at him, only enough to know I was missing fascinating pieces of the puzzle.

He wet his lips, his eyes on my hips again, and then they dropped to the floor and he stepped fully inside, his head remaining bowed with the ceiling bumping against the back of it. I was tempted to offer him a seat, but he would take up so much room, fill my space even more than he already was doing.

"You're right. I shouldn't have picked at you and Evie like that," he said.

I sighed a little and nodded, tossing Ronan's shirt to the chair and pulling the dress on over my head. "I don't blame you for being nervous. I'm nervous."

"I was... You're never late," Nireas said, gaze flicking up through long, dark lashes.

"Technically, I was here the whole time," I pointed out, and my heartbeat stuttered when his lips twitched with a smile. "They'll find Margaret, or she'll turn up and we'll wonder why we ever worried."

Nireas's eyes narrowed slightly, but he nodded, his head thumping lightly against the ceiling of my dressing room. I smiled at the sight of him, clumsy and too big for the room— pretty too—and he answered me with a fuller smile of his own, one so rare it took my breath away. I hadn't seen that smile in years.

And then he turned, and the light from the hall cut around him.

"Oh, uh—"

I blinked at Ronan's voice and Nireas didn't say another

word, didn't look back once, simply ducked again and left the room, making room for the imp. Ronan entered, looking over his shoulder, a plate of steaming food balanced on each hand.

"What was he doing here?" he asked.

"I don't—He apologized for, you know, upstairs," I said, waving a hand.

Ronan raised his eyebrows and crossed to me. "You mean when he was a hysterical prat because you were an hour late to show your face?"

I blushed and hid it by hurrying over to the chaise, holding my hand out for my food.

"Tell me the truth about you two," Ronan said, not moving from the center of the room.

I stiffened. "What do you mean? There is no truth."

"There's something. You only wear that prim, innocent expression when you're keeping a secret," Ronan said.

I tried to fight my traitorous face, not sure what he meant, and leaned forward to reach the plate again.

Ronan skirted backwards out of reach.

"Ro, I'm starving."

"Then tell me."

"No!"

Ronan blinked at me, grin growing, and raised one of the plates to his lips, eating a bite of the bacon hanging over the edge with a wicked gleam in his eye. "Then you're not that hungry."

"There's *nothing*."

"Eight years together in *this* theater and you never, not once, got a little tipsy and fucked the stick right out of his ass?"

I choked on my laugh and shook my head. "Never. Seriously, Ronan."

"Then why does he look at you like you rebuffed him after he wrote you a book of sonnets?"

This time, I couldn't hide my expression fast enough, my laugh from a moment ago twisting into a tangled grimace.

Ronan inched forward. "Did you? Can I read them?"

I puffed out a breath and pursed my lips. I was hungry. I was tired. Nireas was being *strange* after so long of...of nothing, and

Ronan was a horribly persistent pest who could read me like a book.

"Did you burn them? Were they very bad?"

The words spilled free, easier to speak than to ignore. "I kissed him!"

Ronan blinked at that, head tipping, waiting.

I shrugged and sighed. "That's it. I kissed him. Ages ago. Basically when I started here."

"Kissed? Just...on his mouth?"

"Oh, Ronan, *please*, I hate cold eggs!"

Ronan glanced down at the plates of food like he'd forgotten them completely and grunted in agreement. He hurried to join me on the chaise, passing one plate into my hands before settling himself comfortably, wings tucked to the side to hang over the edge of the cushion.

"There's more to the story, even if it was just a kiss," Ronan said.

"I liked him," I said. "He was... He's different now, but he was nice and funny then. A little protective too, told me what rooms to avoid, until... You know how it is here. Some of the guest acts assume all of us humans are available to try on for size."

"Some of the stagehands too," Ronan agreed with a shrug, and I nodded.

"So Nireas was helpful in that way, he gave me time to find my footing, quietly, without embarrassing me. I thought we were flirting, but it wasn't so *fast*, the way everyone else moved. It helped me adjust a bit. There was someone who just liked talking to me," I said, picking at my eggs for a moment before taking eager bites, suddenly remembering my own hunger.

"For as long as I've been here, I'd assumed he was pining after you. That maybe the pair of you had a romance."

"Just a kiss," I repeated, aware of Ronan's stare on the side of my face. "After a show. An act that made me a little uncomfortable. He had me bundled up on his lap and we didn't talk about it, but I know he was soothing me. And I kissed him."

"Did he kiss you back?"

Arms around my hips, against my back, hands cupping my face as we pressed one kiss into another into another, until I was flat on my back, Nireas warm and heavy and sweet on top of me.

"For a bit," I said, trying to push the memory away, surprised at how vivid it still was after all these years. "And at first, I didn't notice much difference. He talked a little less, didn't find me after the shows. Eventually, I realized he really was *avoiding* me."

"Idiot," Ronan muttered, shaking his head.

I shrugged. "I was...too young at the time to really push him to explain himself. And...and it *was* just a kiss. And the theater can be very diverting," I said with a half-hearted laugh.

I'd nearly fallen in love with Nireas. But I'd nearly fallen in love with a few men in my time at the theater. The only difference was I'd been falling in love backstage with Nireas, with conversations and kindness, rather than under the spotlight, fucked thoroughly for an audience's entertainment. And once Nireas had stolen back that conversation and kindness, it'd been almost easy to fall back out of love with him.

Or at least that was what I told myself.

§ð

"YOU WERE QUIET TONIGHT," Constantine noted, balancing over me, pushing my knee toward my chest in a stretch that made me hold my breath.

"My mouth was full," I answered, but without the teasing bite the words deserved.

Constantine had taken my suggestion from the night before and brought it to life on stage, and there'd been a point deep in the act, when my mouth was stuffed with Antin, right to the back of my throat, and my body was screaming as Con fucked me, that I'd thought I might die.

It'd been thrilling and blissfully distracting from the reality of the day.

"You were worried," Constantine corrected.

Margaret had not turned up for work, nor had anyone seen any sign of her in her neighborhood.

Another theater girl, missing.

"Yes," I admitted softly, breathing out in a huff as he moved to the other leg.

"They're coming down from the stage," Constantine noted, as the thunder of footsteps grew louder from the hall.

He pulled away from the bed, the pair of us naked again, him tending to me after the strain of the act. He wasn't *nice*, this demon, but there was something almost like kindness. At the very least, he seemed determined to manage my physical upkeep.

He extended a hand, and I reached for it slowly, somewhat reluctant to leave the sanctity of this room. No one—except maybe Ronan—would dare interrupt us here. The actors and stagehands were all too afraid of Constantine, and even Mr. Reddy displayed a rare deference to our guest.

Constantine pulled me up, our bodies bumping together. His free hand cupped my ass, pulling me against him, and my eyes widened, staring up at him. He'd put his face to my cunt the night before, sniffed me there after fucking me, and somehow I still managed to be surprised by the tiniest lean in my direction. Then he stepped away, releasing me with both hands.

Strange and curious and just tempting enough to make me nervous.

I braced myself as Constantine turned and opened the door, my eyes widening as I found the hallway more crowded than usual, no one sneaking into their rooms, just hovering in place together. A pair of dark horns bobbed up at the top of the crowd, and Ronan wove determinedly through the bodies.

"Thought you might need this," he said, passing me his shirt from earlier, joining me at the doorway so I was pressed between him and Constantine.

"What's going on?" I asked.

"Reddy told us all to meet down here," Ronan said, a grave hint in his voice in my ear.

The entire cast and crew of the theater was together so rarely, it was suddenly overwhelming to have us all crushed together like this.

"Shouldn't we go up to the stage?" I asked.

"The audience is still milling their way out," Leon said. The vampire's dressing room was across from the guest act's, and he had Alexa tucked against his chest, her teeth nibbling in worry on her bottom lip. "And this is theater business."

They mean Margaret.

I found Ronan's hand brushing against mine and I tangled our fingers together, his grip tight and reassuring on mine. Nireas appeared from the stairs, searching the mass of bodies with a disgruntled frown—he'd never liked crowds—before finding me. He slid against the wall, and we all jostled just a fraction closer together.

At last, Mr. Reddy and Myra appeared, remaining on the first two steps and leaning forward. The murmur of anxious conversation heightened briefly before one after another, we hushed each other and fell into quiet.

"Word came in the first act," Mr. Reddy said, abrupt and firm, his lips carving down his face as he stared out at us. "Margaret was found floating south on the Thames—"

I sucked in a deep breath, turning into Ronan, hiding the blank, washed-out fall of my face towards the wall, his arms circling my back as cries and gasps filled the narrow hall.

Mr. Reddy had been on the stage once, as he liked to remind us, and he let the noise of shock and sorrow rise and fall again before trying to speak.

"I'm not sure what the police have found, but our own sources say..." The words went quiet and the hall did as well, waiting and breathless for the rest.

I set my cheek on Ronan's shoulder, thought of Margaret on the stage with Goliath, giddy and demanding, every bit a girl of the Company of Fiends. So young still.

Mr. Reddy let out a heavy sigh. "Our sources say that it's possible it was the same killer."

"Fuck," Ronan hissed in my ear, squeezing me tight.

And what if the theater has something to do with why she was killed? DS Piper's voice echoed in my head.

They, I corrected. *Why they were killed.*

And now it looked as though the theater may have had everything to do with it.

I pulled free of Ronan's grip and slid through the figures in the hall, the girls falling into the stoic chests of men and monsters, weeping or shivering. Questions snapped at Mr. Reddy, who stood still on the stairs, Myra at his side with red eyes and her head bowed. She would take this hard, our protector.

I fought my way through the crowd like it was a tide, felt a large hand circle my wrist, and pulled myself free, pressing to the wall and lowering my head. I passed a large, hairy figure, white coat dense and soft as he shook and sniffled. Goliath. An eager flirt, but a sweetheart too.

I slid into my dressing room, my eyes shutting before the curtain slid closed on my back. The charm muffled the sounds from the hall, left me alone with my own thoughts.

But those were terrible too. I let out a soft moan of pain for Beth and Margaret, wordless and frightened, my hands covering my ribs as if I could hold myself together.

On a deep breath came a faint taste of summer.

"Little one, why didn't you take the carriage?"

16.

A NEW ASSIGNMENT

I let out a little screech, stumbling back, my eyes flying open even though my brain had already reassured me.

Only Hunter.

He stood from my chaise, eyes wide and hands lifted.

"Forgive me, I didn't mean—Miss Nix?"

I shook, a wild energy whipping through me. I'd slipped free of the crowd, knowing I was on the verge of crumbling and hating the idea of witnesses. And here was Hunter. Comforting and frustrating. As much a mystery to me as Constantine. But it was too late to bury the frenzy climbing up from my chest. The sob clawed its way free of my throat, my teeth aching from clamping down.

I didn't hear him move and my eyes were squeezed shut against tears, so I thrashed at the first touch on my arm. But Hunter, for all his hesitance in so many ways, wrapped warm arms around me, the strength of him a pillar for me to collapse into.

The sounds pouring out of me were painful scratches, my muscles clenching as I gasped for air, and Hunter held me through it all. There were no whispering reassurances in my ear, only the steady grasp of his body around me. I wasn't sure if it was the tight grip of his arms or my reluctance to fall apart in front of someone else, but the shuddering slowed to a stop, my breaths panting into the smooth black dinner jacket I was pressed to.

"I thought you'd be gone," I whispered, turning and pressing my cheek to his chest. My eyes ached and I blinked them slowly, tears clinging to my lashes.

"Withes sent word you'd left the house and not returned."

Withes... Ah, the butler.

I leaned back in Hunter's embrace and scowled up at him. "You can't just leave me your house and carriage without any warning."

His brow furrowed and his head tipped. "Why not?"

"It's... I don't know. It's too much," I said.

"It was for your safety," Hunter answered, his hands cupping my shoulders and straightening me in front of him. "I thought then your neighborhood wasn't safe. Now I *know* you're in danger, regardless of where you are."

"You're the one who told Mr. Reddy about Margaret," I said, my eyes widening.

"Of course," Hunter said, nodding. "I told you I would make inquiries."

I sucked in a slow breath, my gaze traveling through the room as if I were searching for the quiet, predictable life of weeks ago. "What did you find out?" I asked.

Hunter was silent until I looked at him again. "You're distressed. I'm not sure now is the time to—"

"Haze—Oh."

Hunter and I both turned to find Ronan at the curtain, the sobs and conversation from the hallway sliding into the quiet of my dressing room.

"Come in," Hunter said, before I had the chance to even think of issuing the invitation.

Ronan looked at me for permission as I stepped free of Hunter's grasp, and I nodded once.

Ronan cleared his throat, glancing between us before settling on me. "Most of the company is staying here for the night."

"I came to persuade you to stay at my house. It's well charmed," Hunter said.

I lifted my fingertips to my forehead, hiding my gaze from the two men. "Would you...would you be there?"

I peeked out from under my hand as Hunter winced and stared down at the floor. "I do...have to return north. I plan to return to London frequently, but until the matter at Star Manor is resolved, I will be away."

"Is she really safe at your house if she's going to be alone anyway?" Ronan asked, crossing his arms over his chest.

"Of course," Hunter said, and I was surprised by how calm he remained. "The house is secure. My staff would be aware that Miss Nix's safety would be the priority."

"I'm not staying in your house without you, Hunter," I whispered, reaching out to squeeze his hand briefly.

He studied my grasp, answered it with his own, and then glanced between me and Ronan. "You'd be welcome to bring a companion of your choice."

I had to fight my own impulse to gape at Hunter. It was strange enough to have Ronan here in the room with us—any other day, and Myra would've chased Ronan out with a broom for interrupting one of us with a patron—but even stranger still of Hunter to offer to let Ronan come use his *house* with me. Hunter had to be aware that Ronan and I were lovers. He'd seen us on stage together at the least, and I knew orcs well enough to know they had a keen sense of smell.

"Give us a minute," I said to Ronan, who nodded and ducked out of the room as quickly as he'd come.

"You intend to refuse," Hunter said, frowning.

"I do."

"You don't like the house?" he asked. "It does need some attention, the fashions are old—"

He's self-conscious. I rose to my toes and Hunter quieted as I pressed my lips to his. *Alexa has two lovers who enjoy each other's company*, a tiny voice in my head mused.

"Your house is lovely," I said, settling my hands on Hunter's chest. "And your offer is generous. But I meant what I said. I...I look forward to spending more time there *with you*. At least for tonight, I think it might be best for me to stay here with the others."

Hunter stared down at me, his own hands circling my waist.

He was studying me again, examining my words and my face. I had so many questions about how he'd come to be so timid in certain ways, and I still wasn't sure if I had the right to ask.

"The danger..." Hunter started, and then paused. He licked his lips and glanced at the curtain before ducking his head until our noses were less than an inch apart. "The danger may not be *outside* the theater."

My hands on his chest fisted in the fabric, my eyes growing wide. Hunter's hand slid up and down my back as I considered the words.

"You trust the imp?" Hunter whispered.

I nodded immediately. "He was with me all of last night."

Hunter sighed and nodded, relaxing. "Good. Then keep him close, little one."

I opened my mouth to agree, but it struck me suddenly—it was a lie. Ronan had woken me up in Constantine's room. After two, he'd said, and I only had his word to be sure of the time. I'd been asleep for at least two hours after the show ended and I—

I swallowed hard, choking on absurd suspicions now racing through my head. Ronan was jealous, he picked fights, but he was gentle too and took a girl's no without argument. He would never have hurt Margaret *or* Beth. Hunter tipped his head, pressing a soft kiss to my lips.

"Be safe. I'll return for your next performance," Hunter said. His eyes flicked over mine and his hand grasped my chin as he glared sternly down at me. "We will have our time together again."

I sighed and softened against him, shy about what a relief it was for him to say the words. I'd always considered patrons an amusing chore for the theater, or an amusing project of Myra's when she was set to make a match between monster and human. I'd never considered my own exit from the stage until recently, but Hunter was a tempting prospect. Still full of questions, but with a curious promise of a future I wanted to at least explore.

"You can't even stay the night?" I asked, wincing.

Hunter smiled ruefully and shook his head. "I'm meeting with a few friends to discuss the murders, see if anyone can dig for information."

I blinked at that and nodded. "Well, I can't argue with that. Thank you for helping."

Hunter's lips parted and then closed again, pressing firmly together, clearly fighting some speech he was considering. He settled instead on leaning in for another kiss, a slow study of skimming lips and subtle nibbles, soothing some of the ragged edges of stress and worry squatting in my chest.

"Sleep tonight, little one," Hunter murmured, the hand on my chin sliding up my jaw, his thumb brushing under one eye and over my cheekbone. "Your heart may remain weary for some time, but that doesn't mean your body should."

I found myself blushing, leaning into the hand on my cheek, embarrassed and touched by the words. Hunter kissed the center of my forehead, his tusks pressing gently to my skin, and then pulled away, nodding in satisfaction at me once before leaving the room.

Ronan reappeared not long after the orc departed, and I puzzled over my momentary suspicion. What reason would Ronan ever have to hurt one of the other girls, and how could I have considered the idea, even briefly? His smile was pasted on, his own worry and sadness clear in the wincing lines around his eyes.

"Back to the loft?" he asked.

I nodded, accepting his offered hand and following him back up the stairs to the darkened stage. With every step, I played the minutes and hours back in my mind. The night of Beth's murder, when Hunter had walked me home through the park. Last night, asleep after the performance, Ronan waking me.

I felt safe in this theater with my fellow actors and performers, with Hunter, even with Constantine. But as Ronan and I settled into the still tangled sheets of his bed, the moon smothered in clouds and the loft dark and quiet with faint rustling from the rafters, the truth was unavoidable.

I could be truly sure of no one but myself.

❧

"What do you mean, 'no memorial act'?" Evie snapped, rising up from her seat, glaring at Mr. Reddy in his own chair.

"Why shouldn't Margaret have one? Beth did!" Goliath barked from the stairs near the wing door.

"We're not repeating the act!" Mr. Reddy answered, sharp and firm.

"He's an ass. Why isn't Myra saying anything?" Alexa whispered in my ear, leaning forward from the row behind me.

And even though I knew I should bite my tongue, the words slipped free as I stared at the back of Myra's dark head. "They're afraid it will happen again," I answered under my breath. "One memorial is respectful, two is polite, but three and..."

I shrugged as Alexa let out a wounded gasp.

"No," Ronan said, shaking his head, his arm hanging over my shoulder. "Mr. Reddy just doesn't want the audience to know what's happening."

"Maybe they should know," Alexa muttered. "Maybe then something would be—"

"What are you lot hissing about?" Mr. Reddy barked, spinning suddenly to face us.

"Nothing, sir," I answered before Alexa or Ronan could say something that might get them fired. Or, more likely, lectured at for an hour, considering Mr. Reddy could hardly spare us now.

His eyes were a sharper green than ever, outlined in weary red, as they narrowed at me. Had he been crying like the rest of us? Or up all night, planning and plotting?

"Nix. You're taking the piano act."

"What?!"

I hadn't meant to shout, but I also didn't feel that there was a more appropriate response. I turned immediately to the organ, where Nireas was seated on the bench seat, back arms bracing him against the shuttered instrument, another pair gripping the bench, the last folded across his chest. His eyes were down, staring at his stretched legs.

"You know the act, easiest one in the show," Mr. Reddy said. "It's yours this week."

The act was simple, and Mr. Reddy only talked Nireas into doing it twice a year or so. A girl sat up above the keys, Nireas licking her along to the music he played below, the moans and sighs perfectly timed to the notes, right to the gasping, giggling, singing cries of climax. I did know it, but only because I'd been in the company for so long. I'd never once done the part myself, and I'd assumed it had been at Nireas's insistence.

Mr. Reddy turned away when I couldn't think of anything else to say, doling out roles to the rest of the cast, assigning familiar favorite scenes.

"He's avoiding looking back at you," Ronan whispered in my ear. "I bet he requested you."

I scowled, staring so hard at Nireas it made my head hurt, but Ronan was right—the giant never looked back.

"It's more about following the music and making a show of it," Alexa said, propping her elbow on the back of the chair next to me. "To be honest, he's never seemed all that interested. Barely puts much effort in. You'll have an easy time of it."

Why now? I wanted to scream, to march up and shake Nireas's broad shoulders, thump my fist down on his dark hair and yank. Punish him for confusing me eight years ago and again now.

It was just a kiss then, and an act in the show now. I was the one making more out of nothing.

And maybe it wasn't Nireas's request. Maybe Mr. Reddy was simply...running out of girls. I sank back into my seat, breathing out slowly.

"Tell him no, if you want," Ronan suggested.

"Maybe I will," I murmured, my glare bouncing between Mr. Reddy and Nireas.

It wasn't until Mr. Reddy was done, heading into the wings to return to his downstairs office, that I thought of the words.

"Good luck," Ronan said, patting my hip as I jumped out of my chair and hurried to chase our employer down.

I made it as far as the downstairs hall, no one nearby to hear me as I called to Mr. Reddy's back at the far end. "You told me I'd only have one act."

His shoulders slumped, and I thought for a moment he might ignore me as he shouldered open his office door, but he stopped, the door propped open by his large frame, and waved a hand in invitation.

I marched down the hall, footsteps echoing behind me as other members of the company retreated from the stage. Mr. Reddy held the door open for me, and I moved to the chair in front of his desk, gripping the back of it rather than sitting down.

"I did, and I meant it at the time," Mr. Reddy said. "We're two girls down now, and even if I *had* time to find a new girl, it's hardly the appropriate time to be doing so, is it?"

I dropped my chin to my chest and nodded slightly. "I know, I do. But why this act? Why not...not the silks?"

Mr. Reddy snorted. "You and the imp have good chemistry, but you don't perform as well with him and you're shit on the silks."

I blinked at that answer. "What? What do you mean I don't perform as well with Ronan?"

Mr. Reddy arched an eyebrow, rounding his desk and sinking into his chair with a weary sigh. "You're too wrapped up in each other on stage. You forget your lights, to face the stage. And don't think I don't know you two are gossiping through your teeth."

My lips twitched at being caught in such a silly thing, and I pulled the chair out, settling down and crossing my arms over my chest.

"You said it yourself—it's the easiest act. Give it to one of the other girls, and it won't make a difference. Hell, give me one of theirs in exchange," I said.

Mr. Reddy hummed, leaning back in his chair and tapping his fingers on the wooden arms as he thought. "Has he hurt you?"

"What? Who?"

"Nireas."

"No," I said immediately, startled by the question.

"Insulted you?"

I swallowed and shook my head, looking down at my lap, knowing I would have to lie to talk Mr. Reddy out of this plan.

"He requested you. I didn't even have to bully him into putting it on the program for once," Mr. Reddy said. "It's not the most exciting act, but everyone always enjoys it. I can't say no. And you're not giving me a real reason to try."

I stifled my groan and nodded. It was the piano act, for Christ's sake. Was my ego really so bruised from one rejection years ago that I would refuse one of the simplest acts in the show? Fighting the assignment just proved Nireas was more powerful in my own mind than he had any right to be.

"Fine," I said.

Mr. Reddy didn't bother looking relieved. He'd known all along I would relent. Like I always did. "And the act with the Gemini? Do you mind it?"

"Constantine? It's...fine, actually."

Strangely, Mr. Reddy did seem to relax at this. "Good. Glad to hear it. I might move it up to the end of the first act, if you think you can manage the piano after? It shocks the audience. Would be better for a good intermission jolt than a finale."

I mulled this over and nodded. "It should be fine. The pain doesn't last after he stops touching me. I'll talk to him if I think I need any changes."

"He listens, then?"

A small smile curled up my lips. Mr. Reddy would always put the show above any of us, but every so often, he revealed little hints of giving a whit for us as individuals.

"He listens," I said.

Mr. Reddy nodded, back to his usual brusque manner. "Fine. You need anything else?"

"You've accepted Hunter's help in investigating their deaths?" I asked.

Mr. Reddy shrugged, leaning forward to rifle through the papers on his desk, most of which looked like letters. "He's offered. So have others. We'll find the bastard."

I leaned forward too, lowering my voice and glancing briefly at the letters, wishing I could search the words for information without Reddy noticing me snooping. "We're...we're sure that it was a monster?"

Mr. Reddy's head shot up, eyes flashing green in warning, and then he blinked and shook himself. "You know, girl, I forget sometimes. That you aren't one of them," he added as I stared back. *Human*, he meant. My cheeks flushed, and he cleared his throat. "We're sure. Now, go. I have work to do."

I stood, headed for the door, and paused with my fingers hovering over the handle, Hunter's warning in my head.

"Do you think it might be someone in the company?" I asked.

Mr. Reddy was quiet for a moment, papers rustling behind me as I examined the dark stained wood of the door. "Do you have reason to think it might be?"

I turned and glanced over my shoulder, Reddy's gaze hard and fastened on me. I shook my head. "No, sir."

His head dipped down, focused again on his papers, a silent dismissal, and I opened the door. Nireas was hunched in the hall, standing at the edge of my dressing room doorway, arms loose at his sides and ankles crossed. He looked up as I paused on Mr. Reddy's threshold but made no motion to attract my attention. He didn't have to.

I closed the door behind me and considered ducking down the side hall to the canteen like a coward. But Nireas could just as easily follow me there, and it wasn't as though I could hide from him for long now that we had an act together.

His eyes flicked up, watching my feet as I approached and walked around his outstretched legs to reach my door.

"Hazel—"

"Come in," I said, trying not to huff, trying to control my tone and reaction to him.

I crossed to my dressing table and gestured my hand toward the chaise as Nireas walked in after me, hunched and curiously studying the small space. My mouth opened to ask *why*, but I shut it just as quickly. The chaise creaked as Nireas sat down, long legs bent up nearly to his chest, arms stretching out into various resting places.

As many questions as I had, they were too personal to my own feelings to ask. Better to treat this as any other part in the show.

"I know the act and the music already," I said, Nireas finally lifting his face to blink back at me.

"I'm using a new piece," he answered.

I clenched my teeth to keep from frowning. That meant we'd have to rehearse.

"It's... quieter. Slower. More of a moaner than a screamer," he said drily, and my lips twitched. "We can- If you-" Nireas swallowed, eyes growing wide at his own stumbling words, and he cleared his throat before trying again. "How much do you want to rehearse?"

"Let me know when you're ready to play the piece. I'll make sure to come learn it," I said with a shrug. "That should be enough, don't you think?"

Nireas tipped his head in thought, his top eye watching me as the other two blinked and trailed away. "We should practice some of the posing too, since it's new."

The posing of his face between my thighs as he played the keys.

I nodded lamely. "Fine," I said, voice thin. "When?"

"Now? None of the others are rehearsing today," Nireas said, adding quickly, "If you don't want to either, I understand."

I should've used Margaret as an excuse, but the idea felt dingy in my head, using her death to get out of rehearsing with Nireas when I was just being cowardly. And I was trying to pretend I was unaffected, after all.

"Now is fine," I said, unable to keep my gaze on his.

He rose slowly from the chaise, one hand bracing the ceiling to keep from hitting his head. "Everyone...everyone says you might leave the company soon."

I looked up at that, and he was walking slowly closer. "What? Why?"

"Myra found you that orc gentleman. And it's been eight years. That's longer than anyone else," Nireas said.

"Not longer than you," I pointed out, frowning.

He shrugged, body contorted in the small room. "The other humans, I mean."

He was right and wrong all at once, and I couldn't do more than say, "We'll see."

I turned and led the way back out of my dressing room. Behind me, Nireas shuffled softly, murmuring under his breath.

"It's all our loss if you do leave."

My chest panged and my lungs seized. *Not now, Nireas,* I wanted to plead. *Don't do this to me now. Don't come back to me now.* But to speak would be to open up those old wounds, let him see how deep he'd carved his mark. So instead, I marched ahead of him for the stage—the only place where I could expose my emotions and then pretend it meant nothing again as the curtain closed.

17.

TRIM THE ROOTS

Goliath was a quiet companion, his shaggy white hair and beard the only recognizable feature left from the disguise-charmed coat he was wearing. We walked side by side, the evening rosy in my neighborhood, with many familiar faces staring back at me.

"You think they assumed you went missing too?" Goliath asked me, his voice low for privacy.

"Probably hoped it," I muttered.

"You should've stayed at the theater," he said.

Ronan, Nireas, and most of the other human girls had all said as much too. It seemed that perhaps the company's residence in the theater might grow permanent, at least until Beth and Margaret's killer was found.

"I was afraid they might have tossed all my things out to the street and put my flat up for sale if I didn't show my face soon," I whispered back.

Goliath grunted.

The yeti's silence was the first real peace I'd had in days, and I found myself strangely eager for the solitude of my home too. Most of my time at the theater was spent in Ronan's company, and it had been almost terrifyingly good, from the easy conversation to the drowsy sex in the early morning. It was as if my life was sliding in his direction.

No, it was that falling-in-love sensation, for the first time in years, tender roots tangling my heart around the little gestures— his arm around my shoulder, his wing as a blanket in the night, the sly look out of the corner of his eye when someone said something ridiculous.

I needed to snip those roots back, free myself before they grew stronger, more likely to wound me when torn away. If I could just stop picturing Ronan's stony, fallen expression when I refused his company in favor of Goliath escorting me home. And not just him. I'd been hounded by gazes all week, Ronan's flirtation, Nireas's focus from under heavy lashes, and Constantine's watchful glint coming from dark corners.

What a relief it would be to wander my home without anyone watching me.

Goliath and I turned the corner to Wellesley Street, leaving the stares of the neighborhood behind us, and my steps slowed as we crossed to my side of the street. Someone was waiting for me.

Not Hunter tonight, in his lovely black carriage. No, this was just a man in a heavy wool coat, with a dark hat casting a shadow over most of his face.

"There's a police officer waiting for me," I whispered to Goliath. "You'd better continue on."

His steps slowed. "I should stay with you."

Would DS Piper be able to recognize Goliath as the monster he'd seen with Margaret on stage? Probably, if his fae blood was strong enough.

"I'll be safe with him. Go on, get back to the others," I said.

Goliath frowned, the bushy white beard twitching, his icy blue eyes narrowing at the man sitting on my stoop.

"I know him, Goliath. It's fine."

And I did know the detective, in ways no one but his mother and father probably did. I wasn't sure if that was really protection enough, but I didn't want Goliath to know that Piper had found the theater. Strangely, I also didn't want DS Piper to misunderstand Goliath escorting me home.

"Be careful," Goliath said with a huffing sigh, and then he continued on behind me, returning back to the underground station we'd come from.

DS Piper looked up from his knees, rising quickly as he caught sight of me, remaining on my doorstep as I approached.

"Your neighbors said I shouldn't expect you," he said in greeting.

"Come in."

He didn't hesitate, following close at my back as I unlocked one door and then another. My home was cold as I arrived as it'd been days since I'd been back, and I crossed quickly to the fireplace.

"Lock the door behind you. It will set the privacy charm," I said softly.

There was a pause and then the click of the lock. "Have you really been missing for days?" he asked.

I was kneeling in front of the fire, shooing a spider off a twig of kindling, and I heard his steps pacing in a slow circle around the room in some aimless investigation.

"Not missing, but I stayed at the theater," I said, scratching a match to life and starting the fire.

"Because...because you caught me?" he asked.

I laughed and glanced at him over my shoulder. My curtains were still closed, and the few flames in the grate offered just enough light to make him out behind me. "No. I haven't told anyone about that. Have you?"

His head shook slowly and I nodded, turning to load logs on the fire.

"There was another murder, did you know?"

"What? No? When?" DS Piper hurried to the seat by the fire, leaning forward to look at me while I worked.

"Saturday night. They found her in the Thames on Sunday morning. Near Jacob's Island," I said.

"That far from here?" He sat back, blinking. "That explains why we didn't hear about it—different precinct."

"You don't talk to one another?"

"Sometimes, but a woman in her bed versus one in the water, different neighborhoods too... It's not similar enough to be linked with only two bodies. At least not so soon," he said, thinking aloud, his hand rubbing at his jaw. "You're sure it's the same killer?"

I added one last log to the fire, pulling my fingers away at the last second, their tips tingling with warmth. "Whoever is helping the theater is sure," I said, frowning. "I feel as though I don't know anything, really. Speaking of, what's your name?"

"Jude," he said after a moment of pause, staring back at me.

A simple name, but there was something pretty in it too.

"They're also sure that the killer wasn't human," I said, watching the subtle flinch and twitch of muscles on his face. "Did you know?"

"I'd guessed," he said. "There are...gouges on Miss O'Mahony's body. Deep scratches, deeper than nails. Almost like an animal. The assumption is a weapon, but after...after the theater, I thought maybe..."

"Claws," I said, nodding even as my blood froze in my veins. "It doesn't narrow down the possibilities, I'm afraid."

Jude's eyes widened. "You know a lot of...with claws?"

"Monsters, yes. Or species, if you're worrying about offending anyone," I said. "Although, I think the most offense you might cause is confusing satyrs for fauns. Or a púca for a werewolf. They're all very proud, in my experience."

"And at the theater? How many with claws?" he asked, words hushed and urgent, as if we might be overheard.

I shook my head. "I can't believe that anyone in the company would've hurt Beth or Margaret. The company is close, friendly. Little spats now and then, broken hearts, that sort of thing."

He frowned but nodded. "Not the kind of hate it would take to really tear a girl apart."

My heart turned to stone in my chest. It was the most anyone had said about what had happened to either woman. Too much, and not enough.

"Shit, I'm sorry, Miss Nix," Jude hissed, sliding down from the seat he'd taken to the carpet where I was still kneeling. Strong hands wrapped around my shoulders, his head ducking to meet my eyes. "I shouldn't have said that. You don't need to know."

"I think I do, actually," I whispered, blinking slowly, certain the room was starting to spin gently around me. "It doesn't always feel real."

Jude's jaw worked briefly, gaze narrowing. "Do you know who is investigating the murders for the theater?"

I shook my head. "Not really. Sort of."

"Can you... Can you suggest they come speak to me?" he asked slowly.

I pursed my lips and considered. He wasn't asking for Hunter's name, or even Mr. Reddy's. Only that I suggest they consider his help.

"But you'll report to human superiors," I said.

He frowned and released my shoulders, staring down at the floor in a soft surprise, as if he'd only just realized he'd arrived there. "I just want to find the killer," he said firmly, lifting his eyes again. "I'll protect their privacy. I'll collaborate with them too. If nothing changes soon, they'll tuck the case away into a file and not bother with looking for answers. There's too much crime for the police to chase down one John. At least in their minds."

I sighed, glancing at the fire, suddenly feeling the burn of it against my cheek. "I'll think about it. It would be better if...if they considered you one of their own."

He jerked at that but didn't speak.

"That's your decision to make," I said, shrugging. "But I know they would accept a fae's help. Not a human's."

His throat bobbed with a swallow and he nodded. "I'll consider it, then. I should go."

I hummed. The neighborhood would already have thoughts about him being on my stoop, let alone him walking inside with me.

He pushed himself up from the floor, offering his hand to me. His fingers were warm and calloused against mine, and he drew me up with a strength that matched the broad frame under his coat.

"If you're sure the theater is safe, you should stay there," he said, not pulling his hand from mine.

"I have to make sure the neighborhood doesn't sell my home out from under me," I said, shrugging.

He huffed, and for a moment, there was only quiet. His eyes searched my face, studying me, making me almost shy with his focus. Just more eyes watching me. I'd loved the focus of being on stage once. Now I wondered if I hadn't had more attention than one life could stand.

He released me at last, walking toward my door, and I found myself all but gasping for breath, like his nearness had stolen the air from around me.

He stopped at my door and glanced back at me. "You said you noticed my ears?"

I nodded.

The door handle turned in his grip. "I noticed yours too," he said.

I swayed in place, one hand reaching up to cover my ear, but my hair was already doing the work as usual. And Jude Piper was walking out of my home without another glance, his parting words a punch to my gut.

He knew.

Which should've been fair, considering I'd exposed him with the same information, understood the horrified shock he'd worn at my discovery. That horror jolted me in place now like a lightning strike.

We were two strangers who knew too much of each other, knew each other's complicated secrets before the simple facts.

And there was the smaller detail I'd been trying to ignore, but which grew painfully clear as he'd grasped my hand. Simmering attraction, like smoke filling my throat and stealing my breath, caressed every nerve. Nymph and fae weren't so different from one another. Jude Piper was probably the only person in my life who was so perfectly suited to understand me.

For the first time since the early days of joining the company, I found myself slightly self-conscious about my profession. My means of survival was in the world of monsters, masquerading myself as a human. And their world was different from the humans' in many ways. Whoring was an honest and appreciated profession to monsters. Pleasure was applauded, not sinful.

I might be nothing more to him than a whore under a spotlight, I admitted to myself, shaking my head and trying to find the steady floor under my feet again.

I had too many men in my thoughts these days. Too much trouble and worry too. Why add Jude Piper to the mess?

Better to forget him. Trim the roots before they dug holes out of me.

⚜

"You've been quiet lately," I mumbled into the pillows on Constantine's bed, my tongue still a little numb from sucking Con's cock on stage as Antin had licked and fingered me. Con had had to hold my jaw pried open to keep me from biting, his cock like a jolt of electricity on my tongue, but he'd massaged me gently all the while and he'd finished himself off, painting my chest with scorching cum.

Now, Constantine's hands dug out the tension in my back from the arched position I'd held on stage. In truth, I'd started craving these massages during the week. I'd even started craving Con and Antin's power. I'd been tempted to spend another night at home after Wednesday, especially with Ronan nursing his bruised ego somewhat gracelessly, but I took everyone's advice and kept to the theater. Constantine, however, had vanished until just an hour before tonight's curtain.

"I'm always quiet," he answered, dragging the heel of his hands up and down either side of my spine, a soft popping as he reached the base making me sigh and shiver.

"I liked tonight," I said.

His touch paused, and then his hands slid down to my ass, a moan falling from my lips at the dull ache of him kneading his way down the backs of my legs.

"Would you let me bind you?"

I hummed my agreement without a thought. For as shocking and extreme and deliciously torturous as those minutes on stage with Con and Antin were, I enjoyed myself. Constantine was careful with me during the act and gentle with me after.

"Gag you?"

"Sure," I said, shrugging. His breath puffed against my ass, and I wondered if I was surprising him. My lips curled, and I decided it was time for another suggestion. "You ought to fuck my ass and cunt at the same time one night. We can ask Mr. Reddy, but I think it's Saturday that's usually sold out."

Constantine flipped me, and I let out a giggle. The act did that to me too, left me loose and calm, like all the pain rushing through was rinsing me clean, taking not just Con's power but all the worldly problems at my door with it.

He dragged me down the bed so that his face hovered over mine, and I glanced between us. Hmm... I'd never seen his cock grow stiff in this form before. Long and thick, as expected, and two ridges twisting around the length like a gentle corkscrew. That would be fun.

His hand gripped my chin, and I thought for a moment he was splitting in two, before I realized it just hurt a little because it was tight. Not too much, not enough to bruise, but enough to make me stop looking at his cock.

His silver coin gaze flicked back and forth between my eyes. "You're serious."

"I like buggery," I said, smiling up at him. "*Especially* while my pussy is being fucked. Don't know why we haven't tried it for the act already."

This time, it was him looking down at my hips. Was he considering turning me over and filling my ass now?

"You have another performance tonight," he said, frowning.

I frowned too. Rehearsals with Nireas had been awkward. The music was beautiful, and in any other opportunity I would've been happy to perform to it, but for the first time in years, I was afraid I might not be able to deliver a scene.

"You're a very strange creature," Constantine mused.

I'd grown used to his cool tone, the steady pace of his speech, so deceptively unaffected. Sometimes, I even imagined I detected more meaning in little lilts and drops, the curves of his speech subtle puzzles for me to solve.

"How so?" I asked.

His gaze ran over my face and then shuttered with a slow blink. "Your cue is coming soon."

I sighed and let my eyes fall shut for one last minute of the stillness that came with being alone with Constantine. This scene with Nireas felt more like going to war than going to get eaten out by a handsome, six-armed giant.

"Very few would prefer my company," Constantine said.

"Then very few have any sense," I muttered.

I stiffened briefly as silken skin and a broad frame grazed against my bare body. A whisper of breath brushed against my cheek, and then a pair of lips pressed gently to my own in a shy kiss. My eyes opened to find Constantine staring, so close it made me dizzy, a wary, skittish look in those impenetrable eyes. I tipped my chin up, pressing into the kiss, and shut my eyes again. His tongue flicked against my lip, coppery and sweet, lips pressing to mine once more.

He'd never kissed me. Antin did, occasionally, with drugging, ecstatic kisses that stole all thought. This was simpler, almost novice, curious. Constantine was...practicing, or studying, kissing lightly at first with brushes and little nibbles, then deeper, with long presses and the gentle probe of his tongue.

He pulled away just as my lips parted, my eyes still closed.

"Go," he whispered.

The careful weight of him vanished, and my skin pebbled with cool air. By the time I'd opened my eyes, he was slipping out the door.

18.

A MUSICAL NUMBER

The curtain slid shut on the vampire's feast, and Alexa giggled drowsily as Leon scooped her up off the surface of the table, his tongue eagerly lapping clean the small wounds of the bites.

"You took too much, Hubert," Leon hissed to one of the others.

"No, I wiggled," Alexa assured him.

"Hush, off stage, go," Johnny hissed to them, his hand guiding me through the dark.

"I'm all set," I told him, patting his hand on my arm, as I tiptoed toward the sliver of light bleeding underneath our heavy red curtain.

Beyond the curtain, Nireas played a familiar refrain, transitioning from the romantic frenzy of the vampire's feast into the languid almost-moan of his new music. I paused as I found the seam of the curtain. My fingers were trembling, and I clenched them into a fist briefly.

I would not let my own head defeat me in a simple scene. Nireas was a crush from years ago, nothing more. I would pose and feign pleasure like all the other girls. Easy.

I flicked the curtain aside, slipping onto the stage, thrusting my shoulders back and lifting my chin high as the bright beam of the spotlight found me. I was dressed in a white dress shirt, meant to resemble Nireas's own shirt, if not for the remarkably *sheer* quality of the thin fabric.

The pipe organ was to the left of the stage, built into the

high wall in panels of glossy black wood and ornately molded tin pipes. The floor of the stage vibrated with the slow, calling notes Nireas played, his back slightly hunched, four hands flying over the stacked rows of keys—four in total—and long legs working at the dozens of pedals below.

It was a beautiful instrument, seemingly made for Nireas. How a human with only two hands could ever master such a beast of music seemed impossible. At the very least, they would never match the intricacy Nireas put into the notes. I allowed myself a moment of watching, stepping slowly forward, flexing my legs and pointing my toes with each step.

This scene is about his music, I told myself. *Almost like a dance.*

And while we hadn't rehearsed much more than the movements it would take for Nireas to place me on the carefully disguised seat above the keys, I hadn't worked at this theater for eight years and not learned how to put on a show.

As a note lifted and hung in the air, I rose onto my toes, lifting one foot up from the floor and extending it high. Nireas's head turned in my direction, watching me as he played, and I smiled, drawing the hem of the shirt up high to expose the smallest glimpse of my sex to him. His lips twitched, and an idle hand raised from his side, reaching for me, fingers hooking in command.

I darted forward, keeping my steps quiet and quick to match the brief flurry of teasing notes, and then I reached him on his bench. I sighed as I wrapped myself around his back, allowed myself to savor the fresh whiff of him, a scent I'd only caught threads of for years. I didn't need to be afraid of failing this act. Of course not. That was absurd.

I needed to be afraid of how easy it would be to get lost in it.

I hooked my fingers into Nireas's jacket collar, tugging lightly, and one by one, he pulled an arm free, replacing each hand on the stacks of white and black keys before it could be missed in the sweet, pleading music.

"Nice touch," he whispered.

I folded his jacket carefully and set it on the bench at his left, stroking one hand up to ruffle through his dark locks. One of his back arms—thick with muscle and connected from the shoulder blade—reached up and caught my hand, guiding me around the side of the bench. He watched me rather than his own fingers on the keys, his gaze dropping to my hips as I lifted a leg onto the bench. He tugged, helping me stand, and then released my hand. Two hands wrapped around the backs of my legs, balancing me as I stepped over his lap, facing the audience with my barely concealed pussy in his face. Four arms tangled around my legs to play the music, lower notes groaning with need, as Nireas leaned in, chin lifted and all eyes on mine.

He pressed his face between my legs, breathing so deeply I could feel the pull of his breath like a rope being tugged right from my core.

Did his hands notice the faint trembling of my legs? Did his eyes see the shy, nervous skate of my glance? I rocked slightly, found his chin perfectly poised just below me, and ground down with a bend of my knees. A soft vibration shuddered through my sex, the music stumbling briefly as Nireas moaned against me, his eyelids hooding over his dark stare.

Why now?

Fingers tightened on the back of my thighs, and I reached out, grabbing onto the high panels at either side of me as Nireas stood, lifting me off my toes and pushing me back onto the cushioned seat above the keys.

"Step back," I whispered, reaching out and cupping Nireas's cheek for show, scratching my fingers against the stubble on his cheek. "They need to see me first."

Nireas's music was swooning as I leaned back against the singing pipes, but his hands on my hips were fierce as he pushed the dress shirt up, revealing my sex. To him, and only him, his lips in a flat angry line, stare blazing up at me.

"They don't deserve you," Nireas snarled back, the words covered under the pound of notes.

My eyes widened and then immediately slammed shut as Nireas leaned in, delivering a filthy, licking kiss, his tongue stroking every fold and crease, lips pulling at my flesh. I moaned —on cue, but only by chance—as Nireas's tongue dipped inside of me, curling and pressing at my opening. The music pouring from the organ made my whole body vibrate, and I shivered as

Nireas narrowed his focus to a gentle, almost devoted treatment to my clit.

I cried out with a tremble of harmonizing low notes as Nireas pulled away.

"Look at me, Hazel," Nireas whispered.

My eyes were already opening to glare at him, and my hands released the wood I'd been gripping to dive into his hair and pull him back to me.

"Get back to work," I breathed.

He grinned briefly, the hard lines of his face brightening with the rare expression, and then turned his head to bite rough kisses on the inside of my thigh. I gasped, squirmed, tried to force his mouth back to my cunt, even as the kisses ran an aching line right to my core, but Nireas was strong and stubborn. His hands held me in place in an almost bruising grip, his lips thorough in their hungry exploration, up one thigh and across my tummy to the other. My toes twisted and slipped on the ledge, one accidentally landing loudly onto high white keys, a bright scream of sound interrupting Nireas's beautiful, bleeding melody.

He laughed into my skin, the audience joining him as I growled and panted.

Damn him. Damn the girls for assuring me he wouldn't really be interested. They had lied, or...or—

Damn Ronan too, for putting thoughts of Nireas watching me spinning through my head.

"Nireas, please," I begged, not caring if it was the wrong note to plead on, if I was too loud or too quiet.

He groaned, and it fit the music, fit the ache, but even more it suited the open-mouthed drag up my thigh, his tongue licking at my flesh, stroking the crease of my thigh. His gaze bored into me, daring me not to respond, as his mouth wrapped around my pussy again, tongue thrusting inside of me. My head fell back, my own mouth spread as I released a bawdy sound of pleasure, my hips rocking into his lips with the eager help of his grip.

Rehearsals had been useless if this was his plan—to undo me with that loaded dark stare and unravel me with a mouth made for devouring.

"Fuck you," I breathed out, not thinking, not reading the music more than the way it seemed to rise up from the keys he played to sing in my cunt, to join his fucking tongue in leaving me breathless.

He purred or laughed into me, drawing back and sucking kisses over my flesh up to my clit, flicking it with his tongue and then slurping on it till it pounded a drum in my blood. The music poured out of the organ, and I begged and cursed and moaned, not in harmony but in contrast. Nireas was ruining the act—ruining me too—and as a new hand appeared, two fingers pressing up inside of me, I wondered if this was some kind of revenge. It was the only explanation for this determined destruction.

"Nireas, I—" I gasped, arched, my hands flying back, grabbing blindly at pipes so full of music they made my bones numb. I was too close. "It's too soon."

He was curling his fingers inside of me, that same demanding hook, *come closer*, and he lapped once at my clit before speaking softly, pressing the words into my core.

"Not too soon. Long overdue. Come, Hazel."

My eyes opened, chin tucking to my chest, and I was vaguely aware of the music, a somewhat broken, ragged version of the piece we were meant to perform to. Then he gazed up at me through thick, dark lashes and latched his lips to my clit, sucking and licking, kissing and torturing, and finally stroking me with that devoted tongue.

I came with a bright shout, the music rushing through me, the vibration of the organ trembling with my clenching, craving core, shuddering through my veins, tightening and tensing and releasing in a sudden, slow burst of warmth flooding through me.

I sobbed at the release—only half of what I needed, my cunt aching to be filled, begging for Nireas's touch—and the shattered moment, and the sound echoed in the sudden silence. Nireas had stopped playing. I sat up as he pulled away, my mouth open on a question, but before I could speak I was being pulled down from my cushion, two hands holding me as another two reached up to the collar of my shirt.

I gasped, and the organ let out a crashing groan as I landed on the keys, the shirt torn open.

The audience behind Nireas fluttered with murmurs and expressions of surprise, but my gaze was on his face, brow furrowed and eyes narrowed, lips pulling down in frustration. Between us, his other two hands fumbled at his pants, and I'd only just realized what he was doing when—

I shouted, arched in his arms, his grip around my hands pulling them up high behind me as he thrusted inside of my wet and still fluttering cunt.

"Yes!" The word was torn from me, jettisoned up through my lungs and out my lips by the force of Nireas's driving cock inside of me. The organ screamed again with me as he bucked, sinking deeper, then fully, until our skin kissed at the root of his cock.

"Hazel," he choked out, arched over me, eyes wide now, lips parted as I stared up at him in shock. "Oh, fuck, Hazel!"

He fucked me immediately, unapologetic in his need, and the shock evaporated the moment his lips met mine with the same hungry ferocity he'd shown my cunt. Fingernails dragged down my back, trying to dig into me. I fought for air as Nireas pulled me off his cock, bringing my breasts up to his mouth, growling into the nipple he sucked. Nireas looked up at me like I was carving him open, as if it was him submitting to me.

Music was abandoned in favor of the slam of keys as he drove back inside of me, half the notes ringing out endlessly where his foot braced a pedal, our voices moaned with the complaint of the organ.

There was no room for words, not as his mouth traveled up my chest to my lips, our tongues tangling as eagerly as our bodies, his hands replacing his mouth on my breasts. He whimpered into the kiss, fucked me like he was trying to make room for himself inside of me, hard and desperate, his cock beautifully thick and long. That was my specialty, my secret nymph skill for Mr. Reddy, but all I cared about in the moment was that Nireas was filling places inside of me that had been left craving for weeks.

I tore away from the kiss for air, and his teeth wrapped around my neck, sucking the spot, his hand gripping my wrists, stretching me out for the taking. I stared down at him, licked my own lips and found my flavor there.

Why now?

Ronan was right—Nireas had denied himself for years, his control finally snapping here on the stage.

No, not snapping. He'd known all week what he'd wanted.

My eyes fell shut as he pounded into me, my ass bruised from bouncing on the keys, my legs trembling around his waist, arms burning from the stretch. His only free hand squirmed between us, found my clit, and rubbed with all the gentleness he'd abandoned the moment he'd thrust into me. I was the instrument now, and Nireas played me like he was trying to break my strings and shatter my keys, as if he had the right to be furious with me.

I was the one who deserved to be angry. I'd been denied this, rejected, rebuffed. I yanked my hands free of his grip and took his face between my palms, pulled him back to my mouth as I started to cry, sobbing with need and sorrow into his lips.

Why now, Nireas?

His rhythm had never been even, all his musicality crumbling under the pressure of my cunt squeezing around his cock, but I could taste his finish on my tongue as he started to moan and shout. His hips bucked and kicked, pausing as if he could resist the finish as I bared down on him, forcing him to take me with him.

His release was hot inside of me, soothing the burn of his fucking, and his cry of relief pounded out on my tongue with the final stuttering notes of the organ. I barely felt my own release at first, but it wound through me, softening my muscles and melting me in Nireas's grip, as hot and syrupy as his seed now leaking out of me.

Nireas nuzzled my cheek, withdrawing from the kiss, and his breath hitched as his nose brushed my tears. "Did I hurt you?" he whispered.

Eight years ago.

"No," I answered, wrapping my arms around his shoulders as he held me on his cock, and returned to the bench he'd abandoned at the start of the scene. My inner thighs ached as we sat, my body spread over his lap, the audience hushed in their seats.

Two strong arms remained banded around my back, and I hid my laughter against his chest as the rest returned to the keyboard, picking up from exactly where he'd left off after my first orgasm.

The audience roared with cheers and laughter as Nireas rushed the music to a new finish, slightly abbreviated from the original score, a punctuation to the desperate act they'd just witnessed.

"We need to talk," he murmured in my ear. "Wait for me? After curtain call?"

I stroked my hands over his shoulders, to the joint of his arms at his back, feeling their muscles flex under my searching touch. And the same two-word question continued its refrain in my head. *Why now?*

I nodded and Nireas sighed, trilling the music to a close, taking my chin in his hand and lifting it so he could stare down at me.

"Don't look at them. Don't bow to them. This was ours, not theirs," he said.

This could've been ours years ago, I thought, but I nodded again.

His kiss was hard, almost biting, and far too brief, drawing away at the same moment that the organ fell into a gentle parting echo and the spotlight faded. Warm fabric wrapped around my shoulders, Nireas's jacket that I'd set aside, massive on me, shrouding me from anyone's gaze even in the dark.

Nireas lifted me off his cock, our foreheads pressing together as we both hissed at the oversensitive drag of separation. He started to stand as he set me on my feet, and I pressed my palm into his shoulder.

"You have to stay," I whispered.

Nireas frowned, barely visible, but he nodded. I pressed my thighs together, wincing at the hollowed-out sensation left in me, and darted for the curtains, slipping in through the side and ducking my head to avoid anyone's gaze.

Mr. Reddy would have words about the performance, although even I knew they might be approving. And Nireas wanted to talk. After one little kiss and eight years, *now* Nireas wanted to talk. Bastard. I swiped my cheeks with the sleeves of his coat and then breathed in the scent of him at the cuff, relieved that Ronan was busy on stage and unable to fill my head all over again.

What could Nireas say after years of silence? What did I want to hear?

My head didn't want to provide answers to either question.

A rough hand caught my arm as I reached the stairs, and my feet slipped beneath me.

"You all right, Haze?" Eston asked, stepping in close.

"Fine," I snapped, tearing my arm free from his grasp. "You can't just go around grabbing us girls, Eston. We're not on stage."

"I was just being nice," he snarled, stomping off across the backstage.

I righted my footing and hurried down the stairs and into my dressing room, over to the table where a small wash basin waited. The water was cold, stinging against my tender flesh as I scrubbed myself clean.

My heart was starting to pound in my chest again, and my little room was shrinking around me, the weight of the ceiling pressing at my back. There was no reason to be so affected, no reason the stretch of eight years was suddenly so tangible, as if I'd been dragging my heart around on the ground all that time, the tether growing so long I wasn't sure I would be able to reel it back in again.

I didn't want to speak with Nireas, didn't want the answers to my question or his weak explanation for shutting me out, only to suddenly demolish those walls. Those walls had protected me too, and I'd had no say in their ruin.

You'll leave. It's what your lot do, isn't it?

For once, my father's refrain, the words an anvil on my chest for more than half my life, made a kind of sense. I'd been fighting those words, rooting myself into the little apartment and defying my mother's blood by staying with my father when she would not. But I didn't need to stay to hear Nireas speak. I would be trapped on the stage with him tomorrow night and the night after, but I didn't need to wait for him to fill up this little room and suffocate me with confessions.

I shucked off Nireas's jacket, setting it on the chaise, and dressed quickly, yanking on my boots and grabbing my cloak.

19.

WAITING IN
THE WINGS

The night was mild as I walked through my neighborhood, the air hazy and glowing orange with the street lamps. Familiar faces watched me pass, a few heads dipping in greeting. Less suspicious than before, at least.

It's good to return to my pattern, I told myself. And I had seen Evie on my way out, told her to let Ronan know I'd left for the night. There would be hell to pay tomorrow, probably from multiple directions, and I wasn't so sure now that the few hours' reprieve would be worth it.

Everything was quiet after I turned off Jamaica Street, the shadow of the park at my left looming high, the dark as secretive as it was protective. I reached up to a low hanging branch, wrapping my fingers around it and pausing for a deep breath, aware of the life in my palm. The tree called gently, echoing up from the roots, inviting me closer, offering me shelter. But I was too human to slide into that safe, hollow space a tree could make for a nymph. I'd tried as a girl, and while I could confuse my father's eye for a time, blend the edges of bark over my skin, that was all I'd managed.

I squeezed the branch in thanks and released it, crossing the road to Wellesley Street, quiet and familiar. There was a lamp in the window of the top story of my building, but the middle two were both dark.

My flat was cold as I entered, musty with neglect, and I thought I caught the whiff of something just a little too sweet, possibly rotten. Guilt ate at me in two directions now. Ronan would worry, but I needed to spend some time tomorrow tidying and taking care of my home.

I ignored the fireplace in the front room—it would take too long for any warmth to reach the back of the flat where I slept—and headed for the stove in the kitchen.

I was bending forward, turning the handle of the stove door, when I heard the creak of the floorboard from my bedroom. I stiffened, only long enough for the steps to race in my direction, and then stood up, my mouth opened to scream, my heart rioting in my chest with the sudden flare of panic.

But rising gave the intruder the advantage. I saw the thin blur in front of me and raised one hand before the wire tugged tight around my throat, biting into my fingers and pinching the back of my neck. My scream was stifled by the grip of the wire, and my feet stumbled as my attacker yanked me backward.

Remember what you know, I thought, ignoring the burn of the wire against my hand, the ache of pressure around my throat, as I fought to brace my booted feet against the floor. I had one free arm, and I threw it backwards, but whatever I hit was soft, pillowed. Cushioned. I snarled, tried to scream, and kicked my heel behind me. That collision drew a grunt out, too low and muffled to know if it was familiar or not.

Anything, Hazel. Anything!

I flapped my arm, found my counter and grabbed the first thing I could, and flailed behind me. Porcelain hit the wall, shattering, just as a knocking from my front door sounded. My racing heart stuttered at the sound, and my attacker paused in the strong yank of his grip.

My salvation was clear—I didn't need to fight off my attacker. I needed whoever was on the other side of that door to break in. And with my salvation came urgency from behind me, a hard tug nearly dragging me down to the floor, cutting off my air and any sound from my voice.

I made as much noise as I could, kicking at my cupboards, tripping my chair and sending it crashing to the floor, pulling another dish off the counter and smashing it on the stove. I fought for every whisper of air, made a dozen prayers a second, to any god or ghost who might listen. In all the struggle, there was only one thing that called back to me, drawing a tear out of my eye—my small potted rosemary in the kitchen window, offering a little tendril of peace.

For every tiny victory, there was also defeat. Sound was growing foggy, and my fingers were slipping as I reached for my next weapon of clatter. Hot blood was running down my palm from where the garrote had cut into me. A loud crack and crash from in front of me sounded, and I caught the fuzzy vision of my rosemary plant, its pot now broken, spilling roots over the window sill as if they might come to my aid.

My name was being called, but from inside the apartment or out?

And my attacker made not one sound, spoke not one word.

I know you, I thought, arching and twisting. *I know you, and you don't want me to recognize you.*

My knees made a dull thump against the floor before I realized I was falling, and my head cracked against the side of the counter before I realized I'd been released. There was a drum echoing, banging off any sensible rhythm, and my vision was spotty as a shadow lurched through my kitchen, rushing out the back of the building with a series of desperate crashes. The floorboards shook beneath me with my attacker's retreat, and then stilled as two figures surrounded me.

"Hazel? Hazel!"

"Come on, nut, there you are. Breathe, Hazel!"

I was breathing, but it was shallow.

"He cut her throat."

"No, no! No, see, it's her hand. It's just her hand. You're all right, nut."

I was breathing and the room was growing clearer, Ronan and Nireas crowding around me on my kitchen floor.

Ronan grimaced, and I whined as he pulled my hand away from my throat and carefully peeled the wire garrote free of my grip.

"Grab a towel," he said to Nireas.

"I'm okay," I whispered, my breaths growing deeper. I ignored the burning in my lungs, blinked to clear my eyes.

Ronan groaned and shifted me into his arms, my next

breath full of that lovely toasty scent of his, never so comforting as now. His face was in my hair, body trembling around me, his embrace just shy of painfully tight. He retreated after a moment, and Nireas reappeared, eyes wide and face pale in the dark as he pressed a clean towel to my hand, wincing with me as the fibers scraped against my tender, wounded fingers.

"I'll...find a candle. Lamp," he said.

I would heal quickly, too quickly to be explained away easily, and it was decades of self-preservation ingrained in me by my father that prompted me to speak, words stilted, my throat grinding itself together as I swallowed.

"There's a...healing salve. In the cupboard. Third shelf."

"Shhhh, nut, it's all right now. Should we... Fuck, it's too late to chase him down," Ronan hissed up at Nireas.

I leaned back against Ronan's arm, almost amused by the sight of Nireas hunched in my small kitchen, frowning at the matches in his large fingers. Wait...

"What are you doing here?" I asked, twisting toward Ronan.

He glowered back at me, and I was sure that only a small part of the anger on his face, still disguised as human by the coat he was wearing, was reserved for my attacker.

"Have you not noticed that there's some beast going around murdering company actresses, nut?" Ronan snapped.

My mouth opened automatically to say I would be fine, then shut just as quickly at the obvious. I was almost very much not fine. I was only remotely okay because Ronan and Nireas had come chasing after me.

"You took a cab," I whispered.

"Something like that," he answered, hardly softening. Then his anger crumpled, and he leaned in to press a kiss against my forehead, whispering, "Thank the stars."

Nireas lit the small oil lamp on the counter with a huff of breath, quickly finding the little jar of oil I'd used for Pa when the chill had set in. It was fragrant with herbs and easy enough to lie and say it was charmed for healing, and it wouldn't do me any harm. My eyes widened as I glanced behind him, to the window sill, where the rosemary's roots had stretched down the wall and across the counter. Calling to me. Would Nireas and Ronan notice?

Nireas crouched on the floor in front of me, blocking my view, all six arms busy wiping me clean from my hands to my throat. The panic of the attack had finally receded enough for me to realize he wasn't disguised.

"Nireas! How did you—"

"We borrowed a patron's carriage," Ronan said. "And rushed into your building with a bit of force. It was dark out."

"But you could've been seen—"

"It doesn't matter," Nireas hissed, his large hands so gentle as he unwrapped my fist from around the towel. "I should have water, or—"

"The oil will be enough," I assured him.

I bit around my lips as he dabbed the oil onto the deep cuts with a clean corner of the towel, and he was nearly done when we heard the shout.

"Miss Nix?"

Hunter, panic lacing his voice.

Ronan stiffened, his arms gripping me tighter. "It could have been him," he whispered over my head to Nireas, whose eyes narrowed as he started to stand.

"In here!" I called, lowering my voice to the others. "It wasn't. I know...I know him well enough. I would've recognized him."

The sickly sweet smell was all wrong, at the very least.

Still, Nireas rose to as much of his impressive height as my ceiling allowed, and Ronan hunched around me, teeth bared like a guard dog as Hunter charged into the room. He skidded to a stop at the sight of us, gleaming green skin paling as he looked at me, his body growing in his well-cut suit.

"It was the killer," Nireas said, words hard and suspicious.

"Who?" Hunter asked, his shock vanishing beneath stern lines and a set expression. The warrior I'd seen in rare moments.

"He ran out before we reached her," Ronan said.

"I couldn't get a look, and he didn't speak," I added.

Hunter's jaw clenched, ticking with tension as his gaze traveled over me.

"It looks worse than it is," I offered.

"Don't," Nireas snapped at me, head shaking. "You were nearly killed."

"Don't bark at her," Ronan snarled up at him.

"Enough." A general's orders to his men. And proof of Hunter's experience, because the bickering between Ronan and Nireas halted immediately. "He perfumed to mask his scent. I will track him as far as I am able. Comfort her," Hunter ground out at the others.

Ronan bristled, but Nireas nodded solemnly.

Jude needs to know, I thought, but I hadn't told anyone about the detective.

"Her bed is in the next room," Hunter added, and I thought there was just a hint of triumph in the words. He was the only one of the three who'd been there, after all. "I'll return soon, little one."

I nodded and relaxed as Hunter strode out the back.

"You're certain it wasn't him?" Ronan grunted, lifting me from the floor.

"He's right about the perfume. I could smell it the moment I walked in," I said.

"We would've caught it on him," Nireas added softly, hovering in place, the bloodied towel in his hand. "He arrived too quickly."

Nireas was right, and given that both he and Ronan had appeared as well... I sighed and sank into the cradle of Ronan's arms. It'd been difficult to even wonder if Ronan might've been the killer, or Hunter, but the relief of knowing it couldn't be true was a heavy weight lifted.

"Can you get water? I hate seeing the blood on her," Ronan called over his shoulder, carrying me into my bedroom. "And do what you can to lock the doors."

"What you can?"

The faint light through my bedroom window landed on Ronan's sheepish smile. "Told you we rushed in. I picked your building door easily enough, but Nireas had to break yours at the lock. We'll get it fixed. Not that you'll be staying here alone anytime soon," he added in warning.

Only the burn echoing in my throat as I swallowed stopped the perverse impulse to argue with Ronan. He was right.

"He was waiting for me, Ro," I said as Ronan set me on my bed. "Almost no one even knows where I live. You and Hunter and...Goliath. He could've seen me the night they found Beth's body, maybe? Followed me a different night?"

My words were tumbling from my lips faster and faster as the nerves set in. I was starting to shake, the strange calm after the attack dissipating, leaving behind the terror of nearly dying.

"Shhh, nut," Ronan murmured, kissing my forehead and stroking my shoulders. "You're safe now. We'll sort it out. First, let's get you changed." He petted me as he worked, fingers quick on my buttons. "Goliath was still at the theater when we left. He's in the last act, remember?"

I sighed and nodded. "He's too sweet anyway. I'm sorry, I'm all—"

"Hush," Ronan whispered, stroking up and down my spine until I calmed again.

Nireas brought in a pot of water and a candle as Ronan was pulling my dress gently over my hips. I glanced down at where Nireas stared and saw the blood soaking the collar of my slip and streaked across my chest.

"It's all right," I told him.

He blinked at me and shook his head. "No, it isn't."

Which was true, I supposed.

"Do you have bandages for your fingers, nut?" Ronan asked.

"Probably handkerchiefs we could cut up," I said, nodding my head toward the top drawer of my dresser.

Nireas set the candle down and approached me slowly, as if I might run away from him. *Because you did*, I reminded myself.

Ronan stepped away from me, and I turned to Nireas, whispering, "I'm sorry. I should've—"

Nireas shook his head. "I deserved it. It will wait," he added, glancing briefly in Ronan's direction.

He pulled a wet, clean cloth from the pot of water and stared down at me, frowning. "I should've warmed this up. I started a fire in the stove."

"It's fine," I said again, lifting my chin. "You'll see."

Ronan brought me an old sweater from my dresser, a little moth-eaten but warm, and slid it over my shoulders as Nireas started to wash my throat.

In spite of their brief snapping at one another when Hunter had arrived, Nireas and Ronan worked easily with one another as they patched me up. It occurred to me that I'd never actually seen the two interact before. Their personalities were so different, Ronan all play and Nireas so quiet and calm, observing everything.

"A few raw spots, some bruising," Nireas murmured, eyeing my throat.

"Someone should tell Reddy," Ronan said, but he and Nireas only exchanged a long look before he said, "It will wait."

When the backdoor rattled, Nireas bolted from the room and Ronan stood between me and the doorway as he changed me into my nightgown.

Hunter appeared first, jaw still clenched, frustration lining his brow. "I think there was a carriage waiting around the block. The scent vanished abruptly. No one there to ask any questions." His gaze scanned me, and while he frowned deeper at the sight of my throat, his shoulders lowered slightly.

Ronan stepped back as Hunter crossed to me, Nireas hovering in the doorway with his head ducked low.

"You left the theater early," Hunter said, tipping my chin up with a gentle black claw, examining me, no doubt cataloging all the damage done by my attacker.

"I forgot. I was tired...and distracted," I said, glancing over Hunter's shoulder at Nireas briefly. "I didn't mean to miss you."

"You put yourself in grave danger, little one."

"I know. I'm sorry," I said softly, looking again at the other two to include them in the apology. "There's something...something I need to tell you all, actually."

20.

BRIDGING THE DIVIDE

Hunter, Nireas, and Ronan took the news of Detective Sergeant Jude Piper surprisingly well. I'd taken care to describe him as a fae detective, which helped, and covered my silence up to this point by defending his right to secrecy.

"This could've waited until morning," Hunter muttered.

I was pressed to his side in his carriage, Ronan and Nireas crammed in on the opposite bench.

"You should be resting," he added to me.

"And we don't even know that he'll be at the station. It's the middle of the night," Nireas added.

"Maybe not, but the sooner the better, don't you think?" I asked.

"You said yourself the killer could've seen you on the street or followed you home from the theater. We don't know how long he's been planning this," Ronan argued.

Still, here we were, smashed together in Hunter's carriage, pulling up to the police station. I wasn't sure if it was because I looked especially pathetic, bruised and bandaged from the attack, or if they knew as well as I did that Jude was our only law enforcement connection and that could be powerful. Either way, I'd won the argument.

"I'll go in with you," Hunter said.

"I want to speak with DS Piper alone."

"Why?" Ronan snapped.

Hunter ignored him. "Very well, but my human disguise carries influence. Let me help you at least reach his office."

I relaxed at that and nodded. "Thank you, Hunter."

I've had sex with all three of these men, my brain very unhelpfully reminded me, not for the first time tonight. In fact, Hunter would probably still be able to smell Nireas on me. I would've thought an orc was the most likely one to be territorial, but he actually seemed the least bothered. I wondered if that was because of the confidence he claimed or a lack of real interest.

I shooed away the trivial thoughts as we reached the curb in front of the police station. It was a large building, dark brick and thick paned windows well-lit even at so late an hour, with uniformed men milling outside and a cart of what looked like drunks being unloaded and led inside.

I was more grateful than I had been at first as Hunter donned the hat of the small, dowdy man and stepped down from the carriage, his hand waiting to help me. I had Hunter's soft scarf wrapped around my throat, hiding my bruises and scrapes, but I was sure most of the officers watching us enter the building assumed I was a whore, even on Hunter's dignified arm.

There was a small line in front of the gated counter ahead of us, and we were just nearing the officer at reception, Hunter asking for Detective Piper, when I looked in the direction of a hall and saw the man himself, his head ducked and shoulders sagging.

I'd barely bitten his name off my tongue when he looked up, as if he'd heard the thought in my head. His steps stalled briefly as he stared back at me, and then he hurried forward.

"Don't bother signing them in, Stewarts, I'll handle it," Jude said, words almost nervously clipped as he reached the counter. "Miss Nix?"

"I came to speak with you," I said. My voice was hoarse now from talking with the others, my throat swelling, and his eyes narrowed at me before flicking to Hunter.

"I'll wait here in the lobby, Miss Nix," Hunter's low voice offered from the small man's lips.

I nodded to him in thanks before turning to the closely hovering Jude Piper.

"Follow me. I was just on my way out for the night."

"I'm sorry," I said under my breath as I followed him back toward the broad hall he'd just left. "I know it's late."

"Are you all right?" he murmured back.

I pressed my lips together, wanting to wait until we were alone, and Jude and I both picked up our steps. My eyes scanned the hall with curiosity. Clean walls, bright polished tiled floor, broad doorways, and glass windows. It was almost militarily pristine, but there were hints of male chaos in scattered paperwork spied through open doors.

"The inspector left hours ago. We'll use his office," Jude said.

There were uniformed police passing us in the halls, watching out of glass windows, and I kept my eyes fixed to Jude's back as he unlocked a dark office and led me inside.

"Less ears in here, and DI Martins doesn't mind me using it when he's out. What's happened?"

The lamp on the broad desk in the center of the room was lit as I shut the door behind us. It was the nicest room we'd seen yet, and the tidiest. I wondered what Jude's own office or desk looked like, but I was grateful for the privacy.

"I was attacked tonight. He was waiting in my flat," I said.

"You saw him?!" Jude asked, eyes wide and standing in front of the desk.

I shook my head and unwrapped the scarf from around my throat, revealing the marks there from the garrote. I'd applied the oil to them before we'd left, to help explain why they would be gone by tomorrow evening. Hunter had frowned when he'd sniffed the jar, and I was trying not to read into the suspicious look he'd given me.

"Shit," Jude whispered, blushing slightly.

"I didn't see him. And the gentleman who walked in with me —he's not human, by the way—he said whoever it was wore perfume to mask their scent. Which means they know monsters are tracking them too," I said, wincing at the end of my speech.

Jude gaped at me for a moment before shaking himself. "Sit. I'll get you water. Actually—" He passed me on my way to the seat, opening the door and leaning out to call, "Humphries, two cuppas."

I sat, and Jude joined me, taking the second seat in front of the desk rather than the one behind.

"You're all right?" he asked, glancing down at my bandaged hand.

"I will be. Two friends from the theater burst in before... And he took off before they could see anything," I said. "Jude, so few people from the company know where I live. Only a few, really, although—"

"You'd be less difficult to track than you'd think, I'm afraid," Jude said. "Any guess on your friend's part as to what kind of monster? It won't help me, but perhaps all the pieces together might."

"I should've brought Hunter in with me," I said, frowning. "I barely know anything. Oh! I felt... When I was trying to fight them off, it felt like I was hitting padding."

Jude frowned at that. "There was some evidence that the girl in the water may have fought. Anyone wounded recently?"

I wasn't sure I would've noticed, but I shook my head.

"I'll come to the theater, offer to help as...as myself," he said, dropping his voice, as if there were anyone else to hear.

"I did have to tell them that you were fae to get them to agree that I should come speak to you," I admitted.

Jude's gaze dropped and his shoulders drew in near his ears, but he nodded just as the door opened.

"Thank you, Humphries," he said as a young officer carried in a tea tray, neither of us speaking again until he was gone.

"What happened to Beth's roommates?" I asked.

Jude frowned and shook his head. "They never turned up. Dunno if they spooked that hard, their punter did, or—"

"Or if he did something to them too," I finished, and Jude nodded solemnly.

I sipped the tea, grimacing at the burn of the hot liquid down my throat.

"Why did you ask to speak to me alone?" Jude asked, tipping his head.

I sat up, not realizing before that I'd even said those words. And Jude sat across from me, watching me swallow another more soothing gulp of tea as I searched for a reasonable answer.

Except I found myself wanting to tell him the truth, which was the least reasonable thing of all.

"They don't know," I said in a tiny voice that made Jude lean in closer.

"Know what?"

"That I'm not all human," I whispered, my eyes wide on his. Had I imagined the hint he'd given me the last time we spoke? Did it even matter when I knew the truth about him?

He only nodded slowly. "I wouldn't have said anything. Why don't they know?"

I blushed and released a shuddering breath, licking my dry lips. "They can't know. Not while I work at the theater."

Jude's frown grew deeper. "You know as well as I do what it's like to not feel as though you belong in the world you walk through, but I...I'd assumed for you, there, it might be different."

My smile was fragile, so brittle I thought it might crack apart as I spoke. "So did I at one point, but..." I remembered Mr. Reddy's words from all those years ago. "It's humans they pay to see. Not me as I am, but the human fantasy."

Jude's lips pursed, his stormy grey eyes holding mine for a long moment before they trailed slowly down my entire body and then back up again, every inch observed making my skin suddenly tingly and *awake*.

His lips quirked, just the slightest bit. "I very much doubt that, Miss Nix."

Don't flirt, I thought, but I wasn't sure if it was a warning to myself or Jude.

He spoke again before I had time to control my blush or think of a response. "It's late, and you need to rest. I'll come to the theater today, speak with the owner."

"I'll tell Hunter to be there," I said, pausing as a thought occurred. "You may have to prepare yourself to...not look so surprised by everything you'll see."

This time it was Jude's turn to blush, his head nodding and ducking. "Of course."

"They'll need to believe you're...acquainted with their world."

"I understand, Hazel," he said, a faint smile on his lips. "You won't catch me gaping again. Now, let me walk you out so you can get some rest before we meet again. A doctor, do you need—"

"I'll heal in a day, maybe less," I said, and it was so easy to speak the truth I was almost afraid I might forget how to lie in the future. "Perks of my mother's blood."

Jude nodded. "My father's, it does the same for me."

He stood and held out an ungloved hand. His fingers were strong and elegant, and they clasped firmly around mine as I reached for him. Fae were generally aloof, and I wondered if Jude knew his father at all, knew if he was Unseelie or Seelie. He was certainly beautiful enough to be one of the Seelie race, at least from the little I knew.

But as we walked out of the office, Jude tucking my hand around his elbow, the halls were too busy to ask such personal questions.

"Someone should watch your apartment, in case he tries to return," Jude said. "How secure is the theater?"

"Not very," I admitted. Plenty of patrons knew their way backstage, and aside from late at night after the show was over and the audience had left, we didn't keep the doors locked.

"Then don't find yourself alone," he said as we reached the lobby.

I had to search the lobby twice before I remembered Hunter's disguise as the little human man, who was now striding across the checkered tile to reach us.

"Thank you," I said to Jude, squeezing his arm.

He nodded, holding my gaze, the look in those soft grey eyes too familiar to face for long. "Until this afternoon, Miss Nix," he said, his fingers covering the back of my hand in a brief stroke.

I slipped free, and Hunter dipped a low nod to Jude as I reached him.

"He'll help us," I whispered to Hunter.

"Of course," he answered, a touch imperious. "But for now, we'll return to my home."

"Ronan and Nireas—"

"Will join us," Hunter said.

I nearly skidded down the first step of the police station,

only Hunter's arm snapping around my waist keeping me upright.

"You need to sleep. And I have plenty of guest rooms to accommodate everyone," he said, and I thought there might have been a hint of laughter in the words.

"Of course," I squeaked out.

In truth, I was too tired to argue. No one would let me return to my home, which I understood, and the only other option was to stay at the theater, but after my conversation with Jude, I wasn't sure how safe that would be. Better to let Hunter argue his case with the others than to give myself a headache sorting the matter out for myself.

But when we did return to the carriage and Hunter made the announcement, neither Ronan nor Nireas spoke a word of protest.

"Goose down pillows never did a man any harm," Ronan quipped cheerfully.

21.

FIGHTING AND COOPERATING

Ronan was right about the pillows. I'd forgotten how wonderfully easy it was to sleep in Hunter's bed, although I'd been falling asleep in the crowded carriage too, and I wasn't even sure which man it had been to carry me inside as we'd arrived at Hunter's grand house. I knew exactly who was curled up against my back as I woke slowly, the curtains drawn tight to guard against the bright morning sun teasing around the edges.

I rolled over and breathed in the flavor of summer, cuddling closer to the warm chest in front of my nose. The thick staff of Hunter's cock pressed briefly against my belly before inching away.

"Do you hurt, little one?" Hunter asked, voice gravelly and deep.

"No—a bit," I said, wincing at the stinging ache in my throat. I leaned back, the room grey and soft from the muted light, and Hunter's face hovered above mine. I gestured to my throat and he nodded, frowning.

"It's healing quickly, but an uncomfortable process all the same. Can you sit up?" he asked, but he didn't wait for me to try on my own, his arm wrapping around my shoulder and drawing me up to lean against the stacks of pillows at the headboard.

He twisted away from me, and I took the opportunity to nudge at the bedsheets, finding the muscular line of his hip bare at my side.

Hunter growled lightly, correcting the sheets with one hand

and holding a tall glass with the other, a hazy, opaque concoction filled with ice chips.

"This will help with the swelling," he said.

I sipped carefully at first—the flavor was confusing, sweet and herbal and a touch creamy—and then more eagerly as the cold liquid soothed my throat with every swallow.

"Thank you," I rasped, pausing to catch my breath.

Hunter ran a gentle finger over my throat, frowning at the bruises. "The oil you used, where did you get it?"

I licked my lips. The problem with lying was the way it always seemed to pile up. "An apothecary," I said, which was true. "Recommended by some of the girls who used to work at the theater." Which was a lie Hunter couldn't check.

"The smell reminds me of something my parents would rub on my chest when I caught chills as a youngling," Hunter said, brow furrowed even as he smiled. "But this is very effective."

Hunter was right—it was only thieves oil, an effective remedy for a cold, but not much against bruising and cuts.

"How is your hand?"

I lifted it up between us. "We should probably change the bandages, but I think it's okay."

I flexed my fingers and they were a little weak and stiff, but I was right—they would heal fine.

Hunter sighed, a heavy arm wrapping around my shoulders. I sank into his chest eagerly. I was wearing the clean slip I'd changed into the night before, the last of the ones I had, and I remembered Hunter draping my dress over the door of the wardrobe after tucking me into the bed.

I kissed the skin in front of my lips, Hunter's collarbone, and rubbed the cool tip of my nose into the hollow there. Tender claws combed gently through my loose hair, untangling the strands from sleep.

"My task in the north is finished," Hunter said softly.

"Oh, Hunter! Why didn't you—Never mind, silly question," I said. I tried to lean back to meet his eyes, but he held me in place and I was too comfortable to wrestle free.

"I would...like it very much...if you would stay with me this week," he said.

I blinked against his chest. Hunter and I had spent more time discussing the idea of being together in any sense than actually doing so, and it was almost as if I'd never expected the offer to arrive.

"For my safety, or because—"

Hunter growled softly, squeezing me in his arms and then rolling us. My back was cradled as I landed on the mattress, and Hunter's hips fell naturally between my own, heavy and surprisingly comforting.

"Because, little one, I have wanted you in my house, my bed, my company, as much as I could have you, for as long as I have known you. And there finally appears to be time...for us." His gaze was as bright as a spotlight on me, his features sharp and fierce.

"My warrior," I murmured, reaching between us to trace my fingertips over his cheekbones and over his jaw.

I was drawing my knees up to frame his hips when the inside of my thigh brushed fabric on his, just a strip, wrapped around the muscle.

"Hunter, are you injured?!" I asked.

"It's nothing," he said, words rumbling with a content purr.

But that wasn't enough of an answer for me, and I scrambled out from under him, fighting for a grip of the blankets. He huffed, relenting and falling back onto the bed as I tore back the bedding.

I gasped as I found not one, but two new wounds. The bandage around his left thigh was tight and there was still a dressing applied to the inside, but there was also a large square taped around his right rib, a vast, purple bruise spreading around the spot like a spiderweb.

"Hunter!"

"I heal quickly," he said immediately.

"What was your business in the north?!"

"A battle," he said, shrugging his left shoulder. No doubt because the right was still paining him. "We were the victors. These will come off no later than tomorrow evening, little one. Don't fret."

"But it's over now?" I asked, frowning, ignoring the fact that

Hunter was half hard too. *The bruises are more significant than his arousal*, I reminded myself, although there was nothing about Hunter's cock that was insignificant.

Hunter's frown sobered me. "Most likely not. In fact...I believe the theater and my friends at Star Manor may have a common enemy."

I sat back on my heels, blinking back at Hunter. "You...think the murderer was at this house—"

"No, no. I think..." Hunter sighed, sitting up and sliding to the edge of the bed. "This was not the topic I'd hoped to discuss this morning."

Right. Because he'd offered me his home for the week. This time, with him included.

"I do want to stay here with you this week, Hunter," I said. "But I absolutely don't want to be kept in the dark about—about you being injured, or why girls from the theater are being murdered, or—"

Hunter reached for me and I rose up on my knees, crawling over to the edge of the bed, but remaining stiff as he wrapped his arms around me.

"There is a figure in my community, a wretch less than a man, but in some ways more powerful than any monster I've ever met. He influences so many of us and feeds our vices and worst cravings," Hunter said, frowning down at me as he spoke. "He hides his actions well, so we can't be certain, not about the murders yet, but I think he may be responsible. It wasn't him who attacked you last night, but perhaps he is motivating the beast who did."

"And Mr. Reddy? Does he know any of this?" I asked.

Hunter nodded. "He shares my suspicions."

"What on earth would he have against the theater?" I asked.

"I suspect he would like to own it," Hunter said, shrugging. "It's an alternative to his own houses and parlors."

A spike of anger so hot it was like being stabbed with a fire poker shot through my chest, and I stumbled off the bed, ignoring Hunter's offered hands.

"You're telling me that girls, Beth and Margaret and nearly me, are being killed in some—some pissing contest over who owns the theater and Mr. Reddy is just...carrying on?" I shouted. "On with the show, and twice the acts for each of us, so he can hold onto the reins?! He hasn't told us any of this, you haven't told me—and you've known too—"

"Suspected," Hunter corrected quickly, grimacing as I shot him a ferocious glare. "You're right, little one—"

"I'm not little!"

Hunter flinched, but he stood straight and strong, almost as if he was inviting me to strike out, to lash my fury against him. "Hazel. You're right. But believe me when I say Mr. Reddy's determination to hold those reins is a blessing. The theater would not be a safe place for you in Birsha's corrupt grip."

I stumbled back at the name. *Birsha*. Had I heard it before? In the whispers backstage? Had I met the man or only heard of him? Was he a patron?

"The humans in his establishments are only objects to be tormented, to bring out the worst in monsters, reveal our darkest natures," Hunter murmured.

Because a man who would kill women to get what he wanted certainly wouldn't be merciful once we were in his possession.

I was calming, releasing a long breath, when the bedroom door banged open. Ronan strode in, bare chested and dressed in his pants from the night before, his eyes wild and searching the room. I yelped and jumped, and Hunter pulled me close, pushing me to stand behind him.

"Hazel, are you—"

"It's fine, Ronan," I said.

"Sir, I did try to prevent him—" the slow and solemn voice of the gargoyle butler intoned.

I slipped free of Hunter, easing him back and holding up a hand to both him and Ronan.

"I heard shouting," Ronan said.

Behind him, in the doorway, the surprisingly harried-looking butler was jostling with Nireas.

"Leave, Withes, it's fine," Hunter said, calm as ever, one hand stroking my back. "Come in, both of you."

Ronan blinked at that, clearly not expecting a naked orc to

invite him to intrude, but he didn't hesitate, and I hurried to the foot of the bed to meet him.

"I was getting upset over information to do with the murders, it wasn't Hunter's fault," I said, turning back to find Hunter wrapping himself in a handsome black-cherry velvet robe. "It wasn't your fault."

"You should've been informed sooner," Hunter acknowledged with a nod. "Why don't you soak while I arrange breakfast for all of us. I'll explain the argument to—"

"I think I'd like Hazel to be the one to explain," Ronan said, jutting his chin out at Hunter. "I want her side of the story."

"Your throat looks much better," Nireas murmured to me.

"It is," I answered, but my eyes were bouncing between Hunter and Ronan.

"Then you're welcome to join her, if she's amenable," Hunter said, shrugging.

Hunter was a little taller and broader than Ronan, but the imp's wings were flexing open slightly, as if to make up the difference.

"Someone hand me that glass," I said, pointing to the drink Hunter had prepared for me. All three of them jerked, as if they might fight to see who was quickest. Nireas was closest, and I thanked him as he passed it to me, trying to decipher what Hunter was up to. Wasn't he meant to be chasing other men away from me, not inviting them into my bath?

Was this a test to see if I would take Ronan with me? Was it a test for Ronan? Was Hunter trying to prove something to me— that I had the right to choose, that he was confident enough to not be jealous? All the possibilities made my head spin.

"Ronan, go with Hunter," I murmured, turning my back to all of them. "I trust him and whatever version he gives you."

"But someone should help with your hand," Ronan said.

"No. I'll manage on my own. Thank you," I added, not looking behind me as I shut the door on the bedroom, alone in Hunter's beautiful marble bathroom. I sighed at the ensuing silence. Yes, this was better. I needed to retreat and order my thoughts again. It was too impossible to keep my head straight when surrounded by the three of them.

And worse, there was something exciting about the past twelve hours, about the lot of them fussing over me, fighting and cooperating, crowding me.

Being alone made more sense.

Moods had settled again, theirs *and* mine, by the time I found them in the dining room. Hunter had left another outfit for me, this one a simple, pretty sky blue blouse with embroidered vines running down the buttons and purple blooms at the collar. There was a dark blue skirt and jacket to match in a lovely, thick twill. I dressed slowly. My hand was still healing, but I'd taken the bandage off and cleaned it thoroughly. As long as I was careful, it wouldn't bleed again.

Hunter smiled brightly as I met them in the outfit he'd left for me.

This is the man who might give you a life outside of the theater, I told myself, smiling shyly back at him.

But as much as I tried to avoid the urge, my gaze trailed down the table to Ronan and then to Nireas. Ronan surprised me with a gentle smile. No hard feelings, then, for me walking away earlier. And Nireas was only studying me, all the passion from last night's moment on the stage hidden away once more. It was what I wanted, but it made breakfast taste bitter on my tongue.

Make up your mind, I told myself. But it was my heart's decision I was growing wary of.

22.

ASSEMBLING

I wasn't prepared for the spectacle of returning to the theater. We arrived at the stage wing door, and the moment we stepped inside, voices were shouting our names.

"They're back!" Frank shouted.

"Who's back? Ronan? Did you find her—Oh! Hazel, thank god!" Evie cried out, rushing at me from up the stairs, throwing her arms around me and sending me stumbling back to bump into Hunter's chest. "I shouldn't have let you bolt last night, I don't know what I was thinking, what if you had—Oh! Hazel."

I reached up, pressing my hand over the bruises lingering on my throat where Evie's gaze had snagged.

"It's not as bad as it looks," I said.

Her eyes narrowed and she stood straight, jaw clenching. "Did you see him?"

"Who was he, Haze?" Eston asked, approaching from the other wing, arms crossed over his chest, electric blue eyes glowing in the dark.

I shook my head. "Still no idea, I'm afraid. I never saw anything clearly. Is Mr. Reddy in?"

"He's downstairs with that detective. Who asked for you by name, I might mention," Evie said, some of her usual flirtatious teasing returning, a slight smirk on her lips.

"Ju—Detective Piper is here already?" I asked, glancing over my shoulder to the others. "We should join them."

"You're all right, though? Really?" Evie whispered, clutching my arms.

I nodded and offered her a half-smile. "Nothing a little stage paint can't cover."

Evie huffed and rolled her eyes. "Only Hazel Nix would be nearly murdered one night and then powdered and painted and under the spotlight the next."

"You're not performing tonight, nut," Ronan said, huffing a little.

"But—" We were down two girls already, and I...I glanced at Nireas. I didn't really want the girls standing in my scenes, I realized. Not with Constantine, and not because of the pain. And not with Nireas either.

"Reddy will cut the scenes for tonight," Nireas said.

"He won't like that," Frank laughed.

"We should go down," Hunter prompted.

"I'll... I just need a moment, I'll meet you down there," I said.

Hunter, Ronan, and Nireas all narrowed their eyes at the same time, and it made Evie snort.

"Go on," I said, nodding my head toward the stairs.

They trailed away at a reluctant crawl, and Evie's smirk strengthened as she waggled her eyebrows at me.

"I bet that lot was very attentive last night," she said.

"Hush and go bend over for someone," I answered, a little bubble of lightness in my chest at her answering laughter.

I slipped away from her to where Eston was turning around.

"Hey, Eston, wait," I called. He stopped in place, shoulders rising, and turned slowly to face me, gaze wary. "I'm sorry for snapping at you last night."

He blinked and then his lips quirked up, opal horns at his temples and along his jaw glowing and shining faintly pink. "Don't mention it, Haze. We all get prickly around here, don't we?"

I reached for his arm, but he was already patting my shoulder cheerfully and walking away. I headed back for the stairs, greeted with warmth by some of the other actors and stagehands on my way down, before they all slipped by. And there, at the foot of the stairs, staring up at me with his high horns and silver coin gaze, was Constantine.

A week or two ago, and it would've been alarm racing through me at the sight of him looming there, clearly waiting for my arrival. Now it was something like relief.

"I'm okay," I said immediately, even though there was no clear reason to read worry in that impassive expression.

"You've been injured. You've bled," he answered.

I stepped down to the last stair, and I was nearly tall enough there for us to be nose to nose. I raised my hand between us to show him the slightly red but mostly healed cuts on my fingers.

"I'll be better by tomorrow," I whispered.

He caught my wrist in a strong grip, lifting my palm to his face, breathing in deeply, his nose wrinkling. He tugged me closer, and I tipped my head to the side to allow him to scent my throat too.

"You washed."

"Hunter, the orc, he tracked the attacker last night, but the scent was disguised," I said.

Constantine grunted, and his grip eased slightly. "You should not have been touched."

"I shouldn't have tried to go home on my own last night," I said. "I got lucky."

Constantine stepped back into the light, his brow tangled slightly, clear frustration lining his jaw. He looked down the hall, and I realized suddenly that we had an audience, Hugh and Isabella crowded together at his dressing room door, watching us.

"You're not like them," Constantine whispered in my ear.

I stiffened, wanting to ask what he meant and also already knowing. I'd known from the first moment he'd called me "sweet creature," although neither of us had even been direct enough to address it before. Constantine knew I wasn't human.

"Hazel?"

I stepped down, and my foot landed hard, Constantine twisting and taking my place on the stairs. At the opposite end of the hallway, Jude Piper waited in the doorway of Mr. Reddy's office.

"She doesn't belong in this conversation." Mr. Reddy's voice carried to my ear, and Jude's eyes rolled.

"I have to—" I was turning to Constantine as I hurried to join the others, but his back was to me already, halfway up the stairs.

Jude held the door open for me, in spite of Mr. Reddy's increasingly vocal protestations as I ran down the hall.

"She's the only one who's dealt with the killer and lived," a low, heavy voice answered Reddy's snarls. "I don't see why you're keeping them in the dark in the first place."

"Because he's afraid we'll leave," I said, stepping inside and stopping immediately. Lord, it was crowded.

Mr. Reddy was in his usual place behind his desk, but Nireas was standing to the left of him, leaning against the wall, low arms crossed over his stomach. Ronan was in the chair across from Mr. Reddy, Hunter at the wall to his right, and the unfamiliar voice belonged to an enormous man with a bullish face, tan horns, and lovely, gleaming bronze skin. A minotaur! Right there, sitting at Myra's desk. I'd never met a minotaur before!

"Where's Myra?" I asked Mr. Reddy, who in spite of declaring his lack of use for me at the moment, seemed pale and relieved to see me.

"Resting," he said. "You gave us a scare."

"I'll look in on her when we're done here," I said before taking the only bit of space in the direct center of the room and crossing my arms over my chest. "What on earth have you been thinking, old man?"

Ronan snorted and then hissed as Mr. Reddy kicked him under the desk.

"I'm protecting the lot of you."

"Maybe by refusing this, this—"

"Birsha," the minotaur supplied.

"—but not by keeping us in the dark. Not by refusing to warn us of what was coming or what was being risked."

"We don't know—"

"But you thought it might be a possibility, Reddy!" I snapped. "You thought it might be him. When? Margaret? Or even as soon as Beth?"

"No," he barked, face red. We glared at each other for a long moment, and Nireas cleared his throat, almost in warning. Mr. Reddy sighed and sank in his chair. "Somewhere between the two. More so after Margaret."

"Not that I don't think this lovely young woman deserves the right to string you up for your crimes, Reddy, but I'm afraid the situation may be growing worse," the minotaur said.

"Hazel, this is my friend Asterion," Hunter said, gesturing to the man. "He was with me at Star Manor and has been acting as a spy for us in Birsha's house here in London, the Seven Veils."

"Why is it getting worse?" Jude asked.

"Birsha's focus has been split. He was planning an attack against Star Manor, his second effort at destroying Magdalena Mortimer's house," Asterion explained.

"House?" Jude asked.

Oddly, the minotaur appeared to blush.

"It's a place for courtesans who serve monsters," I said, and Jude only blinked and nodded.

"Star Manor was prepared, and she prevailed, at great cost to Birsha's allies. He lost—we all lost some impressive monsters of the community," Hunter said solemnly.

"His temper will be up, and unless he decides to act against Mortimer again, I suspect he'll turn his focus in your direction," Asterion said to Mr. Reddy.

"Politicking," Ronan muttered, shaking his head. "Makes my head hurt."

I flicked him gently on the back of the head, and he twisted to flash me a smile.

"The company has allies too," Mr Reddy said, puffing his chest.

"Of course we do, but have you told them what's going on?" I asked.

"Christ, it's like there's a second Myra buzzing around me," Mr. Reddy muttered.

"Did you write to the sphinx?" Hunter asked, offering to the rest of us, "I only know of one person who injured Birsha directly, physically, and she's in Egypt with several of our kind. I believe they're digging into Birsha's origins.'"

"I did. No word back yet," Mr. Reddy said.

"We need help we can call on from closer than Egypt," Nireas said quietly, and I was surprised to find Mr. Reddy listening, nodding along in answer.

"Please tell the rest of the company what's happening," I urged, ducking my head until Reddy was forced to meet my gaze, his jaw grinding.

"If the patrons find out—"

"Your patrons will want the theater to remain in your hands," Hunter snapped.

"In spite of what Birsha would like to believe of us, there are more who seek out places like Mortimer's, entertainment like yours, than what he offers us. Why do you think he's so determined to crush you? He acts as though he is one of our kind, when really, he seeks to fashion us in his own image," Asterion said. Minotaurs were rare, and we'd never had one perform at the theater while I'd been here, but if they were all like Asterion—so eloquent and reassuringly calm—they would've had their pick of the company girls during their stay.

"It seems to me that until we're able to discover the killer, your company is safest if they know what they're up against," Jude offered.

"I suppose it might keep foolish girls from running off in the night before curtain call," Mr. Reddy grumbled, glaring at me.

"It would," I said, tipping my chin up at him. "Evie and Alexa and I can convince the others to weather the storm, if you'll give them better security."

"With Star Manor settling, Hunter and I may have some trustworthy volunteers," Asterion offered.

I'd known Mr. Reddy for eight years. We weren't friends, exactly, and everyone was right that he took as much advantage of me as I allowed him. Still, we had a moment of shared amusement at Asterion's offer.

"You know the girls appreciate new faces backstage," I said lightly.

"Your dance card is full, nut," Ronan whispered, not quietly enough for my taste. He laughed as I swatted him again.

Mr. Reddy sighed so heavily I knew he was faking, a natural melodramatic, always destined for the theater he found himself presiding over. "See who you can find," he said to Asterion before turning to Nireas. "Gather everyone together on stage. I'll be up in a moment."

Nireas nodded and pushed off the wall. Had he and Reddy always been like this? As if Nireas was the right hand? I'd thought that place had been Myra's, but she was really the advocate for the humans, not for Reddy's orders. More often than not, she was fighting those orders on our behalf.

"Everyone out but the two of you," Mr. Reddy said, pointing to Jude and I.

"I'll wait for you. Upstairs or your dressing room?" Hunter offered.

"Upstairs," I said, and he nodded before he, Ronan, and Asterion passed by me on their way out.

"Detective, sit. Hazel, the door."

Jude's eyebrows were up, glancing at me in a need for what was probably reassurance.

"He's just a snarling old guard dog," I said in a false whisper.

I closed the door behind us and returned to stand at Jude's side, where he'd obediently settled into the chair.

"You don't look full fae," Mr. Reddy said to Jude.

"I'm not," Jude admitted, refusing to balk. I wondered how it had gone without me, when he'd been in the room with an orc, a minotaur, an imp, and a gegenees all in their own skins, undisguised.

Mr. Reddy glared up at me, and I nodded. "He knows about me. He found the theater weeks ago and has kept us a secret so far."

"You should've told me."

"You should've told me lots of things," I answered back, voice tart.

Mr. Reddy growled, but it was half-hearted. "Fine." His focus returned to Jude. "You expose us, you're exposed with us."

"I assumed as much," Jude said with another abrupt nod.

"I want to know everything you know," Mr. Reddy pressed.

"I've already reached out to the Jacob's Island precinct for details. I'll bring it all to you. My DI certainly isn't pursuing the case."

Mr. Reddy snorted and clapped his hands against his desk, bracing himself and pushing up from his chair. "That's it, then. I'd better go face the executioner."

"Fudge the news if you have to," I said, rolling my eyes. "Tell them you only found out today. Just tell them, Reddy."

He rounded the desk and approached me, and I squared my shoulders as I faced him.

He stopped in front of me and reached up, almost touching my throat while a frown carved lines over his face. But his hand settled on my cheek, patting gently and pulling away.

"There would've been hell to pay if we'd lost you, Hazel. And I know I'd have myself to blame," he said.

My chest panged at the words, and none of my own came to mind, even after Mr. Reddy had left the room.

"I learned new interrogation tactics from that man," Jude said from behind me.

I snorted. "I'm sorry I wasn't here earlier."

"Don't be. I'm glad to see you looking better."

My cheeks warmed, and my thoughts hissed, *You can't encourage him. There's enough men circling you already.*

"Did you have any trouble with him?"

"A bit at first, but your name helped, especially when I told him I'd spoken to you the night before. He was relieved you were safe," Jude said.

There was that pang again, with a bit of a twist. I opened the door of Mr. Reddy's office wider for us to leave and paused at the sight of Hunter and Myra standing at the bottom of the stairs. Myra's back was facing me, and the pair of them were too far to hear the words passed between them, but I frowned as Hunter handed Myra a bulky fold of paper. I'd seen him do something similar before and then quickly forgotten it, but this time it was sticking.

"What are the performances like?"

The words roused me and I glanced to Jude, eyebrows raising. "Here at the theater?"

His smile was small, slightly crooked. "Where else?"

"They're... You know what they are," I said, scoffing, trying to ignore the rise of heat in my cheeks.

"I have an idea of them. Perhaps I should see one for myself," he said, staring at me.

There'd never been anyone in my life who'd known me from outside of the theater and then walked into a performance. The idea of Jude, who knew the singular secret I possessed, seeing me on stage, made me feel edgy and vulnerable.

"It's your world now too," I said. I offered him a tenuous smile. "But our seats sell out fast most nights."

"Hazel, lovey," Myra cried out, a perfect excuse to escape the squirming nerves of the conversation with Jude.

He followed me out of the office but passed me as Myra hurried over, gathering me up in a tight hug. Myra was petite, but her hugs always seemed to consume me, and I accepted this one gratefully, searching over her head for Hunter. He was missing from the hall, probably upstairs waiting for me in the audience, and it was on the tip of my tongue to ask Myra about their exchange, but she rattled in my ear.

"I've been sick with worry. I knew something like this would happen. I told Reddy. I never liked that horrid little man. He's been sniffing around the company for ages, and he's got the look of a rabid bloodhound. And then for him to send us that Gemini, as if it were a gift, and—"

"Wait, Myra, what? The Gemini? Constantine?" I asked, even though I knew there wasn't another. "Constantine came from Birsha?"

"On loan," Myra whispered, face fierce with distaste, lips twisted.

"Loan a demon?" My eyes searched over Myra's head for a glimpse of Constantine, but he'd been heading up the stairs. Had he left, or was he hiding in the shadows again?

"And I told Reddy not to accept. He thought it would keep Birsha out of our hair, but obviously that isn't the case at all. For all we know, it was the Gemini who—"

"No," I said. Myra blinked at me, and I realized how sharply I'd spoken. I shook my head. "No, it wasn't Constantine. I—He was upset when he saw me. He really is kind, Myra. In a way."

"Ah, well," Myra said slowly, clearly unconvinced.

You should never have been touched. Those were Constantine's words. Myra was chattering again, but I was thinking of Constantine's apparent anger and what he'd said. He knew something.

"But a whole week. That'll give you plenty of time together, finally," Myra said, catching me again.

"A week?" I asked.

"With Hunter," she pressed, eyebrows waggling briefly before her head tilted. "You do like him, don't you?"

"I do! Very much," I said, scrambling to keep up with her bouncing conversation.

She sighed and nodded. "Good. I thought you would. Yes, a week will be just what the pair of you needs for him to settle the matter."

I laughed at her obvious scheming. "Reddy will have something to say if you manage to ship me out of the theater to a patron."

Myra snorted. "His roaring is just hot air. Come on, lovey. We'd better get up there and make sure he's not selling them all a rotten load."

Her arm linked with mine, tugging me along at her side toward the stairs, my thoughts bouncing from one man to the next. Was Myra right that Hunter would make me some kind of fashionable offer to be his live-in mistress, or whatever deal it was that Myra seemed to work for other girls? Were Constantine's words a cryptic confession, or just an oddly protective speech? Was he working for Birsha, or did Birsha own him in some way?

But when Myra and I made it to the stage, as Mr. Reddy and Jude were peppered with questions, I searched the audience. Hunter was there, waiting for me a few rows back. Nireas was already at his bench by the organ, the sight of it reminding me of the crashing keys and groaning notes from the night before. Ronan was in the front row, long legs stretched and hoofed heels propped on the stage.

Constantine was nowhere to be found.

"Go on to your gentleman, lovey," Myra whispered in my ear. "I'll fix it so you don't have to come in tomorrow either."

Unlikely, I thought as she winked at me, but perhaps Mr. Reddy's guilt might buy me two nights off.

Ronan nodded to me as I passed him, gaze trailing after me briefly. If I did settle down with Hunter, that would be a goodbye to Ronan, wouldn't it? Why did the idea of that sting so deeply?

Hunter had chosen one of the bench seats, and he was warm against my side as I sat down.

"He's very sly with his words, but he's managing the truth," Hunter whispered to me.

"He's only direct when he's telling us all how shit our scenes look in rehearsal," I answered. "We can leave soon, if you like."

Hunter's hand found mine on the seat, our fingers tangling. "Have you been to Kew Gardens?"

I blinked and shook my head, the question entirely unexpected.

Hunter smiled and nodded. "I think you would enjoy it. Unless you'd rather return for sleep."

I was used to running low on sleep and curious about the idea of a garden as a destination. "I'm happy to go anywhere with you," I said.

But my eyes trailed back to Nireas and Ronan as Hunter guided me up from the seat and toward the back of the theater. I wanted to be with Hunter. I was excited to spend the week with him! And yet I couldn't shake the sense that I was leaving something rather important behind me as we walked away.

None of it matters if they don't know who you are, Pa's voice reminded me.

They could, I thought.

But a bolt of fear struck my heart like ice at the idea and my fingers tightened around Hunter's. What if my father was right? If Mr. Reddy was right too? If Hunter and the other monsters only wanted the human girl—the delicate and pretty toy so many monsters coveted—then I might be worthless to them. The only way to know would be to ask, and I couldn't bear the thought of seeing disappointment in Hunter or Ronan's eyes.

I pressed my lips firmly together to seal the secrets in and followed Hunter out of the theater and into the hazy light of London.

23.

THIRTY POUNDS' WORTH

I t was as if some madman had grown a forest inside of a glass jar. Or as close to a forest as I'd ever witnessed.

"It's small," Hunter said to me, our arms linked and his head ducked close to mine to keep our conversation private. He was wearing the new top hat, so his features were a human version of his own, but even so, I missed the yellow of his eyes and the way his tusks pressed into his cheeks when he smiled.

"I was just thinking it was enormous," I said, laughing, my face flushed and warm from the humid air of this greenhouse, as Hunter called it. My gloves hid the cut on my hand, and the high collar of the jacket Hunter had gifted to me hid most of the bruising on my throat. Together, we looked like any elegant couple in London.

"Do you like it?" Hunter asked.

There were walking paths through the building, with enormous, thick, waxy leaves reaching over their stone-lined beds. They looked more like exotic fans than any plant I was familiar with.

"It's my favorite place in London," I said immediately.

From the moment we'd walked into the gardens, I'd experienced a sense of settling. Kew Gardens made Stepney Green feel like a patch of lawn, infinitely vaster and more relaxing than my little neighborhood park, both familiar and strange at once. I'd never seen so many varieties of trees and flowers in my entire life.

"Mine as well," Hunter said. And he did seem lighter as we

walked. He'd come from mountains and forests, he'd said, and I now understood with more clarity how vastly different the city really was from the natural world.

Tears stung my eyes and I blinked quickly, not wanting to alarm Hunter. My father had stolen me from this, from the woods he'd met my mother in. The only park I'd been afforded growing up was Stepney, and it now seemed so shabby and young by comparison.

I wanted to climb off the path and into the heavy and unusual plants surrounding us, to disappear into lush foliage. For the first time, I offered sympathy to the mother who'd abandoned me. Of course she couldn't have tied her life to my father's, not when this was where we belonged, when this was the life she'd really known and loved. I only regretted that she hadn't kept me with her.

"Are you hungry?" Hunter asked.

I blushed. "I am, but...I don't want to leave."

Hunter grinned, and I wished we were alone so I could kiss that delight on his face, let it mingle with my own.

"I arranged a picnic for us," he said.

"I've never had a picnic," I admitted. I'd seen them on the green as a girl, had even considered enjoying one by myself after my father's death. They looked whimsical and leisurely.

"I haven't either, actually," Hunter said. "Unless I ought to count eating in fields with other warriors before a battle."

I grinned at that. "I can't imagine you out of your lovely waistcoat."

He arched an eyebrow, leading us toward the grand, tall doors of the greenhouse. My steps slowed with an instinctive reluctance, and Hunter's smile broadened.

"There's even more outside, little one," he said. "Entire woods where we might get lost together."

That *was* tempting, and I followed cheerfully. The walk away from the greenhouse and into the arboretum was long and decorated with new trees, an entire collection of species arranged together. They had unfamiliar voices, but they all called to me.

Hunter guided us into a clearing, away from the arboretum and toward the edge of a lake. A small man was already waiting by a spread blanket, a wicker basket resting on the corner. A few other visitors to the gardens were passing, giving the picnic arrangement a curious glance. Was this the kind of life I might lead with Hunter? I'd never been to a fine restaurant or a fashionable dressmaker, or a theater where girls weren't streaking across the stage, chased by monsters.

"Being here makes me miss home sometimes," Hunter said, voice low and quiet, almost anxious in honesty.

"How long has it been?"

"Almost three years since I visited. I think you would like it there too," he said. "There's majesty in mountains, unlike anything men can fashion."

"I've never traveled...but I would like to."

Our steps were slow, words careful, and I looked over to find Hunter already staring back at me. His hand covered mine on his arm, stroking the back of it through my glove.

"Dens might not be the most appropriate place for a woman," he said, frowning slightly. "But there are other mountains we might visit than those of my home."

"You might be underestimating this woman," I answered, softening my teasing with a gentle smile. "You usually do."

Hunter wet his lips but didn't argue, just guided me to the blanket, his gaze trailing over the still water thoughtfully.

"Mmm, I've been wondering how you always managed to do this without waking me," I mumbled as Hunter lowered my head gently down into his pillows, my blouse draped over his forearm.

There was a small fire burning across from the bed, and it gave the dark room a warm glow. I glanced out the window to my left and found the sky dark. We'd left the gardens before sunset, but all the walking and the harrowing night before had left me exhausted. I must've fallen asleep in the carriage again.

"I work very slowly and gently," Hunter said, smiling at me.

I looked down and found my skirt already unbuttoned, and I waved him away as he reached to help. "I can manage this."

I slid up out of the skirt, watching Hunter reach for his own shirt buttons. My feet were sore, and the nap in the carriage was enough rest for the moment. It felt incredibly decadent to not be at the theater, probably my first real night off in months, if not years.

"Hunter? Do orcs give foot rubs?" I asked, grinning as he laughed.

"With a little instruction," he said, nodding. His skin glowed in the firelight, and I was especially delighted when he continued to undress until he was completely bare, this time also lacking any of the shy reserve from the first night. It was good to see progress in my orc.

I watched his back and ass flex, musing on the question of whether such a beautiful view might ever become mundane as he crossed the room. He returned to my side with a small tin.

"For aches," he explained, sitting down at the edge of the bed and patting his naked thigh for my feet.

I settled on my back, propping my ankles up on his warm skin. "How are your wounds?"

"Nearly healed," he said, opening the tin and smearing the salve into his hands, the scent of rosemary sharp in the air. "And yours?"

"Mm, same. Ohhhh," I groaned as he lifted my foot from his lap and gently rolled his thumbs up my arches. "Ohhh, Hunter."

He huffed, and I grinned, aware of the nature of the sounds I was making in response to his touch.

"You'll have to instruct me on how to repay this favor," I said, my voice a little tight as I squirmed. The ache in my foot and the relief of his touch was blatantly erotic.

"Your company is already more gratifying than I could hope for," Hunter said.

I giggled and opened my eyes. He'd twisted to face me at an angle, and he was watching my face rather than his own hands at work.

"The strangest part is that I think you're serious," I said softly.

"Why should it be strange?"

"Why should you find my company such a treat? I know...I know not all human women might accept an orc, but any of the girls at the theater would consider themselves lucky to be in your company."

Hunter's brow knotted. "Tolerant, perhaps."

It was my turn to be puzzled. "Hunter, I mean it."

"Would you prefer it was another girl in your place?"

I balked at the question, trying to sit up, but Hunter kept my foot clasped gently but firmly in his grip and I could only push up on my elbows.

"Of course not! In fact, I would be very jealous!"

Hunter's touch paused, and he blinked, cheeks darkening and lips twitching. We stared at one another for a long stretch of quiet until I grew restless, wanting to shake his thoughts from his head.

Finally he spoke, slowly and quietly. "Would you have preferred I had taken you shopping today? To a jeweler's? To have dined at a hotel rather than on a blanket in a garden?"

"Absolutely not," I said easily.

"Would any of the other girls have preferred that version of the day?" he asked.

Probably all of them. Maybe not Alexa, but she was already in love twice over.

"I suppose you and I are more enthusiastic about a garden than most," I admitted. "Does the idea of spending money bother you?"

"Of course not," he said, and this time, it was his turn to sound defensive. "Today was more than worth the price."

He sat my right foot down and added more salve to his palms, warming it before picking up the left.

"Price," I repeated.

"Mm," he said, blinking at me.

Earlier, with Myra, he'd handed her... Could it have been money? Wrapped in an envelope, perhaps? And the other night too? Cold settled in my bones, disappointment and heartache chilling me in that warm room, on that decadent bed.

"Hunter, stop," I said, and he stilled immediately, only squeezing briefly around my ankle before letting me slip free. I sat up completely, drawing my legs under me and inching a little closer. "Hunter, did you... What do you mean by 'price'?"

Hunter blinked back at me for a moment, head tipping. Did he feel the same chill creeping in from the windows that I did? The sinking weight in his chest?

"The thirty pounds for this week," he said. "I gave it to Miss Jones earlier today."

"Thirty pounds?" I squawked.

"Is that not enough?" Hunter asked.

I gasped and his eyes widened. My face was numb, my head pounding, and I wanted to scramble out of the bed, out of the house.

It's not as though you're not paid to have sex on stage, I reminded myself. But certainly not thirty pounds a week!

"Hazel, please," Hunter said, reaching for me.

I wanted to slap him, but it wasn't his fault. And the truth was, sex had always been a kind of transaction for me. Except what I'd gained was a fleeting kind of approval, the gratitude of my partner. And money too, through the theater, but...not like this.

"Is this the first time you've paid Myra?" I asked, words almost at a whisper with how strangled my throat was.

"I paid her after the night at your home, I hadn't expected—"

"Oh!" This time I couldn't resist, nearly falling out of the bed in my haste to escape. My feet were greased with the salve from Hunter's hands and stiff from walking all day, and I nearly slipped as I marched off the carpet and onto the floorboards.

I braced my hands on the back of a velvet armchair that faced the fireplace, aware of Hunter's approach, fighting down the urge to storm at him or out of the house and back to the theater to tear into Myra.

"You didn't know?" Hunter asked, and my slip brushed against my back where he stroked a tentative line down my spine.

The question brought a rush of relief. He'd seemed surprised for me to ask anything about a price, as if it wasn't meant to be a secret kept from me. But I'd never heard even one of the girls mention making money from their nights with patrons. The hope was always that you'd catch one who'd build you a life outside the theater, not that you might make a living from bedding them.

"Was it just a price for me?" I asked.

"The understanding that was shared with me before visiting the theater was that Miss Jones was the woman who might arrange the liaison," Hunter said. "With any girl."

How does she work it when we don't fuck them? I wondered. A deposit up front? Or does she trust them to pay up afterwards?

Does Mr. Reddy know?

"Lit—Hazel, forgive me, but...that night..."

The night we'd seen Beth's body in the street.

I spun to face him, and the worry creasing lines around his eyes softened the bitter edges carving through me. Hunter had thought this whole time that I'd been receiving money for fucking him.

I told him the truth. "I needed you. I wanted you that night, I still do, and I've never needed any money to—"

Hunter's arms wrapped around me, drawing me roughly to his chest. The rich scent of him eased the tightness in my chest, and I sagged in the embrace.

"I'm sorry for contributing to any deception against you little —Hazel, but this is an incredible blessing to learn," he said, arms squeezing.

Myra, how could you? I'd thought she was our advocate. I thought she was seeking better lives for the girls in her care, when really, she was mining monsters' pockets. I hurt for them too now. Hunter had believed I was entertaining him for my own profit. No wonder he'd been so cautious to push any little liberty.

I wrapped my arms around his waist and tried to grip him as tightly as he did me. He grunted, and I remembered the wound on his side, but he didn't let me release him.

"Fuck the jeweler's and shopping and dinners, and fuck the thirty pounds," I mumbled against his chest. I tipped my head back. "I'm here because you're here."

Hunter groaned, his yellow gaze shuttering briefly before opening again, a predator's stare hot and determined on my face. He ducked, lips latching to mine before I could think, tongue thrusting in and stroking, wrapping around my own. His arms around my waist lowered to my hips, lifting me from the floor and spinning me back toward the bed, my calves hitting the mattress with two long strides from him.

He dropped me there, lunging over me and pushing me onto my back. He bowed and I gasped as he licked a long stripe up my throat and then again, starting from the collar of my slip and my breast, his wet tongue dragging hotly all the way up to the lobe of my ear.

"And you are surprised that your company is a privilege to me, little one?" he rasped, lowering himself slowly down on top of me, grinding against my thighs. "That I'm grateful for such a beautiful woman to need me? Desperate to plunge my cock inside of her, to find her wet and wanting?"

His growl gave me shivers that transformed into licks of heat. Myra had denied him the truth and *my god* did it change everything. I gave him more.

"I'd thought I would go mad if you didn't fuck me that night," I said, marveling as Hunter groaned again, as if he were already inside of me, or like I was dragging pleasure from him with my lips wrapped around his cock, rather than only speaking honest words.

I reached up, combed my fingers through his beard and hair, smiled at the blissful droop of his eyes at the touch. Was this the reason for his reserve before now?

"And now?" he asked, a whisper, still nervous.

I spread my legs around his hips, and his hands pushed my slip up around my waist and then continued over my breasts, not hesitating. At fucking last.

"And now I believe you promised me your tongue on my cunt, sir," I said, smiling at his growl.

Myra was still there at the back of my thoughts, a traitor or a blessing or both, but I couldn't blame Hunter, not when the lie had hurt him too.

"I only ever wanted you for my own sake," I said before lifting my breasts and pulling the slip off over my head.

Hunter panted, his hands cupping around my back, holding me in place as he suckled on my breasts, gasping against my skin like he could feel my own pleasure. I tangled my fingers into his hair, sliding them around his braids.

"I want the kindness you've shown me," I said. "And I want your hunger and lust. It matches my own, Hunter."

And then I pushed gently, Hunter snarling as I guided him down my body, his tongue lapping eagerly like I was denying him the right to taste every inch of me.

This was my only defiance, I decided.

"You'll get your thirty pounds' worth like this," I said, my breath hitching as Hunter's hands slid up to grip my breasts. "With your mouth full."

Hunter growled and I lifted my head, grinning at the bright yellow of his gaze, glaring up at me in hungry approval. Then his tongue thrust in, as eager and hungry as it had been in my mouth, and I collapsed in the mattress with a happy cry.

24.

TRAINING

"Are you sure you wouldn't prefer I speak to her?" Hunter asked, his palm resting in a possessive spread over my back.

"You can for your own sake, but not for mine," I said.

Hunter only smiled as we stopped by the stairs that led down to the dressing rooms. It was late afternoon, still hours away from the Sunday night performance, but the theater was unusually quiet.

"I'm sorry, for interrupting our day," I said, and meant it.

Hunter had kept his previous promise, and I'd woken with his face between my thighs and my cunt still tingling from all his efforts the night before, and a few of my own for him in thanks. We'd bathed and spent the day in his house, with him giving a bashful tour that ended in his office, where he'd explained his cargo and exportation business with a charming excitement that did nothing to actually make any sense of all the terms and names and numbers. It didn't matter. I'd liked listening to him speak with confidence.

"We have tonight, tomorrow, the rest of the week," he said, shrugging. Then he beamed at me and added, "Longer, if you like."

It was as sweet a statement as it was troubling. Was that all it would take? The offer of staying longer, and then I would vanish from the theater? Have a life with Hunter? Never see Ronan again, or give Nireas the opportunity to explain himself?

"Come and wait in my dressing room for me," I said, and Hunter followed me down the stairs.

Even downstairs was uncommonly quiet, although I thought I caught the whisper of voices in some of the dressing rooms we passed on the way to mine. Stranger still was the sight of Nireas hovering at Mr. Reddy's door, his back to us.

Hunter squeezed my hand, slipping under my curtain, and I walked slowly toward the giant at the door. He turned before I reached him, and his eyes widened in bright alarm, a finger raising to his lips as my mouth opened to ask what he was doing.

He jerked his head toward the door and my eyes widened. Nireas was snooping? I tiptoed closer and he bent to my ear, whispering.

"Birsha. He's here."

I froze, immediately understanding why the theater was quiet, why everyone was hiding. Our boogeyman was here in Mr. Reddy's office.

"I've heard the act was a success for you," a smooth, cold voice spoke, not loudly, but just clear enough for Nireas and me to listen.

"It certainly added variety," Mr. Reddy grumbled.

"I'd like to offer you another two weeks of use. I plan on viewing the performance myself this evening."

"You've been generous enough already. And I'm sorry to say, but it won't be on tonight's bill."

"You cut the act?"

I flinched at the sharp note of Birsha's voice, and one of Nireas's hands reached for mine.

"Our actress was attacked on Friday," Mr. Reddy snapped, just shy of the actual accusation. "And I don't have any to spare."

"Ah, yes. Miss Nix." His voice was crisp around my name, the bite of sharp teeth through a fresh apple. "My man speaks very highly of her."

Constantine, I mouthed. Mr. Reddy grunted on the other side of the door.

"I'm looking for new stock myself," Birsha continued. "And surely by now your audience tires of a girl so long in the tooth. I could buy her off you."

Nireas stiffened and our fingers clenched, the bite of pain distracting from the urge to storm inside the room.

"You know I don't sell my girls," Mr. Reddy said.

There was a pause of quiet, and I was afraid to breathe or be heard.

"We'll speak frankly. I know what she's worth and I'm prepared to retreat, to offer you the price that would save your pathetic little stage and curtains and timid little beasts who perform in exchange."

Nireas was pulling me slowly and gently closer to his side, a long arm at his back circling around my shoulders. Because neither of us truly knew in that moment what Reddy's answer would be. Or maybe I had a guess, and I was already preparing to ask for Hunter's help, anyone's, to save me from the man that cold, sharp voice belonged to.

"No, my girls aren't for sale. Not at any cost. And if we are speaking frankly, I don't believe there's a prize you could win or steal or buy that would satisfy you," Mr. Reddy said.

Nireas tugged and guided me back from the door. "Come on," he whispered. "You don't want that man to see you."

But I resisted, some note in my ageless employer's voice telling me he wasn't finished.

"And of all my girls, Hazel's the last one I'd let you take. Not because of what she's worth, but because she's been loyal to me for as long as I've known her. I'm a burden on that girl's back, and she's been carrying me without complaint for almost a decade. I'm almost sorry for you that you'll miss her tonight; she's a sight to be seen. But she'll never serve in one of your houses, not while I live."

"Very grand and dramatic," Birsha said, clipped and cool.

My eyes shut as Nireas pulled me away, a moan trapped in my throat that I refused to let escape.

"You need to get out of here before he, I don't know, sniffs you out," Nireas hissed.

I shook myself and brushed the heartache stirred up by Mr. Reddy's words out of my head, then led Nireas to my dressing room. He stopped as I pulled back the curtain and stepped inside, Hunter waiting casually on the chaise inside.

"Never mind. Wait here. I'll let you know when he's gone," Nireas whispered. I nodded, and he pulled the curtain shut again.

"How did it go?" Hunter asked.

I shook my head and crossed to him, holding my hand up for him to stay put and then helping myself to his lap.

"I didn't speak to her. Birsha is in Reddy's office," I said.

"What?" Hunter hissed.

I shared what I'd overheard, and Hunter settled slightly.

"We expected this. I'm glad Reddy's proving he has some spine, but I'm afraid there will be consequences," Hunter said, hands stroking my back. "And Miss Jones? What will you do about her?"

I didn't know if Myra was taking the money from patrons for herself or for the theater. I did know that in spite of the greed, she made happy matches for the girls. I wasn't inclined to forgive her yet, but I didn't want to start a fight today, not after what I'd overheard.

"I don't know," I admitted. "Just don't give her any more of your money. Ask for it back, if you want."

Hunter nodded and shrugged. "I'm not concerned about the loss, but if she wants a donation for the theater, I wish she would simply ask for it, like she did with your costume."

I groaned at that reminder and pressed my face against his throat.

"I...I told you I was a patron of Magdalena Mortimer's former house? Rooksgrave Manor," Hunter said.

"You implied," I said, shifting to face him.

"Mm. The young woman who entertained me there was... I believe the word is mercenary," Hunter said, frowning. "I paid my membership for the house, for my visits to her, but also she required... Presents were to be expected, but she preferred coin." Hunter blushed. "Specifically in exchange for certain requests."

My eyebrows bounced before I could school my expression, and I stroked my hands over his chest to encourage him to continue.

"She wasn't fond of me. She didn't want me or need me as

you do, little one," Hunter said, voice purring. "And she led me to believe..."

"That a human woman wouldn't accept your desires?" I supplied, the pieces fitting together at last.

"Or my features," he said, grimacing. "My piercings. My speech."

"Fuck her," I bit out sharply.

The grimace curled up into a smile, Hunter's eyes crinkling at the corners.

"I thought the girls at those houses were meant to be delighted with monsters, or at least accepting," I said. Mr. Douthwaite had offered me a house like that as an option for my future after my father died, but I'd thought the theater would be less confining.

"Most were accepting. Some delighted." Hunter nodded. "Mary had nowhere else to go, and she saw an opportunity in me. I sought to please her and realized too late I could only do so with money. She betrayed the house eventually, and I was relieved to be released from the arrangement."

"And you didn't renew. Good, that madame should've done better for you than some—" My words were cut short by Hunter's kiss, firm and sweet, lingering on my lips as his claws bit gently into my hips. A question slid into my head as Hunter kissed me and burned in my thoughts until I had to pull away to ask. "What kind of requests did you make?"

I reached up and cupped Hunter's cheeks as his gaze flitted away from me. This horrible woman had made Hunter nervous about his own desires, and it was now my mission to undo her work. I ought to have been more sympathetic, but instead I felt like I'd won another woman's reward.

"Hunter, I honestly can't think of anything you might ask of me that I'd refuse. You've seen me on stage," I soothed.

"I have," he growled, his brow furrowing.

"You make me feel like a wild, hungry creature when you touch me," I continued, grinning as I recalled the night before and the many moments of pleasure Hunter had offered so eagerly. "So tell me."

He growled softly as I scratched my nails into his beard and then back into his hair.

"I'd do anything you asked, Hunter," I purred, knowing the moment I was succeeding by the slow close of his eyes and the heavy weight of his head leaning into my hands.

"You would obey me?" he asked.

"Of course."

His eyes opened, their color golden and bright as he gazed back at me. "At home, the best warriors have their pick of pleasure pets—women who come to the mountains to seek strong males' beds."

I grinned as Hunter searched my face. "Do you miss having a pleasure pet?"

"I never took one. They were for men who were settling, their blood cooling and bodies retiring. I moved on from the mountains before I felt ready," he said.

"And what does a pleasure pet do for her master?" I asked, feeling victorious as Hunter's eyes blazed at the word *master*, claws digging into my hips and ass as he tugged me closer.

"Wait at his feet, for his need," Hunter rasped. "Be fed by his hand. Reveal herself to his gaze. Obey."

Such simple requests, and he'd been shamed? An orc who loved to feast on a needy pussy and gave gentle, thorough massages and was so happily generous? Of course there would be women who objected to being called "pet" or being told to kneel or obey, but in a house meant to serve monsters' pleasure, obedience seemed like the least of a girl's worries.

"Sometimes, the women are harnessed or leashed," Hunter added, wincing at me.

"Now we're getting interesting," I said, making sure to tease gently.

The wince vanished. "You're not disgusted?"

"I meant it when I said I would do anything you asked. And I think I would make a very pretty pleasure pet, don't you?"

Hunter growled and surged up, arms wrapping around my back, one hand cradling my head as he twisted and lowered me to the cushion of the chaise, tongue twining with mine.

I tugged my lips away, turning and offering my throat as I continued. "Do you have a leash for me?"

Hunter shuddered on top of me, and I grinned.

"A harness," he said, the words dragged from his throat in a snarl, his tusks scratching over my throat.

With my head turned toward the doorway, I caught the flash of the curtain opening, Nireas's dark gaze landing immediately on me and Hunter.

"A pretty one, with a strap across the back I can grip as I fuck you, pull you onto my cock," Hunter continued, not noticing or caring about our audience at the door.

Nireas's head tipped, and I arched up into Hunter's body at the vision of his words. Hunter's tongue stroked from my throat up to my ear, taking the lobe between his teeth and sucking on the spot, a warm, echoing pulse in my cunt answering the treatment.

Nireas nodded toward the hall and then stepped away, the curtain fluttering shut. I ignored the faint whisper of disappointment at his departure, intrigued by the idea of being watched with Hunter, and turned to steal a kiss.

"Then I think you should take me home and put me in my pretty harness and train your pet how to please her master," I whispered.

I STOOD in front of the large mirror in the corner of Hunter's bedroom, twisting on my toes and examining myself. In spite of Hunter's eager response in my dressing room—warring briefly with himself over fucking me directly on the chaise before all but dragging me back out of the theater—by the time we'd made it back to his house, his control had returned.

We'd had luncheon in the dining room, and I'd gently pried information about being a pleasure pet from Hunter's lips. I wasn't sure if playing the part of a pet would be exciting for myself, but it was obviously thrilling to him and that was a powerful enough incentive. I'd played so many roles for the theater, putting on another for Hunter would be as easy as it was gratifying.

I ran the brush Hunter had offered me through my hair draped over my shoulder and then set it aside on the table by the mirror. I was freshly washed from head to toe, copper red locks still a little damp, and I pushed my hair back over my shoulder, arms stretching to braid it tightly under his instructions, my eyes glancing to the clock. Nearly time to meet him.

"I can send all the servants to the kitchens, serve dinner myself," Hunter had offered.

"I don't mind. I'm only for you to touch?"

"Tonight, yes," Hunter said, *an intriguing possibility left for the future in the statement.*

I found the leather tie left on the table for me, and my braid slapped between my shoulder blades. I looked at the clock again and bounced on my toes. Was I allowed to be early? It was still twenty minutes to seven, when Hunter had told me to come join him in his office, but I was jittery and buzzing with curiosity.

Would I be chastised if I was early, or rewarded? Either option was intriguing. It was like I was getting ready to walk on stage, except the audience was private tonight, only Hunter, a more intimate experience. More important too. I wanted to be perfect, especially after learning about the woman before me.

Deciding that eagerness might please him, I turned to go and find Hunter. I was more aware of my own nudity here in this grand house, with soft carpets under my bare feet, than in the crowded and chaotic backstage of the theater. There, I usually wasn't the only one naked, and I certainly wasn't running past fine art and beautifully made furniture.

A house elf passed by the doorway that led to the dining room as I made it downstairs, but he didn't glance at me. I was only for Hunter's gaze tonight, and the thought made my skin warm and overly sensitive.

My steps slowed as I neared his office, the door only partially ajar. The tile on the floor here was cold and a little slippery, and I shivered as I stopped just short of the opening. The air coming out of the room was warm, and I could hear the soft crackling of a fire inside and little whispers of a pen scratching over paper.

"You're early."

I jumped in place and then inched toward the door, hand outstretched but hesitating.

"I...I was excited," I called softly into the room.

A chair squeaked and fabric rustled, but I remained on the other side of the door, determined to wait for permission.

"Come."

I stepped inside and found Hunter immediately, his back to the fire, jacket off, eyes fixed to me.

"Kneel," he said. The short commands turned my familiar orc into a stranger, imposing and almost dangerous.

The office had carpets spread out and layered, and the wool was thick and scratchy against my knees as I obeyed.

Hunter moved forward in one long step and then stopped himself abruptly, and I smiled at the glimpse of the orc I knew, his face open with hunger and surprise at the sight of me.

"Crawl to me."

I leaned forward, my hands sinking into the dense weave of the wool, my braid sliding over one shoulder to sway with my movements.

"Shoulders back, chin high, little one," Hunter purred, regaining some of his previous control.

I slowed my crawl, focusing on the arch of my spine and the tilt of my chin, creating a pretty view for him to enjoy.

"Very good," he said, when I'd nearly reached him. "Sit up and rest your palms behind you on your heels."

The position made my thighs burn and thrust my breasts forward. I ducked my chin, imagining what obedience might look like, but Hunter growled in response.

He bent and lifted my face again, gazing warmly down at me. "No. I want you as proud of yourself as I am proud to possess you now."

A warm flush ran through me at the praise, and I strained as I stretched toward him. He rose again and stared down at me, gaze vivid and sharp with hunger.

"Beautiful," he murmured. He stared at me for a long time, pacing slowly around my back, stopping there. "Now, hands together on the floor in front of you, and lower your head to meet them."

Face down, ass up. Just like stretches with Myra, I thought. I bent down and rested my forehead on the back of my hands, shivering as Hunter's foot slid between mine, tapping side to side.

"Spread."

My breath shuddered out of me, a gentle ache building in my core as I spread my knees wide apart, leaving a clear view of my ass and pussy for Hunter's eyes.

His breath rushed gently over the cheeks of my ass, and one hand stroked over the backs of my thighs, squeezing and testing the muscle. I whimpered against my hands as his fingers stroked over my puckered hole and then down to the lips of my sex, spreading them open and then rubbing them together. Heat bloomed in my core and seeped out, and Hunter purred with approval.

"You please me."

"Thank you, master," I gasped out, the words shockingly natural to say in the moment.

Hunter's hand left my pussy, and I bit my lip to stifle my objection. He rubbed at the back of my neck briefly before gathering the base of my braid in his hand and using it to guide me back up on my hands and knees. His other hand reached to my hips, gently arranging my legs closer together. His hands smoothed over my hips and shoulders, pushing and adjusting me gently, until my back was straight and flat, eyes on the floor.

"These are three positions I would like you to remember. Can you do that for me, little one?"

"Yes, master."

Hunter stroked over my spine and I held still, even when I wanted to arch into his touch.

"I admit I like when you call me master, but will you save it for when I please you?"

I grinned at the floor, twitching under his hand slightly. "Yes, master."

Hunter chuckled and stepped back. "We have ten minutes until dinner, and I need somewhere to put my teacup. Follow me."

He glanced back at me, smiled when he saw my chin lift exactly as he'd instructed the first time, and then settled into an armchair to the right of the fire.

"Here," he said, pointing down at the floor at his side. I crawled to the spot, flinching slightly at the scratch of the carpet as he looked away. He lifted a cup and saucer from a small side table—so much for not having anywhere to put it—and watched me as I straightened my back and pointed my nose down to the floor. His hand smoothed over my spine, down to my ass, where he patted lightly.

"Very good. This is warm, but it won't be hot," he said. "If you grow too uncomfortable, tell me. I don't want to hurt you, little one."

The porcelain was pleasantly warm as it touched my back, and the cup immediately rattled in its saucer as I took my first breath.

Was this a request he'd made of Mary? I smiled at the thought, slightly less frustrated with the woman. If I didn't already know Hunter's kindness and incredible passion for pleasing me already, I probably would also be offended at being turned into a table. But I'd once had my wrists and ankles tied and hung from a beam while two werewolves used my mouth and ass. This was infinitely easier and more relaxing.

I giggled and then sucked in my breath as the china rattled on my back.

"Do you hate it?" Hunter whispered, his shy nerves slipping out.

"No," I said quickly, wanting to sit back and look up at him so he could know I was sincere. "No, master. I was only thinking about much less comfortable tasks I've been assigned. I'm happy."

Which was strangely true. The carpet was unpleasant, and the task was odd, but Hunter was trusting me with a part of himself he'd been convinced was wrong to crave. And there was a calming quality to the stillness, even as my arms and back and legs started to ache from holding the position.

Hunter's claws traced aimlessly over my shoulders, the weight of the cup lifted, saucer left behind, and then returned again. The carpet was floral, leaves and blooms twisting and folding together, a pretty pattern to study as I tried to remain motionless.

"You're starting to arch," he warned gently.

I straightened my back, and he pet my head as the china rattled and then quieted. "Good girl."

My cheeks warmed at the praise, and I licked my lips. "Am I allowed to speak?" I whispered.

"Of course. Always."

"Will you...will you put the harness on me?"

"You really want it?"

I nodded, ignoring the chime from my back, since Hunter didn't seem to mind me making noise.

"Then if you behave well for me at dinner, I will put it on you after," Hunter said, and I thought he sounded a little breathless. "Before I fuck you."

"Then I'll behave at dinner," I said brightly.

Hunter drank from the cup again, and I made sure my back was straight before he returned it to the saucer.

"Do you want to know the truth, little one?"

"Yes."

"It's taking all my control as a warrior and a gentleman to keep from throwing this tea aside and pulling you onto my cock at this very moment," Hunter rumbled warmly.

The china sang as I gasped and shivered, my cunt clenching on nothing, begging for the very thing Hunter was denying us both.

"But you're offering me an incredible gift," he said, voice calming to a tender murmur, claws dragging back and forth over my shoulders. "I don't want to waste it."

"My obedience won't expire, Hunter," I said.

The door to the office creaked slightly, light from the hall falling in across the carpets, and Hunter stood, moving to stand behind me, no doubt blocking me from view.

"Dinner is ready, sir," the butler said.

"Thank you, Withes."

The light softened, and then the porcelain was lifted from my back.

"Walk with me," Hunter said.

I sat back on my heels, immediately tucking my hands, and his eyes widened, lips curling at the sight of me.

"You don't want me to crawl?"

He purred again, fingers stroking my cheek. "Later. This is training, and I don't want you sore too early in the evening."

His hand waited for mine and he pulled me onto my feet, my body protesting and settling into standing again.

"Also, I want to do this," he said, claws biting at the cheeks of my ass as he pulled me into his chest, mouth slanting over mine with a soft growl. My arms were trapped under his so I grabbed at his waist, our hips grinding together. I moaned into the kiss, bucked into the rigid length of his cock through his pants, aware of my own slickness seeping through the fabric.

His claws scratched up my back, his hands clasping around my arms to push me away, chest heaving with deep breaths as he licked his lips.

"Am I still behaving if I say I can't wait for dinner to be over?" I asked.

Hunter grinned. "You are, barely. Come, or Withes will fuss."

And in spite of our roles for the evening, Hunter tucked my hand into his elbow and walked me down the hall of his home, past the charmed windows that revealed his busy street but disguised my nudity and his true nature, as if I were not his pet, but his dinner guest.

I laughed again as we arrived in the dining room. The table was dressed in candlelight and glittering glass and gleaming china, but there was only a plate and silverware for one, a seat at a slight angle at the head of the table. And at the foot of the chair, spread over the floor, was a large cushion in pale blue velvet.

Hunter led me there, seating himself in the chair with his thighs spread wide, his cock clearly outlined through his pants.

"You'll sit there. I want you kneeling as much as you can, but don't be afraid to shift or adjust," he instructed.

I sank down onto the cushion, settling into my kneeling position from before, blooming under Hunter's answering smile.

"I'll feed you as I eat," he said, studying me. I nodded and waited. A brief war waged on his face, his lips pursing like he was fighting words, or trying to force them out. "When you want to rest, or you are full, your mouth should take my cock. You won't suck. You won't lick. You won't finish me, little one. Do you understand?"

"Yes," I said, arching an eyebrow and leaving off the "master." Hunter laughed at my show of defiance, but then his hands were at his pants, opening them and pulling himself free.

I leaned forward immediately, lips parting, only hungry for one thing, the beaded and weeping head of his cock in front of me. Hunter growled, his hand wrapping carefully around my throat before I could reach him, delicately cupping to avoid irritating my bruises.

"I'm not hungry," I said, remembering my instructions. "And I'm tired."

Hunter huffed out a laugh, the mask of the stern master cracking with his smile. "I haven't even been served, little one. Therefore, neither will you be," he teased.

Be good, I reminded myself. I pressed my lips together and held my position, and Hunter pet my throat before nodding and leaning back in his chair, scooting it closer until his cock was only an inch or two away and his long legs acted as a shield around me. I didn't care what the servants saw, used to being nude and being seen, but I liked this protective or possessive quality from Hunter, the illusion of privacy. Above my head, he gestured to Withes, his gaze holding mine.

A dish rang against the serving, wine splashed in a cup, and through it all, Hunter and I stared at one another. The cushion under my knees was dense and comfortable, but I was grateful he'd given me permission to move throughout the dinner, already aware of stiffness settling in my limbs.

Footsteps echoed away from the table, and Hunter's gaze finally lifted, glancing at his plate. He sat up straighter, shifted forward, and I sighed as the gold beads bolted through his cock bumped my lips. They parted and I leaned forward, drawing him in eagerly. Hunter snarled, hips bucking, cock sliding along my tongue with every bump of a piercing on the underside, and nudging briefly at the back of my throat.

Claws stroked through my hair, and I whimpered as Hunter forced me back, yellow eyes blazing down at me.

"No," he snarled.

My mouth was still open, tongue extended to stroke his length just a breath away. His flavor was fresh, his scent filling my lungs, and I leaned forward, moaning at the pull of my hair where he gripped it. He grinned at me, but there was danger in the sharp bite of his teeth.

"You're misbehaving," he warned.

I whined, my lips shutting and swallowing his flavor, and I stopped straining against his grip.

"I'm sorry," I said. "I like your cock."

Hunter laughed and shook his head. "It likes you too. But this is training, little one. You have to be good for me. Show me how well you behave. Now, open your mouth."

I had to take a deep breath, stiffen my muscles, brace myself to not just suck him down. Something about being refused the right to suck cock made me suddenly desperate to do so. I opened my mouth and held my breath as Hunter slid forward in his seat, staring down at me as his cock nuzzled between my lips and settled on my tongue.

"Nothing more," he warned.

I considered nodding or mumbling my answer, just to be a brat, fairly certain Hunter might enjoy punishing me as much as he would rewarding me. Or perhaps not. I might have to coax him into spanking me someday, reassure him it wouldn't send me running.

A knife scratched lightly on a dish and Hunter's cock rested heavily on my tongue, his deep, fresh flavor slipping off his head and down my throat, my own arousal gathering between my thighs.

I swallowed slowly, waiting to be scolded, but Hunter's hand only pet over my head, a new rush of fluid pooling on my tongue.

"That's very good, little one, but you must eat," he said.

I pulled off his cock slowly, pausing as it twitched on my tongue, and gasped as he slipped free, his hand appearing in front of my lips with a cut of meat pinched between his fingers. I accepted the bite, surprised by how juicy it was, and licked Hunter's fingers clean, pleased when I didn't get in trouble.

This is easy, I thought. And not only easy, but strangely calming. My role was simple—to obey and please Hunter. My instructions were clear, even if I might've preferred the right to lap and pull at his cock with my hands, please him as a show of thanks.

"Another?" Hunter asked.

I glanced between his face and his cock. But I would have the cock all night. And the food was delicious.

"Yes, please, master," I said.

Hunter petted me as he fed me, my careful braid growing a little loose around my face. He ate his own bites of food between mine, and when I shook my head at the offer of more, he waited a moment before sliding slightly forward. My mouth opened eagerly, and his rich arousal mingled with the salt of the meat. I couldn't help my hum of pleasure.

Hunter huffed but didn't correct me, and it was a whole new battle with myself to keep from dragging my tongue up and down those lines of beads.

"The next course is arriving," Hunter said as footsteps approached.

"Course?!" I squawked, but the word was unintelligible with my mouth full, and Hunter bucked in my mouth, grunting briefly before sliding back in his seat and drawing free.

"Five in total," he said, smiling down at me as the butler served the dish over my head.

"Will I be one of the courses?" I asked hopefully, already aware of slick arousal now sliding against my inner thighs near my sex.

Hunter's laugh was rowdy and bright, and he leaned back in his chair, throat flexing as his head fell back, a feast for my gaze. I helped myself to a mouthful of him when he didn't answer. Apparently, I was in for a long evening.

25.

REWARDS

By the fourth course, my legs ached and my jaw was tired from holding Hunter's thick cock on my tongue in between bites of food. I'd rearranged myself on the pillow, aware of the slightly damp mark I'd made, but my arousal had calmed with hints of boredom.

Hunter brought me up to perch on his lap for the fifth course, poached pears and ice cream, and I thought he might have been growing impatient too, based on the quick trading bites he fed us with.

"You did very well tonight, little one," he said, hand stroking up and down my back as my skin developed goose bumps from the ice cream. I leaned into the heat of his chest, pressing my face to his throat to protest another bite.

"Thank you, master," I murmured, my lips brushing his skin as his hand twined around my braid.

"Are you tired?" Hunter asked, spoon scraping against the glass bowl we'd been eating from.

I huffed against him and caught his hand as he raised the spoon to his lips. He allowed me to put the spoon back in the dish and guide his fingers down to my lap, then between my thighs, purring as I pressed his touch to my sex.

"I know I am here for your needs, master," I said, trying to keep my voice sweet as I shifted to smile at him.

"But you need my cock, little one?" Hunter asked, eyes bright and lips twitching.

He was fun to play this role with, as delighted by my interest as I was to see him reveal a new side of himself.

"Yes, please," I said, batting my lashes and dropping my gaze to where he was still half hard. The power of an orc's arousal.

"You were made to be a pet," Hunter murmured. "Or you are a very good actress. Stand up."

I hurried to standing, and his eyes narrowed as I grimaced, my ankles and feet still stiff from kneeling so long.

"If I harness you now, will you crawl to bed for me?" he asked.

Which wasn't the same as being bent over the table and fucked till I screamed, but I was curious about the harness, so I nodded eagerly.

Hunter grunted, and I tried not to pout as he tucked his cock into his pants and stood from his chair.

His hand reached out, cupping my sex, fingers patting lightly as he leaned down and kissed the top of my head. "Don't move."

I remained stock still as he left the room, as the butler Withes returned and cleared the dishes without so much as blinking at me, even as I heard Hunter's steps return, metal clinking lightly with each step. But I couldn't keep my eyes from investigating what he brought with him.

The leather was a deep, warm brown, embossed and blackened with a simple vine pattern—a motif Hunter seemed to prefer for me—just wide enough to fill the thin straps. Hunter held the harness on two fingers spread between him, and it took me a moment to translate all the lines, buckles, and silver rings. There were two triangles made up of decorated leather straps, and I realized as Hunter neared me that the triangles would surround my breasts like a frame.

I was too busy marveling at the contraption to notice the guarded stillness on Hunter's face until he was right in front of me. He was nervous again. Waiting for my rejection.

"You don't have to—"

"It's beautiful," I said, reaching for the leather, marveling at its buttery softness between my fingers, the lovely texture of the pattern. Even the silver rings were etched, I realized as I brushed one. "Put it on me?"

Hunter stared at me, and I held my arms out in front of me in invitation.

"Turn," he rasped finally.

I spun on my toes, and Hunter's heat stroked over my back as he raised the harness up over my head and around my front. I put my arms under the main straps immediately, shivering as Hunter slid the leather up into place on my shoulders.

"Cold?"

I shook my head, although in truth, I was a little chilly and the silver rings were sharply cool against my skin. Hunter's hands covered my breasts, warming and groping them, as if they might need his help in finding their place too.

The harness tightened as he buckled me in, careful to be sure it fit but didn't dig. Strangely, the structure made me feel a little less exposed and also more possessed. I was fitted to my master's liking, and there was a silver bar over one strap on my back, somewhere for him to grip and hold me as he fucked me, just as he said.

"Did you order this for me?" I asked, whispered in the quiet moment between us.

"I did."

"When?"

"After you told me you liked what the Gemini did to you. It's not the same, I know, to play the part of a pet, but...what you said gave me hope."

I reached behind me and Hunter found my hand, squeezed it in his.

"Now, will you crawl for me, little one?" Hunter growled.

With the leather around my shoulders and ribs and breasts, I settled into my role. I sank smoothly down to the floor, ignoring the bite of the carpet and the ache of my knees.

"Do I follow you?" I asked.

"And deny me this view?" Hunter chuckled.

I grinned and put an extra arch in my back, widening my legs a little as I moved forward, his stare hot on my ass, the rumble from his chest rising in volume.

I crawled slowly out of the dining room on my hands and knees, blushing at the bustling activity of Mayfair just outside of the windows we passed, and Hunter's footsteps vibrated against the floorboards behind me. The tile was painful, too hard and cold, and a little noisy too, hard to travel smoothly over, but all the sensation was dull beneath the awareness of Hunter's stare following my every move.

"Are you intentionally trying my patience, little one?" Hunter asked, rough with warning.

We'd just reached the main entrance, and I turned to face the stairs, my ass towards the sealed doors.

"What would you do if the doors opened right now?" I asked, sharing a coy smile with Hunter over my shoulder.

"Make enemies," Hunter snarled, and he stepped between me and the door. "Crawl faster."

I hurried forward, ignoring the thunk of my knees on tile, the scratch of the carpet as I reached the rug on the stairs. My heart was pounding in my ears, too loud to make out Hunter's steps behind me, and the grin on my face stretched my lips wide and made my cheeks ache.

"Spread your legs, little one."

Crawling up the stairs was awkward and uncomfortable enough, my back and arms straining, but spreading my legs for his view I was sure made me look ridiculous.

But it wasn't Hunter's intention to look. The stairs below me creaked briefly, and then his shadow layered over mine on the thick paisley carpet. I gasped, reaching up for the next step, the harness snagging possessively around my body as claws slipped under the grip bar and I was yanked to a stop.

"Take your master here, little one."

It was all the warning I received before a blunt, slick cockhead was pressing at my cunt. I cried out, voice echoing in the grand room, as Hunter thrust inside of me, the force pushing me forward, my hands bracing on the stair above me, the carpet abrasive against my nipples. I wasn't quite ready for Hunter, but he eased himself in with commanding and careful thrusts, the slight sting of his cock stretching me a familiar stimulation.

Fingers tangled in my braid, twisting and pulling, bowing me in an arch that forced my gaze up to the ornate ceiling and bright chandeliers.

"Oh god, Hunter, yes," I gasped out, forgetting our roles briefly in that first decadent seat of his cock fully inside of me, the length and girth everything I'd remembered from weeks ago, my body eagerly adjusting, hips rolling back to try and take more of him. "Oh, I've missed this. You feel so good. Please, more."

I didn't think what the words might mean to him, an orc who'd been scorned and used by his last bed partner. They were stolen from my lips by the snap of his hips, my thighs pressed to the ledge of a stair, just honest and unintentional confessions.

Hunter groaned, his weight on my back, body flush with mine, holding me still and in place, his tusks scratching against my shoulder, tongue licking me.

"Please fuck me, master. Please, I need you. Please." Begging came naturally, the only thought available in my head when Hunter was buried inside of me but not moving.

His claws gently scratched my scalp, taking a firmer grip of my hair, and I moaned as he drew slowly out of me.

"You are so much more than I'd hoped for, Miss Nix," Hunter rasped, driving back in with shallow, gentle thrusts, wetting his cock on my rapidly growing arousal. "More than I deserve."

"No," I gasped as he slid out to just his tip again. I fought against his grip on me to force him deeper, my toes slipping against the stair, ass grinding backwards. "No, you deserve this. You deserve a pretty pet who wants your cock and claws and tusks. Bury yourself in me, Hunter. Every inch of you. Please, I need you."

Hunter roared, retreated, but then he was bucking forward, stealing my breath and sense in one thrust, filling me to the hilt, his balls slapping against my clit.

"Take me, then," he grunted.

I braced myself, mouth open on a slow wail as Hunter fucked me with all the abandon I'd fought for weeks to drag out of him. He was as brutal as he was thorough, shifting and twisting until he stroked inside of me so perfectly that the note of my voice raised. He huffed in victory as my nails raked through the thick carpet, my breasts aching from the frictious burn, thighs bruised from Hunter's pounding pushing me into the stair.

I liked the pain, Con had proved as much to me as a fact, but even more, I liked Hunter's selfishness, so rare from him.

"What a good pet. What a lovely, wet cunt," Hunter snarled, hips clapping into my ass, piercings rubbing at my front walls like playful little fingers.

"Your cunt," I panted.

"Yes, mine. Mine tonight. Oh, how I will use you, little one."

"My mouth is yours too. My ass."

Hunter's steady drumming pace stuttered briefly, paused, and then resumed with a harder snap that made me gasp with every collision.

The hand in my hair pulled free and dove under my hips to rub and circle my clit as I whined. My forehead touched the stair, and Hunter's knuckles rubbed against my back, his grip tightening on the silver bar. The leather straps pulled at my shoulders, and my body snapped backward, a bright cry on my lips. Hunter used the harness to fuck my body onto his, crude and rough and delicious, his hipbones bruising my ass and the jerk making my head shake.

I still loved it, loved the almost useless flop of my body under his command, the inevitable end rising up as he played with my clit and started the quick bloom of heat in my core. We both groaned as it spread to my cunt, making me flutter and clamp down around him, his thrusts deeper and quicker to keep me from squeezing him out.

There was no audience but Hunter and perhaps his servants, so the long, howling groan rising up from my chest was entirely involuntary, forced out of me by the swirling, smothering pleasure spinning through me. Hunter bellowed and snarled at my back, buried himself deep and nudged and ground out his orgasm inside of me, hot and silky and extending on and on till it started to run back out and down my thighs.

I was still in the throes of aftershocks when he pulled free, scooping me up off the stairs and thrusting several fingers inside of me like a plug. I yelped and squirmed, but Hunter's grip was steady, his march up the remaining stairs determined.

I reached a shaking hand up to his face, and he turned his head to kiss the tips of my fingers, his features still sharp with predatory intent. The door to his bedroom banged open, and I'd barely caught my breath before it gusted out of me again, my back landing on the mattress of Hunter's bed. His hands gripped my thighs, spread them wide, and then he was thrusting inside of me again, as hard as ever as I arched and shouted, his fucking immediate and relentless.

I reached for him and Hunter fell over me, snatching my hands up and pinning them over my head with the grip of one hand, the other sliding under my ass to hoist me up and put me at the angle that made our slick hips kiss and his eyes flutter shut on a growl.

"You must tell me if I hurt you," Hunter ground out, brow furrowing, forcing his gaze back to me.

"You won't. Don't stop, master," I said, wrapping my legs around his back to draw him closer. When he frowned at that, I added, "Hunter, you have no idea how good you feel, how good you make me feel. Please, don't stop."

His kiss was rough and clumsy, and he released my hands when I fought him. I wanted him closer, and I tore at the fine clothes he wore, ignoring the snap of a button as I pushed fabric away to hunt for skin.

Hunter could do more damage than Con, it was true, but he didn't want to hurt me and I healed quickly. A rough fuck was a specialty of mine, and with Hunter it was too full of pleasure, affection, to ever be a chore.

I managed to wrestle Hunter's chest bare as he fucked me, to push his pants farther down his hips so I could grab and scratch and grip at decadent flesh. Our breaths were rough and ragged, our kisses messy and biting. I didn't know if I was still his pet or simply his lover, only that we were fighting to claim one another at the basest level, teeth marking with bruises, nails and claws writing primitive names on one another.

My mouth found its way to Hunter's ear, teeth latching on the pointed tip. Hunter howled, his release sudden and surprising inside of me, hips snapping and driving me farther across the mattress. I soothed the nibble with my tongue and lips as he grew heavy, expecting him to settle. I whined as he pulled away.

He only took the time to finish undressing, another telltale rip of fabric sounding, and then his hands grabbed my hips and shifted me to the center of the bed, his shoulders falling between my thighs.

I gasped as his tongue thrust inside of me, mingling with our releases, forcing sticky fluid out of me. His hands pushed my thighs up and back, and my eyes widened as his coated tongue slid back to my tight hole.

"Oh god, yes, yes, yes," I squealed as his tongue breached my ass. "You meant it. Tell me you meant it that you would use me all night."

Hunter growled against my cheeks, tongue probing and slicking my hole. He pulled away, flipping me roughly onto my belly.

"Tell me you meant it when you said this was mine," he answered, a finger taking the place of his tongue, stealing cum from my cunt and using it on my ass.

"I meant it," I said, lifting my ass to drive his digit deeper. "Oh, fuck, Hunter, I meant it. Please, master, use your tongue again."

Either I was a very lucky pet or Hunter was just delighted at my choice of demands, because he dove down, eating my cunt and ass with starving enthusiasm. Orcs had exceptionally long tongues, and Hunter used every inch of his as I thrashed and howled into his sheets, clawing the lovely bedding. There was a wad of sheet under my hips, and the friction against my clit sent me gasping and falling over the edge again, Hunter snarling as he hurried to catch every drop that splashed out of me.

The bed shook as he crawled up, wedging his tip gently into my ass and then allowing his weight to bury him deeper as I gasped for air. The burn was exquisite, the stretch overwhelming, the tease and press of the piercings even clearer against this more delicate place.

Hunter was spread out on top of me, his arms sliding underneath my limp body to cradle me close. Every breath I took shifted Hunter's cock in my ass, but the sting and pressure made my entire body more sensitive, my heart pounding and my pulse heavy in my clit. Sweat broke out and goose bumps raced up to chase shivers.

Hunter's lips brushed my ear, down to my shoulder, one hand cupping my sex and two fingers pressing slowly and gently inside of me as I moaned, the pressure growing heavier but sweeter too.

"I feel more myself now, with you, than I have in years, little one," Hunter breathed into my skin, a private admission that brought tears to the corners of my eyes.

He moved like water, body surging so gently and slowly that I answered the motion like an echo. I was too breathless, mindless to answer, and too afraid of the words floating through my head to speak them, but Hunter didn't care, just fucked me slowly, his fingers holding still inside of me to rub onto as we moved, the heel of his hand a steady press on my clit.

My orgasm was heavy and gentle, with no clear edges and never relenting, only occasionally rising up again with Hunter's patient and powerful fucking.

❧

"IT'S NOT BAD," I said as Hunter's thumb stroked over my red, irritated knee where it peeked up from the bubbles of our bath.

I was covered in Hunter's cum by the time he was done with me—using my breasts once when my body had protested any more—and nearly asleep, but he'd washed me tenderly in the bath, surveying all the marks he'd left on me as he worked.

The carpet burns seemed to be the only marks that really bothered him, and I suspected it was because he hadn't been the one to make those, not directly.

"But I would look pretty in a harness that extended down my hips," I added.

Hunter hummed in thought at that, his palm covering the red mark. "You would," he said, head turning and lips kissing my temple.

"And with handles on my hips, you could teach me how to ride your cock," I added.

Hunter wrapped himself even tighter around me in the water,

lips sucking droplets off my shoulder. "My clever pet," he rumbled into my skin.

He'd been quiet all through the bath, although very cuddly, and I stroked my hands over his arms, waiting for him to speak and growing too impatient when he didn't.

"Go on, ask," I whispered. He stiffened and then relaxed again as I cuddled closer, preferring his heat even to the bath's. "Ask me what's running through your head."

"You... Did you truly enjoy that? Dinner and the harness and..."

"And you fucking the air right out of my lungs until I was a filthy limp rag doll of a pet on your cock?"

Hunter's hands tightened on my sides, his cock twitching with an impressively persistent interest.

"I loved it," I said softly, rubbing my head against his jaw. "But something to protect my knees while I crawl would be nice. And I really think I ought to be allowed to get you off when I have my mouth on your cock."

Hunter laughed, arms loosening and hands stroking up my ribs to my breasts and collarbone and down to my hips. I hummed and sighed at the touch, body worn out but heart touched by his care.

"I will take my pet's suggestions into consideration. For now, I have need of her again," he said.

I twisted and wrapped my arms around his shoulders as he lifted me from the water. He carried me toward the towels stacked on a table, and I expected him to set me down to dry us off. Instead, he sat me down on the stack of towels, spreading my knees apart as he stepped between them.

"Oh! Ohhhh," I laughed as Hunter fit the head of his cock at my entrance and pressed slowly forward. I was tender and swollen from the night already, every little bead pushing past my entrance a notable intrusion.

"Forgive my hunger," he whispered.

"I love your hunger," I assured him, leaning in for a lazy kiss, as leisurely and aimless as his slow and uneven thrusts inside of me. I pulled away when I needed breath, and Hunter's hands on my ribs balanced me as I lowered myself back on the table, my hands tracing around my breasts. "Bring your hunger here, if you wouldn't mind."

Hunter laughed and I grinned in victory as he bent forward, that elegant, long tongue of his circling and teasing around my fingers.

"Oh, yes, that's very nice," I praised, my eyelids fluttering softly closed as Hunter licked and suckled, careful with his tusks to be both gentle and teasing.

"Perhaps we ought to have you play the master next time," Hunter mused.

At the thought of Hunter bent forward, legs spread so I could see his ass and sac and cock hanging and ready for me—and the thought of him strapped in leather too—I clenched around him.

"You like that," he hissed, bucking into me and groaning.

"It's a very clever idea," I teased.

And in fact, it gave me another rather good idea.

26.

Vulnerable Honesties

"You want us to *what*?" Eston squawked.

The company was gathered together on the stage. It was Monday, and it was time to plan a show for the weekend.

"I want the monsters to take the submissive role this week," I repeated, not bothering to look at Eston. It was Reddy who mattered, and he was staring back at me from the front row, eyes narrowed.

Myra's gaze bounced between Reddy and me, her lips twisting. "Hazel, lovey, that's a very unique idea, of course, but—"

"Myra Jones, you can't tell me that in all your time at the theater, you never once had a monster ask you to stick something up his ass, or—" There was a great burst of gasping and chatter and laughter from the company, and I knew I'd won already when Mr. Reddy snorted and glanced away, lips twitching. "Or to call them names or have you take charge during sex. We're only showing half the fantasy. It's predictable."

Mr. Reddy scowled at me for that, but I bucked my chin up and continued, "This competitor of yours is treating us humans like we're disposable collateral. Powerless. What better way to piss him off than by giving us the reins for a week?"

"Hazel is right," Evie said, stepping up to my side. And I could've sworn the lights glowing at us grew just a little brighter. The pixies always did seem to like Evie best. "I once had a giant ask me to stand on his cock for a full twenty minutes. The floor was so slippery by the time he let me walk away, I nearly slipped and broke my neck. We are not just playthings to be spanked and fucked. We can master your lot too."

"Just to be clear, I personally am not objecting to being toyed with and mastered," Ronan called from the foot of the stage, shrugging as some of the other men laughed. "Particularly by you, nut," he added, grinning and winking at me.

"And how exactly would Hazel be able to dominate you?" Eston asked with a roll of his eyes. "You can fly. It's not realistic."

"I'd catch him in a net, string him upside down, and tickle him until he came all over himself," I said at once.

Ronan's skin started to produce tendrils of smoke, his naturally red skin flashing orange with flames as he stared back at me. He liked—no, *wanted* this scene. I blushed too, slightly embarrassed by how easily the idea had come to me. I'd once accidentally tickled Ronan into orgasm, and I'd been fascinated by the possibilities ever since.

"We all have our weaknesses," Ronan bit out, possibly a warning to me.

"And you are his," Evie teased me in a whisper.

I ignored her and turned back to Reddy. "It's just one week. You've tested concepts you weren't sure would do well before."

"It's a good concept," Hugh called from the seats. Isabel was cuddled to his side, their closeness a new development or one I'd missed. "We deserve a chance to be in control."

"But—"

"If you hate the idea, sit out a week," Mr. Reddy snapped at Eston.

"Shame," Evie muttered. "I would've liked to take one of his horns and shove it up his—"

I hushed her, trying to stifle my own laughter. I'd owed Eston a few jabs myself, and Evie had taken my place with him ever since Constantine arrived.

Speaking of my demon, I searched the theater for him and found his tall frame lurking in the shadows of the wing to my left. I itched to cross to him suddenly. I hadn't seen him since the morning after my attack when Reddy had been forced to come clean to the company. I was surprised Constantine was still here. Both Reddy and I knew he was Birsha's man, at least in some regard. I didn't believe he was the killer, or at least not the man who had attacked me, but that didn't make him less of a potential threat. And yet, all I really wanted was to go speak with him. Did he hate my idea? How could I take control from him when my body forcefully surrendered to him at every touch?

"We'll include our audience in the third act. Draw out volunteers to endure your human mercies," Mr. Reddy was saying, pacing in front of the stage as his thoughts started to brew. "We'll call it...*Fragile Dominance*. Ideas like Nix's. Emphasize our weaknesses, or control in subtle ways. Partner up, plan an act."

I was looking at Constantine, considering slipping over to him, when Reddy called.

"Nix, with me for a moment."

"If this goes well, you'll be more his favorite than ever," Evie said, nudging her shoulders against mine before hurrying over to Goliath. The yeti would be a good sport for a scene like this, and a fun partner to work with.

I crossed to the end of the stage, and Ronan rose to meet me. "Sorry for blurting that out," I whispered.

"I don't care," Ronan said, his hand wrapping around my arm. "Just tell me you'll go through with it."

I blushed as his stare blazed down at me. "I'll tell Myra to buy me some feather dusters," I said, smiling. "How often can you come in, say...fifteen minutes?"

Ronan laughed, his fingers tightening. "You want them to have to mop the floor when you're done or something?"

"Maybe."

He pulled me closer, and we both took a deep breath. Oh, I'd missed him. I'd loved every minute of the days with Hunter, but I'd missed Ronan. It wasn't fair to have everything be so right and yet so incomplete too.

"I can teach you a few secret spots to use," Ronan murmured, gaze hooded with interest.

I nodded, suddenly looking forward to rehearsals for once.

"Nix!"

I jumped, and Ronan pulled away as I hurried toward where Mr. Reddy was waiting in the center aisle.

"We need to talk," he said in greeting, nodding his head toward the back of the audience. Myra watched the pair of us walk back. I hadn't spoken to her yet about Hunter, and I briefly debated asking Reddy what he knew but decided against it. Myra taking money from patrons was about us humans first, the theater second.

"I haven't told the others that Constantine comes from Birsha," Reddy said as soon as we were out of earshot. "But I'll throw him to the curb if you want."

"No," I said immediately, and Reddy's eyebrows bounced. "I don't know what the connection means, but he's...nice, actually. And whatever he is to Birsha, I don't think he wants," —*me*— "any of us hurt."

Reddy nodded slowly. "He was the first one I had followed. But he never went near your or Margaret's apartments, we know that for certain."

"I knew it wasn't him," I said, shrugging. "He was angry when he discovered what happened. On my behalf."

Mr. Reddy looked surprised by that. "He cares what happens to you."

"He likes me," I said with confidence.

Mr. Reddy smiled and huffed. "Of course he does. You like us, all of us, even the ones like him, where we're not sure what to make of them. Fine. He may come of use yet."

I nodded. Could I use Constantine to learn more about Birsha's plans? Perhaps, although I wasn't sure I had the nature of a spy or that I wanted to use Constantine's interest in me like a tool.

"We'll need you in the third act," Mr. Reddy said, slower, something almost apologetic in the statement.

"A scene in each act, then," I said, thinking for a moment. "I'll open the first with Ronan. Constantine and I will cook something up for the second, and I'll help with the audience in the third."

Mr. Reddy's answering smile was grim. "You're a good girl, Hazel. Actress, help, whatever."

"Don't get soft on me, old man. We have a show to put on," I said, laughing and turning away as Mr. Reddy growled.

Myra was still waiting at the stage, and my heart sank slightly at the sight of her. Now was as good a time as any for a conversation I didn't want to have in the first place. I caught a quick, steeling breath and approached my old friend.

"WHAT'S THIS ABOUT, lovey? Not enjoying your week with Mr. Hunter?" Myra asked as I pushed the curtain shut on my dressing room.

It was a good opening for me, an easy route into the topic at hand, but my tongue was thick in my mouth as I turned to face Myra.

"I am, very much," I said. Myra beamed at me, floating about my dressing room and tidying the space as if it were her own. "But...thirty pounds, Myra?"

Myra stiffened, her back to me as she smoothed the gown Hunter had purchased for my scene with Constantine, hands fisting into the silk fabric.

"He told you?" she asked, the corner of her frown just visible over her shoulder.

"I saw you in the hall with him. I asked."

Myra remained still and silent for a moment before finally releasing my gown, giving it a gentle pet to erase the wrinkles from her fist, and then turned to face me. Her lips were pursed flat and her chin jutted forward. I forgot sometimes that Myra was growing older, changing with the other humans, not frozen in time like me. But it showed on her now, the changing landscape of her features, the gathering lines over her brow and around her lips.

"It's for your own good. For all of you."

"So it isn't just me you were profiting off of?" I asked, crossing my arms over my chest.

"It's not profit!" Myra caught a deep breath and then shook her head, gaze dropping. "Not much, at least. I do... I have taken a little, when I had to. But so much is saved, Hazel, I swear. Enough for three or four girls."

Irritation pricked at my spine and made my words sharp.

"What do you mean, 'enough'? Myra, you've been scamming the patrons!"

"Well, why do we call them patrons if they aren't going to do more for the theater? For the actresses they come to gape and paw at?!" Myra snapped. "So yes, I take a little here and there. No more than they're very willing to pay. And I put it aside, just in case."

I stepped forward and paused as Myra flinched. "In case of what?"

"In case a charm fails and a girl gets pregnant. In case one of you wants to leave the theater without beholdening yourself to a man," Myra said, eyes wide.

My mouth hung open and I blinked at Myra. A charm had never failed, as far as I knew. And no girl had ever retired from the theater with some secret gift of money to live on.

"You never told us," I said, jaw clenching as Myra's gaze glanced away. "Myra, you've been hoarding away money, and whether it's for you or for us, you made it from our bodies and our time without our knowledge. Who is going to know to ask for help when they want to leave if they don't even know the money exists to help them? I don't believe you!"

"What do you want?" Myra asked, arms flapping at her sides and an urgent squeak in her voice, her eyes glancing over my shoulder at the doorway. "Do you want the money from Hunter? I have this week and the time before. You can have it."

"No!" I cried out, and she fell back a step. "Myra, it meant a great deal to him to find out I was there with him for my own pleasure. Those monsters have as much right to know we're with them by choice, as any of the girls have to know there's money being exchanged!"

"It's only to help," Myra whispered, turning to the side, shrinking in on herself.

"It hasn't helped. Not anyone but you, as far as I can tell. And Reddy—"

"Don't you dare tell him," Myra hissed, spinning to face me again, charging forward, all her nervous apology vanishing in feral anger. It was my turn to lean back, stumble away, but she didn't spare me an inch. "Yes, I saved, and yes, I might need it in the future. I chose that man when I could've had...had dozens of others. I love him, I do. But I'm aging and he's not, and every other month there's a new girl in here and—"

"Stop."

"—his eyes will wander eventually, and I'll have nothing. No beauty left, no money. So I am saving, more than I need, but it's not just for me, Hazel."

"Myra, enough!" I shouted.

This time she stopped, her chest heaving and throat bobbing as she seemed to swallow down the flurry of words that had exploded from her.

"No more," I whispered, staring at her, those pretty dark eyes of hers now creased at the corners, slightly puffy dark circles remarking on years of lost sleep. "You have enough saved for yourself?"

She swallowed again, then nodded.

"No more," I repeated, frowning. "Ask the other girls what they want."

"Reddy would strangle me if he knew I was—"

"I don't care what you tell him or don't tell him. He...he'd probably take a cut for the theater, and he has less a right to it than you. But if you make any more deals with patrons, you do it on the girl's behalf. With her knowledge, Myra. I will find out."

I held her gaze, watched the anger fizzle into worry, through shame, and back to a firm, cold strength, her chin lifting again.

"Fine. And you don't want—"

"No! No, I was—*am* with Hunter because I like him. I slept with patrons and guest acts because I wanted to, to enjoy myself. And those men deserved to know that. They *should've* known that, Myra. There's no shame in making sex our work, but you've muddled it all up, for them and for us. I don't want the money. I never did."

"Then you never needed it, not the way some of us do," she whispered, looking away, wrapping her arms around her stomach. "Fine. It's done."

I nodded, not certain if I could believe her now. I would talk to Evie. She was usually very welcoming of patrons and probably had helped Myra save a good deal of money without realizing.

"If you change your mind about the orc, I can still help you," Myra said, walking toward my door.

Maybe Myra was right. Maybe a rich monster's pocket book was our only way out of the theater. Maybe all my time spent considering a future with Hunter was just the same thing as accepting money from him for sex. But I wouldn't be just fed and warm and housed and taken care of with Hunter, I would be happy too. Because Hunter was kind and sweet and passionate, he had a good sense of humor, a wicked hunger for sex that matched mine, and a desire to *know* me, just as I wanted to know him.

"Reddy loves you," I said, watching Myra walk away.

She shrugged. "For now. For years to come still. But not as much as he loves the theater. He takes care of the company first. I take care of myself first. It's how we work. I'm sorry, lovey. I meant well."

She slipped out of my dressing room, the curtain fluttering shut behind her.

<h1 style="text-align:center">27.
RENDING AND
MENDING
HEARTS</h1>

onan shuddered, wings trembling inside of the gentle net surrounding them, his cock bobbing and weeping a drop into my palm. He looked like a smoking, red bat, and I wasn't sure how well the net would hold up if he couldn't control the occasional flare of impish flames while I teased him. He was always careful when we had sex, but apparently, being left to another's mercy made Ronan especially fired up...all pun intended.

"Louder!" Evie heckled from the audience.

I grinned as Ronan released a loud groan, arching where I had him suspended upside down.

"Tickle his balls again," Alexa hollered through giggles.

"We're rehearsing the blocking, ladies," I answered, rolling my eyes.

"But do it," Ronan rasped to me, pressing his chin to his chest to look up, flashing me a grin.

I snorted and brought the feather duster to his dark sac, teasing gently over the spot, Evie and Alexa both hooting in enthusiasm as Ronan started to buck and thrash. His chest heaved with breaths, garbled moans and sudden flashes of laughter bursting from his lips. *God, he'd look pretty in a harness like mine*, I mused.

"Wings," I reminded him, but I had to pull the feathers away from his skin before he could focus. "Wings, Ro."

Ronan howled, but the claws at the tips of his wings wiggled and then cut through the delicate net holding them trapped. The vast black stretch of flesh and bone flashed free, net still strapping Ronan's shoulders, and I brushed the feathers over the membrane of one wing, Ronan's gasp drawing a smile to my lips. His wings stretched wide, an invitation to continue my tickling, but I pulled the feathers behind my back.

"Boo!" Evie cried.

"Finish him off!" Alexa crowed.

Ronan laughed in his suspended trap, twisting in the net and harness to grin at me. His cock was stiff and tempting, little dribbles of precum on his chest and jaw.

"Don't tell me you're going to leave me...hanging," Ronan said, eyebrows waggling as I groaned at the terrible pun.

"I'll finish him off, but not for you perverts," I called to the girls in the audience.

Ronan stilled at that announcement, as Alexa and Evie cursed me. I wasn't sure how all of the monsters who worked in the company felt about this week's theme, but us humans were in high spirits.

"Will you?" Ronan asked as I nodded at Billy, who lowered the rope and harness slowly to the floor.

I knelt, wrapping an arm around his back to keep him from landing in a messy heap.

"I have to find Constantine later to talk to him about our act, but I have time," I said, smiling at Ronan.

His gaze was bright on mine, but he was quiet for a moment, his hips touching down and wings spreading out flat. "What about Hunter? He'll smell me."

I blinked at that. Hunter had woken me with his face between my thighs and his fingers slipping into my ass. In the carriage ride to the theater, he'd put me on the floor and let me suck him off. He would be waiting for me tonight when rehearsals ended, and he'd promised to put me back in the harness for the evening. Things with Hunter were...wonderful, actually. Fun and sweet and incredibly erotic all at once. Easy too. We were still in a bit of a sexual frenzy together, learning every little detail of arousal, but the moments of quiet and calm were equally sweet, full of honesty and affection.

It reminded me of how things were with me and Ronan too.

"I've missed you," I said to Ronan, staring back at him, unbuckling the harness—inspired by the one Hunter had made for me—and pulling his arms free.

"Is this the last week you'll spend with him?" Ronan asked, the words simple, carefully placed one after another, and heavy with meaning.

I shook my head, trying and failing to ignore the seize of my heart. I would not be done with Hunter at the end of this week. I didn't want to *ever* be finished with the orc if I could help it. What that meant for Ronan and me... My heart panged again, and I could've sworn I felt it tear, bleeding a bittersweet poison into my chest.

His eyes closed and that poison burned, teasing through my veins, punishing me for the truth. Was Ronan finally learning the lesson I'd taught myself years ago? That one by one, we all left the theater eventually, and so rarely together.

"Then I don't care what he minds," Ronan said softly.

I had no reason to know, but I got the feeling Hunter wouldn't mind. Not yet, at least. It wasn't as though I'd quit the theater. He knew I was still working, still fucking monsters for work. I could easily pretend he smelled Ronan on me because of rehearsals. But I also knew that if Hunter asked about Ronan, I wouldn't lie.

"You're up," I called to Evie.

"Saddle my beasts!" Evie hollered, triumphant and almost diabolically gleeful.

Ronan's hand clasped around mine, and I tugged him up from the floor, keeping hold of him as I led us offstage. There was a beating, living creature between our clasped palms. Our hearts probably, ready to break when we released one another. I meant to take Ronan down to my dressing room, but we hadn't even made it to the stairs when he shouldered open a narrow door, dragging me inside.

My back hit a shelf as he squeezed the door shut behind us, something metallic chiming as it rattled. The prop cupboard, I realized, as Ronan gathered me close.

"I've missed you too," Ronan whispered, his nose dragging

along my jaw. "It doesn't have to be him. You could wait. Myra will find you another. Or—"

I found Ronan's face in the dark and pulled it to me, took his lips in a deep kiss he answered eagerly. A kiss intended to apologize, but what quickly became a plea. A begging press of my lips to his, to forgive me, to pretend with me that I wasn't saying goodbye.

The truth was that I missed Hunter now too, right here in this tiny cupboard. I was thinking of Jude, of how he was the only person who knew the truth of me. Still full of questions for Nireas, wondering why he'd turned away eight years ago. Still curious about Constantine, his intentions and interest, needing to know why he looked at me like he saw right through me and still didn't believe I existed.

It wasn't fair to any of them, and it was entirely unfair to myself to be doing this, pulling my skirts up as Ronan and I gasped and clutched and fumbled closer.

"You like him," Ronan hissed.

"Yes," I admitted, my heart pounding. *More than like, I think.*

"And you'll miss me."

I kissed Ronan again, cried out into his mouth as he lifted me in his arms and then speared me onto his cock, a sudden plunge that struck my heart like a spear.

"Yes!"

Ronan's nose nuzzled against mine, and he shook as I grasped one wing and one horn in either hand.

"Then you'll break my heart, nut," Ronan breathed against my lips, tongue licking out to erase a tear that clawed down my cheek. My breath hitched as he rocked in and out of me. "But not until you tell me to stop."

I whimpered and Ronan silenced me with a kiss, tongue thrusting in time with his cock.

Stop, I thought, but I bit down on Ronan's lip to keep from speaking the word. Would I be able to do it? Be able to walk away from Ronan? And if not him, Hunter?

How long could I get away with never saying the word 'goodbye'?

I sucked on Ronan's tongue, wrapped my legs so tight around

him, I was sure his hips would leave bruises on the insides of my thighs, more evidence for Hunter to find.

I would ignore the truth until they reached down into my chest with their claws and tusks and talons, and dragged the bleeding, broken heart out of me.

꒰ঌ

THE ATTACK CAME FAR SOONER than I expected.

That very night, in fact.

Hunter's claws dug into the base of my neck, and his other hand had a firm grip of a cheek of my ass. The desk drawers of his office rattled, the beautiful wood sticking and dragging at my bare skin as Hunter rutted behind me.

"Oh, fuck, Hunter, yes, harder!"

There was a whine in my voice, a tight pinch in my throat, and a sting in my eyes. I was still sensitive from hours with Ronan. I'd refused to tell him to stop, and he'd taken it like a challenge, although I wasn't sure which of us it was for. All I knew was that Hunter's eyes had glowed brighter than ever as I'd stepped into his carriage, barely cleaned and tidied, still full of Ronan's release.

I'd been stripped, harnessed, and fucked within five minutes of stepping into his house.

Hunter's chest was hot on my back as he bent over me, denying me my request and grinding slowly against my ass. His lovely moss green hand left my ass and reached out to my grip at the edge of the desk, stretching me further, tangling thick fingers with my own.

"Do you want to know the truth?" Hunter growled.

My head shook in refusal before I could think straight, but Hunter either didn't notice or didn't care.

"I like the scent of the imp on you," Hunter hissed, his tongue lapping around the shell of my ear.

The shock of the words was immediate, all the swirling guilt and worry bursting free of my chest in sudden sobs.

The creaks and thrusts and fucking ceased immediately. Hunter cursed and a rougher wave of tears rose up from chest in garbled, wet gasps, drawn by anger at myself for ruining this moment. But Hunter's hands were gentle as he peeled me up from his desk. I hunched as he turned me to face him, trying to hide, but I was weak and wobbly and no match for Hunter's tender strength.

"Forgive me, little one. What did I say? Did he hurt you? Did *I* hurt you?"

I was crying too hard to catch my breath and speak, but I wailed a little and shook my head. The fire was blazing as Hunter bundled me in his arms and carried me over to the large armchair, settling me in his lap, and the heat reminded me of Ronan's touch.

A claw skimmed my back, and the leather straps of the harness loosened. He was taking it off of me! I'd failed him, failed being his pet!

"No! No, I'm sorry. I'm sorry, please, master, I'm so—"

"Hazel, shhh, hush little one," Hunter answered, soft but almost frantic. His fingers released the clasps and he started to stroke my back with long sweeps of his hand. "Shhh. The imp, Ronan—"

"He-he didn't hurt me," I forced out between gasps of air.

Hunter was blurry through my tears, but his hand on my back was helping, and I twisted on his lap, cuddling closer and breathing in his scent.

"Then I've hurt you?"

A distant part of me was proud of Hunter for his question sounding doubtful. A month ago, he probably would've banished himself from the room. Now he was holding me in his arms, determined to be the one to take care of me.

"No! Not at all," I managed, squeezing his shoulders in my grip.

Hunter settled at that answer, petting my back and hair, guiding my breaths with deep inhales of his own.

You fell in love, you fool, I thought. And not just once. Had I ever really managed to avoid my own emotions, or had I simply been breaking my own heart for all these years?

"Are you angry with me?" I asked.

"No," Hunter said firmly, and then added, "What for?"

"Because I had sex with Ronan." Would he be able to tell the nature of it? Was that ridiculous? Was there a particular scent for hours of desperate, emotional, heartbroken sex?

Hunter shook slightly, and it took me a moment to realize he was trying to hold in laughter. I wiggled free of his close grip in order to find his twitching lips and furrowed brow.

"No, little one," he said, managing to remain sober as he spoke.

"It wasn't... I didn't..." *Why are you trying to ruin this?* I screamed at myself in my thoughts. He wasn't angry. I didn't have to explain why he ought to be.

"You didn't have to. You wanted to," Hunter said gently. I nodded, watching him, waiting for some sign of anger or... No, he wasn't jealous. "You prefer him?"

"No!" I blurted out, jaw hanging open.

Hunter frowned and looked down between us, and I realized I was still naked and his pants were down, and the whole situation seemed suddenly absurd and humiliating. I'd burst into tears at a simple...

"You like his smell on me?" I asked, suddenly remembering the words Hunter had slipped into my ear.

"Let me take the harness off. I hate to see you upset in it," Hunter said, frowning.

I opened my mouth to object. Wearing the harness was a sign of his approval of me, taking it off would mean I made a mistake as his pet, surely? But maybe for him, watching me sob while wearing it was equally uncomfortable. I turned and waited as Hunter unbuckled me.

"Why do you like his scent on me?" I asked, frowning and finding it easier to think as the harness slipped down my arms.

"He smells like toast," Hunter said.

A hysterical, exhausted burst of laughter cracked out of me at the statement. Hunter was right, and yet...

I twisted and found him smiling, wondering if he'd said something so ridiculous on purpose.

"I can smell him and your own pleasure. And yet, you're here with me too, and I bring you that pleasure as well," Hunter mused, studying my face. "I also like smothering his scent with my own," he added with a sharp grin, tusks gleaming in the firelight.

I stood, and Hunter's grip faltered, freezing as I lifted his shirt from the rug where he'd dropped it and then slid my own arms into the sleeves. His smile softened again as I climbed back onto his lap, facing him.

"Do you want me to leave the theater?" I asked.

Hunter's eyebrows bounced. "Do you want to leave the theater, little one?"

I blinked at him, surprised to find no answer on my tongue. Hadn't it been *yes*? Wasn't I tired? But today's rehearsals had been fun. The company was like family to me, and my family was under attack. How could I leave the theater and leave Ronan? Leave Nireas? Even Myra and Reddy, when I wanted to strangle them. All the other humans and monsters.

"Not yet," I whispered.

Hunter leaned forward, and I twined my arms around his neck as he kissed me. "I love to watch you on stage. Here, you are my little pet and my exquisite Hazel," he said, brushing my cheek with his knuckles. "And there, you are equally vibrant, but I share my joy of you with so many."

"And that doesn't bother you?" I asked.

Hunter shook his head, but his gaze trailed away thoughtfully. "Is it ugly of me to say that it is like the privilege of witnessing a beautiful work of art on display, and then to be alone and enjoy the art as she breathes and lives and thinks in her perfect," he kissed my brow, "exquisite," my nose, "honest form? The woman, not the canvas, that is."

I blushed at the comparison and took his lips with mine, lingering until a smile interrupted the kiss. "I'm not sure. I don't mind it. And you're certain I won't hurt you if I step out of that frame with...Ronan?"

"Little one, correct me if I'm wrong, but I'm under the impression that if anyone should be offended by an interloper, it is him, not me," Hunter said, arching a lovely coppery eyebrow.

"I'm not sure I really understood the connection until recently. I am especially susceptible to affectionate feelings lately," I said with a heavy sigh. But Hunter's smile was too huge and dazzling for me to be annoyed by my own rebellious heart for long.

"You're a very rare woman, Hazel Nix," Hunter said, hands sliding under his shirt and up my back to draw me closer. "Someone so precious ought to be loved by many."

My cheeks warmed again, and I reached down between us, but Hunter caught my hand before I could distract him from his sweetness.

"We should've talked about this before. I didn't realize it was disturbing you."

"Neither did I. Or not so much," I admitted, frowning. "If I didn't feel so equally for you—" I hummed as his lips pressed to mine, yellow eyes warm and hooded as he pulled away again. "You know that, or you should. You could be a guest act or a company member or yourself. I want you, with or without grand houses and pretty harnesses."

"Thank you, little one," Hunter said with another long kiss gifted to my lips, and his hands no longer fought me as I found his cock and stroked it to eager arousal. "You should be tired."

"I'll be tired after," I said, kissing each of his cheeks and then the tips of his tusks. "You'll make sure of it."

Hunter chuckled, and I held my breath as I turned the sound into a moan, drawing him inside of me and sinking down, watching his eyes fall shut and his tongue wet his lips.

I'm free, I thought, my own breath coming short. To stay with Hunter. To remain at the theater. Hunter might buckle me into the harness, tell me to crawl for his pleasure, but he would be the first to hand me back up to the stage or to carry me to bed or to see me home to Stepney Green in his carriage, if that was where I wanted to go.

My knees sank into the cushions on either side of his hips, his hands on my waist helping me slide up and down his cock.

"Are you attracted to Ronan?" I asked, still thinking over that little note about Ronan's scent.

Hunter huffed and blinked at me, lips parted on a soft pant. "I'm attracted to the sight of him touching you, feasting on your cunt, fucking you. Alone...no, I don't believe so."

I smiled at that, rewarding my orc with a nip on his lip.

"Would it be terrible if I say I am going to be very possessive of you?"

Hunter's eyes widened, and a soft moan escaped his lips as I started to ride him a little faster, rolling my hips in a forward circle to make those tip piercings rub inside of me.

"You know me well enough to know how much that honors me, little one," Hunter said, words ragged.

"Then you are mine," I said, gasping as he bucked up at the words. "My gentleman orc. I ought to share you with others like you've offered to me, but I won't. I will possess you with all the greed in me."

Hunter groaned, his claws scratching down to grip my ass.

"Mine," I whispered, nibbling on his tipped ear. "My orc. My master."

"Hazel!"

"And I want your seed in me. I want you to fill me up and make me filthy. I'll let them all smell you in me tomorrow," I said, my eyes widening, understanding my own power and privilege as I watched Hunter unravel at my words, my touch.

Victory was as bright as Hunter's eyes blazing up at me, as sharp as his claws gripping my flesh, and as hot as the burst of his release in my cunt as he bellowed his joy and took me down with him.

28.

CONTROLLING A DEMON

"What did Mr. Reddy want?" I asked as Hunter returned to my dressing room. He'd accompanied me to the theater again the next morning, a note in hand from Mr. Reddy to come and see him.

"Is it private here, little one?" Hunter whispered, double-checking my curtain was shut behind him.

My eyes widened and I nodded, ushering him to where I was sitting on the chaise. It struck me as he marched forward, with no hesitation, how much more assured this version of Hunter was than the one I'd met weeks ago. Was that because we knew each other better now, or because I'd made Hunter more comfortable with himself in the process? Either way, it left me grasping him eagerly as he joined me on the cushions.

"Mr. Reddy has collected a list of suspects," Hunter said, his voice lowered. "Within the company as well as the audience."

"No," I said, shaking my head. "It can't be—they can't be in the company. I...know everyone, and..."

But how well did I know them, how well had I *allowed* myself to know them?

Hunter's hands reached up to cup my face, and it struck me how large he was, how easily I could tuck myself into Hunter's embrace, feel small and safe with him.

"Not many," Hunter said gently. "But yes, a few. And there aren't enough people we trust to track them."

Oh. "You have work to do," I guessed.

"Tomorrow I will," Hunter said with a grimace. "And as

much as I'd like to insist you make use of my home in the evenings, I thought perhaps you might like the opportunity to remain here while I'm away."

His thumb brushed my cheek as I blushed, thinking of our conversation the night before and Hunter's easy blessing in regards to the other men in my life.

"You know who is safe. Ronan and Nireas were with you that night. Stay in their company, little one," Hunter said, a slight growl rumbling through his voice. I nodded, and he leaned forward, kissing the center of my brow and a line down my nose. "I'll be at the performances. Perhaps this matter will resolve quickly. In the meantime, speak to your lovers."

"My lovers?" I repeated, eyes widening at the plural.

Hunter's head tipped. "The imp. The gegenees."

My teeth carved into my bottom lip as I stared back at Hunter. We'd never said anything about Nireas. But he was right. I did need to speak to him. I'd been running from the conversation for days already.

"Perhaps the demon too?" Hunter mused, lips twitching.

"You're teasing me now," I said sharply.

"Oh, and the detective."

I gasped. "Hunter!"

He grinned and huffed as I dove closer, wrapping my arms around his shoulders and slanting my lips over his before he could list any others. Not that there *were* any others. Was I that transparent?

What good was running from my feelings if they were plain as day for anyone else to see?

"But tonight, you're mine?" I asked, pulling away, breath slightly short.

"Every night, little one," Hunter purred. "But yes, tonight we'll be together at my home."

AND YET, it wasn't Nireas or Ronan or even Jude I went in search of after Hunter's departure. Perhaps Hunter had spooked me and I was afraid of the conversations I might have with the others.

Running away, my father's voice hissed in my head as I knocked.

Constantine opened the door to his dressing room, his flat, silver gaze landing directly on my throat.

"Healed," I said, and he nodded, stepping aside to grant me access. "I'm sorry I haven't come to find you sooner."

"You've been busy," Constantine said. There was a slight lilt in the words, as if he were joking.

"And stumped. Have you thought about our act at all?"

"I suppose me binding you is now off the table," Constantine said, watching me as I crossed the room to sit at the end of his bed.

"On stage it is," I said, smiling as Constantine's head tipped curiously.

"You don't mean that."

I blinked at him. "Of course I do. It doesn't suit this week's theme, but that doesn't mean I wouldn't enjoy myself."

"From one of the others, perhaps, but not—"

I rose and crossed to Constantine, reaching for the layers of strange clothing he still wore, frowning up at his blank expression.

"What's wrong? I've meant what I said to you every time, Constantine," I said, searching his face for any hints.

"I'm here to be feared. To cause pain."

"I like pain," I said, shrugging. "I like *your* pain. I like the way it cuts through all my fears and worries and stresses. It eliminates everything cluttering my mind and—"

I gasped as Constantine's arms snapped around me, hauling me up off my toes and drawing me up to his mouth, my own lips ready for the furious kiss. Constantine in his full form was neither pain nor pleasure, but his touch was charged and heavy, his tongue on mine sending a current of buzzing energy rushing through me right down to my core. I moaned and clutched him in return, aware of the sway of my feet as he carried me to the bed. His lips pulled away briefly as he laid me down, and the glare of his gaze was almost hateful.

"You're pretending. Acting."

I blinked up at him and reached for his face. He flinched and then froze as my fingertips framed his cheeks. "You think I'm capable of acting when you touch me?"

He stared back, brow folding between his eyes.

"I can't be the first person to enjoy your touch," I said, my expression matching his in confusion.

"There are those who savor the oblivion of either side of me, even together, but not..." Constantine's frown deepened and his gaze flicked away.

Not *him*, I realized. The pain, the pleasure, but not the man who offered them.

"I was frightened of you when I met you," I said, pulling his eyes back to mine. "Terrified and excited, ashamed of how much I enjoyed what you could do to me. You're very careful with me."

"I'm dangerous," he said.

"So is everyone here," I answered, shrugging. "Not everyone is careful. So yes, I'd like it if you tied me up. If Con and Antin fucked me at the same time, or if just you and I lay here together, touching and kissing, talking. I want to know you, and I like the little you've shared so far."

Constantine stared down at me for a long time, his body lowering to the mattress, pressed close against my side. He wasn't scorching hot like Eston, but he warmed the longer we touched.

"I am here at the command of another," Constantine said slowly.

I sucked in a slow breath, considering my next words carefully. Constantine's disbelief in my interest reminded me of Hunter, and it made me more determined than ever to prove how worthy I found him. Lies wouldn't cut it, not with this demon.

"Birsha," I said, and Constantine jerked his head in a rough nod.

"I did not go to him...voluntarily. Although his houses offer me a considerable outlet, his preference for Con's skills is clear," Constantine said, frowning. "I fought the orders to come here, of being reminded how objectionable most find me. And yet...I am more feared by Birsha's terrified, trapped animals than by anyone here."

Which wasn't saying much, considering almost everyone but me still avoided his company.

"What do you mean, you didn't go to him voluntarily?" I asked, reaching for him, tracing the muscles of his throat under my fingertips as his lips pressed flat and his entire body tensed. Not at my touch though...something internal. "You can't say?" I guessed.

He relaxed slightly. "I haven't hurt anyone here. Aside from you," he said.

"Good, I'd be very jealous if you had," I said, my mood brightening as a surprised little smile curled up the corners of his lips. I would ask more about these terms he was bound by, but first..."And Antin?"

Constantine's smile grew again, a rare warmth of expression transforming his eerily beautiful features. "Received a request."

"From whom?" I asked, sitting up and glaring at the door.

"They were denied," Constantine said. I hiccuped with surprise as he pulled me closer, rolling back until I was seated on top of him. "You know Birsha's name because you know he is likely responsible for the death of the human girls?"

I nodded, freezing at the reminder that Constantine seemed aware of what I was, or at least wasn't, in spite of not saying so directly.

"I had no knowledge of his plans when I came here, and nothing has been shared with me when I ask. If he discovers what you are, he will almost certainly take steps to acquire you for his collection," Constantine said, gaze growing dark as he sat up slowly. "And if I am asked..."

My breath froze in my chest, my eyes growing wide. "He asked about me."

Constantine blinked, shook his head. "No...no, I would've been forced to speak. I said nothing, sweet creature, I swear it to you."

"No, Constantine. He asked Mr. Reddy about me," I whispered.

Constantine's eyes flashed, and his hands gripped my hips for a moment before his head dipped down. "Then I've given away my own interest to him and put you in danger."

I reached up to the horns framing his head, studied their texture from tip to root, where Constantine hummed at my touch. Sensitive then, like Ronan.

"You don't care about the human girls, do you?" I asked.

Constantine lifted his head and hesitated, nodding it side to side in ambivalence. I was a little disappointed but not surprised. Humans were coveted by some monsters and dismissed by others. And I doubt many had given Constantine a reason to feel especially protective.

"Would you help us, though? If I asked you to? Or are you loyal to Birsha?"

He growled and shuddered under my touch. "Not loyal, the opposite. But I'm not free to act against him, as much as I might wish, even for my own selfish reason," he said, frowning. "I would help, if I were able."

Understanding trickled in slowly, little whispers of information I wasn't meant to know, not as a human girl in a monster's world. But they'd reached my ears, and I'd never had cause to wonder about the laws of demon blood until now. My breath hitched, and my hands slid down the sides of his smooth face to his jaw. "Constantine, are you bound?"

A demon could be held against its will by a witch or warlock. All it took was finding the demon's mark, their talisman, and I supposed the skill in magic to perform the summoning. It was absolute possession, an almost complete loss of the demon's will, as far as the summoner commanded it. Horrifying.

"Not by Birsha's hand," Constantine said, flinching again.

My hands tightened briefly before I realized, and I pushed them down his back, drawing him roughly against me. Constantine was *bound*.

"Where is the talisman?" I hissed. "Who is the summoner?"

Constantine's face turned, his breath rustling against my throat. "I would rather remain bound for another century than involve you in that net, sweet creature. You are my only haven, after so long."

I let out a wounded sound, tried to pull away. "But—"

Constantine's arms tightened around me, kept me close. "I'll speak with Mr. Reddy. Offer the little I know and am able to share."

"Wait, I don't want you risking yourself for—"

Constantine shifted, his mouth sliding over mine, his tongue catching and twisting around my own, my body arching into his as that returning current of power raced through me.

I whined as he pulled away, opened my mouth to continue the argument, but Constantine spoke before I could.

"I've considered your theme for this week, and I have an idea you might enjoy," Constantine said.

"You can't distract me from this—"

"As Con and Antin, I can choose whether or not to use my gifts on myself."

My mouth remained hanging open, but no words came out in response. *Don't let him distract you, this is important.* And yet, what could I do? Constantine would be bound to serve and certainly bound to secrecy. No warlock who kept a demon for a century would be idiot enough to miss that step.

"So with that in mind, perhaps it would be time for you to make demands of me on stage," Constantine said.

I was a little embarrassed by how readily my mind offered up suggestions in the wake of such a serious conversation.

"You'll speak to Mr. Reddy?" I asked.

Reddy might decide to help Constantine of his own volition, but if he didn't, I felt sure I could pressure him. Hunter might even volunteer if I told him. In fact, I would absolutely see he did. And as many other friends I might be able to call on. Demon blood might demand this sacrifice from Constantine, but I demanded that he be free. I knew what it was like to be trapped, bound in a way, on a much smaller and more loving scale.

"I will speak to him."

I stroked my hands over his back, up to his throat again, studying the muscles under my touch, Constantine still and patient under my hands.

"I want you free," I said.

His eyes flashed. "And I want you unharmed, safe."

Constantine's throat flexed as I tipped his chin up, lowering my face to hover my mouth over his.

"I'm not giving up on this conversation. But...yes. I have some ideas. Can you control how much your touch affects me?" I asked. Because if either Con or Antin laid a finger on me, I would have a difficult time doing anything other than screaming and begging.

"Not much, but a little," Constantine admitted.

"And how much it affects yourself?"

"Yes, easily," Constantine said, nodding his head.

"Is it like touching yourself?" I asked, squirming with my own curiosity.

Constantine's lips curled up again, his gaze narrowing to slits. "Oh, it's *much* better."

I stared at him for a moment, holding my breath, before making up my mind. "Show me."

His head tipped. "Show you? Are you taking control *now*, sweet creature?"

I nearly said "can I?" before catching myself, rising up from the bed. "I am."

On stage, I usually missed the dizzying moment of Constantine splitting into two, and I'd almost forgotten how disorienting it was, as if there were suddenly two realities to choose between. The sensation settled as Con and Antin shifted apart, Con's gaze hungry and cautioning, Antin's crimson hand reaching for me.

"No," I said, the word rare and powerful on my tongue. They both froze in place on the mattress. "Undress each other. Don't...don't use your powers yet."

"Should I call you 'mistress'?" Antin asked, lips quirking.

Part of me wanted to laugh, but heat pooled in my core at the word, and I nodded. "Here. And on stage."

Con's eyes blazed as Antin reached for the buttons of his starched collar, but there was no anger in that fierce stare. No, that was excitement. Blue hands reached forward, and I gasped as Con tore open Antin's tunic, earning him a tut of displeasure from the red demon, who continued in his more careful work. They were as much as opposites as they were part of one another, equal halves of Constantine.

"I feel as though you show me more of Antin than Con when you're whole," I mused as they bared each other's chests. "Stand up."

I moved back and Con glared at me, yanking Antin up from the bed by a hooked grip on his trousers, his long, blue fingers sliding down into the fabric. Antin hissed, but it was in relief, not pain, as his other half took him in hand.

"I am the preferred," Antin said, adding with a smile, "By most, at least."

"I prefer you equally," I said, my eyes fixed to the bobbing fabric of Antin's pants, his red throat flexing, horns arched back.

Antin groaned, and then his fingers made quick work of Con's own buttons, pushing the fabric down dense muscular thighs. "We believe you, but even your body needs more care than it does pain. Trust us, mistress, you are more than generous."

"Antin, show me what it looks like when Con feels pleasure," I said.

Con's eyes widened and Antin's lips grinned, his red hand snapping forward and taking Con's hefty, blue cock in a firm grip. Con had no voice to speak with, but his body said more than enough, tensing and twitching, releasing his grip of Antin in favor of reaching up to red horns, hips bucking forward. His legs trembled and his stomach flexed, ass clenching, a perfect vocabulary of muscle and skin fighting the torment of pleasure.

"He wants your mouth," I noted, watching Con's hands tighten on Antin's horns, trying to force them down.

"Can you blame him?" Antin laughed.

Con's eyes rolled back, cock pounding into the grip of Antin's fingers.

"Stop," I said, and Con's glare turned to me as Antin released him before allowing him to come. I smiled back at my blue pain demon. "It's your turn, Con."

His narrowed eyes flicked toward Antin, and I expected his fury to be as strong and violent as his pleasure, but instead, he only reached up and cupped Antin's face with a gentle touch. It was all he needed to do. Antin didn't scream like I did, but his body tensed and his breath came out in wounded whimpers and anxious pants. His knees folded, sending him kneeling on the floor. Even without lips, I understood the victorious smile in Con's eyes as Antin crumpled forward, his face perfectly poised in front of Con's bare and stiff cock.

Con was taking control.

"No," I snapped harshly as Con started to aim the head of his length at Antin's open mouth. He ignored me for a moment, and Antin moaned around his flesh. "Step *back*."

Antin pulled away, still moaning in agony, and Con's head thrashed as he dropped his hands to his sides.

Antin gasped for breath, hands braced on his knees and head bowed as I stepped forward to address Con.

"You're not naturally obedient, are you?" I asked, smiling.

Con shook his head, and Antin huffed.

"Lie down on the bed, Con."

He didn't move at first, his stare sharp, the pair of us equally aware that all it would take was for him to grab my wrist and I would be at his mercy completely. Which was why it made me so breathless as he stepped around Antin to spread himself out on the bed, hard cock standing and pleading to be touched. And ohhhh, how I wanted to.

"On your belly," I said.

Con froze, but he didn't look angry at all as he rolled over, adjusting himself, and Antin smiled up at me from the floor.

"Do you... Have you ever...?" I asked, glancing between them.

"What wouldn't you do to yourself, if you had the chance?" Antin asked, grinning.

Not much, I admitted. "Don't use your powers," I said, rounding the bed to sit at the head. If Con stretched, he would be able to reach me, but I wasn't really afraid. He'd behaved so far, more or less, and I liked his horrible touch anyway.

Antin stood, finally shedding his loose linen pants, and then gently pushed Con's legs apart, kneeling between them. He sucked on a finger, and I watched Con twitch as Antin burrowed it between his ass cheeks, just circling and pressing at first. Blue hands clenched at the sheets, Con's hips bucking into the mattress. I wanted to touch him, either of them, pet them and praise them, but I wanted to be lucid even more.

"Be good for me, Con. Relax and show me what you can take."

Con's glare wasn't a glare at all—it was the visual of a growl. One of desire, not temper. Antin hummed in approval as his finger sank into Con's ass.

"Now make him feel you," I said to Antin, who nodded, horns bobbing.

Con's hands clawed at the bed, his body thrashing.

"Another finger," I said, watching his back tense, but Antin was already stretching Con. "I want you to use his ass to your finish."

"He won't be able to control his power," Antin warned me.

"Try for me, Con," I murmured. "As long as you can."

Con's face was rocking into the bed, his hips rising to chase Antin's fingers as they pushed and pulled, split and surged to stretch him open.

"He loves pleasure," Antin murmured. "That's his secret. He's greedy for it. And until you, there weren't many who found it with him. Not the way we do."

I braced myself and reached out, smoothing my hand over the back of Con's head, gasping and holding onto the bed as the fiery agony surged through me. He lifted his head into my touch as I pulled it away, something new in his stare. I caught my breath and smiled at him.

"Be good for me," I said.

Antin lurched over Con, the contrast of his warmth and Con's cold color beautiful and blurry. Con's eyes rolled up to white as Antin sank slowly into his ass. He fucked himself onto Antin's cock, and the shudder raced through him with eloquent trembles from his eyelashes down to his bracing toes. Antin's brow furrowed and his voice yelped as Con squeezed around his cock. Red hands braced on either side of Con's shoulders as Con tried to rise up for more, and the bed started to shake with their movements.

They were like a storm together, bodies crashing like thunder, Antin's cries of pain and grunts of pleasure the strike of lightning. I wanted to slide under the pair of them, pull Con into me, but as he lifted up onto his knees I had the view of his cock jerking, fluid gushing eagerly out of the tip, dripping to the bed and running down his length to his balls.

"Look at me," I pleaded to him, and he did immediately, all the pleasure he craved written out in that wild stare. He came again, and Antin hissed but didn't stop his thrusting. "You're both so beautiful."

Antin gasped, and Con's fingers twisted and crawled closer to me. I held my breath, swallowed my groan, and petted up his arms, embracing the pain and withdrawing before I grew too weak.

"I'm close," Antin gasped out, head tossed back. "I want his pain!"

I nodded at Con and then Antin was howling and Con was gushing again, Antin's arms wrapped around Con's chest as Con sat up, hips snapping back on Antin's cock.

I crawled forward on the bed, and Con's gaze snapped to me as I raised my skirts, revealing my own damp sex.

"Give me Constantine."

The shift was sudden, the pair so closely fused together already. Constantine's eyes were as wild as Con's, his mouth still opened on the moan from Antin. He shimmered gold and violet, the colors racing over his skin with the flush of release, but his cock was still hard as he reached for my ankles. His grip was tight, and my breath rushed out of me as he dragged me under him.

"I don't have their powers," Constantine rasped.

"You can give me pleasure and pain without demonic gifts," I said, reaching up to grasp his shoulders.

"Gladly," he gasped, a slight whine in the word.

I arched and cried as he thrust inside of me, my own arousal and his slippery cock making the sudden plunge as smooth as it was shocking. Our voices chorused, Constantine's eyes wide and mouth open as I pulled his face to mine and took his lips in a needy, messy kiss—a demand and a gesture of thanks.

He was almost a novice at kissing, I realized, chasing after me, clumsy and catching up. But he learned quickly, his hands roaming over my body, searching and pulling at fabric.

"I want your skin," he hissed, and I laughed at the words,

pushing on his chest and helping him yank the dress up over my head.

He tugged my hips close and I groaned, seated fully on his cock, my thighs stretched wide and my back sticky with Con's cum left on the bed. Constantine sat up and stared down at me, his expression slack with wonder for a moment.

"It's been centuries," he said, possibly to himself.

Centuries since...

Oh.

Since *Constantine* had been the lover, rather than his two halves. His eyes narrowed on the corset stays I wore, a simpler, shorter version that kept my breasts bound, and I had barely raised a cry of objection before he was tearing it open.

My complaint died as Constantine lunged down, mouth wrapping around a nipple, horns nudging my face away. I laughed at his urgency and then moaned and ground myself up and down his cock as he suckled me roughly, the echo of pressure ringing down to my cunt. My hands grasped his horns, steering them carefully and pulling Constantine's mouth to the neglected breast. His hands stroked my bare waist, down to my hips, squeezing there and pumping me on his length.

Would Hunter like Constantine's spice and sugar scent on me as much as he liked Ronan's?

"Will you make up for the lost years?" I asked, whining slightly as his lips moved up to my throat.

Constantine bucked inside of me. "I will. I will fuck every inch of you, sweet creature." I shivered at the promise and then whimpered as Constantine scooted back, lips abandoning my skin as he sat up and stared down at me again. "In fact..."

He pulled free of me, and I gaped at him, a refusal or a plea on my tongue. And then his hand cracked down from the air, landing sharply on my sex, snapping on my clit. I screamed and twisted, barely catching a breath before he did the same again. My sex throbbed hotly, my eyes wide in shock at the revelation of the pain and the deep burn of hot pleasure.

"Again," I gasped.

He obeyed and I screamed, my hips humping the air as the sudden crack of pain turned into a pounding throb not unlike being fucked. And then Constantine grabbed my hips and pulled me onto his cock, and I came in earnest, back bowing and hands fisting in the sheets as I soaked his cock with my eager release.

He pulled out before I'd settled, and I sagged on the mattress, sucking in air as he crawled up over my chest, all the way to my face.

"Now clean me, suck me, and drink me down, and then we will begin again," he said, gaze glinting down at me.

If this was Constantine bound, I would tear that warlock to pieces to know my demon untethered. I opened my mouth, my eyes fluttering shut at the mix of flavors on his length, mine and his mingling together like a bitter treat. I would free this demon, and then I would possess him as much as he might let me.

"Pretty lips. Pretty creature," Constantine groaned.

29.

IN UNISON

The canteen was busy for lunch as I entered the next day. Hunter had kissed me goodbye, thoroughly and extensively, in the carriage outside, before leaving for a mission for the next day or so to track the suspects. I was in the care of the company for the night. One member in particular, I hoped.

I paused in the doorway, studying every familiar face in the room. Every actor and stagehand, monster and human. Was one of these faces, people I trusted with my body at its most vulnerable, the killer? Someone who knew Beth's laughter and Margaret's shy smile?

My gaze drifted over the table to where Isabel and Hugh were still snuggled together—a few stray glances from nearby monsters studying the pair with open jealousy—and then over to the corner, where an unexpected duo was bent over their plates, not speaking.

Nireas rose from the table, arms shifting, head ducking as he spoke to Ronan across from him. The imp looked up from his food to nod, expression uncommonly somber, and then his gaze caught mine, eyes widening with brief surprise. Nireas slowed as he approached me.

"I've been avoiding you," I said when he was near enough for me to speak softly.

"I could tell." He didn't sound offended, but I wasn't sure I still remembered how to read this man.

"I'm sorry. It's... You..."

"I waited too long."

I stared at him and wet my lips. "I don't know. But...would you wait a little longer? Not much. Just give me a little more time."

Nireas's lips pressed flat but he nodded, slow and deliberate.

"Thank you," I said, reaching out and squeezing his arm, not pulling away as he slid his arm through my touch, allowing me to feel the flex of dense muscle, before he grasped my hand tightly. But he let me go as I stepped forward, and he was gone from the room when I glanced over my shoulder as I walked up to a watchful Ronan. "Are you two friends now?"

Ronan's spoon stirred aimlessly through the stew and rice on his plate. "We have...things in common. You arrived late."

I hesitated, glancing at the bench across from Ronan before rounding the table and squeezing in at his side, his arm curling around my back automatically. "I did. But I'm staying the night."

His spoon stopped in his bowl "With me?" Ronan whispered.

I arched an eyebrow at him. "Unless you've found another bed partner."

I'd been teasing, but Ronan grunted as though I'd just punched him in the gut. "Hazel."

"Sorry. Sorry, that was careless," I whispered, turning my back to the rest of the room, offering Ronan a shy smile as his wing lifted to shield us. "Hunter smelled you on me that night."

"He was angry?" Ronan asked, and to his credit, he didn't look pleased.

I shook my head. "He didn't mind."

Hunter also hadn't minded the smell of Constantine in the least, from what I could tell, although he hadn't remarked on it with more than a sniff and a wicked smile.

"Then he's an idiot."

I glanced down at the table, at Ronan's fist wrapped around the spoon. He loosened his grip as I reached for his hand and let me steal a large bite of food. It was cool, proof he'd been mulling over his dinner more than eating it, but it still tasted good. Johnny was a better cook than a stagehand.

Ronan was jealous, possibly even possessive. The truth was that just because Hunter had offered me freedom, it didn't mean

Ronan would be equally eager to share me. Maybe now, because he had to, but...for how long?

"I really care about him, Ro," I said slowly.

"I know you do," he said, frowning.

"As much as I care about you," I continued, trying to keep breathing even as my lungs tightened and my eyes stung.

Ronan's arm tightened around me, his voice lowering, ragged at the edges. "He can take care of you, nut. I hate it, but I understand it. Just don't tell me we're done already."

"It's not—I'm not with Hunter this week because of money, Ro!" I said, indignation helping distract from the worry.

"I like him too, as it turns out, as much as I hate him. But it makes sense, and it's not as though I want you trapped here just because we don't have anywhere else to go together," Ronan rushed out.

"No. No, no, you're not—you're not *getting* it," I said, fighting to keep my own voice from rising. The tears were gone now, at least. "Ronan, I'm asking if...if it's unfair or cruel of me to...to want you both. To keep you both."

Ronan's eyes were a vivid amber, as bright as coals. His hair was mussed, and there were dark circles under his eyes.

"Both," he repeated.

I swallowed hard and nodded, my heel jiggling against the floor as I waited for his answer. This was somehow more stressful than fighting against an attacker with a garrote around my throat.

"But, Hazel. I..." He frowned and blinked as he looked around us. "Does that mean you'll be stuck here at the theater?"

"No, not stuck," I decided. "But I'm not sure I even want to leave the theater right now."

"It's not safe here," Ronan hissed.

"Well, then you'll have to keep an eye on me," I huffed.

Ronan's lips opened and parted a few times before shutting again, seemingly stumped for anything to say. But when I reached for his hands, he grabbed onto me with a fierce and determined grip.

"My only hesitation with Hunter this whole time has been the idea of...losing you," I said softly. "Except he's not asking me to walk away from you or the theater or anything that makes me happy, which includes him. I don't know how it will work yet, but I just want to know if you would....would want it to work too."

Ronan's eyes widened. "Nut, are you mad? Of course I would!"

My breath gusted out of me, and I threw myself forward, Ronan quickly releasing my hands so we could wrap our arms around one another.

"I've been in love with you ever since you asked me how flexible my tail was," he muttered in my ear before kissing the lobe.

I laughed, and it was teary, so I tucked my face into his shoulder.

"Or at least since you asked me if I wanted you to help me oil my wings," he said, squeezing me tighter. "And I know you'll probably hate to hear it, but if you've made your mind up to keep me around, I'm afraid you'll have to grow used to the words. I love you, Hazelnut."

I clutched hard at his back, smothered my face in his skin so I could fill my mouth and lungs with him. Like toast, as Hunter had said. I'd heard those words very little in my life, and there was a part of me screaming to *run* at the sound of them. But it wasn't my mother's blood at all, I realized. It was the knowledge that the love I'd known before the theater had latched around me like a cage, had been built out of fear and anger.

I hadn't run from my father, and I wasn't sure if that was for good or ill. But I didn't need to run from Ronan or from Hunter, or even from how they made me feel.

"I don't mind it, actually," I murmured, lifting my face just slightly, tucking my nose against his jaw.

"No?"

I nuzzled against him as I shook my head. "I might even like it. Not sure yet," I teased.

Ronan huffed and his breath tickled my throat, drawing goose bumps out. "Well, we'll practice it, then. For now, are you hungry?"

I pulled away slightly, trying to fight the absurd grin on my face, at least until I saw an equally ridiculous one on Ronan's. "I am, actually."

He nodded, gaze winking with mischief. "Good, because mine is cold. Go get a plate so I can eat some of yours."

I rolled my eyes and swatted a hand at his chest. "Pfft, bastar—Mmph!"

Ronan's arms snapped around my waist, full lips snatching at my own in a deep and heady kiss. Someone across the room whistled at the pair of us, and a few whispers rose up as I wrapped my arms around him and leaned in for another press before he pulled away.

"Since you're staying the night, we ought to practice your tickling technique," Ronan said, eyebrows waggling.

"My technique?" I asked, eyebrows rising high. "With the feather duster?"

"Mm, it could use a little work. It's a bit of a limp delivery."

I snorted and tried to wrestle free of his arms. "I've changed my mind. There's no living with you."

"No, it's too late," Ronan said, grinning. "You've compromised me. Everyone in the room saw. I'm yours now."

I laughed and squirmed as Ronan peppered kisses over my throat and cheeks. We were gathering stares, and for all I was a girl who exposed herself on the stage, I still wanted to crawl under the table and hide from the attention. Because this wasn't an act, and I couldn't even pretend it was. It made me feel wired and confused and happy and terrified all at once.

Run, my head urged. *Run, before it's—*

But it was too late. And I wasn't my mother *or* my father.

"We'll figure it out, nut," Ronan said, almost echoing my own thoughts.

I settled against his side and nodded, helping myself to another cold bite of stew.

There was a killer to catch and a madman to deal with. Constantine was bound to a warlock, and Nireas and I had yet to face a conversation that was eight years overdue. I wasn't sure how it would work with my men, if indeed it worked at all.

But we would figure something out, if it didn't all go to shit first.

§

IT FELT like it had been a long time since I'd really been present at the theater. Since Beth's death, at least. And even though the whole company was trapped together, aware of the trouble lurking in the shadows around us, it was almost like things were back to normal.

Evie and I paced up the spiraling stairs into the attic of the theater, well above the pulleys and levers, the spotlights and mezzanine seats. I had a tray of cake in one tired hand and a stack of plates in the other, and Evie's arms were loaded with jars of honey and pitchers of milk for the wee folk who kept the roof on, picked loose change up from under the audience's seats, worked the lights, and mended the clothes we never got to.

"I thought you were settling down with the orc," Evie said.

I blinked up at her swaying hips. "Who says I'm not?"

She huffed. "You and Ronan have always been thick as thieves. You're worse than ever now." I smiled at that, but Evie wasn't done. "And don't think I didn't hear you begging for your life and sanity in the guest act's room yesterday." My smile widened, and Evie stopped at the top of the stairs, glaring down at me. "Lord, look at how smug you are."

"You lot claimed to want nothing to do with Constantine—that's not my fault," I laughed, following her up and nudging her aside with my hip.

"Oh, I tried my luck with him, but he wouldn't give me the time of day," Evie said, shrugging.

My hand clenched on the railing. *Evie* was the girl Constantine had mentioned. Why did I have the sudden urge to send her toppling down the stairs?

I shook myself—he'd refused her, and she'd only asked for Antin, foolish woman—and remembered her question.

"Who says I can't have the orc, the imp, *and* the demon?" I asked.

Evie's eyebrows bounced up. "Oh, is that how it is?"

"Alexa sets a good example," I pointed out. Alexa seemed quite settled with her vampire and her handsome enchanted statue.

"I sort of assumed that was because Leon liked a stiff pair of fingers up his ass," Evie said with a shrug. Her eyes widened. "Oh! Is Ronan—"

Now there's a thought. Ronan had performed with Hugh in the past. *Would* he want sex with Hunter or...

"Nothing there yet," I answered before she could ask. Although there was certainly potential in Constantine, given his self-serving proclivities. And in spite of my rather possessive feelings toward all the men, that was a *very* tempting picture forming in my mind.

"Then you're just lucky," Evie said, turning on her toes and heading for the little nest Myra had built up here.

Broken doll houses and forts built from scraps of leftover fabric all sat cluttered together in the corners of the attic. I'd never seen any pixies myself, although I thought sometimes I heard them scuttling around my dressing room as I returned from my scenes.

"I am," I said softly, smiling to myself, ignoring Evie's snort.

"I thought you were a bit of a stalwart, like me," she said.

I shrugged. "So did I. And then suddenly... It's a bit like a game of dominoes. I fell over for one, and now I can't seem to stop myself. Speaking of new developments...Hugh and Isabel?"

Evie hummed, and we stopped outside of a dollhouse, a little flicker of light winking and then vanishing from one of the windows. "I don't know what Hugh's thinking, but it's going to cause trouble."

"You think he'll get jealous?" I asked.

"No, he has too much sense and he's been with us too long. But the monsters aren't happy, are they? Isabella was already a little too free with her opinions about them. Now she's gone and made it obvious she'd prefer a human."

I pressed my lips together. I believed her, but I'd been out of touch with the others. I could imagine it, though. Two humans choosing each other rather than the monsters. It was only a game of odds, really, bound to happen eventually, but it would wound pride and confirm certain monsters' fears of human feelings.

"The worst part is I'm not sure if she really gives a shit about

Hugh, or if she just realized she's in over her head here and wants a way out," Evie continued.

I set two plates down in front of the dollhouse door, scooping out cake from the pan. Evie joined me, drizzling honey over the crumbs, and then pouring just enough milk to fill to the brim of the plate.

"Could it just be love?" I asked.

"Sure. If you believe in that sort of thing," Evie said flatly.

I did, although I'd certainly tried to avoid it as long as I could. I suspected Evie had once too, and I hoped she got to again.

"There you are, my little darlings," Evie cooed to the house. "And I'll be back tomorrow morning to clean up. Have a lovely night."

"Softie," I whispered to her.

She rolled her eyes and tossed her hair. "I get best lighting for a reason, don't I?"

30.

THE EAGER
AUDIENCE

"**D**o you have someone picked out yet?" Ronan whispered in my ear, his chin resting on my shoulder as we waited in the wings.

"Hunter ought to be here tonight," I whispered back.

It was opening night of *Fragile Dominance,* and so far my theme had been a hit with our audience. In our first scene, Ronan's capture in my nets had drawn a collective gasp from the crowd, the introduction of the feather duster had brought out laughter, and by the time Ronan's body was thrashing in the trap and spurting cum down his own chest, I'd spotted no fewer than four audience members with their hands very much occupied. Self-pleasuring was always considered a good start to a show at the Company of Fiends.

My time with Con and Antin had been equally successful and a wonderful excuse to shower more touch onto Constantine, who soaked up every brush of fingers and lick of a tongue like a sponge.

In fact, every act had been met with enthusiastic applause, more so than usual, and a few patrons had snuck downstairs during intermissions to beg for humans to spank or demean them. Perhaps it was because the change in dynamics was so surprising, so out of the norm for our company, but the humans as masters was a hit. Reddy was prowling around behind the curtains with a bright gleam in his eye, and I knew he'd be mining for donations and funding from the audience at the end of the night.

"Did you see who else was out there?" Ronan asked.

"I didn't really look," I admitted, shrugging.

"Mmm...well, there's a surprise for you in the fifth row, stage left, near the aisle," Ronan said.

On the other side of the curtains, the audience was settling in their seats, the lights dimming from the end of intermission.

"What surprise?"

"Can't tell you a surprise. That's the point of one," Ronan said, lips twitching.

"That's a secret, not a surprise," I hissed, but Billy was whispering orders to us. Ronan kissed my throat and slipped away before I could grab at him. This scene was only for the humans —and our audience, of course.

And Ronan would have plenty of time with me later, since Hunter was...well, hunting this evening. I missed my orc, and as the lights rose gently on the stage and we tiptoed into the small doorways that led down to the audience, I knew I would find him in the crowd and bring him up to the stage with me. I'd already considered what I might like to make him do—bend over and let me play with *his* ass for a change.

Except Ronan's teasing was echoing in my head, and as I followed Alexa out of the shadows and into the audience, I couldn't help but count the rows.

One, two—oh, there was Hunter to the right, with a burly and shaggy redhead at his side—three, four...

My steps down the short staircase paused as my eye landed on my "surprise," as Ronan had put it. Jude Piper, just a couple seats left of the aisle, without his usual bowler hat to obscure those beautiful cheekbones and ice blue eyes.

Hugh nudged my back gently, and I nearly slid off the edge of the last stair, gathering myself at the last moment by luck.

Jude was here. In the audience. He'd watched me tickle Ronan with a feather duster, for Christ's sake, and command Con and Antin, and spread my legs for Constantine's mouth, my breasts nearly spilling out of my leather and lace-trimmed corset. The one I was still wearing, the one Jude's gaze glanced over, down to my stockinged legs and back up again, those eyes as sharp as a hook catching in my throat, calling me closer.

I stopped at Hunter's side and settled on his lap as Hugh passed me, following after Alexa, hunting through the crowd along to Nireas's playful and plodding musical guidance. Hunter's lap was warm under my bare thighs, and his hands helped themselves to a gentle grip of my hips as my arms circled his neck.

I pulled my stare from Jude at the last moment and smiled at Hunter, lowering my lips to hover over his. "I've missed you," I murmured.

"And I you, little one," Hunter answered, smiling.

"You ought to introduce me, Hunt," the jovial man at Hunter's side said, leaning close enough to brush his shoulder against my back.

"I certainly won't, Conall," Hunter growled, leaning in and grazing his tusks against my throat, breathing me in up to my ears.

Conall the Red Wolf, of course—the monster who'd introduced Hunter to the human world. I offered him a brief smile of acknowledgement and tried to shake off the gentle tugging still lingering in my belly, calling me across the aisle and up a few more rows.

"Will you be here tomorrow night?" I whispered to Hunter.

My orc grinned. "Yes, and I'll ferry you back to my bed after too," he answered. I kissed him, and one hand slid up to my ass, squeezing gently as he pulled away. "Go have fun, pet."

Not just permission, but encouragement.

I wiggled on his lap and grinned as Hunter's gaze brightened, his cock twitching with interest against my ass.

"Pick me," Conall whispered, grinning as Hunter shot him a glare.

"But sir, you don't strike me as one to kneel and obey," I said, batting my eyelashes.

Conall was handsome, remarkably hairy with wild auburn waves of hair, and charmingly roguish, with scratches across his cheek and through the opposite eyebrow. He reminded me of all the monsters who'd passed through my bed in the years past— interested in a mutually pleasurable fuck, but not in staying. I was spoiled now, and he didn't suit me.

"Clever girl," Conall said with a grin, a pair of bright, sharp canines winking at me from that feral smile. He was by far the most obvious werewolf I'd ever met in my life, and the only one I'd heard of with a title for himself.

I kissed Hunter again and lingered, brushing my nose against his, and then stood with his hands guiding me, helping themselves to a final pat and squeeze before I slipped away.

Jude was still watching me. Hugh was already escorting a giggling female troll—head and shoulders taller than him and blushing like a school girl—up to the stage, and Alexa had a hoard of monsters at the back begging for her favor. Christine, Evie, and Isabel on the other side of the room were in the middle of choosing their own guests for the scene, coaxing and flirting and teasing the monsters.

Jude looked human enough on the street, in daylight, but here, surrounded by other monsters, he glowed. He might not be the most obvious example of a monster, but his beauty was too remarkable to be mistaken.

The gentlemen at his side, a pair of feathered incubi, reached for me as I slid in front of them, but their touch paused as I tutted and shook my head.

I stopped in front of Jude and he scooted forward in his seat, his hands reaching out and wrapping around the backs of my thighs, balancing me as I straddled his lap and bent over him. The row in front of him twisted to watch, their murmurs of appreciation and jealousy covering the sound of my whisper.

My lips grazed his ear, heat bubbling through me as his calloused fingers stroked up my thighs. "What do you want?"

Jude leaned in. Sitting up on my knees, his face was close to my breasts. His breath ghosted over my skin, bristled cheek turning to graze against me. He tilted his head back, soft strands of hair landing in my reaching fingers.

"To know what it feels like to be all of myself at once," he whispered back.

The words gripped me, a concept I'd banished from my own heart years ago. To be human *and* monster. He was fae, and he hardly knew that part of himself, even less than I knew my own nymph blood.

"And you," he added, the words pressed to my pounding

pulse through full lips.

I didn't even have to pull. It was as if that stare that had hooked me minutes ago had locked us together. I slid off his lap and he rose with me. The incubi tucked their legs to the side, making room for me to lead Jude out of the audience, into the aisle. On stage, Hugh was already being gently feasted on by his adoring troll, her huge hands petting playfully as she lapped at his cock with enormous lips, his face dizzy and blissful. Isabel looked significantly less blissful as she ordered an elegant vampire into the stockade at center stage, but the vampire didn't seem bothered and the troll only had eyes for Hugh, so I assumed Isabel could be left to her own devices. Jealousy wouldn't serve her long in this theater.

I caught Jude's hand in mine, considered my former plan for Hunter, and then blushed and discarded the idea. I knew Jude almost as well as myself and yet hardly at all. Especially not when it came to sex. And as much as the theme meant I ought to make him submit, I looked at the stage and all our toys—chains and paddles and phalluses and clamps—and knew there wasn't one I wanted to introduce to Jude. Well, not tonight at least.

I drew him into the shadows of the small staircase to the right of the stage, and Jude crowded close.

"I'm nervous, suddenly," he whispered. "Do you get nervous?"

Not anymore, I thought. But I didn't answer.

I reached for his face in the dark and pulled it to mine, as I'd been craving to do for what felt like ages. His arms snapped around me as our mouths fit neatly together, and there was no evidence of nerves or hesitance as his tongue met mine, stroking and twining and chasing for more. *This man knows me in ways no one else does*, I thought, twining my own arms around his neck, pressing my hammering heart to his through our chests.

He tasted a bit like pipe smoke and bitters, earthy too, and he felt familiar in my arms even though we'd never kissed—a destination I understood intimately even if it was my first visit. I sucked at his lips, rocked my hips into his, and pulled away with a few quick kisses.

"I'm less nervous now," Jude said, voice lowered, honeyed and warm, nuzzling his cheek to mine. His hands cupped my ass, rubbed me against his hip, the ridge of his cock growing stiff in his pants.

Strange, because I was more nervous now.

"Jude...do you have any fae features?" I asked, inching us slowly toward the door that led to the stage.

"Wings," he whispered. "I keep them hidden."

Wings. That was right, he'd said so before. Webbed like Ronan's, or feathered like an incubi? The last Unseelie I'd met didn't have any wings.

"Tonight you'll show them," I said.

I didn't give him a chance to argue. That would be my dominance, I decided, because everything else I wanted to do to Jude probably wouldn't match. Reddy and the others would forgive me. I pulled Jude out onto the lights of the stage, past Evie, who was undressing a pretty demon woman with chains jangling over her arms, and into the center of the floorboards.

His eyes were wide and shockingly pale, pupils shrinking at the glare of the spotlight, and his steps stumbled into place. I circled to his back, leaving him to the stare of the audience, and brushed the nape of his neck with my fingers.

"Just look confident," I whispered in his ear, tugging at his collar to warn him.

He straightened, shoulders broadening, and he didn't flinch as I pulled his jacket down his arms. The back of his white shirt was cast in shadow, and I blinked and puzzled over it for a moment, tossing his coat to the floor. The shadow shifted, trailed down to his thighs, tickled against mine, and it struck me suddenly. Not waxy membrane or feathers. I reached up and stroked the shadow, felt the whisper of Jude's wings rustling and flexing against my touch. Jude groaned and shuddered. Had these wings *ever* been touched? Not likely, given I was the only person aside from his mother who'd known what he was.

Which presented an intriguing possibility about Jude's experience with touch in general.

"They're not strong," Jude gasped.

Because they'd been trapped under coats his entire life, prevented from stretching and beating freely. But in spite of his claim, the shadows began to spread out, shrouding Jude's head through a dark film, tickling and teasing me as they started to stretch. I rounded them carefully, the spotlight making their outline clearer on stage than they would be in the dark. I stroked my fingers over them, the sensation cool and pleasant, just shy of tangible but not entirely.

Jude's head was dropped, his chest heaving, his wings flirting eagerly with my hands.

"Look up," I said, not performing for the audience anymore, not even aware of what the others were doing.

Jude's eyes were hooded as he lifted his chin, lips wet and parted on a pant. I stroked his wing closest to me again, and those eyes shut as he released a moan. Softness nuzzled into my palm, his wing still stretching. I guided it out, my own lips parting on a gasp. They were huge, perhaps even growing to spread into the light, to swallow it up in that gauzy, glittering shadow. I stepped in front of Jude, and he blinked dazedly at me.

"I want everyone to see you," I said.

He blinked again, eyes flicking over my shoulder and then to me. "I want *you* to see me."

So I unbuttoned his shirt, watching and studying the way his wings only really had to flutter to shed the fabric. Pure shadow. I'd never seen anything like them, and from the murmurs of wonder behind me, I had a feeling neither had some of the audience.

Jude's skin was pale under the spotlight. Of course, because he could hardly waltz around without his shirt with those great black shadow wings. At least not in the middle of London. But his body was lean and his muscles were clean and carved, almost like he'd been made of ivory. I stepped in closer and pressed my lips to his shoulder, feeling the pound of his heart under my palm as his fingers tangled in my hair, holding me to him.

"It's...it's been a long time," he whispered, voice catching as my other hand trailed down to his waistband.

"I won't embarrass you," I reassured him, licking at his collarbone next. I knew how to delay a man's relief as well as I knew how to call it on faster. I also knew monsters and their own arousal better than Jude. "Pleasure will never embarrass anyone in this theater."

Jude groaned and bucked into me with a *whoosh* of air as his wings flexed and beat at my trailing touches. He would put on a beautiful show.

"I want to taste you," I murmured, kissing his skin, his fingers flexing and tightening in my hair. "I want them to watch me please you. To watch a spectacular male fae fall to pieces at my touch."

And I wanted to wrap my lips around Jude's cock and gaze up at him as I made him come apart.

Jude's fingers in my hair tugged, just the slightest encouragement for me to move lower, and I offered him a bright smile before bending and doing exactly so. There was an appreciative chuckle from the audience at the view of my ass as I kissed down Jude's chest, and his stomach jumped as I licked the ridges of his abdomen, ticklish and sensitive. But when I knelt, burying my face in the fine hair leading down from his belly button below his half-open waistband, Jude's legs were spread to make room for me and his wings were a commanding presence at his back.

I looked up and smiled again at his hard stare and clenched jaw, the muscle ticking as my palm covered his hard cock through his pants and squeezed. His stare flashed in warning, and I released him. The audience wouldn't see much of my work from this angle, and I didn't want them to. I wanted their eyes on Jude.

Mr. Reddy would know more about him, or at least what branch of the fae he might've come from with wings like that. I was more certain now that it was Unseelie, and probably impressive. Fae princes did love a human dalliance, according to folklore, and folklore was often right.

I kissed Jude's hips, sucked on the muscle that carved a line down to his cock, and carefully pulled his pants out of my way, making sure not to stimulate him. But his cock was long and pleasantly thick, and it bobbed against my ear. Jude gasped as I rubbed my cheek against him, my hands stroking his thighs.

"Take my face," I whispered, kissing the base of him as his trembling hands reached for my cheeks, cupping them gently.

I tapped my fingertips up his chest and back down again,

poising my lips against the twitching, slick, red head of his cock. His brow was furrowed, breaths ragged.

He wouldn't last, and it brought me a wildly inappropriate amount of pleasure. Any sex he'd had must've been clothed, or at least in the dark, and probably brief. And not recent, according to his own claim. I ran my tongue over his slitted tip and his head fell back, fingers biting around my cheeks but not pulling me closer.

Did he even know his own body? His own pleasure? I suspected not.

And if I couldn't delay his release, then the answer was simple.

I wrapped my mouth around his head and suckled him, kissed him as if it were his lips against mine, teased my tongue at the tiny opening, and hummed as sweet and bitter fluid pooled on my tastebuds. Now he couldn't resist, his hands tugging me closer, my lips greedily sucking and pulling him deeper, tongue stroking.

Jude was loud, and it took all my concentration to fight my smile. His hips were bucking and his hands demanded more and his moans carried up to the ceiling, out to the audience. I reached for his grip on my face, held it there when he started to pull away, and then taught him how to make me pace up and down the length of his cock. I hummed again as he started to thrust against my tongue, rubbing himself to the roof of my mouth.

Oh, he was beautifully eager and sweet. As unpracticed and unguarded like this as he was somehow shy too.

He sounded so disappointed as he started to swell in my mouth, hot and hard and as desperate to hold off as he was to come.

"Oh god, Hay—" He swallowed my name, and I sucked in my cheeks as he bellowed wordlessly, hips arching forward, wings beating in time with the throb of his release.

His taste was fresh and bright, like a hot swallow of syrupy-thick, dark tea. I didn't waste a drop as he shuddered and flinched, shoulders slumping and fingers petting my face. I didn't release him either.

Jude strangled his shout and shivered as I licked him clean, dug my fingers into his hips, sucked on the tip of his cock. I reached below his length for his sac, now that I was sure it wouldn't send him immediately to a fast finish. He barked in surprise at my touch, and I was glad the audience wasn't laughing. No, they were behind me, gasping and touching one another, a worthy finale—the response Reddy liked best.

And above me, Jude's eyes widened as he realized the truth of my earlier guess. He was sensitive but not flagging, still hard and still weeping eagerly on my tongue, against my cheek as I pulled away to catch my breath.

He stared at me, mouth open, and I smiled at him and mouthed the word. *Monster*.

Most races were considerably more virile than the average human man. Sometimes, it wasn't exactly a blessing, but in this case...I certainly didn't mind.

I kissed his tip, squeezed his sac, and caught a quick, deep breath as Jude's hands tightened on my face, as his feet braced the floor, and the shock in his eyes turned to determination.

I relaxed my mouth and body at Jude's first thrust, rewarding him with a moan around his length. He was a good size for me, not too big to take fully like this, just enough for him to grow a little rough and demanding. His hands knotted in my hair, thumbs stroking my cheeks, and I let my hands play as he controlled my mouth.

There was a frenzy on the stage, Hugh and Evie both groaning wildly, and the rough slap of a paddle rewarded with a cheerful yelp at the back. Jude's wings stirred the air, the breeze rushing over my skin, tickling me and acting as a kind of caress.

I scooted closer, grunting as Jude's cock hit the back of my throat, pressing my breasts to his thighs, my hands gripping his ass. He was certainly the dominant, in spite of my initial coaching and encouragement, but who would care in this moment? And there was nothing I could see but the flex of his stomach, his hungry stare as he thrust and used me.

I wanted hands on me, mouths, something to treat the ache of need growing in my core. Jude was gasping, and I hadn't even realized I'd wrapped a continuous whine around his cock, the sound's vibration making him a little ruthless and desperate. Close again. Which was good. Nireas's music was storming now —it was time to wrap up the act.

I tugged on Jude's balls, pulled back a little against his hands to focus on his tip, wrapping my other hand around his base to squeeze and pump him.

I knew my work very well.

Jude groaned and leaned into me, the shadow of his wings snapping backwards and arching high as he flooded my mouth again. This time, some fluid slipped out of the corners. I pulled away, heaving for air, letting him splash his finish against my breasts—he would like that once he'd settled—and stroked him root to tip. His belly jumped against my lips as I kissed him there, and his weight pressed into me as strength rushed out of him with a final spurt of fluid striking my chest.

I leaned back and caught him against me as he dropped to his knees, the music pounding and the view of the others clear over his shoulders. Everyone was in the throes of release. I didn't care. I pressed my face into Jude's throat, his arms clasping weakly around my back, embracing me, lips murmuring senseless words against my shoulder.

The audience was cheering or coming, and the curtains were sliding shut for the moment, and still the moment was somehow private. Just for me and Jude. I didn't want to pull myself away from him, drag him into the wings of the stage so we could take our bow. I wanted to simply stay here, wrapped up in him, for another hour at least.

"Quick, Hazel," Hugh hissed, brushing his hair out of his face, guiding his besotted guest by the hand.

I would've ignored him too, my least professional choice at the theater in all my history, probably, but Jude heard the words.

He leaned back, a sloppy, boyish grin on his face, and then kissed me once, firm on the lips.

"Thank you," he said, hauling me up from the floor, guiding me after the others as if I were the guest and he the actor. The words were annoying, impersonal, but then he squeezed me close and whispered in my ear, "I can't wait to return the favor in private, Miss Nix."

31.

THE OVERTURE

"In private" ought to have taken place immediately, in my opinion. Or at the very least after curtain call, a rare evening where I hadn't managed to skip it, given I was already standing right at the edge of the stage.

Instead, I found myself in quite the opposite situation in my dressing room. Not alone with Jude or Hunter or Ronan either, but quite crowded in by all of them, including Constantine, Nireas, Mr. Reddy, Conall, and even the minotaur, Asterion.

Jude wasn't even close at hand. He stood near the door, his shirt hanging open on his shoulders, the shape of one shadowy wing outlined by the candle behind him, chatting amiably with Hunter, Conall, and Ronan. Nireas, Mr. Reddy, and Asterion were gathered together in another pocket, slightly closer to where I was wrapped in my robe, settled against the back of my chaise with my knees bent and my feet in Constantine's grasp.

Constantine was doing his usual post-stage treatment of massaging me, although in truth, I'd had a surprisingly easy night for once. But I wasn't about to turn him down.

Lord, they're all just...in here, I thought, my eyes bouncing between them again. Constantine, Jude, Ronan, Hunter...even Nireas. I wasn't even sure why. Hunter was keeping an eye on the hallway, and I suspected that he might've been waiting to follow someone out of the theater. I supposed I was the excuse for his presence.

"I'm going to talk to Mr. Reddy before I leave for the night," Constantine murmured, surveying our companions with me.

"Do you have to leave for the night?" I asked, frowning.

He nodded. "I'll be called back soon."

By the warlock, or Birsha, calling the shots from a distance. Using Constantine like a pawn could've been the man's only crime, and I still would've hated him. I reached out for Constantine's hand on my ankle, wrapping my fingers around his wrist and catching his eye.

"Grab him now. If he won't try and help, I'll ask Hunter," I said, leaning in to whisper. Ronan was watching us from the door, but he wasn't frowning, just observing.

Constantine blinked at me. "He would grant me his help for your sake."

I opened my mouth to disagree, but I wasn't sure. Hunter didn't know Constantine, although I wanted to believe he was the kind of man who would be as disgusted by Constantine being summoned and bound as I was.

"Does it matter?"

"Debts are complicated. But it might be an improvement," Constantine said.

He rose up from the chaise, tucking my feet against me, and the crowd in my dressing room—the air now hot and fragrantly male—jostled to make room for him. I stood too, catching his hand in mine before he could slip away and rising to my toes without thinking about the many eyes that might watch. Constantine was still, impassive, but he bent enough for me to press a kiss to his lips, my own eyes falling shut as his widened.

There was the slightest stammer in the rhythm of conversations around us, but it was gone by the time I landed back on my heels, squeezing Constantine's long fingers. He moved to Mr. Reddy, and I slipped past Asterion's massive frame to the small crowd at the door. Ronan and Hunter had just enough room between them for me to squeeze in, and I stiffened briefly as Hunter's hand cupped my waist and Ronan's arm slung over my shoulder. Neither of them retreated or seemed to take much note of the other, although Jude studied the arrangement casually.

"Detective Sergeant Piper is assisting us this evening," Hunter said.

"Shadows aren't a perk I get to take advantage of in my regular work," Jude said, excitement bright in his eyes, a flush of pleasure still on his cheeks. *I put that there*, I thought with a glow of pride.

"I was thinking of joining them too," Ronan murmured in my ear.

"You were?" My eyebrows rose, and I tried to push down my own disappointment. No Hunter, Ronan, *or* Jude?

"We could use a man in the air," Conall said.

"And we have the charms ready to keep him safely out of view," Hunter assured me.

"I feel quite left out," I said, fighting the pout on my lips. "I suppose you decided I won't be any help?"

"You'd be bait if anything, girlie," Conall said, and Hunter let out an immediate growl. "And we can't have that."

I wasn't entirely defenseless, but then again... Jude and I glanced at one another, his eyes wincing. He was free now, able to explore a part of himself he'd kept hidden for most of his life. I was madly jealous and furious with my father, with Mr. Reddy, and with myself too. Hunter and Ronan needed to know the truth about me, and now was not the moment to tell them.

"I'll stay if you'd rather," Ronan offered, speaking softly into my ear. "If I go, you'll need to keep close to Nireas."

I jolted but didn't shout the man's name like I wanted to. "I can stay here and wait—"

"There's not even a decent door on your dressing room, nut," Ronan said. "And I'd put you up in my apartment, but we don't know what we're up against. They might be able to fly too."

"Nireas is safe," Hunter said, with an authority that was as comforting as it was infuriating.

"I can stay," Ronan repeated, a lifeline for me to grab if I wanted it.

I didn't sigh. Nireas might've heard every word we were speaking. It wasn't as if my room was big enough to hold private conversations. "No, go. I've been meaning to speak with him. This will be the right time." And only partly because I had no choice now.

"Yes, it will," Ronan said, lips twitching.

"Conall," Hunter said sharply, nodding toward the door. "Time for us to leave. Jude—"

"Ronan and I will follow," Jude said easily.

Hunter's grip on my waist tugged me free of Ronan, his kiss firm and sweet but far too brief. "Tomorrow night, little one," he growled, and I nodded, my fingers gripping his coat anxiously. *He will be fine*, I told myself. The killer was only a threat to women, as far as we knew. I just missed him.

Hunter slipped away and Ronan turned me toward him next, a sly smile on his lips, glancing at Jude out of the corner of his eyes. "I'll be in the hall, Piper. Give you a moment." But before Jude or I could answer, Ronan's mouth was on mine, his tongue slipping between my parted lips, thrusting playfully and suggestively against my own.

I was breathless as he pulled away, and deeply annoyed with him, although I wasn't sure if it was for the blatant claiming or the fact that he wasn't following through on the kiss. He ducked out into the hall with another quick, smacking kiss on my cheek, and I found myself laughing. Jude's lips were curved in a smile, and it took me a moment to realize we were nearly alone in the room, only Asterion and Nireas behind me now.

He stepped closer and my laugh stilled in my throat, my eyes widening.

"You see how it is," I said, bracing myself.

Jude glanced at the curtain the men had just left through, then back to me. "I do. Was that for the audience, or—"

"You," I whispered. The more honest I was, the harder it was to come up with lies. Not that I wanted to give him one. "On stage. That was for you. And for me."

Jude stepped closer again, and my head tipped back just a bit to meet his gaze. "And if I want more?"

My breath caught. I wanted more too. "Well, that was my plan, but now you've decided to do your job and—"

His kiss was sudden—*that's four in a row*, I thought—and a little rough, abrupt, but I smoothed my lips against his and took his face in my hands to teach him the act. He groaned slightly, and we took turns suckling at each other, tender exchanges that made up for the rush of connection we'd had on stage. His hands searched me and pulled me closer, a slow study.

"The others—" I started as his mouth trailed to my jaw.

"I don't care," he rasped.

"—aren't going anywhere. They're mine."

"I don't care," he repeated, pulling away, smiling, his stare bright and cheeks flushed. "Aside from perhaps the difficulty of finding time with you."

"I'll sort it out," I said.

"At least one private moment," Jude continued, a shocking grin growing on his face. "And then I'll learn to share."

I had no right to blush. Sharing was hardly out of my normal repertoire, and yet the thought of Jude and Ronan and Hunter *sharing* was—

His parting kiss was soft, trailing across my cheek over to my ear. "Thank you."

"We'd better leave now," Asterion announced, and Jude was vanishing out the door like the others, his chin high and shoulders broad, a smile still stretching his cheeks.

Which only left...

I turned and found Nireas sitting on the chaise, two hands gripping his knees, another two the cushion.

"I can stand out in the hall. Keep an eye out so that no one bothers you," he said.

"Are you offering to let me avoid talking to you, or are you no longer as eager to—"

He rose up suddenly, cursing under his breath as his head hit the ceiling, hunching and stepping forward. He was still in his suit, the fitted black sleeves tight around his many arms, long tail resting patiently on the floor behind him. He was a bit of a chimera, this gegenees giant.

"I'm not eager, Hazel. I'm *desperate*. Desperate for you to listen to me, for me to finally quit being such a coward. Desperate to touch you, kiss you, watch you falling apart in my arms again." His voice was torn, agonized, all three eyes pinning me in place with tangible gutting, like he'd just thrust a sword through me, to the wall. "Desperate to apologize, and desperate for you to forgive me. Desperate to know if...if it even matters."

I wet my lips, heart drumming in my chest. Nireas was an old wound, freshly irritated from our time on stage together. A wound that should've healed over and stopped throbbing years ago. It was only a kiss. A kiss and a friendship, a kindness I'd never encountered in my life at that point. My first love.

A speech like that would make any girl swoon, I told myself. But I wasn't swooning. My eyes were stinging and my heart was panging, my hands clenched to fists at my side.

Eight years of silence was the infection that had never allowed me to heal. As much as I wanted to run from Nireas now, it wouldn't make things better.

"It matters," I said.

Nireas let out a heavy breath, his shoulders slumping somewhat, and a hand reached for me.

"Not here. Someone will interrupt," I said, studying him.

He nodded and let his hand drop. "I know where we can go. Will you follow?"

I bit down on my lip, gathering strength, and when I didn't find enough, I pretended there was more there. I was an actress, after all.

&

NIREAS HAD an apartment in the theater, like Ronan's, although his was in the stage right wing. We took a ladder up, the pipes of the organ rising around us like columns, hidden in the walls, and we stopped at a tall but narrow door that Nireas had to walk through sideways.

The ceilings were high and the windows were tall, facing the blank brick wall of a warehouse next door. Nireas lit a small lamp and I stopped still at the entrance, marveling at the room. Ronan's apartment was sort of perfunctory and bare, a landing place for an imp that rarely stopped moving. A nest for sleeping and not much more.

Nireas's was...cozy. Beautiful, actually. There were carpets layered over the floor, and large solid furniture that was clearly well cared for. He had bookshelves stuffed with thin spines and loose papers—music perhaps—and a small piano, ill-suited to his size, pressed to one wall.

"How long have you lived here?" I asked.

"Over sixty years," Nireas said.

He didn't even look sixty years old. He was probably centuries old. A millenia even?

The apartment was his home. The theater was his home.

"Reddy was a stagehand when I came to play the organ," Nireas said, watching me from yards away.

His bed was to the right of him, a structure clearly built for him in mind because it was enormous. Comfortable and simple. He cleared his throat, and I pulled my stare away, looking for anywhere else to sit. A small table with a single seat sat near the window, and the piano bench was to my left.

"I fell in love with a girl my first year here," Nireas said.

I shut the door behind me as the words rang in my ears. So we were starting now—starting with a former love. That bleeding space in my chest throbbed.

"And she left," I said.

"She died, actually."

I froze, my eyes wide, staring back at Nireas.

"She died shortly before you arrived," he said, his smile fragile. "No. It was...a year or more. Short for me. We didn't stay together the whole time, and we weren't lovers at the end. She did get sick of the theater in time. I tried playing human for, but I hated it, stuffing myself into spaces that were too small. But we loved each other through all those years, even if the nature of that love changed over the decades."

Mr. Reddy would've known, but who else? If the woman had left the theater years before—and surely she must have, because she would've been at least eighty by the time she'd died—there wouldn't have been anyone else around long enough to know about her.

"You were still mourning her," I said, thinking of the Nireas I'd known when I'd arrived. Quiet, kind, protective. I'd been smitten, soaking up a tender kind of attention I'd never known before, ripe for falling in love with him. And he'd been suffering a quiet, patient heartbreak.

"I was. I *am*. I will still mourn her," Nireas said, shrugging. "It's no excuse."

"It's a better excuse than I thought you had," I admitted.

He sighed and moved to the bed, arms tangling in front of him as he shook off his jacket and uncuffed his sleeves, an entrancing confusion of limbs moving together familiarly.

"Not for ignoring you, refusing to speak to you. It's not that you remind me of Louise," he said, looking up, two hands unbuttoning the front of his shirt. Was he undressing? No, they stopped halfway down his chest, revealing a glimmer of iridescence that glowed by the lamplight. "It's that I remembered the feeling, that sliding sensation of falling into another person. I felt guilty that it was happening again so soon after she'd died. Mostly, I thought I could stop it, for both our sakes. It's... Hazel, it's such a hard journey," he whispered.

I groaned softly and stomped forward, landing heavily on Nireas's absurdly large and surprisingly soft bed. "You were too late for me."

He reached out with one hand. "I'm sorry."

And maybe it was a mistake, but I scooted back out of reach, deeper onto the bed. "It's not the loss of the romance that hurt me. Or maybe it was, but... You were my *friend*."

"I am your—"

"No." I shook my head, ignoring the way my body wanted to flinch at the same time he did. "No, you *were*. And you broke that. You stopped speaking to me! That's not going to...going to heal quickly."

"I didn't mean for eight years to pass," he said, frowning and twisting to face me. "I was waiting...and then I realized you would be leaving soon, and I'm an idiot, I know that. Because eight years is nothing to me, but—"

"It could've been a year and it would've been just as bad. You withdrew completely! Barely a word. And then suddenly, you *demand* me on stage with you and fuck me—"

"I'm so sorry, Hazel," he rushed out.

I shook my head. "Shut up, you can't be sorry. Not for the— If you apologize for that moment on stage, I'll throttle you to death."

His lips pressed shut, eyes watching me, and I glared down at his hands on the bed. Two of them had absolutely managed to sneak closer to me. I tucked my legs underneath me, widening the space, but what good would it do when I was cornering myself on his bed? What good did I want it to do?

"I have money saved. If you want to leave the theater, it doesn't have to be with Hunter or me. You can have the money, live your own life," Nireas said, eyes widening. "Or settle down with the detective. He could protect you too."

"What?!"

"I don't want you to leave. I'm not saying you *have* to leave. I want the time to make things up to you, to see if you can forgive me, but...but I can't ask you to stay. You've been miserable this past year."

"Not miserable."

"Not happy," he countered quickly.

I'd lived with my father's grip on my wrist my whole life. Telling me I would leave, emotionally cuffing me in place to deny me the privilege. And maybe no one at the theater had forced me to stay. Maybe I'd created that sense of being trapped, chained to the stage, on my own, so used to the idea.

"I would do anything in my power so that you could just feel...free," he breathed.

The words shocked me, so far from the voice I'd grown up with, so far even from the twist of my own thoughts. Sweet, and honest. Why I'd fallen in love with Nireas in the first place, because yes, he had been the first and most fragile of them. I wasn't forgiving him for eight years of cold silence. Not yet. He couldn't be my friend again until that was fixed, but it didn't stop me from needing him in this moment in a visceral and painful way. As much as the ancient wound hurt, so did staying in this tiny corner of an enormous bed, with a man I...loved reaching out to me when I so badly wanted to be touched.

Nireas gasped as I threw myself forward, but his arms were ready, snapping around me and clutching me to his chest, toppling us down into the mattress.

32.

IN HARMONY

The kiss was slow and thorough, our tongues twisting, thrusting, not teasing but feasting. Eight years of avoiding one another had only been eight years of denying each other what we'd wanted from the start, and I'd had such a small and shocking taste on the stage.

I wanted more.

I wanted to see him.

Nireas's busy hands made short work of my robe, twin grips on my ass eager and drawing me up to press to his hips. My legs twined around his waist, and he was huge and heavy, having to hunch over me to hold the kiss. He let me turn us over on the bed until I was on top, two of his hands cupping my face, two cupping my ass, and the other two arms splayed out on the pale blue sheets.

I sat up and stared down at him, a flicker of panic flashing over his features until my hands moved to the remainder of his buttons.

"We don't have to—" Nireas started.

"Are you going to deny me anything after eight years?" I asked, a low blow, but an effective one.

He gaped up at me and then shook his head. "Nothing."

I finished with his buttons, shoving the shirt back, twisting to let the light strike his chest. His skin was a vivid green sheen with a glittering rainbow shifting over his muscles as he caught his breath. He sat up with the smallest tug from me, and I threw my robe back on the floor as he pulled his arms free of his sleeves.

The pair of limbs at his shoulders were the thickest, the arms just under those slightly more sinewy. I lowered my head to his shoulder, found a surprisingly soft and fresh scent on his skin. His back arms reached around, grabbing at my bare waist and hauling me closer. I was still wearing lacy drawers and garters, but I'd taken the corset off the first chance I had, and Nireas lifted a hand to one bare breast, cupping it as he stared up at me.

His hair was short and black, shaved close at his sides, and I ran my fingers through the bristles. His three eyes hooded as I drew his face to my chest, sighing as he licked and kissed and wrapped his mouth around my nipple. His tongue swirled, laved, lips puckering and pulling away with a wet *pop!*

"You could have any of us you wanted," Nireas whispered.

"And if I intend to have you all?" I asked, not even considering the words. They came naturally, encouraged by Hunter, and Ronan now too. Even Jude.

Nireas's tongue flicked my nipple again, and I shivered and then moaned as a heavy, thick tail, ridged and scaled, stroked the backs of my legs, wrapping around my thighs and tugging me down so I was pressed firmly over Nireas's rising erection.

"That's probably for the best. With four of us, we'll be less likely to make stupid decisions," Nireas said.

Which was almost certainly the opposite of what was likely.

"Five," I corrected as he moved to the other breast, his kisses and my slow grind over his lap putting me in a hazy, aroused state where my tongue was too loose.

Nireas paused in his work, fingertips twisting my nipples and drawing a bright cry from my lips. "Oh! Five, seven, however you count the Gemini. I see. He's wrong about the act. I would play music that made the pair of you even more—"

He hissed as I grabbed the roots of his hair and yanked. "Focus on *me*," I snarled.

But when I looked down, the smiling face I saw was so familiar, it took my breath away. I hadn't seen Nireas smile like that in years.

"That's been a personal habit of mine for *years*, Hazel," Nireas said.

And then he was flipping us easily on the bed, pinning me down, his mouth back to work on my throat and down to my breasts, teeth and tongue dragging over my ribs. I grabbed his shoulders and arched into that hunting mouth, my eyes falling shut on a sigh. Tonight's show had been exhilarating, and I hadn't been the focus for once. My blood had simmered in my veins for hours, then kissed to a frenzy by the others before they left. And Nireas had been a fantasy I'd coveted for too long.

He can be my lover without being my friend, I told myself.

He stood and my eyes opened, but I was too stunned by the sight of him to speak. I'd never seen him nude before. He looked more enormous than ever. More handsome and monstrous too. Black scales framed his hips and covered his shins, matching his long, dark tail. The iridescence over his arms and shoulders glowed in the light, surrounding him with a blazing halo. Beautifully inhuman, I decided.

And my god, that cock was enormous. It suited him, he was a giant after all, but the girth alone left me breathless. Or it would.

"Come here," I said.

He knelt on the bed, and I spread my thighs wide.

"Did I hurt you before?" he asked, frowning.

I shook my head. "You were perfect. It made me angry how good you felt inside of me. I've been thinking about it all—"

Nireas cut me short with another deep, probing kiss. Two fingers pushed inside me, his thumb circling my clit gently, and I moaned around his tongue. He only toyed with me long enough to make sure I was slick and desperate before nudging at my opening with his tip. I found his hips with my hands, drew him closer, and caught my breath as he pulled his mouth from mine, his gaze dark and fixed.

"The way you fit me feels like madness," Nireas whispered, sinking easily and slowly into my cunt.

"Yes," I agreed, or encouraged. "Yes, Nireas."

He arched down to kiss me and fuck me at the same time, but he didn't complain as his mouth found mine, our moans echoing together. This *was* like madness—it felt that way with the others too. Madness and relief and still the ache of a healing injury, a fresh bruise. Still tender, almost uncomfortable, but I couldn't stop myself from pressing it, making it hurt just a bit.

I was gasping and I couldn't breathe, rocking myself up into Nireas. His hands were everywhere, each one doing more work for me than an average man's effort in bed, massaging my breasts, tugging on my hair, rubbing and rolling my clit. Pausing their torture to wrap all six around my body and hold me so tight against him, our heartbeats struck through our chest to hammer at one another.

"If you walk away from me again, I will cut your tail off," I cried out as he shifted, drawing my hips higher, stroking deeper inside of me until my throat was tight and my pulse pounded in time with his rhythm.

"I swear I won't," Nireas gasped. "I can't. I can't now, Hazel."

I keened as he kissed my throat, a pair of arms tying around my back as the others went back to their busy work of stroking and gripping and fondling. My cheek ended up over his heart-beat, an urgent percussion in my ear. His grunts were strained above my head, hands still working to take me with him. And he would. I was already there at the edge, fighting my own finish, as if I might steal it back from him, refuse us both the satisfaction.

I dug my nails into his shoulders, the only punishment for our time apart I could think of, and then rewarded him as I clamped down on his length, moaning into his hard, glimmering skin, shuddering and riding him through a desperate finish.

He was trembling slightly above me as I settled, and I turned my face to see one of his hands clenched hard in the bedding. He hadn't finished. He was holding himself back.

"What are you doing?" I asked, arching and blinking up at him.

He pushed himself slowly up to hover above me, flexing his hips and making me shake with a flutter of hot aftershocks.

"I rushed the first time," he said, jaw flexing as he shifted inside of me again, testing both our responses. "I want this time to last. I want you slick with sweat and begging for rest. And I deserve to wait for my own release."

I licked my lips, half-tempted to prove how easy it would be to take him down with me. But there was no cue to meet, no audience waiting for the climax of our scene. And Nireas was right—he owed me.

"Pay your penance then, Nireas," I said.

He nodded, brow furrowed around his top eye, and started a slow, steady rhythm that made my toes curl in the sheets.

MUCH LATER, after we were both slick with effort and release and I'd pleaded for rest—a few tears tucked carefully into Nireas's shoulder—our bodies went still and languid. He was warm enough to curl up with on top of the covers, his arms covering much of my back and ass and thighs.

"I don't want to leave the theater," I said slowly, before exhaustion and limp satisfaction could pull me to sleep. "Not yet. And if I am with Hunter, or Jude, or you, or by myself, it won't have anything to do with that decision."

Nireas was still, frozen, holding his breath.

"I haven't been happy here until...quite recently, but that's to do with me, not you or Reddy or anyone else," I continued.

"I hurt you," Nireas said.

"You did. You were hurting. I'm not forgiving you for how you handled your feelings, but...eight years was brief for you and long for me. You weren't the only man to disappoint me in all that time. And I've been living with someone else's rules in my head."

"Mr. Reddy's?"

I snorted, although maybe that was almost true. "No. My father's. He wasn't a happy man. I don't think he wanted me happy either. But I *would* like to be."

"I want you happy."

And even if Nireas and I weren't solved, I was grateful to him for saying that. I kissed his throat and he sighed, one hand aimlessly stroking the back of my head and my shoulders.

"We'll see you happy," Nireas said softly.

I hummed, not sure if he meant me and him, or him and the others. It could wait until morning. I was tired now, and Nireas was warm and had worn me out. Peace had to be stolen lately, and I was all too eager to take some for myself now.

&a.

I DREAMT I had wings of shadow, spread out under the bright stage lights. I dreamt of claws on my fingertips and the flesh of men scratching themselves on my touch. I dreamt I had a bright set of fangs and tough scales and a long, playful tail.

I dreamt I was a monster, and when I woke, I found one of Nireas's pillows soaked with my own tears.

Nireas and Ronan said they wanted to see me happy. Hunter loved that I'd accepted every part of him. I wanted that too. And I knew it wasn't my lovers who were holding me back from having all of that and more.

Nireas protested as I tried to rise from the bed, his top eye blinking open. "Don't go," he whispered.

As far as Nireas knew, we were running out of time together. I would age like his human lover, we would grow apart, and I would die. How much time did he think he had left with me?

"I'll come back," I said, ducking down and kissing the top of his forehead above his third eye.

He huffed a sleepy breath but didn't untangle his arms, and it took me a few minutes of gently maneuvering him and untwisting his tail from around my right leg before I was free. There was sunlight bouncing off the warehouse wall outside the window, enough to assure me it was late morning.

My stockings were torn—probably from Nireas's tail—and the room was far too chilly for just my robe, so I stole one of Nireas's shirts and tied the extra arms around my body to fashion something like a short, fitted dress. I found a pair of massive wool socks under a chair, then slipped out of the room and into the rib cage of the theater, a narrow spiral staircase leading my way around the organ pipes and back down into the wings.

The underbelly of the theater was already thrumming with life, the canteen full of chatter with everyone more or less living together in the building. Mr. Reddy's office door was cracked open, and I approached it with shuffling steps, pausing outside just long enough to hear murmurs of a gentle conversation.

I knocked, and Reddy called me in. Myra was sitting on his lap, their arms twined around one another, her head on his shoulder. There was a bittersweet contentment between them, a familiar gentle pain in the air as I entered, and Myra slid off Reddy's lap with his arms dropping reluctantly to his side.

"I've told him already," Myra said, shooting a sullen glare at me out of the corner of her eyes.

The money she'd been collecting, I recalled. It'd only been days, and yet it felt like ages since we'd spoken.

"That's not why I'm here," I said. Reddy didn't look angry, and I refused to feel sorry for Myra.

"Get something to eat, Missy," Reddy said, patting Myra's bottom, a heavy sigh shifting his broad frame.

Myra and I passed without another word, and I landed heavily in the spare chair in front of Mr. Reddy.

"What is it then?" he asked, not unkindly, but with all the weight of a man who had too much on his plate and was afraid of another helping.

"You can fire me if you want, but I'm sick of keeping my mother a secret," I blurted out. The door was still hanging open, and I had a jittery thrill at the idea of someone overhearing us.

"Your mother," Reddy repeated, blank confusion washing over his face.

I flushed. We'd had the single conversation almost a decade ago regarding my heritage. Had he *forgotten*?

"That I'm..." *Say it! Just say it!*

"Oh!" he recalled with a shake of his head. He frowned at me, and I braced myself for the fight. "I'm not firing you, Nix. I'm not even sure what we're going to do when you leave."

"If I leave," I said.

Mr. Reddy blinked at me, tensed in his seat, and the keen, beady look he got when he thought of money and business and asses in seats took him over. "'If,' you say?"

You've been a fool, I thought to myself. Eight years ago, I was a novice at sex, new to the theater, and I'd needed my job more than Reddy needed me. How long had it been since the opposite became true? I was the girl who could take a centaur. A giant. Who could be tortured with pain and pleasure and walk away with a smile on her face. The Company of Fiends needed *me*.

"I haven't made my mind up yet."

"You don't like the orc?"

"Hunter is wonderful and I plan on staying with him as long as he wants me to, but he doesn't mind my work here at the theater. Most of the time, I don't either. But there are people I care about here and I'm sick of lying to them. Or feeling as though half of me is meant to be a dirty little secret," I said, gripping the arms of the chair I sat in.

Mr. Reddy's lips pursed. "You're not an attainable goal for our entire audience when you're something so rare."

It was almost flattering, but he hadn't meant it to be and I scowled back at him. "I'm not asking you to put it on the marquee. I'm telling you that I'm going to talk to Ronan and Nireas and—"

"You haven't yet?" Mr. Reddy asked, eyes wide.

I gaped back at him.

"You're the only woman I've met who can keep a secret," Reddy said, then huffed and growled. "No, I suppose that's not true now. Myra managed it well enough till you caught her."

"Are you saying you don't care?" I asked, breathless.

He blinked at me and then shrugged. "It's your personal relationships you're talking about, not your business ones. And hell, two weeks ago, I thought we'd never sell shows where human girls were leading monsters about on a leash, but the crowd went wild. Maybe I'm wrong about us halflings too."

I sucked in a rough breath and let it out slowly, staring hard at Mr. Reddy's heavy, leather-bound ledger, wondering how much damage I might manage if I beat him over the head with it. But he was right. I'd kept the secret as much out of habit, and the fear my father'd instilled in me, as I had because Reddy told me to.

Because my father had been unable to love me. He'd blamed my mother's blood, and thus so had I, when really it was his own fault.

"Maybe you are," I said in a small voice.

"A few more girls and boys like you, and we'd have quite a pretty show on our hands," Reddy mused. "You're not leaving?"

"Not yet," I said, blinking, my eyes drifting aimlessly somewhere north of his head as my thoughts spun.

"That's a boon, Nix. You don't know how glad I am to hear it. And I'll tell you what. Think of another clever theme, a few more standing ovation acts, and I *will* put it up on the marquee," Reddy said. He was leaning back in his chair, his pointed boots rising up to rest his heels on his desk, and the gears were turning in his head. Damn. Now if I wasn't quick, he'd spread the news before I got a chance to talk to my men.

Money-minded, miserly bastard.

"Are you angry with Myra?" I asked.

Mr. Reddy stared back at me with his hard, calculating gaze. He could easily lie to me one way or the other. He didn't. "I'm mad I didn't think of it first."

I snorted and pushed my chair back. I needed to tell Nireas. No, Ronan should be first. Or Hunter? Perhaps it would be best to gather all three of them together at once.

"If you make money off us, we get a cut, you unscrupulous twat," I said. "And not *me*. I work on the stage, and that's it. The rest is selfish."

"You're selfish on the stage too," Mr. Reddy said with a laugh, but he nodded in agreement. "S'pose your evenings are already spoken for anyway."

I certainly hoped they would be. I waved my hand at him as I turned for the door.

"You're a good girl, Hazel Nix. You deserve the lot of them, and however many more that please you."

"Five should do the trick, I'd think," I huffed. But I grinned at Mr. Reddy over my shoulder as I opened the door wide. "And a raise, perhaps."

"Out!" he barked, but I heard him laughing as I hurried down the hall.

33.

THE WEIGHT OF A BURDEN

Nireas took the invasion of his apartment fairly well. Hunter, Jude, and Ronan arrived at the theater just as I returned upstairs, freshly dressed and mulling over my conversation with Mr. Reddy. I'd grabbed them impulsively, dragging them after me.

"Are we having an orgy?" Ronan asked as we headed up the stairs.

"Don't get me wrong, I'm intrigued, but I haven't slept in ages and I wouldn't mind being alone with our girl for the first proper time," Jude muttered from the back of the line.

"A conversation," I said crisply.

"Not as much fun," Ronan said, then paused and asked, "A conversation about the orgy?"

I heard a smack and Ronan's hissing laughter, and I figured it was Hunter who'd thumped him for his remarks. I would thank him later.

And I would apologize to Nireas later for bursting through the door while he was still sleeping, with three men in tow. He glared at us, face still pressed to his pillow, and then groaned and rolled over onto his back, sheet barely covering his hips. I stared at him in the hazy morning light, the shifting colors of his skin softer and paler, his hair rumpled, a bite mark I'd left on his chest clearly visible.

He'd denied me this for eight years? I was angry all over again.

"Put on pants," I snapped.

His eyebrows rose, and I regretted my order as he sat up slowly, muscles flexing and skin shimmering. As if one pair of strong arms wasn't distracting enough. I paced to the window before he stood from the bed.

"I don't mind, exactly, but I'm not sure my bed is big enough for all of you," Nireas said, and Ronan laughed.

It was Jude who followed me to the window, who rested a hand on my back and waited for me to look up to meet his gaze. It was one thing to tell Mr. Reddy that I was going to let them know. He already knew the truth about me. Jude knew. Even Constantine knew. But I'd never actually had to confess the words to someone who might be surprised by them.

Jude's smile was soft, his pale eyes skimming over my face.

"Hazel?" Hunter called. "What's wrong, little one?"

Jude knew why I'd brought them here. He nodded at me. "You won't regret it," he whispered.

I swallowed hard and turned to face them. Nireas was buttoning up his pants, Ronan had already helped himself to the chair at the round table in the center of the room, and Hunter was still standing by the door, waiting for some explanation of my sudden demand for an audience.

I swallowed again. It was a simple thing to say. Just a handful of words, but they seemed to cling to my teeth like they were trying to fight their way back down my throat. I spat them out in a clumsy rush.

"My mother was a wood nymph."

Jude's hand stroked my back, trying to soothe me through the way I coiled up with tension, my eyes bouncing between the three other men. They wore similar expressions of empty shock. Not horror, or anger, or anything so illuminating that it might give me some idea of what they were thinking or how they were feeling. Just flat, open surprise.

"My father was never very forthcoming with the details. But he had a farm near a forest, and he met her there, and...I suppose she seduced him, or vice versa, and then...then she left me at his door," I said.

"You just found out?" Ronan asked, the question painfully sincere.

My cheeks were hot and my mouth opened and closed on nothing, his eyebrows rising in understanding.

"Hazelnut...why?" he asked, leaning forward.

"It was always a secret!" I cried, shaking myself and trying to gather back my calm. Jude's hand squeezed on my shoulder. "Obviously, living with my father, I had to pretend to be human. He thought he could hide me here in the city. But after he died and I came here, Reddy said not to say—"

"Bastard," Ronan growled.

"That monsters wanted *humans*, and I was so used to just... hiding it. Lying. And then I suddenly realized how much I hated that, and how miserable I was becoming because of it, and..." I hiccuped and blinked. My face was wet. How embarrassing.

I rubbed the tears off my face and squared my shoulders, catching my breath and shaking my head. "I never told anyone who didn't already know. It's been just buried inside of me for almost forty years."

"Forty," Nireas gasped. He stumbled back, sitting roughly onto his bed, and I winced.

"Oh. Yes. Thirty-eight to be precise, although that's been a secret too," I said softly.

Hunter's gaze was warm on me, studying, impossible to decipher. Ronan looked bowled over once again, and Nireas was shockingly pale as the obvious sank in. I wasn't aging like a human woman. I wouldn't age like one.

I pressed Jude's hand on my shoulder and then left him at the window, crossing and kneeling in front of Nireas.

"I'm sorry, I didn't know," I whispered to him. My aging would've almost certainly been a fear for him after losing his last lover, and the glassy cast of his gaze confirmed as much.

"I'm twice the fool now," he answered numbly, blinking at me. "I should've realized. You haven't changed. I thought I was being romantic, but... Fuck. Hazel."

Six arms snapped around my back, drawing me into Nireas's grasp, his face pressed between my breasts. I stroked over his head, down to the tops of his arms and back again as he shuddered.

"This is why Reddy gives you all the roughest guest acts. The hardest jobs," Ronan bit out.

"Better me than the other girls," I recited gently, and Nireas's arms tightened.

"Bullshit," Ronan snapped. "That's his excuse. Don't make it yours."

I flinched at Ronan's tone, and Hunter let out a low growl. "There's no need to be angry."

"I'm not angry! No." Ronan cleared his throat and huffed. "I'm not angry with *you*, nut."

Nireas loosened his hold, his face rising and lips brushing over my cheek. I turned, and he settled me on his lap, facing the others. My hands twisted in my skirt. Nireas was relieved. That was one good thing. The others...

Ronan pushed himself out of the chair and crossed to me with his wings rustling in agitation. "I'm an idiot for not thinking of it sooner," he said, sighing. He bent, hands around the crown of my head, and kissed my hair.

"You don't mind?" I whispered, that ancient comment of Mr. Reddy's squirming in the back of my thoughts.

"Mind?" Ronan barked.

"Now I'm angry," Nireas mumbled, but a pair of his hands rubbed my hips gently.

"I don't know. I mean, there are houses and theaters meant for monsters to enjoy humans, right?" I asked, a fluttery panic rising in my chest. "And I am, but I'm—"

"Enough."

Hunter's command was familiar and final, making my teeth snap shut with a clack, and he marched over to the bed. Jude smiled at me from where he watched by the window.

Gentle black claws clasped my chin, lifting it to stare up at Hunter's stern face. "You haven't changed. Why would our feelings for you change?"

Warmth pooled in my cheeks and washed slowly down into my chest and my belly. I shook my head, unable to answer his question, blinking back the tears that tried to rise again.

"They won't," he said for me.

"There are plenty of places in our world where monsters are

falling in love with and chasing after other monsters. Where it's only fae with fae, or satyrs desperate to catch nymphs, or vampires lusting after werewolves," Ronan said with a shrug. "Reddy's a shit, and he knows less than dirt about love."

I squirmed at the word *love*, and Hunter grinned down at me.

"I find your news illuminating and full of potential," Hunter said, a rough hunger in the gravel of his voice. His claw scratched my cheek and Ronan smirked, glancing between us.

"I find it a relief," Nireas said in a gust, his lips landing against the back of my neck.

"I've just realized you're seven years older than me," Ronan said, grinning. "I always knew I liked older women."

I rolled my eyes and relaxed in Nireas's arms, a kind of soft lethargy rolling over me that I usually only knew from a post-sex high.

"You're tired, little one. Rest here, and we'll discuss this more tonight after your performance," Hunter said, and this time, the pad of his thumb ran the same line over my cheek as his claw had. "But *know* with absolutely every fiber of truth that no detail of your birth or parentage could ever change my devotion to you. You have given me *everything* I've wished for. I intend to do the same for you."

The words were too much. They made me want to burrow into the mattress and hide away. They also made me want to stretch under the force of the praise, bathe in it like a cat in sunshine. Hunter bent his head, grazed a simple kiss with a flick of tongue over my lips, and stood straight, smiling down at me. I unwound under his warm stare, curling up, and Ronan and Hunter stepped back, allowing Nireas to settle me into the bed.

"You'll be here for the show, won't you?" I asked Hunter.

"I believe it's my turn on stage tonight, if Mr. Piper doesn't mind," Hunter said.

Nireas's pillows were warm, and Jude approached the bed. "I don't mind."

"Do you know how to fly?" Ronan asked Jude.

I smiled at the boyish wonder on Jude's face. He looked so much younger without that silly bowler hat and heavy coat. More fae too, beautiful and otherworldly.

"I've never had a chance to try," Jude said.

"Come downstairs and we'll give it a go," Ronan offered.

I yawned and blinked at all of them. "Constantine knows too. He guessed," I said.

Nireas petted down my side and then pulled a sheet up over my hips. "You're wearing my socks," he noticed.

"They're warm."

"I've been meaning to speak with the demon. I'll find him," Hunter said. He arched over me, kissing my brow gently, nuzzling the spot so his tusks bumped my skin. "Keep her company, Nireas."

Nireas stretched out at my back, two arms over my side. "Gladly."

Jude crouched in front of the bed, our hands linking eagerly at the edge of the mattress. "Nice, isn't it?"

My smile was watery as I nodded. I stretched up and he met me in the kiss, lips soft and eager and sweet. "Steal me away tomorrow?" I murmured.

He kissed me once more, lingering until I realized I'd forgotten to breathe, and I gasped as he pulled away. "Tomorrow," he said.

Nireas waited until the door shut behind Jude before tugging me and turning me over in the bed to face him. He was still a little pale, his eyes wide, their sharp green almost electric.

"Are you all right?" I asked.

"I feel like an idiot. Like Ronan said, why didn't we realize? I've known you for eight years."

"You've been keeping your distance," I reminded him, softening the words by stroking my hands over his bare chest. Or maybe that was for my own benefit. It was a very nice chest. I reached up and tucked my hair behind my ear, the gesture strange and unfamiliar. I usually made sure my hair covered my ears. I turned my head, and Nireas was quiet for a moment before sucking in a quick breath. "I don't even remember it. Pa probably had it done as soon as he could find someone who wouldn't ask too many questions."

I shivered as Nireas leaned in, kissing the top of my ear

where a scar so old it was barely noticeable shimmered faintly on my skin.

"If I'd known..." He shook his head, and I smiled at him as he leaned back.

"You were still freshly heartbroken," I said.

"Maybe just four years, then," he said roughly, frowning.

I covered the expression with a kiss, Nireas's arms drawing me in close. Damnit. Maybe I did forgive him. Maybe I didn't care either way. He knew. They all knew now.

"I don't know how long I'll live," I murmured, tucking my face into his throat.

"I don't care. Eight years, five hundred. It's not going to hurt less later, and I want every minute of it," Nireas whispered. "I wasted enough of them already."

This wasn't the wild celebration Jude had on the stage the night before. This was quiet and private, and somehow a little sad too. My body was heavy, as if the battle of keeping my secret was now lifted, and I was twice as weary and limp in my victory. I didn't fall asleep, although Nireas was humming something sweet—the song he'd played the night of our performance—and his arms cradled me perfectly.

I lay in the hazy light of the comfortable apartment for a long time, an hour or more, listening to that song and thinking about the future I might have. And when my eyelids did grow heavy, my muscles giving up completely and demanding rest, I heard Nireas's whisper against my ear.

"Sleep, nymph."

34.

BREAKFAST AND CARRIAGE RIDES

I stretched in Hunter's bed the next morning, a gleeful groan echoing in the large room as I admired the ache and strain of my body. My orc had been holding back. I stroked an aimless hand up my ribs and over one breast, delicately testing the marks his tusks had left on me, just shy of breaking the flesh. There would be pretty twin bruises decorating me now, playful bite marks creating a pattern of passion. Ronan would have to help me cover them up for the stage. I giggled, already imagining all his jealous griping.

A soft knock on the door stilled my hands, and I tugged the sheet up and tried to tame the copper nest of hair on my head. Hunter had already left for the morning, and I vaguely recalled a gently growled promise of a surprise.

"Come in," I called, expecting Hunter's butler.

The door opened slowly, and I kept my sheet in place as I sat up at the sight of the heavily laden breakfast tray. But it was Jude and not the butler at all who stepped into the room, and my hand on the sheet slipped as I gasped. He stopped in place, staring back at me, and dishes rattled on the tray as one of his own hands started to drop. He caught it quickly, sky blue eyes blinking.

"I..."

There wasn't much I found more flattering than a man who failed to recall his own powers of speech when he looked at me, and I took my time in drawing the sheet up again and tucking it under my arms.

"Brought me breakfast?" I suggested gently.

Jude cleared his throat, then glanced out the door as if looking for backup. He let out a small puffing laugh and shook his head, nudging the door shut with his foot and then crossing to me. He was dressed in light, clean clothing, that heavy black coat that disguised his wings gone, and as he stepped into a ray of sunlight I saw them slightly shuttered at his back.

"I can't decide if I should ask you to take mercy on me and dress, or if I'd rather burn all your clothing to make sure you don't," Jude said, settling at the edge of the bed and putting the tray down between us.

I laughed and slid out from under the sheet, holding Jude's wide gaze as I moved to the armoire, where my robe was hanging over the door. I put it on slowly, turning on my toes to give him a good view, before finally tying it around my waist.

"Better?" I asked, returning to the bed.

Jude swallowed and cleared his throat, but his voice still came out in a growl. "Not exactly."

I grinned, ignoring the fabric of my robe as I crawled forward on my knees toward him, knowing it would reveal plenty of skin as I moved. "You don't have to resist, you know."

His eyes were growing black, but he reached out and stopped me with a firm hand on my thigh. "I don't...but I have something of a plan for us today, and if I'm going to get you back to the theater for the show, we'll have to behave...this morning."

I sat back on my heels and reached for a piece of toast. "That's intriguing enough to pause my seduction, I suppose. Are we going somewhere?"

"We are."

I raised my eyebrows. "But you won't tell me where?"

"You won't have long to wait," Jude said, shrugging and lifting a bite of sausage up on his fork, arching an eyebrow. "Provided you don't dawdle."

"And whose idea was it for you to bring me breakfast?" I asked.

"Hunter's," Jude said, glancing up at me. "Do you mind?"

"Not at all. But I'm beginning to realize that some of my men are a bit high-handed."

"Consider it a testament to the inspiration you provide."

"Inspiration? Am I inspiring you, sir?" I teased him as I sat forward, the robe slipping and gaping at the collar, Jude's stare falling eagerly into the shadows.

He had his legs crossed, but it wasn't enough to hide his arousal. "You're very cheerful this morning."

"I was very well-bedded last night," I purred. "I could be very well-bedded again."

Jude's cheeks were flushed and he glared at me, picking up a strawberry and trying to stuff it between my lips. I nipped his fingers, and he groaned and stood up from the bed, pacing along the edge as I laughed.

"You must be very proud of your plan," I said.

"It'll be worth the torture," he agreed, taking a deep breath to control himself.

I shouldn't have provoked him. It was fairly obvious to me he hadn't had many occasions to indulge in physical desire. Not if he'd had to hide those wings.

"I had no idea what a relief it would be to tell them," I said, rearranging my robe and returning to my food.

Jude sighed and settled back on the bed. "I had no idea what a joy it would be to actually feel...fae. Anything of my father, really. And since you gave that to me, I'd like to do the same for you."

I tipped my head and tried to fight my smirk. "I believe I've explored my nymph qualities quite thoroughly on stage. And we could certainly do the same in the bed."

This time, it was Jude who looked smug. "Maybe. But let's see if I can't surprise you. Eat your breakfast and dress. If you try and tempt me any more, I'll have to go downstairs and wait for you in the carriage Hunter has left for us."

I opened my mouth to do exactly that, and Jude raised an eyebrow, challenging me. Fine, better to behave and find out what surprise he had in store. I grabbed a piece of bacon and smiled angelically back.

❧

FED, washed, and dressed, and an hour later, we were in the carriage. I made a few wicked suggestions of how we might pass the time, mostly to rile Jude up, but he tangled our fingers together and found the words to derail me completely.

"Tell me about your father."

My breath was deep and rough and I twisted away, staring out the carriage window, as if I could erase the request by ignoring it. Jude didn't say anything else, just sat in the quiet of the ride as we wound our way through the streets of London. He didn't retract the words, didn't add to them, didn't apologize. It wasn't a demand, but it tugged at me like one until it was a pounding refrain in my head, a story begging to be let out, exorcized from me.

And if I would tell anyone, Jude would be the one.

"My entire life, every day, he told me I would leave. That it was in my blood to run like my mother," I said at last. And once those words were spoken, so many more wanted to follow. I sighed, turned back, and let my knees hit Jude's. I rested my head on his shoulder, and his thumb stroked at the back of my hand. "I wanted to. So badly. Every second of every day, I wanted to run from him. And I refused to, because she had run from me, and I wanted to be anything but like her."

Jude *hmm'd*, his cheek resting against the top of my head. "You wanting to run had more to do with him than with her."

I nodded. "I know that now. I'm still scared I'll run, and I'm still terrified that I might not when I ought to. I don't want to prove him right."

"That doesn't mean he deserves to have any influence over your decisions now," Jude said.

It was true, of course. I knew that. "He didn't want me," I said in a small voice. "I think I made a romance out of them when I was a little girl, but when I think about them now...he was barely twenty and just out of the army. He met a nymph in the woods, and I don't know if he chased her or she offered herself up willingly, but...it was just sex for them, wasn't it? It wasn't love. And then I appeared on his doorstep."

"There are no excuses, Hazel," Jude whispered.

Weren't there? Maybe not. I didn't know. "You're right. I need to carve his voice out of my head," I said.

"It takes time." Jude turned his face, kissed the top of my head. "All my life, my mother told me my father was an angel or a prince, that I was a blessing, even as she struggled to feed us both, to find us somewhere to live when it was so clear I was a bastard. I could never reconcile her words to what I knew was true. My father burdened my mother with my birth."

It was my turn to offer comfort, and I curled into Jude's side, wrapped an arm over his waist, and listened with the same quiet patience he'd offered me. It had been an even exchange between us since the beginning, a perfect balancing of scales.

"I had to do everything I could to be that blessing, to make her life easier," Jude said. "But...sometimes, I just wanted to prove the truth to her. My father had taken advantage of a girl and then left her with the consequences of his actions." He paused and then whispered in my ear, "I'm sixty-eight, by the way."

I snorted and slapped his chest lightly. "Old man!"

"Spinster," he answered, chuckling.

We rested in the quiet of the carriage. It was sunny out, and the houses were thinning into smaller neighborhoods, estates, and parks.

"We are proof that the two worlds we are made of refuse to fit together," I said softly.

"Perhaps," Jude said, shrugging. "Some bridges take time."

I sighed and nodded, then gently extracted myself from Jude's embrace. He blinked, leaning back against the leather cushions of the carriage, watching and waiting for whatever I said next. I'd never expected to find the truth so easy to share in my life, and with Jude, it was getting more and more natural to let the words spill free.

"I've spent all my years at the theater trying to train myself not to fall in love," I admitted.

His brow furrowed slightly, but he kept his tone neutral. "And now you feel you can't?"

I huffed a sigh, wrinkled my nose, and held his stare as I answered. "And now I'm frustrated by how easy it still is."

Jude's smile was gentle, and so were his hands as he pulled me closer. I arched and met his lips, studying him briefly as his eyes shut and his face smoothed. My own eyes fell shut as his tongue licked at my mouth, begging entrance, which I offered eagerly. When I grew greedy for more, trying to suck that tongue and wiggling myself closer, he pulled away with a laugh.

"Oh no, you don't. We're too close to the destination now for you to disrupt my control."

"We really need to get you more in touch with your monstrous side. Less of this human nobility, if you please," I said, grinning as he laughed, all of the somber detective vanishing from his expression. He was incandescently beautiful.

"You know there are others," I said, biting my lip.

He blinked at me and then realized my meaning. "Of course I know. You said and I've noticed. I've met them. I don't care."

I nodded and relaxed, then realized he was debating something in his head, his eyes drifting around the carriage.

"Tell me," I prompted, tapping a finger on his chest. "If it bothers you, *please*, tell me."

"It doesn't. Honestly. I just... How does it all...go with so many of them?" he asked. "In sex."

I laughed, and Jude's arms circled my waist as I melted into giggles. "I mean, I have some ideas, but we haven't gotten that far yet."

"It just seems like an awful lot of work for one person," he said.

"Are you offering to help?" I teased.

But his cheeks pinked and his eyes ducked. "Maybe. With some of them."

Ronan and Jude were getting along, I'd noticed. Flying lessons and hunting the killer together. This opened up a sudden, delicious world of possibilities.

I kissed Jude again before he could worry. "I'd be *more* than happy to accept that help," I whispered, nuzzling his ear, grinning at his pant of breath. I tried to slip my hand on his chest down to his groin, but he caught me before I could succeed.

"Don't make me handcuff you," he said, then groaned as my eyes lit up.

"Oh, but that's such a lovely—Mph!" I softened in the kiss, and moaned as the carriage came to a stop. Jude pulled away grinning.

"Finally," he gasped, shaking himself loose of me and pushing the door open.

I opened my mouth to tease him again for running away from me, when the lush and damp air of the woods rushed into the carriage and filled my lungs. Outside the carriage was a dense woods, quiet and misty and filled with birdsong.

Jude stood at the door, hand extended to help me down. "Ready?"

Not at all, I thought, but I accepted his hand.

35.

WOOD NYMPH

"Are we on someone's estate?" I whispered, although it was hardly worth trying to keep quiet with all the underbrush crunching under my boots.

"Asterion's," Jude said.

"Oh!" I looked around, following the lead of Jude's hand. "It's so wild. I can't see a house anywhere."

"It has a charmed boundary as well, to keep any humans from wandering in. He lets weres and other monsters use it," Jude said. "Hunter helped me arrange it for us."

My cheeks were starting to hurt from all the smiling. "When did the pair of you find all this time to plot together?"

"Yesterday, while you were resting with Nireas," Jude said, smiling over his shoulder.

"And tromping through the woods is the best you could come up with?" I didn't mean it, and Jude didn't take me seriously. I was practically jogging to keep up with him, my boots already muddy and my new light skirt possibly ruined. But I was beaming, my face almost constantly tipped up to breathe in the fresh air, to feel the sun dappling over my cheeks through the branches.

"Here we are."

My eyes were shut, trusting Jude as my guide, and sunlight stroked over my relaxed features as he spoke. I blinked into the glare of the rays, lowering my chin. We were standing at the edge of a good-sized clearing, a stream running through the woods on the other side of the grass. There was a red wool blanket spread out just in front of us, and another picnic basket from Hunter.

Jude released my hand, and kicked his shoes off and shed his jacket. His wings were hazy at his back, just barely visible as they blended into his own shadow cast on the grass. He sat down on the blanket, his bare feet oddly arousing, a strangely intimate sight. I watched, mesmerized by his beauty, as he rolled his shirt-sleeves up his forearms and leaned back, ankles crossed.

"Are you coming?" he asked, lips an enticing curve as he waited, all long limbs and elegant features.

I sat down on the red blanket, and Jude helped with my boots before I could even ask. "Tell me your plan," I said.

Jude set my boots carefully to the side of the blanket, and my eyes grew wide as he reached for my feet again. His eyes held mine as his hands stroked up my leg, over my knee and all the way to my thigh, helping himself to the tie of my garter.

"I assumed London might not be a very comfortable place for a wood nymph," he said.

"But I'm not—"

"You are. Part of you is. And I don't think an eager appetite for sex is your only inheritance. How do you feel here?"

I licked my lips, thoughts bouncing between Jude's slowly exploring fingertips as he drew my stocking down my leg. If I'd known this was his plan, I wouldn't have bothered with them.

"Comfortable," I said. Jude nodded, encouraging me to go on. "Um...relaxed, like I can breathe more deeply."

The stocking was off, twisted and folded in his hands. I wiggled my other foot, and Jude smiled as he repeated the slow and soothing process on my other leg. I spread my knees apart, my skirt still hiding the view, but his smile only twitched. He knew what I was up to.

I moved one hand off the blanket, into the grass, and closed my eyes again. In my head, I could picture our surroundings perfectly, the presence of the trees as tangible in my heart as they were visible to the eye. There were more varieties here, like at Kew Gardens, and new songs to listen to.

"I can hear them," I murmured.

"Wood nymphs live in their trees," Jude said.

I opened one eye to look at him. "Mmm, but then where would I put you and the others?"

Jude just smiled calmly back. On this thigh, his hands took different paths, one drawing my stocking down and the other continuing a tiptoeing path up the inside of my leg. "Lie back," he said.

I hummed and fell eagerly back on the blanket, spreading my knees a little farther again.

"Can you speak to them?" Jude asked.

I snorted. "Hello, trees."

He pinched the inside of my thigh, high near my center, and I squealed. "Don't be a brat," Jude said.

I sighed and shifted on my back, wiggling to get more comfortable. "I don't know how."

"I didn't know how to stretch my wings until you drew me up on stage. Didn't know I could pull shadows around me until Ronan suggested it while we were tracking together," Jude said. "I thought my only gift from my father was being able to catch a lie, but I'd never had the chance to search for others. Just close your eyes and feel the woods around you."

I closed my eyes as Jude pulled his hands out from under my skirt. I floated in place for a moment, aware of the strength of the trees, of their energy branching up overhead and burrowing down in the ground, but not knowing how to bridge the gap from here on the blanket. I thought of the flower pot in my home, the way it had cracked during the fight with my attacker and the roots that had been stretched out in my direction.

Hello, trees, I thought, but I knew immediately it hadn't reached them.

"You're overthinking it," Jude said.

"How can you tell?"

"Because you're frowning."

"Well, I'm concentrating."

"So stop."

"First you tell me to focus and then you tell me to—Oh!" I arched as Jude's touch reappeared, directly on my sex. It was a simple, gentle stroke over my lips, up and around my clit and back down, and then as quickly as it had arrived, it vanished. I moaned, hips lifting and bucking, chasing the touch, trying to draw it back.

And all around us, leaves rustled.

"That's a start," Jude said, and he was grinning as my eyes flew open and I pushed up on my elbows, staring between him and the trees.

"Was it a breeze?" I asked.

"You tell me," he said.

I pursed my lips and tipped my head. "You'd better repeat the experiment."

Jude leaned over me, lips hovering just out of reach even as I craned my neck, and his hand petted up one thigh and down the other, making up for all the torment I'd given him earlier.

"Jude," I pleaded.

"This is as much for my own enjoyment as it is about you learning what you're capable of," he said.

His thumb found my clit before I could complain, just pressing gently. I breathed through the dull, sugary pressure of the touch, and he lowered his face just enough to brush his lips over mine.

"Please," I whispered, trying to rock myself into his hand, but he was careful to move with me, never growing lighter or firmer.

"The trees," Jude prompted.

I groaned, closing my eyes and finding their strong, old souls around us again. And as I groaned, they did too, an ancient and dangerous and slow moan of roots and branches and thick, sturdy trunks. I gasped, laughing, and then whimpered as Jude rewarded me, swirling his thumb, petting at me with a few fingers.

"More," he said.

But I was already there, my heart pounding through the ground, into the tangling net of roots that burrowed their way toward the water beneath our blanket. I opened my eyes, and above me stretched the future ghosts of branches, a hundred years or more from now. The sun was skimming and feeding me by the edges of their leaves.

Jude pressed two fingers inside of me, and his mouth kissed

my slowing pulse in my throat. I was languid, falling into the patient life of the trees, ready to rest and grow and feed the earth.

And then Jude pulled away again.

I whined and the branches rustled, complaining on my behalf. I blinked up at Jude to find him grinning, and this time, I was still connected to the woods around me, not pulled entirely out of the moment.

"Undress," I murmured.

"You don't want to keep—?"

"I do. Undress," I said.

He had nice hands, those fingers that had touched me shining faintly with my own eager interest as he reached up to pull at the buttons of his shirt. I rolled on the blanket, rising to my own knees, unfastening the waist of my skirt and eagerly tugging off the blouse I'd been wearing. The woods were protected, and Asterion knew we were out here. We'd be alone.

"Come here," Jude said, shedding his shirt and reaching out to me with dark eyes and a silky smile.

But I rose up, wearing my white slip and nothing else, and danced out of his reach. The trees were laughing with me, Jude's open desire written plainly on his handsome face. He was bare chested, wings growing denser as we both grew more comfortable out in the woods. This lovely place was well-suited to a fae too. And he was right—there were still parts of myself I didn't know yet.

"Catch me," I said.

Jude's brow furrowed, and then his eyes grew wide as I dashed for the tree line, my feet bare and my hands pulling the skirt of my slip up to make it easier to run.

"Hazel!" he cried, but I heard his own steps follow.

These woods were wild, thorny, but the undergrowth parted for me as I ran into the shade, soft moss blooming under my steps. His laugh was low behind me, and I picked up my pace, wanting the chase, wanting to play and tease and tempt Jude. I pulled the thin slip higher and then gave into the urge, drawing it up and over my head completely, tossing it into the air. The air was sharp and cool on my body, nipping my breasts and stroking between my thighs as I ran.

I'd played games of chase on stage before, barely a dozen meters to run, the scene controlled. This was so much better, wilder, and it made my muscles eager to win, to keep running, to never be caught.

I was headed straight ahead, grinning and prepared to close my eyes, when a sudden tall tower of shadow rose up ahead of me. My steps stumbled and I swerved, glancing back over my shoulder to find Jude behind me. His wings were massive, brushing against tree trunks as he passed.

"We'll both learn new tricks out here," he called.

He was right. These woods were nothing like Stepney Green Park. London was somewhere in the distance, a brick wall to the endless stretch of comforting wild around me. It was easier to find my mother's blood in my veins, to touch the trees around me, when I was so far from the busy city and the curious eyes of humans.

I ran for a cluster of beech trees, two trunks growing together in the ground with a cradling V shape between them. My body felt lighter, my feet steadier, and I climbed up into their shelter. Jude's shadows caressed me, a cool lick between my legs, a soft brush down my back. I lay down against the reclining tree trunk and offered Jude an inviting glance as he prowled closer.

His hands were on the front of his pants, his grin sharp, and he leapt up into the heart of the trees, stretching over me, balancing with his hands placed above my head.

"I knew you were too beautiful to be human the moment I saw you on the street that night," Jude said, his face hovering over mine.

I nearly abandoned my plan at the praise. I closed my eyes and softened on the rough tree bark, Jude's weight slowly pressing into me, comforting and complete. His lips brushed my cheek, and then I wrapped my head around the slow, quiet pulse of the beech and vanished into its solid presence.

"Hazel!"

My name was faint, muffled. I opened my eyes, and it wasn't a hollow tree trunk around me but threads of life, trails of color in front of my eyes. The path of the water up through the roots, the beat of the sun soaking into the leaves, and the little traces of creatures and insects that made the tree their home. It was peaceful and fascinating, and I was sliding down, down into the heart, where the trunk reached the forest floor.

"Hazel! Where are you?" Jude's voice was moving away. He was so light in this place, his shadow mere whispers, his footsteps like gentle knocks above my head. I followed them, and it was a sluggish version of swimming.

"Hazel!"

He was worried now, and that was all it took to draw me out of the reverie. I followed a new, more lively set of roots and came back up in a new heart, a younger oak.

"Fuck. Hazel, where are—"

I reached out of the oak and grabbed Jude's hand, laughing at his bellow of surprise. I'd barely stepped out of the tree, drawing him closer, when I found his mouth and kissed him roughly. The taste of the earth was on my tongue, but it was replaced quickly by Jude's gentle smoke and shadow.

His hand found my hip and gripped it tightly, no doubt trying to keep me from slipping away again. I didn't want to. Coming back out of the oak was a reminder of life, of my own faster and more frantic energy in comparison to the woods. I wanted Jude, wanted to remember my body and how much pleasure it could offer me.

I pulled my second leg into open air, my hands wrestling into Jude's pants. He groaned as I cupped his cock, gripped and stroked it, and then he was hauling me up from the moss at the foot of the oak.

My arms circled Jude's shoulders as he spread my knees wide. Our eyes met as the head of his cock kissed my sex, his wings casting us in a hazy shroud of privacy from the rest of the woods, the bark of the oak biting into my bare back. And then he was driving inside of me, my relief a sharp cry into the air, answered by the birds in the trees as they took to the sky.

Jude growled in my ear, pressed me into the trunk of the tree, hid his face in my throat. I stroked my hand over the back of his head as his arms tightened around my back.

"Thank you," I whispered to him, remembering he'd said the same after the scene on stage.

He huffed. "We're not done yet, Hazel Nix. I won't be done with you for *a long* time."

"Good," I said, starting to move, to roll my hips for friction.

Jude grunted and then his mouth found mine, tongue stroking in as he pulled slowly out. The branches shook as he thrust back in, as I trembled and moaned. The ground rolled in time with my pleading whines, my twisting hips.

"You'll bring the trees down when you come if you aren't careful," Jude rasped, laughing as I shuddered and a few old, brown leaves floated down to us.

I doubted that. I might've discovered my stronger gifts, but the trees would only let me have my way so long as it pleased them too. Still, I drew Jude's kiss back and settled in my own skin, releasing my connection with the woods in favor of finding it with the fae in my arms. His wings brushed up and down my sides, a cool and ticklish sensation.

"Christ, you feel so good." He bucked his hips, his brow furrowing. I smiled and clenched on his pumping length, sighing at the pound of pleasure it created for me too, as Jude let out a shout, his fingers digging into my ass. "It's a good thing you already proved I can stay hard, or I'd humiliate myself every time I fuck you."

"It's not humiliating if you know how to use your hands and mouth," I gasped. The tree had grown moss for my back, and it was silky-soft as Jude started to bounce me on his length.

"Ahh, clever girl," Jude murmured.

His hand fit between us with a determined press to my clit as he fucked me eagerly. Even without drawing the woods into our frenzy, the joy in my head was echoed through the trees, the birds and wild animals crying out with us. The sun flashed through the leaves and Jude's shadow, sounds and colors growing brighter as his demanding fingers drew me to the edge.

He roared, his rhythm erratic and his weight pressing me into the tree, while the rough and ragged strike of him inside of me brought on my own release. I had no idea what fanfare the woods made on our behalf, too lost in my own pleasure, arching and rocking and grinding into Jude until the wave finally crashed softly on the shore inside of me, a last tremble running down to my toes.

Jude sighed, kissing my shoulder, and for a moment our hearts beat together, pounding through sweat-sticky chests. He pulled away sooner than I wanted, and I whined as he slipped free of me. But then he was sinking to his knees, the thigh wrapped around his waist now gently draped over his shoulder. My mouth was open in an O of surprise, and Jude's eyes were pale and blue again as he gazed up at me, his smooth cheek stroking against my inner thigh.

"Hands *and* mouth, you said, yes?" he asked.

I bit my lip, bracing my heel on the forest floor, combing the wild strands of silky brown hair back from his face. "Oh, yes. Preferably in tandem."

"Don't be afraid to offer direction," Jude said.

I wouldn't have hesitated, but in truth, he was a natural.

36.

A WITCH'S HELP

The absence of the woods as we returned to the city, to the high warehouses and close brick buildings, was a tangible cage rising around my heart.

"We'll go back again," Jude said, noting the gradual change passing through me. London was heavy in my bones.

I nodded. "Now that I know what that feels like..."

Jude huffed in agreement, wrapping his arm around one of mine, tangling our fingers together. "I'm dreading reporting to the precinct tomorrow."

"Because of the case?" I asked.

Jude shook his head, a rueful smile on his face. "Beth's case is falling under paperwork. No, I just...hate the idea of hiding under that wool coat again for days on end. Only seeing one side of the city."

"Would you ever become a private investigator?" I asked.

Jude's eyebrows rose, and he stared across the carriage at the blank wall opposite us. "I hadn't thought of it. What would it change?"

"You have connections to both sides of London now," I said, shrugging and resting my cheek on his shoulder. "You could investigate for humans and monsters."

"Actually...that's a smart thought. I've been around a little long already. A new name and neighborhood, a new office." He twisted and smiled at me. "One where I can make my own hours and pick my cases. I like this idea. Thank you."

I leaned into the kiss on my forehead he granted, and we

pulled to a stop along the side of the theater. "I need to change neighborhoods too. I've already waited too long, but it's..."

"The first time for you," Jude said, nodding. He opened the door and helped me down, holding onto my hand and offering it a supportive squeeze. "I've heard Mayfair is nice."

I blushed, and he smirked at me. Hunter's house was in Mayfair.

"Better parks too," he added.

"Hush. Don't you have murders to solve?"

Jude grinned and followed me to the narrow alley door just off the right wing of the stage. It was a heavy old beast of a door with a screaming face for a handle, but it knew who belonged on stage, and it let me in with only a slight groan of protesting effort.

A dark figure darted in front of the door and out of sight, and Jude pushed me aside, staring after it until I shoved him in and pulled the door shut behind us.

"Don't get skittish. That's just Myron. He's a ghoul," I said.

"You have an act with a ghoul?"

"No, he's shy of the spotlights. But ghouls are good guards against trespassers," I said, and then rose up to whisper in Jude's ear. "And he likes to watch."

I couldn't see his glare in the dark of the theater, but I was pretty sure I'd earned a roll of his eyes. "Sometimes, I think you're teasing me."

"Sometimes I am teasing you. Doesn't mean it's not true."

"Hello?"

Jude and I both stiffened at the woman's voice, calling from the empty hall of seats. I tiptoed toward the curtains and Jude followed, trying to tuck me behind him again like he had at the sight of Myron.

"Hello? I'm looking for—Oh!"

I pushed the curtain aside, and the pixies raised the lights for me, just enough to cast a glow over the genteel woman at the foot of the stage. She was tall and slim, with delicate and distinctly feminine features, a black netted veil only slightly obscuring her beauty. She looked fairly human, but there was a bright energy to her, a sheen over her deep red dress, that spoke of magic.

She reached up, raising the veil, a crisp white smile framed by a broad pair of lips. "You must be Miss Nix," she said, and my eyes narrowed. "I'm Magdalena Mortimer. A friend of Hunter's."

Jealousy spiked in my chest. Magdalena Mortimer was beautiful and sharp and eerie. And then I remembered what he'd told me of his time before meeting me.

"You're the madame that arranged to have Hunter paired with a woman who made him feel like he was lesser for what he wanted," I said, raising my chin and staring down to the audience floor.

Magdalena's smile only grew broader, but her cheeks flushed a pretty shade of pink and her head ducked. "Right in one, Miss Nix."

I pressed my lips flat and crossed my arms over my chest. "I suppose I might thank you, but I won't. Why are you here?"

"A courtesy visit. I heard the theater and I have a common enemy," Magdalena said, shoulders squaring and her calm authority reclaimed. "I'm only here to offer what little help I can."

I chewed over the words. Hunter said he still respected Mortimer, and I supposed that would have to do no matter what pain she'd indirectly caused him. I sighed and nodded. "Doorway to your left. I'll take you to see Mr. Reddy."

"Aren't you a fierce protector," Jude whispered in my ear as Mortimer followed my directions. "Shame Hunter wasn't here to see that."

"He's too sweet. It would've embarrassed him," I answered back.

I met Magdalena at the doorway. "There's not much we can do about the dark back here."

"I have remarkably good eyesight, Miss Nix, don't worry about me," she said.

I led her to the stairs, Jude in tow. "Hunter said you were successful against Birsha."

"Mm, I don't know that I'd say that. We survived the first attack, won the second. But both were bloody affairs and not without losses. He's a cockroach," she said, voice dark and vehement.

Eston was at the bottom of the stairs when we arrived, and he stopped at the sight of Magdalena, in all her lace and velvet and beading.

"New girl?" he asked, black eyes huge and bug-like.

"No, not that it's any of your business," I answered, shooing him away.

"How flattering," Magdalena said brightly, and I thought she might really have meant it. "I do have a flair for the dramatic, or so my partner tells me. But I'm more of a voyeur, I think."

"Reddy's office is just this way," I said, battling my smile and fighting my rising appreciation for this woman.

I knocked on the door, and he grunted in answer. Magdalena didn't wait, strolling in ahead of me as I pushed the door open.

Mr. Reddy startled at the sight of her, blustering in his tilted-back chair and nearly falling out of it as he rose to standing, his face going red.

"Fuck! Mags, who let you in here?!"

"Alphonse," Magdalena said with a firm smile and a dip of her head. "I let myself in, of course, although I do congratulate you on your wards. They are very tidy. Who do you use? Don't tell me. It's Nathaniel, isn't it?"

"Alphonse," I repeated, sounding the name out, my eyes growing wider. I'd assumed Mr. Reddy had a first name, but I'd never heard anyone, not even Myra, use it before. "Alphonse."

"You, out!" Mr. Reddy snapped at me.

"No, let her stay. I like her very much," Magdalena purred. She drew a black handkerchief out of the collar of her fitted bodice and wiped it over the back of the spare chair before helping herself to a seat.

I snorted and shook my head. "You two talk business. Jude, you'll stay, won't you?" I asked. He nodded. Good. This way, he could report back to me on anything interesting between the pair. "Do you need anything, Alphonse?"

Mr. Reddy glared at me, and I thought at any moment, that stare might shoot flames. If he'd been part imp, perhaps it would have. "Find Constantine," he bit out, sobering me. "Bring him here."

I nodded, catching Jude's kiss on my cheek, and left them to their discussion.

Constantine was easy to find, sitting on the bed in his dressing room, but I stopped short in the doorway all the same. Ronan and Nireas were in the room too. Nireas was seated on the floor, long legs stretched out in front of him, two crumbling old books held between his six hands. Ronan was sitting backwards on an old wooden chair, tail coiled around one wooden leg, and another book in front of his nose.

"I told them not to bother," Constantine said to me as I stepped inside. He was also holding another book.

"Bother with what?" I asked.

"Hello, nut," Ronan greeted with a stretch of his wings.

Nireas tipped his foot to the side and it nudged my ankle, but he didn't tear any of his eyes off the pages in his hands. "We're studying up on demon bindings and deals. See if we can't find a loophole or the like."

"We can't," Constantine said flatly.

"He's a bit morose, but I don't mind him," Ronan told me, his head tipping. "What is it with you and serious men?"

"I have you for balance," I said to Ronan before turning to look at Constantine.

Constantine ignored our comments, shaking his head. "There's only one way to free me."

"Which is?" I asked, crossing from the door to sit at Constantine's side. His hand slid over my knees, drawing me in closer, and Ronan and I shared a smile.

"To convince the warlock to release him," Ronan said.

"Two ways. We could kill them," Nireas added, matter-of-fact. "But Constantine can't tell us who or where they are."

"Why are they doing this?" Constantine asked me, brow furrowing, glaring at the other two. Ronan was right—he *was* morose. Frustrated and weary at the idea of being helped.

"Because I like you, and they like me," I said, checking on the others for confirmation. Nireas's lips twitched and he shrugged, nodding. "But actually, Mr. Reddy wants to see you. I think there's a witch here."

"A witch?" Nireas echoed.

"No good can come of a witch," Constantine snapped, but his hand stroked over my thigh absently.

"Maybe not, but this one called Birsha a cockroach, so she doesn't seem too terrible," I said, nudging Constantine's side. "I'll come with you. Leave these scholars here to do the work."

Constantine stared at me for a long moment, glanced at the others out of the corner of his eyes, and then slid a long arm slowly around my shoulders, drawing me closer. His kiss was tenuous, fragile, like he was waiting to be interrupted. I pressed into his lips, stroking my hand over his sharp jaw, and then drew away.

"All right," he said mildly.

I nodded and rose up, and Constantine followed. "Maybe the loophole we should look for isn't how to get him out of the binding, but how to find out who the warlock is," I said to Ronan and Nireas.

"I don't want you near him," Constantine said, hard and crisp, his arm tight around my side.

"So it's a him!" Ronan noted brightly.

"We'll look at everything," Nireas assured me, leaning forward and reaching out to me with a free hand, cupping it around my ankle for a moment, his thumb stroking and sending bright darts of interest up my body.

Constantine and I left them to their work, and the hall was growing busier, filling up with monsters and humans.

"Hazel? Have you seen Hugh?" Isabella asked me, stepping out of Hugh's dressing room.

My heart went cold at her question, but then down the hall Evie answered, "He's upstairs, planning something with the stagehands for the third act."

I blew out a puff of breath and ignored Isabella's pout as she shoved past me and into her own dressing room.

Evie rolled her eyes and shook her head at me. "I think Hugh's soured a bit on little Isabella," she whispered to me.

"See if you can't talk to her," I said, laughing as Evie's beautiful features twisted with revulsion. "We need all the peace and harmony we can get."

"I suppose," Evie said with a heavy sigh, pushing off the wall and following after Isabella.

"The witch won't be able to help me," Constantine said, frowning and hunching to meet my eyes as we neared the door. "You and the others should—"

I rose up to my toes, my hand on the handle, and pressed a quick kiss to his lips, hushing his objections. I pushed the door open and caught the tail end of the conversation taking place.

"Khepri is calling them closer as quickly as can be managed. We will have allies and information soon, Alphie," Magdalena said.

Oh lord. Alphie was even better than Alphonse. Myra was in the room now, sitting on the arm of Reddy's chair and only looking a bit ruffled and nervous about the stunning and strange woman's familiarity with Mr. Reddy. Jude stood as Constantine and I entered, and he pushed the chair from Myra's desk closer, offering it to Constantine.

My demon looked nervous, and it hit me at once that it was the same stiff, frozen look on his face he'd worn the day he arrived. I followed at his back, my hand on his shoulder, and he jerked down into the chair, leaning away from Magdalena and into my touch.

"How do you do," Magdalena said coolly, dipping her head. "Alphonse informed me of your situation. I can't do anything directly, but—and feel free not to comment, I know how tight these contracts can be—I will look into the matter as discreetly as possible and bring my findings here, with your consent."

Constantine stiffened, his eyes darting between Magdalena, Reddy, and me. "No."

Magdalena's lips pursed, and Reddy blustered. "You can trust the witch. She's a rare decent one," Reddy said.

"It's dangerous," Constantine answered, his eyes flicking to me once again.

"It's already dangerous around here," I said, kneeling down at his side and turning my back on the others. "Do you want to remain bound?"

"No," he bit out.

"I don't want that for you either. And if Madame Mortimer doesn't look into the matter, then you know I'll have to stick my nose into Birsha's business—"

"You'll do no such thing!"

"Absolutely not."

"Hazel!"

The chorus came from behind me, and Constantine's eyebrow arched, his lips twitching for the first time today.

"Please let us help," I whispered.

Constantine glared down at me, a low and velvety snarl in his throat. Con would make me pay for my needling, later perhaps. Not that I would mind. That silver stare glanced up at Magdalena.

"Very discreet."

"Positively clandestine," Magdalena answered sweetly.

Constantine's head tipped in a faint acknowledgement, and I squeezed his hands in mine.

⚜

"I HAVEN'T BEEN this titillated since Lilith's musicale during the Black Death," Magdalena Mortimer giggled, her pale eyes wide as Goliath squeezed past her in our crowded hall, his cock fully erect and wrapped in Evie's hand as she guided him through the mass of people. "We really ought to collaborate, Alphie."

"When all this is settled and it's safe, we could use a girl or two, if you could spare them," Mr. Reddy said.

I leaned against my dressing room doorway, watching the cheerful bustle of backstage with a smile on my lips.

"I'm not sure my patrons would appreciate that," Magdalena said, but her head tilted in thought. "I could, however, be prevailed upon to scry for the right candidates."

Red arms circled my waist, tugging me slightly back into a warm and familiar chest. "Did you have fun tonight, nut?"

"I did," I said, leaning my head back and letting my eyes fall shut as Ronan rubbed his cheek against my hair.

Hunter hadn't arrived for the show, so I'd pulled an enthusiastic cyclops from the audience and paddled him for the third act finale. And for the third night in a row, I was left simmering with interest at the end of the show. I wiggled backwards in Ronan's embrace, and he huffed.

"Don't worry. We have plans for you," he said in my ear.

The crowd was starting to thin in the hall, and I twisted in Ronan's hold, craning to look over his wings. Nireas, Constantine, and Jude were all gathered behind us in my dressing room.

"We?" I asked, eyebrows raising. Four would be a challenge, even for me. Five even more so, if Con and Antin were part of the plan. But I liked to be challenged.

Ronan lifted his wings and kissed my cheek. "Mm, you'll see."

"Miss Nix."

I jumped and found Magdalena Mortimer facing me, her cheeks flushed, lips stretched in a smile. I had a feeling she, Reddy, and Myra had been drinking together during the show.

"I wonder if I might steal a moment of your time?" Magdalena asked.

"Oh! Sure," I said.

Ronan slipped his arms from around me. "You two settle in here. We'll go...get things ready," Ronan said with a cryptic wink for my benefit.

Magdalena brushed the curtain of my dressing room with an appreciative study. "That's a tidy charm. Nathaniel is an utter prick, but he does good work with fabrics," she mused.

"What are you up to?" I mouthed to Jude as he filed behind Nireas, and the four of them trailed out of the room under Ronan's command. He only shrugged in response, eyes glittering with excitement.

"You remind me of a friend," Magdalena said, her back to me as she surveyed my tiny, shabby room. "The pair of you have that equally large and incredible capacity for loving, and loving with such a lack of reserve."

I blinked at the praise. Was Magdalena thinking of someone else?

She turned and found me stock still and baffled, and her smile stretched. "Only those who love so deeply it consumes them, find themselves fighting so strongly against the emotion.

Why fight an airy, passing love that can do very little harm? No, it's only those feelings that run bone-deep that threaten to shatter us."

Her words gave me chills, reminded me of all my fears, all my struggles against Ronan's steady friendship and the offer of more. The empty ache left behind after Nireas's rejection, the way it lingered for years.

Magdalena stepped forward, reaching out and clasping my chin in a gentle grip, drawing it up as she stared into my eyes. "I find it often worth the risk," she said.

She released me and I caught a deep breath, wanting to skirt away from the unnerving woman, to go and find my men at whatever mischief they were up to.

"You were right. I failed Hunter while he was a member of my house," Magdalena said, nodding slowly. "I could be coy and claim it led him more easily to you, but in truth, I was occupied by blindspots at the time. He deserved better. I only wanted to say how grateful I am that he found exactly that."

My lips pursed, a puff of breath released, tension bleeding out of me. "I suppose I am a bit pleased you gave him such a horrible girl for a partner," I said, offering a half-smile. "If she'd been even halfway decent, he would've devoted himself to her, and I..." I wouldn't say it to Magdalena before I said it to Hunter. "I would've missed having him for myself."

Magdalena nodded, one shoulder rising and falling. "These matters have a tendency to work out once the stars start turning in their favor. It appears I'll miss seeing Hunter on this visit. I'll be back soon, but give him my regards in the meantime."

"And you'll search for Constantine's warlock?" I asked.

"With all the subtlety and care I possess," Magdalena said.

Which was reassuring, in spite of the fact that it came from one of the most dramatically-presented women I'd ever met. We nodded to one another, and she glided out of the room with a whisper of jasmine floating behind her.

37.

A PRIVATE PERFORMANCE

I was turning for the stairs, ready to hunt Ronan and the others down, when I ran bodily into Nireas at the bottom step. He caught me by my waist and shoulders, and I reached up for him, rising to my toes.

"What are you up to?" I asked before pressing my lips to the glimpse of his shimmering throat at his open collar.

His hands on my waist lowered to my hips, and then I was up off my feet and held to his chest. "Good. You didn't dress."

"I assumed any plans probably weren't formal," I said, grinning and wrapping my arms around Nireas's shoulders.

"There was a debate on that," Nireas said.

"Who won?"

His smile was rare, and it transformed his usually solemn face into something bright and beautiful that made me ache. "I did."

"If I'm your prize, I think you ought to take me now," I said, waggling my eyebrows.

Nireas huffed a laugh. "Tempting, nymph. But I'm looking forward to your surprise." He brought a length of black silk out from behind his back and held it between two hands. "May I?"

"You may," I said, my eyes narrowed. "But what's a surprise I can't see?"

"It won't be on for long," Nireas said, and I shut my eyes as he wrapped the blindfold and tied it in place.

"Has there been any word from Hunter?" I asked softly, my body rubbing against Nireas's as he turned us and headed up the stairs.

"We're keeping you occupied until he arrives," Nireas said, a free hand rubbing my back. "He's fine."

Nireas had to duck to exit the stairs, and he cupped the back of my head and held it to his shoulder as he did so. I took advantage, my mouth on his throat, helping myself to a taste of him, clean and velvety. Nireas stifled a groan, his footsteps shuffling and tail dragging over the floorboards.

"There she is," Ronan murmured. "Her seat is saved."

"I told everyone else to leave us the stage, but I'm sure some will come snooping," Nireas said to them.

"Are we putting on a show?" I asked, leaving Nireas's throat with a farewell nip.

But no, Nireas was carrying me down a set of stairs, one that ended quickly. Oh, we were moving into the audience.

"You've done your work for the night, nymph," Nireas murmured in my ear, his lips grazing my lobe and summoning goose bumps over my throat and down my arms and chest.

"This show is all for you, Hazelnut," Ronan called, his voice softly muffled.

I laughed as Nireas set me down on the dense velvet cushion of one of the bench seats, my toes digging into the thick fabric. All six of his hands soothed over my shoulders, down my ribs and waist, stroking my hips, until my robe was loose and slipping off. I'd put on a lovely chemise that Hunter had tucked into my wardrobe, the ties around my shoulders loose enough for the short sleeves to droop, and Nireas cupped a breast through the fabric.

"You can take that off too, if you like," I offered, arching into his touch.

"Mm, no. It's very pretty, and I wouldn't want you to get cold," he said.

I was lifted into his many arms again, turned, and this time I landed on his lap, the slip conveniently hiked up so that it pooled over mine, but left the thick wool of Nireas's pants pressed to my bottom. My legs were spread over his, my back pulled to rest against his chest, and my body was draped in heavy, warm arms, breasts and pussy cupped in large palms. I sighed, wiggled on his lap, pushed myself into his touch, but Nireas didn't move until I settled and relaxed.

The blindfold came undone but revealed only the dark theater, curtains closed and the moment still and quiet.

"The other girls...they're not..." I bit my lip, a small, bitter spike that ought to have been irrational but persisted nonetheless burrowing through me.

Nireas turned my face, kissing the corner of my eyebrow near my eyelid, the spot unexpectedly tender and sensitive. "It's just us, Hazel."

I sighed and then gasped as the spotlight flared into life, the curtain a bright bloom of stunning blood-red velvet appearing before us.

"Well, us and the pixies," Nireas allowed.

A warbling, slightly staticky note of music appeared from behind the curtain, and I twisted to smile at Nireas. "You didn't want to play?"

"Someone had to make sure you didn't get lonely," Nireas said, his smile small and sly.

I hummed, shaking with repressed laughter, and settled back into his chest as the curtain started to part. My breath caught in my chest immediately.

The elaborate bench used for my scenes with Constantine was center stage, and spread on top of it, limbs tangling and bodies rubbing together, were Ronan and Jude. Ronan had Jude pinned down, red hands wrapped around pale wrists, Jude's white shirt pushed open. Ronan's wings were stretched back, taut with tension and desire. Their lips were crashing together, hips grinding, and Jude let out an eager moan as Ronan pulled away, trailing his mouth down to Jude's chest. Ronan's long, black tongue circled around Jude's nipple, drawing a loud groan from the half-fae's lips.

"He's as noisy as you," Nireas said in my ear, one thumb circling around my own nipple in time with Ronan's tongue on Jude.

"They're beautiful," I murmured, watching Ronan press sloppy, wet kisses down Jude's stomach, his long red fingers working at the front of Jude's pants, stroking his crotch and loosening the buttons.

"Mmm," Nireas hummed noncommittally, thick fingers finding the tie at the collar of my chemise and pulling it loose.

I suspected his view was pointed downward, not on the stage, which suited me just as well. He pushed the collar open and then down over my breasts, hands returning to my exposed skin. His touch was warm and heavy, impossibly patient as he rested his palms over me, just cupping.

Ronan and Jude were significantly less patient, Ronan yanking Jude's pants down over his hip and Jude practically falling off the bench in his haste to stand and kick the fabric off. Ronan was on his knees, and he pulled Jude to the side with a wink to me, keeping my view of them clear on the stage. Jude grabbed his face, pulled him in for a thrusting, biting kiss, and then tackled Ronan around to lie flat on his back. Their chests heaved as Jude straddled Ronan and the bench. Ronan was already bare chested, propped up on his elbows, and Jude crawled up, knees framing Ronan's ribs. Jude's flushed and weeping cock was wrapped in one pumping hand .

"Oh, lord," I whispered, my eyes wide. Only Nireas's gentle hold kept me from running onto the stage.

Ronan's eyes were tilted up to stare back at Jude, his tongue flicking out over his lips before his mouth parted in invitation. Ronan slipped his arms beneath Jude's legs, and Jude's free hand went to the back of Ronan's head as he rubbed the head of his cock around Ronan's lips.

I squirmed and gasped as my sex rubbed against Nireas's fingers. I repeated the motion and my giant chuckled, his tail lifting and draping heavily over one of my legs, holding me in place.

"We're only just beginning. You must be patient, nymph."

Ronan moaned as Jude fed him his cock, removing his hand and bracing it against the back of the bench as he started to thrust gently. Ronan's hands were rubbing over his own groin, pulling open his pants, drawing out his dark red cock. I was so fixated on the pair of them, I missed the shadows moving out of the wings until they'd nearly reached the bench.

My breath hitched at the same moment that Jude released a bright bellow of pleasure, Antin's red hand stroking up his spine. Creamy fluid spilled out over Ronan's lips, and Antin stepped back next to Con.

"Up," Antin said, even as Jude still trembled and dripped onto Ronan's chest.

But they shuffled obediently, Ronan rising and pushing off his own pants, Jude catching his breath, his wings a restless, billowing shadow behind them.

"Touch me," I whispered to Nireas.

And this time, he listened, pulling up my nightgown and teasing my damp sex with two hands, spreading my arousal over every fold and quivering inch.

Antins's red flesh was a cooler shade than Ronan's, a subtle contrast as he braced the imp, and Con brushed a blue hand over Ronan's nipple. Ronan's eyes were wide and his skin flickered with flames, wings beating as he howled with pain. But his long cock was stiff, a visible bead of slick arousal pooling at the tip. Con and Antin both pulled away, and Ronan sagged and groaned, chest glittering with sweat as he gasped for breath.

"Fuck. Fuck," he whispered. I braced myself, waiting to see if he'd enjoyed it as much as I had or if he would only prefer Antin's gift of pleasure. He shook himself and then straightened, head turned toward Con. "Fuck, that's good. Again, but just you this time."

I grinned and then squirmed as Nireas swirled his fingertips over my clit, one digit sliding easily inside of me. He was being gentle, two more hands playing softly with my breasts, the last two holding me in place on his lap, petting my shoulder and stomach, maintaining my arousal as I watched the foursome on stage.

"Together," Jude said, shuffling forward on his knees until he and Ronan were kneeling within reach of each other, their cocks rubbing together.

Con reached for their faces with both hands, and Antin smiled—for me, I thought—and slipped his red hand between them. Jude and Ronan jerked as Con's hands grasped the backs of their necks, and their mouths slammed together in what had to be a brutal, bruising kiss, all teeth and tongue. And then Antin took their cocks together in one hand, and they were bucking, shouting, kissing, fucking the red fist that held them, their bodies tense under Con's sapphire touch.

I shuddered, riding Nireas's fingers as I watched them. Ronan's tail was whipping wildly, his wings beating and providing momentum to his thrusts. The heads of their cocks were rubbing against each other's stomachs, painting sticky streaks in their wake that caught the stage lights and glistened.

It was Ronan who came first, pulling away from Jude's kiss, leaning into Con's stroking hand that tangled in his hair, howling up to the rafters. Con tried to pull away, and Ronan grabbed him by the throat, making Con's silver eyes wide.

I tried to scramble off Nireas's lap, but he only allowed me to move up to my knees. It was enough. Ronan's tail was circling around Con's back, his hand reaching for Con's cock, and I gasped as Con went rigid, eyes rolling back and body trembling. Ronan yelped, his tail vibrating up to his spine like a strike of lightning running through his body, but whatever he was doing to Con, he didn't stop, and Antin soothed him with another stroke down his chest.

"Let's join them," I breathed to Nireas as he pulled me back to his chest.

"No," he answered, and then he drew me down, right onto his thick cock.

I hadn't noticed him readying himself, the man had too many damn hands, and I arched and moaned as his length stretched me. In the throes of my shock, Jude grasped Antin's face in his hands, pulling him in for a kiss.

The performance was messy chaos. They hadn't rehearsed, and I could barely see half of what I suspected was happening, but it was a beautiful tangle of bodies I knew and appreciated intimately. I was riding Nireas without thinking about it, my body following the same pace as Jude's thrusts in Antin's hand. Ronan was pulling Con onto the bench, between himself and Jude, the demon surrendering to their clamoring touches, his eyes wide with some mix of passion and surprise.

The vision was shrouded, briefly, as Nireas pulled my chemise off over my head, and then revealed again, Antin now tangled in the middle, his and Con's backs to one another as Jude and Ronan attacked them with desperate kisses and an unrestrained frenzy of need. Their bodies bucked together, cocks grinding and spurting, arms circling and legs bracing, folding, until they were one intricate knot of muscle.

"You made it," Nireas said, his breath a little short as he worked me on his length.

I blinked and realized Hunter was approaching from the aisle, sparing an appreciative glance for the stage. His hat was off, coat over his arm, and I whined as Nireas shifted inside of me, sinking deeper, rubbing at my front walls.

"I did. And our darling girl looks as though she's appreciating the efforts on stage," Hunter said, smiling down at me, watching me rise and fall on Nireas's thick cock.

"I am. Very much," I panted, my eyes trailing back.

Ronan's tail was in Antin's ass now, the red demon thrashing with delight, Ronan all but collapsed in Con's embrace, his face tortured with sensation.

"I won't interrupt your view," Hunter said, sinking to his knees.

Nireas spread his legs, and mine with them, and I managed one quick whimper of understanding before Hunter was kissing my sex, long tongue stroking, lips pulling and pressing around my clit. Nireas shuddered and groaned in my ear, his fingers on my breasts pinching a little tighter as Hunter's tongue circled his pumping cock, even dipped inside me with his thrust.

"Oh, Hunter. Fuck, Nireas, I—I'm so close," I whined. "You feel so good. Please don't stop! Don't tease."

Hunter licked me like he was greeting me after not seeing me for weeks. There was nothing like his tongue, his hungry lips, his tusks pressing and spreading me open. Nireas's hands combed through my hair, and I brought one of his hands up from my hip to my throat, teaching him how to grip and hold me as he fucked me. He was gentler than Hunter, but he learned my taste as I started to flutter and thrash on his cock.

Antin was sucking Jude's length, Con in his ass now and Ronan's tail around his blue cock, and Ronan was fitted to Con's back, furiously bucking even as he whined in pain. Jude looked as though he might've forgotten to breathe, one lone taut arch of pleasure, glittering with cum and sweat dressed over him.

I came as they all did, screaming with them, my cunt bearing down and Nireas's grip biting erotically around my throat as I took him with me. Hunter cleaned us both as we shuddered through wave after wave, and Con and Antin blended back into Constantine, his face pressed to Jude's hip, Ronan limp over his back, wings drooping down to the floor.

Hunter kept licking, summoning fresh shivers of release, until Nireas lifted me off his cock with a groan. I was passed down into my orc's arms. He stood, cradling me, and Constantine blinked wearily at us, a rare smile gracing his lips.

"Are you tired, little one?" Hunter asked, lifting my fevered body up to the cool floorboards of the stage.

I was exhausted. I was only just beginning.

I shook my head as Hunter jumped up and then lifted me again. "No. Let them watch?" I asked.

Hunter nodded toward the bench, and with soft protests, my men rolled slowly off the structure, sliding in a heap together on the floor and no farther. Nireas came up from the audience, pants just barely closed, and sat down in front of the bench, his hair rumpled and his smile lazy as he watched Hunter lay me down. The bench was messy. I would owe the pixies extra cakes for cleaning up after us.

"This isn't a performance," Hunter said, arching an eyebrow at me as I shifted and preened and adjusted my position.

"I know," I said, trying to sound innocent, even as I spread my legs wide and glanced down the length of the bench to where Jude was leaning back against Ronan, the pair of them staring with a drowsy kind of hunger in their eyes.

"What happens between us," Hunter said, and my heart stuttered as he turned and nodded to the others to include them, "will always be personal and private. No matter how many witnesses we have...watching from the wings."

"Hunter," I murmured, reaching for him.

He was stripping slowly, the spotlights bright on his piercings, and he paused, head tipping and waiting for me.

"Come here and touch me, my love," I said.

The pet name was almost accidental. He stiffened, bright eyes blazing, and then he rushed to kick his clothes off, climbing onto the bench between my spread legs. I was stretched out in offering, my body languid, already satisfied and yet eager for more.

Hunter's head bent, lips wrapping around my nipple, and I sighed, sliding my fingers into his hair, turning my head and smiling at the others. Hunter rose up again, braced above me, and he nodded his head without me having to ask the question out loud.

"Everyone touch me, please," I said.

They slid closer, wings and claws and horns and tails all reaching for me. My men. My monsters.

38.
PROGRESS IN SMALL MEASURES

A fingertip traced over my lips, and a soft puffing breath tickled the hair at the back of my neck. Another hand brushed strands back from my face, and a third hooked two fingers into the sheet covering my breasts. Still half-asleep, I smiled as I realized who was in front of me.

My eyes blinked open slowly, sunlight bright in Hunter's bedroom, and I rolled back into Ronan's chest, drawing a sleepy murmur from my imp. Nireas was seated on the bed, leaning against the heavy and swirling headboard, staring down at me.

"Hunter and Jude left?" I asked in a whisper.

"Jude did. Hunter's downstairs," Nireas answered.

Constantine had left us while we were still at the theater, called back by that horrible tether the warlock had over him, and this time it wasn't just me unhappy to see him go. After cleaning ourselves up, Ronan, Jude, Hunter, Nireas, and I had stuffed snuggly into Hunter's carriage and traveled to his home. I'd woken once in the night, tangled between three bodies all of a mind to make me scream and beg for release, but it took me a moment to sort through the foggy, pleasure-hazed memory to sort out who was who.

"You didn't sleep with us last night," I said.

Nireas shook his head, wearing a wry smile. "There wasn't room. Don't pout, nymph, I didn't mind."

I pressed my lips flat to try and hide the supposed pout, rolling back and pushing Ronan. I let the sheet slide down as I moved, stretching my limbs out in invitation to Nireas.

His tongue flicked out over his lips, eyes studying me at odds. I was still mostly covered, but my body warmed with every pass of his gaze until his eyes all flicked up to the ceiling in unison and his head shook slightly.

Now I was certainly pouting.

"Asterion just arrived. I think he might have some news, and I came to see—"

Nireas didn't need to finish the sentence. I was already sitting up and scrambling for the edge of the bed. Ronan groaned, reaching for me and coming up short.

"What news?" I asked, bouncing off the side of the mattress and racing around to the wardrobe. It had more new items—it seemed to accumulate clothing for me like something out of a fairy tale—and Hunter was learning my tastes at last, the new garments simpler in design but still made of luxurious fabrics.

"Not sure, but I know you don't want to be left out of the conversation," Nireas said.

I paused in dressing long enough to offer him a sincere smile. "Thank you."

He nodded and rose from the bed. "Here, bring all your buttons and laces to me. I have six hands and they might as well be of use."

"I feel as though I've been simultaneously run over by a carriage and gone for a bath in some sort of holy pool of rejuvenation," Ronan muttered, rolling to his side and making no effort to cover himself as he stroked his morning erection with aimless attention. He grinned at me as I hurried to Nireas for help in dressing. "Constantine *is* a revelation, isn't he?"

I arched an eyebrow at Ronan. "I told you." I wiggled in place as Nireas finished lacing the corset, then reached back behind me, but he swatted my hands away. "Bit tighter," I instructed, laughing.

"You know your orc—"

"Hunter," I corrected, rolling my eyes at Ronan, just as the light cotton skirt billowed over my head.

"—opened his house to all of us last night," Ronan finished.

"Obviously," I said, waving at the pair of them.

"No, he means...Hunter made it clear that we were every bit as welcome to make a home here as you are," Nireas said.

My cheeks flushed, and Ronan smirked. "I've never thought of being a monster's kept lady, but I have to be honest, it doesn't sound so terrible," he said.

It was partly presumption—had Hunter even said the words to me directly yet?—and partly the usual openhearted generosity I was used to from the orc, but it made me rush to dress a little faster, combing my fingers through my unruly red waves until Nireas shooed me away, three of his hands making quick work of a French braid.

"Are you coming down with us?" I asked Ronan as Nireas finished tidying me.

Ronan's hand was still around his cock, and he grinned at me, head shaking. "I plan on having a very long and very pleasurable bath to myself, as a matter of fact. Feel free to come and join me and catch me up when you're done."

I snorted and turned, taking the hand Nireas offered and smiling as another arm wrapped around my waist and a third over my shoulders. We left Ronan to his wickedness, and I fought the impulse to study the house in a new light as we walked downstairs. The paper on the walls in the upstairs was old and dark, showing its age and making the more narrow halls feel somewhat oppressive by comparison to the bright rooms on the first floor. It would be nice to make some small improvements...to stake a claim on the space, but it also felt as though I was still an infrequent guest in the house.

"Thank you for last night," I said to Nireas as we walked down the stairs, his hand on my shoulder toying with the tail of the braid he'd fashioned. I glanced up and found him blushing.

"It was really Ronan and Jude's idea. I was just the lucky bastard who got to keep you company," Nireas said softly.

"Just the idea that any of you, *all* of you, are willing to work together for my enjoyment is a gift on its own, Nireas," I said, squeezing the hand I held.

He stopped us at the bottom of the stairs, moving me to stand in front of him, all six hands holding onto me. He bent slightly so I didn't have to crane my neck to meet his gaze.

"You've made five very unlikely men into friends, something I... have somewhat foolishly been avoiding for quite a few years. It's lonely to be without a lover, certainly, but even more so to be the idiot who hasn't *anyone* to speak with, to share with. So the gift is mutual, nymph. In fact, I'm still not certain the odds aren't in my favor."

I sighed and rose up to my toes, reaching for Nireas's face. He leaned down the last few inches, lips tender and insistent against mine, hands drawing me in to press to his front.

"I missed you for so many years," I whispered.

"No more," Nireas answered, temple stroking my cheek, mouth trailing to my jaw and neck before he stood upright again, his smile tenuous. "No more, I promise."

I drew in a deep breath, accepted the ache of my heart in my chest as a sign of it still being capable of growing and beating, and together, we turned and walked toward the dining room, Nireas leading the way.

The mood was grave as we arrived, Asterion sitting at the table without a plate and Hunter leaning back in his own chair, wearing a deep frown. They both rose at my entrance, bowed to me as if I were some woman of consequence, and ignored my flapping hands urging them to sit again.

"What is it? What's happened?" I asked, hurrying for the table.

"It's news related to Miss O'Mahony," Hunter said, drawing out a chair at his side for me.

"Related to?" I repeated, sitting down.

"It's her roommates," Asterion said. "Jude mentioned they'd gone missing."

Guilt struck me, sudden and woozy, and I leaned heavily back against the chair. I'd forgotten about Beth's roommates, forgotten they'd gone missing in the wake of Beth's death. Part of me had assumed they'd reappeared again or had moved on to a different apartment or neighborhood.

"Have they been found?" I asked, voice thin.

"Not for certain. However, I returned to my post at the Seven Veils this week to discover Birsha had...new women available," Asterion said carefully, reaching up to scuff one of his broad golden horns in obvious discomfort. "Human girls. Absolutely not there of their own volition."

I sucked in a rough breath. The table was laid out with a king's feast of breakfast foods, and not a bite of it looked appetizing at the moment.

"Jude provided me with enough details to assume I'd come across the missing roommates," Asterion said.

Nireas took his own seat on my other side, and both he and Hunter offered their hands. I latched on gratefully.

"What about Margaret? She wasn't living alone either."

"We have someone keeping an eye on her own roommates. It's difficult to...protect women of their profession, but we're doing what we can," Asterion said. "Margaret was killed on the street. Whoever is acting for Birsha must not have been able to snatch the girls at the same time."

"This is the best evidence we have yet of Birsha's responsibility in Beth and Margaret's deaths," Hunter said.

"Was there any doubt?" I asked, frowning.

"Little," Asterion said, shrugging. "But it would hardly serve us to focus an attack on Birsha and his business if the culprit weren't connected. He's no easy foe to challenge."

"And how do we challenge him?" I asked.

Asterion's brow furrowed, and he glanced between Hunter and me. "Those discussions are still in progress. And while I don't doubt your determination to see Birsha and his accomplice brought to justice, the battle wouldn't be a safe place for a human woman."

I blinked at him, my answer ready on my lips, when I stopped myself. Hunter shifted in my direction, and I turned to him, caught his smile and the squeeze of his fingers around mine. I didn't have to keep the secret. Not if I didn't want to.

"I'm not human," I said, and the truth came awkwardly to my tongue, so rare and so long held back. I turned back to Asterion. "Not entirely. And anyway, human women might not be strong enough to fight monsters face to face, but I'm sure girls like Alexa and Evie and me would like to be of *some* use. We're as much a part of your world now as you are."

I hadn't considered it before, but it was true. I'd spent eight years thinking I existed in some in-between place, not allowed to belong to the world of monsters, incapable of continuing to be entirely human. The knowledge of monsters, the nights and days spent in their company, made us every bit as much a member of their community, whether they wanted to believe it or not.

"She has a warrior's heart," Asterion said to Hunter.

My orc grunted, drawing my eye. His gaze was warm, lips curved, and his thumb stroked gently over the back of my hand. "Actually, she has two warriors' hearts in her possession."

I flushed warm, melting into the chair as Hunter lifted my hand to his lips, kissing my skin and drawing a shiver through me as his tongue flicked out to taste.

"Consider it three," Nireas murmured, squeezing my hand. "But, Hazel, it doesn't make me less reluctant to have you involved."

"He's right," Hunter said. "Whatever role you take, your safety will be my first priority."

I wanted to argue but suspected there would be little chance of success, especially at the moment. I turned back to Asterion instead. "Can anything be done for Beth's roommates?"

Asterion grimaced, baring his blunt teeth briefly. "Not enough thus far, but I'm in talks with a few acquaintances to try and come up with a plan."

"We still need Asterion to remain under Birsha's nose without arousing suspicion," Hunter said.

Asterion let out a huffing grunt, nostrils flaring. "He's saying that as much as I'd wish to, I can't carry all of Birsha's wares out the front door without losing my head in the process. But I've been doing my best to bring in more sympathetic clients who might be able to help."

He didn't look proud. It wasn't enough. But it was something for those men and women and monsters Birsha had his grip on. I offered Asterion a gentle smile and a dip of my head.

"Some rescues take more time. It doesn't make you less of a hero," I said.

Asterion's cheeks flushed, and he turned his eye toward the front windows, another flustered huff puffing from his nose. "Thank you, Miss Nix," he grumbled.

39.

EXIT,
STAGE LEFT

"The carriage will be here for you this evening, little one," Hunter said, handing me out into the theater's alley.

Nireas had already unfolded himself out of the narrow door, and Ronan was following after me.

"I'll have dinner waiting. Jude has already confirmed he'll return for the evening." Hunter's gaze flicked over my shoulder to Nireas and then back to me, a slightly expectant rise to his eyebrows.

I wanted to tease him for inviting Jude already, but in truth, we would all be guests in Hunter's home. He had every right to issue the invitations. And I would be contrary if I pretended to wish for Ronan and Nireas to remain here at the theater.

"I'll bring these two wastrels along with me," I said, winking over Hunter's shoulder at Ronan.

"Oh, you will, will you?" Nireas asked. "Never mind that I have my own apartment to retire to." I spun to face him and found him smiling. "I'd be delighted."

Hunter kissed my cheek as Ronan descended and then stepped back into the compartment of the carriage. "Until this evening, friends."

"Reddy will give the three of us hell for being late," Ronan said.

"Reddy won't say a word," Nireas said with absolute certainty. "If he tries, I'll remind him I own fifty-one percent of the theater."

My jaw dropped at that, and Nireas opened the side door that led to the stage left wing before I had time to form the words for a question.

"Did you know?" Ronan whispered in my ear.

"What do you mean he's working with the man who killed Beth and Margaret?!"

The shouted question, coming from inside the theater, wiped away all my plans of quizzing Nireas with a sudden blow of surprise and worry. The three of us rushed inside to find the company gathered together on and around the stage.

Alexa was standing at the foot of the stage, glaring up at Mr. Reddy.

"He's *not* working with the bastard," Mr. Reddy said.

"But..." Myra murmured, staring up at Reddy.

"But what?" Alexa asked.

"Myra, but *what?*" Evie echoed, sitting in the front row with her arms crossed.

"Don't lie," Eston said. "I heard you talking about him. Birsha *sent* the demon here."

Realization was cold and cutting, the meaning behind the conversation suddenly clear. I marched forward onto the stage, searching the room for Constantine and finding him in the shadows on the opposite wing.

"He's not here for Birsha," I said immediately. "Constantine might be here *because* of him, but not *for*. He's—"

Constantine stepped out of the shadows, head jerking at me once in refusal, eyes glinting like a mirror's reflection caught by light. *Quiet*, that look said. *Don't tell them.*

"He's not a danger to us," I said instead.

"You just don't want to give up your starring act," Eston snapped at me.

I scoffed, and Ronan marched ahead of me. "Eston, don't be an idiot. If anyone is jealous of Constantine's presence here, it's bound to be you."

"Birsha *bullied* Red into bringing him on!" Myra said to Alexa, her head shaking and eyes wide. "We were under so much pressure."

"Missy, *hush*," Reddy hissed to his partner.

"Constantine is *not* working with Birsha. He never touched Beth or Margaret," I said. "This is mad! How did this even come up? He's been here for weeks, and we lost Beth before he ever arrived!"

"The timing is close though, isn't it?" Goliath asked, glaring at Constantine from the stage.

"Listen, all of you—" Reddy tried, hands raised in a useless placating gesture that would only rile more tempers than it soothed.

"Answer for yourself, Gemini," Evie said, rising, glaring at Constantine. "Are you here at Birsha's bequest?"

Constantine stepped forward, and my heart sank as everyone on the stage—everyone in the audience, even—inched back.

"Yes," he said.

I tried to intervene again, shouldering Eston out of my way. "But—"

Evie held a single finger up in my direction to hush me. She alone didn't flinch in Constantine's focus, and she refused to look away. I loved Evie. She was brave and stern, and a little bitter, like I'd been recently. And Evie loved this theater. As long as Constantine posed any kind of threat, she would never accept him.

"Are you reporting back to him? Giving him information about what's happening in the theater?" Evie asked.

Constantine's head tipped to the side. "Yes."

"Constantine," I gasped out. I turned to Evie. "He's not helping Birsha."

"Not voluntarily," Constantine said.

Damnit, stop! I wanted to shout at him.

"Hopefully not at all," Constantine added, one shoulder rising and falling in an abrupt shrug. "But I am forced to speak with some truth."

I held my breath. The words were damning. Honest too, which was worse.

"It's not his fault," I whispered, but I saw the look on all the faces in front of me. Anger, fear. No sympathy. Constantine had not endeared himself to the other company members. I looked back at Ronan and Nireas, found them frowning. They looked worried, but I wasn't sure if that was for Constantine's sake or mine.

Evie tore her stare away from Constantine's and looked back at me, cold and determined.

"He can't stay," she said. "He stays and I leave."

"We leave," Samson said, now standing at Alexa's side.

Alexa's eyes bounced between me and Constantine, her lips twisting and pinching. Behind her, others rose, echoing the threat to Reddy. Alexa finally stared back at me.

"I'm sorry. He might not want to help Birsha. But that doesn't make it safe for the rest of us."

"She's right, Nix," Reddy said at my back, a heavy sigh in the words.

My hands clenched to fists at my side, my heart pounding all the way up in my throat. My eyes were stinging as harshly as the first time I'd stared into the spotlight. Constantine turned away from everyone, facing me, his steps a steady thudding.

"You'll have to leave," Reddy said, adding more softly, "I'm sorry."

"It's not his fault," I hissed again, whipping around to glare at Reddy. And those stupid thick hands of his remained opened at his sides, as if he could feign helplessness.

Constantine's shoulder brushed mine and I grasped his arm in my hands, but it didn't stop his march and I found myself jogging along at his side.

"You don't have to—"

"I do," he said, glancing down at me.

"But we promised to help you."

"And I told you it wasn't possible," Constantine said.

"Constantine."

He didn't shake me off but he didn't slow down, and everyone moved aside. I felt like a child clinging to their parent's leg, trying to hold them back from walking out the door.

"Go to Hunter's house," I whispered.

"I can't."

"You can. I'll tell—"

Constantine pushed the side door open, and I winced against the glaring sunlight, my feet tripping beneath me.

Constantine spun away and I cried out, but he wasn't leaving me. His hands grasped my elbows, and he yanked me against his chest. I snapped my arms around his waist, burying my face in the layers of soft fabrics he wore.

"I would be an even more dangerous spy in the orc's home than I am here, sweet creature," Constantine said. "Your friends are right. I'm not safe for you."

"But that's only because—"

"It doesn't matter." Constantine's hands moved to my face, cupping it and pulling it up a little roughly. He was actually beautiful in broad daylight, more an angel than a demon, the sunlight striking the gleam of his skin and giving him an unearthly glow. "My intentions don't matter. The risk remains. And you know... you must know..." Constantine swallowed, a rush of blue flickering over his skin, an electric prickling licking my cheeks from his hands. "I've remained at his bequest. It is a relief to know I will no longer pose a threat to you or those you care for."

"I care for you!" I cried out.

Constantine's kiss was a rough, hungry press of lips and teeth, my breath whooshing out of me. I teetered on my toes, arching into him, gasping at the sudden slam of my back into the brick wall of the theater. I licked at his lips and demanded his surrender when he parted them for me, as if I might convince him to stay, as if I might convince the whole company to offer him safe haven with something as simple as a kiss.

Constantine groaned, one hand leaving my face to wrap his arm around my bottom and lift me. He was heavy against me, stealing the breath from my lungs, and his tongue twisted around mine. Soon my victory was turning into surrender as I grew soft and languid in his grasp. He would stay. He would stay because it was what I wanted, what we both wanted. As if my affection might be a solution to the laws of demon blood.

We settled into softer sips and licks until finally, Constantine nuzzled against me, the both of us catching our breath.

"That is both my consolation and my motivation to leave, sweet creature," Constantine said.

I whimpered as he pressed a soft and fragile kiss to my forehead.

"You brought me back balance, Hazel Nix," Constantine said.

"You are *not* saying goodbye to me," I moaned, head shaking and cheeks wet. "I refuse. We will find your horrid warlock and—"

Constantine hushed me with another firm kiss. "I believe you," he said, setting me back on my toes. His smile transformed him once more, and I couldn't speak because I couldn't find the air in my lungs when I looked at him. "I will await you."

I tried to tighten my arms around his waist, but he unwound himself without any trouble, kissing my knuckles on one hand and then the other.

"Don't leave me," I whispered.

He paused, then blinked at me, that beauty crumbling with a frown, the first real glimpse at his own fears, his own worries and anger, twisting over the polished features, slumping his shoulders.

"Don't leave," I repeated.

"I must," he said.

The door banged open and I jumped, my hand clapping over my chest as I turned to find Ronan waiting there. That was all the time Constantine needed to turn and stride away. Ronan caught my wrist in his grip before I could chase after the demon.

"Wait, nut," Ronan said. "Wait, you know that's not the end."

My breaths were short and ragged, throat crumbling in on itself. Ronan reeled me in closer, drawing me into his chest as little whimpers and gasps started to break free from my lips, tears rolling over and down my cheeks.

"That's not goodbye, Hazelnut," Ronan whispered in my ear. "You know we'll track him down." He shouted over my head, down the alley to where Constantine was disappearing around a corner. "We'll track you down, mate!"

I shuddered and fell into Ronan's chest. *They always leave*, a cruel little voice whispered in my head. But for the first time, I knew that the person walking out of my life hadn't done so by choice. I hated to admit that Reddy and the others, even Constantine, were right, but I knew the truth. Birsha might force him to reveal plans or to risk another girl's safety. He had to leave.

It didn't make it hurt less.

"What if something happens to him?" I asked, swallowing my tears, strangling myself in the process. "What if Birsha is angry that he's been kicked out?"

Ronan's hand stroked up and down my back. "He's got good reason to lay low and stay safe. He hasn't given up hope, and neither should you, nut."

My nod was feeble and my breath shuddered, but it brought a deep lungful of Ronan's homey scent into my chest and it acted like a drop of laudanum. I sagged in his arms and let my eyes fall shut. I wasn't sure if Ronan was right about Constantine, I'd seen the resignation on my demon's face, but I would make sure Ronan was right about me. I would not give up hope. And I would not surrender Constantine to Birsha's grip so easily.

"Hunter will help," I said.

"Of course he will. We all will. For now, come inside. I'll take you up to my room, and you can rest there until Hunter's carriage comes back for us," Ronan said, guiding me back to the door.

Comes back for us. *We're an* us *now*, I thought.

Constantine would be part of that, even if I had to find my way to the Seven Veils and steal him back from Birsha with my own two hands.

40.

WELCOME PUNISHMENT

Three days later, with no sign or clue of Constantine's whereabouts, my hope was dwindling and my determination met one brick wall after another.

"I'm sorry, little one," Hunter said, stroking his hand over my shoulder as we watched Asterion walk out of Hunter's front door with a final tip of his hat.

"Why wouldn't he tell us where the Seven Veils is located?" I asked, my fingernails biting into my palms.

Behind us, Nireas scoffed and Ronan's wings rustled. Hunter's eyebrow arched as he stared back at me. "Because he knows better than to lead you directly into Birsha's clutches."

"But—"

"But nothing, Hazel," Hunter said firmly. "Entering Birsha's territory without a plan, or even knowing for certain that's where Constantine is, is the surest way to jeopardize your safety."

"Hunter..." I sighed and tried to look away, but Hunter's hand snapped out and caught my chin in a firm but careful grip, turning me back to him.

"And where you go, we will follow, no matter the risk to ourselves," Hunter said, nodding his head back to Nireas and Ronan.

That roused my common sense at last, and I shook myself out of the fog I'd been dropping in and out of for days. "You're right," I said. *I don't want to risk them. I can't.*

Hunter's grip on my chin turned into a caress, his palm sliding up my cheek, a sympathetic and weary smile curving his lips. He stepped forward, kissing my brow. I looked over his shoulder and mouthed "sorry" to the others.

"You're not worrying alone, nut, I promise you," Ronan said.

"I don't mean to be so focused only on Constantine's absence," I said, leaning back to meet Hunter's gaze too. "It isn't as though I haven't enjoyed what... You all..." I blushed as my tongue tied itself into a thick knot over the words.

It's wonderful, all of us being in this house together. There, was that so hard? In the privacy of my own thoughts, the words were easy. I hadn't managed them out loud yet.

"You are mourning a missing lover," Hunter said, shrugging.

"Yes, but I'm not less grateful for the four who are near," I said, relaxing at managing to speak sensibly at last.

"We know that, nymph," Nireas said.

"Speaking of four, Jude should be returning soon. Perhaps it's time we prepare ourselves for supper in the dining room," Hunter said. He turned us toward the stairs, nudging me forward. "I...took the liberty of laying something out for you to wear, little one."

My eyebrows rose. Hunter certainly played the role of an English gentleman to perfection, but that had never extended to dressing for dinner. At least not while the others had been staying here too.

"Go up and see if you approve," Hunter urged, pushing me gently again. "We'll wait for you in the study."

"I'll come up with you—" Ronan started to offer.

Hunter cut him off abruptly. "No. No, I have...something to show you."

My orc was being mysterious. Which was often a good sign.

"Go on, I'll be down shortly," I said, hurrying to the stairs on my own now, reaching out to pat Nireas and Ronan as I passed between them.

I had an inkling of what might be waiting for me, and the thought thrilled me, rushing my footsteps, warming my cheeks. If I was right, Hunter knew me perfectly, knew exactly what to offer to draw me out of my worries and my occupation over Constantine's absence and back into the present with him. And now with Ronan and Nireas and Jude too?

I held my breath as I pushed open the bedroom door, but it only took one glance at the bed for all the air to go whooshing out of me.

Spread over the lovely quilt, carefully arranged so that every strap lay flat and every ring gleamed in the lamplight, was the harness. And now there was one for my hips and knees too.

I stepped inside, immediately reaching for the buttons of my skirt with one hand and the pins in my hair with another. Taking the role of pet would apply order to the chaos in my head again, simplify and narrow my world down to a single point. Or perhaps four points? Was Hunter going to put me on display for the others' envy or make me a shared object between them? Either was an intriguing prospect, making both my breasts ache and my nipples tighten and my cunt clench.

Undress, wash, put on the harness.

I had tasks now. Goals. No more watching the minutes and hours pass, waiting for change. It would all be pushed aside for the night. Tension was already bleeding out of my neck and shoulders as I shrugged off my blouse and stepped out of my skirt.

Thank you, Hunter.

THEIR VOICES CARRIED out of the open door of the study, Jude's low melody now included. I licked my lips, smoothing my hands down over my bare thighs, down the leather straps there. If I waited too long, Hunter would catch my scent and call me in. I wanted to take them by surprise instead.

I lowered myself to the floor—the thin knee pads of the hip harness would be a blessing, I could tell already—and then reached out, pushing the door open wider to make room for my shoulders.

Their eyes were high as I crawled inside, searching where they expected to see me, and it was Hunter whose gaze dropped first, his smile growing wide.

I arched my back as Nireas found me on the floor, slinking forward, and his jaw dropped open, voice mute.

"By all the stars in the northern sky, look at you, Hazelnut," Ronan said, voice breathless and eyes wide.

I stopped, knelt, and rested my hands on my heels behind me, posing and blushing at the collective intake of breath from my men.

"Very good, little one," Hunter said, and then he patted his thigh.

I sank back into my crawl, fighting a grin as Nireas groaned. "Is this...am I allowed to say how much I like this?" he whispered.

"Usually, a pleasure pet only belongs to one warrior," Hunter said as I stopped at his side. I rose up to my knees and pressed my entire body to his leg, panting at the texture of the wool against my bare sex, my eyes falling shut as his claws stroked gently into my hair. "However, I think we will make an exception in this pet's case. She is more than capable of serving all our needs tonight. Aren't you?"

"Yes, masters," I said, rubbing my cheek against Hunter's thigh.

"Fuck," Jude whispered.

"Very good. Stand for us, little one," Hunter said, extending his hand to help me balance as I rose up. "Turn." I made a slow spin, the carpet squishing under my bare feet. "Good. Now, allow them to inspect you."

"Inspect her?" Ronan squawked, echoing my own thoughts.

But I stepped forward, shoulders back and chin high—as proud to be their pet as they would be to claim me, just like Hunter had told me the first night—and adjusted my stance to spread my legs slightly.

Ronan didn't hesitate, stepping between the others and me, eyes still wide and bright, dark tongue flicking out over his lips. His gaze met mine, searching, and I nodded as he reached for my face. Two fingertips patted lightly over my bottom lip.

"Open," Ronan said. Those fingers stroked over my tongue as I opened my mouth, their flavor slightly salty and bitter. "Suck." All three of my new masters groaned as I hollowed my cheeks and sucked on Ronan's fingers, treating them as though I had a cock in my mouth. "Good girl," Ronan rasped.

Ronan and I had an evenly matched relationship. He was rarely completely dominant with me, and I was surprised by the heat that pooled in my belly at those simple words of praise from him. I continued to suck, humming slightly with hunger and desire, slipping my tongue between the two fingers to lick the skin that joined them. Ronan hissed and pulled the digits free of my lips. He loomed forward, head ducking to kiss me, when a hand reached between us, holding him back by the chest.

"My turn," Nireas said.

Ronan rolled his eyes, but he was smiling and he stepped back without further complaint. Nireas tipped my jaw up high with one hand, stroked down my throat with another, and for a moment, it was just him staring down at me, gaze warm and approving. Then suddenly there were two fingers spreading the lips of my sex, stroking, and two hands plucking and plumping my nipples, making them hot to the touch and rosy with pinches. I moaned, and Nireas gazed smugly down at me. Five hands...five hands touching me all at once, and where was the—

"Ah!" I jumped as the sixth hand appeared, a single digit burrowing between my cheeks, searching and then pressing at the tight rosebud of my ass.

"Relax," Nireas said.

I panted but forced myself to soften under his touch. The finger didn't do more than probe, even as I tried to flare my hole and welcome him. The hand on my pussy only petted and stroked, finding arousal at my opening and spreading it over my lips.

"Pretty pet," Nireas said, the words dark and lovely. I shivered against all of his playful hands, parted my lips as his thumb stroked there. His hand on my sex lifted, and I blinked with heavy eyelids as he drew the fingers that had touched me into his broad mouth and purred with approval. "She tastes good."

"Let me," Jude said at my back.

Nireas retreated one hand at a time, until only the finger at my ass remained, just barely dipping inside before pulling away. This time, Jude didn't take his place.

"Bend over, Hazel," Jude said.

I started to bend, and Hunter cleared his throat. "This is a pose we haven't practiced yet. Widen your stance, little one, and wrap your hands around your ankles."

I did as instructed, my braid hanging awkwardly at the side of my head. I was rewarded by a chorus of approving groans, and this time, my blush ran all the way from one pair of cheeks to the others.

Jude's shoes were dusty, the knees of his pants slightly loose and worn. I recognized him immediately as he sank down behind me. His cock was tenting the fabric, and I licked my lips as he adjusted himself briefly.

"Stay still."

I froze as his hands cupped the backs of my thighs, thumbs pressing into the base of my ass, spreading my cheeks. His breath was hot and rough against my exposed sex, and I bit my lip as it grew heavier, closer, dampness calling out more arousal. His tongue wasn't a surprise, but I trembled and jerked all the same as he licked me from clit to ass in one long, smooth stroke.

"Mmm. Very nice. Is it time for dinner yet? Because I'm starving for dessert," Jude growled.

❧

"FUCHS. She's meant to be holding still," Hunter said, his voice muffled through the table.

Ronan paused in his slow, subtle thrusting, and my eyes watered, the head of his cock buried at the back of my throat, his hands tightening in my hair. "She is," Ronan said, but his voice was ragged. He groaned, rocking and rubbing his length on my tongue. "I'm the one who's moving."

Someone, Nireas or Jude, chuckled and I had to fight my own smile.

"Stop," Hunter said, the word hard around the edges. "You'll ruin my training of our pet."

"A good girl holding still and letting her master fuck her pretty mouth isn't so bad from where I'm sitting," Ronan moaned, picking up his pace.

But Hunter's command was sinking into me, if not Ronan, and I started to pull away. Ronan let out another clear groan, his fingers slipping free from my hair. In the shadow of my spot beneath the table, Ronan's cock looked bruise-purple as I pulled away, and the head was glossy and pooling with eager need, pearly and tempting to my hungry tongue. I sat back on my heels.

"Sorry, master," I said, to both Hunter and Ronan.

"Come here, little one."

Ronan sagged in his chair, his own hand reaching beneath the table.

"It appears we have two naughty pets at the table this evening, gentlemen," Hunter announced. "Piper, perhaps you might assist me with Mr. Fuchs."

"Wait—wha?"

I grinned as I crawled over to Hunter's side, watching the shuffle of Jude walking around the table, then dragging Ronan's chair backwards.

"It's a shame we don't have the harness from the theater for you, Ronan," Nireas said, his quiet tones only audible as I slid out from under the cover of the table.

Hunter studied me, a frown on his lips but laughter in the creases at the corner of his eyes. He patted his thigh. "Up here. You'll enjoy this."

I climbed eagerly onto Hunter's lap, his arm wrapping around my waist and hand immediately coming to cup my sex. Ronan was a foot or two from the table now, one of Jude's hands holding him down in his seat.

"Remove his shirt and lower his trousers to his knees," Hunter said. "Nireas, if you wouldn't mind grabbing the case from the sideboard, there are some objects I believe we'll find useful in our necessary punishments."

I leaned into Hunter's warmth, nuzzled my sex against his fingers, and pressed my lips to the lobe of his ear. "Just so you know, I want to ride your cock so hard I feel it all the way in my lungs right now."

Hunter's fingers dipped inside of me, and he hummed at how slick he found me.

Nireas opened the case and laughed at what he found, carrying it to the table.

"Wait a second. How come I've gone from master to pet all of a sudden?" Ronan asked, although he didn't seem very put out.

"You made it evident you don't have the control necessary to be a good master," Hunter said, shrugging, lips twitching. "In fact, I rather suspect you won't even be a well-behaved pet like our Hazel. You'll have to use a firm hand, Jude."

"Gladly," Jude said, grinning and glancing down at a blushing, pouting, squirming Ronan.

"Are all of these toys for him?" Nireas asked.

"Just the collar and the cuffs. Hazel will need a punishment too, for allowing Ronan to make her disobey my orders," Hunter said. I bit my lip and stretched, trying to see what else was in the case, but Hunter settled me, squeezing his arm around my waist. "He didn't feed you enough either. Eat from my plate now, little one."

I hadn't minded, but Hunter was right. Almost as soon as my lips were around Ronan's cock he'd forgotten his duty of feeding me, a right he'd all but begged Hunter for, in favor of using my mouth. I'd enjoyed his eagerness as much as I'd enjoyed the fun of disobeying.

"You can always say no, Ronan," I said.

Ronan glanced between Nireas, who approached with a pair of leather cuffs and a leather collar, and Jude, who held him in place. Finally, he looked at me, flashing a grin. "I know. But where's the fun in that?"

Nireas and Jude wrapped the cuffs around the arms of the backless chair—something Hunter had made so Ronan could sit comfortably with his wings—and Ronan's wrists, pinning him in place before Jude took the collar.

"Since you were so eager to finish before the rest of us, I'm going to make sure you finish last," Jude said, wrapping the collar around Ronan's throat, buckling it as Ronan groaned softly. "But I'll keep you hard. Dripping. Begging."

"Jude's very good at this," Hunter said in my ear as I nibbled on his steak and watched the pair of men with wide and delighted eyes.

"I suppose he's used to bossing lots of men around," I mused.

Jude glanced at me, his smile sly and wicked. "Yes, but not usually ones so pretty."

Ronan's cheeks darkened, and he gaped back at me in surprise. Jude took his jacket off and rolled up his sleeves as Nireas joined me and Hunter at the far end of the table. The box was closed now, and I was enjoying watching Jude and Ronan too much to ask questions.

"Now, I've been dying to do this ever since I saw the act on stage," Jude said. He reached for Ronan's wing, gently grasping and watching Ronan as he went rigid, glowing eyes rolling back slightly.

"Be careful," I warned Jude. "He won't tell you when he's close."

Jude nodded, gently expanding the wing to the side as Ronan trembled in place. We all waited, watching, as Ronan breathed and settled. And then just as the imp looked calm, Jude brushed a delicate touch over the finely veined flesh of the wing.

He was tickling Ronan.

Ronan bellowed and his hips bucked, and Jude grinned, retreating immediately and watching Ronan's cock weep. Ronan's head fell forward, chest panting, and Jude waggled his eyebrows at the rest of us.

"That will do very nicely for Ronan. But now it's time to serve your punishment, little one," Hunter growled in my ear, his claws scratching the nape of my neck.

My breath hitched and I nodded eagerly, setting down the fork. Hunter leaned around me and pushed the plate to the side, and Nireas pushed the wooden case in front of me.

"Open it," Hunter said.

My hands trembled as I set them against the polished wood, lifting the light lid back on its hinge. My pulse hammered as I gazed at the box's contents. I recognized the larger of the three items immediately, although I'd never seen one so ornate before. The plug was made of clear glass, with what appeared to be a little flower bud trapped inside of the bulb. I pulled it out of the blue velvet cushion and realized that the bud was also made of glass too, a perfect illusion. It was heavy and cool in my palm, and my ass clenched instinctively at the weight and size of the plug. The taper thickened quickly. It would be a struggle to fit, but the reward of the stretch promised a very exciting evening for me.

"It's beautiful," I said, turning to offer Hunter a sincere smile.

And because he was Hunter, he released a small sigh of relief. He would never take my acceptance for granted, would never force me to try anything new. It made every eager "yes" all the sweeter for how happy he always was to hear them.

The other two items in the box were a matching pair, sweet little blossoms in the same style as the jewels Hunter had ordered for my performance with Constantine. The reminder of the demon caused a soft pang of worry to run through me, and I closed my eyes, accepting the pain as if it were Con's touch. He and Antin weren't here tonight, but Hunter's gifts promised me some of the same pain and much of the pleasure the pair did.

"I've worn nipple clamps before, but never ones so pretty," I said, twisting to kiss Hunter. "Which first?"

"The plug," Hunter said immediately. "I want to watch you squirm on it when I pinch your pretty nipples with the clamps."

Well then.

I pushed the box my presents had been in aside and slid off Hunter's lap, pressing myself to the smooth surface of the table.

"Plug my ass, masters," I breathed.

Ronan moaned and shuddered without any encouragement from Jude at all.

41.

POSSESSED

Squirm I most certainly did. And moan and whine and sweat and beg for mercy. It took three of Nireas's thick fingers to prep me for the plug, and what I suspected had probably been a small bottle of lubricating oil.

Finally, just as I considered giving the effort up, Nireas murmured simple words in my ear.

"You're going to fit me here later."

Well, that was a goal worth striving for. A little swirling touch on my clit, a kiss on my spine, and I relaxed enough for the plug to settle in place. I was stuffed. Obscenely so. I groaned and softened on the polished table, my face slack and eyes drooping briefly.

My main consolation in the process had been watching Jude slowly and meticulously tease and torture Ronan to an equally delirious mess in the chair. And still not allow him to come. I admired them now, Ronan glittering with perspiration, his lap a mess of eager pre-cum, muscles tense and veins popping on his throat. Jude, for all his control, was starting to look equally strung out, running his tongue up Ronan's twitching length, whining and stroking his own arousal as he forced himself away before Ronan could come.

"Good boy, Ro," I murmured, and Ronan shook and growled at me.

Hunter turned me over onto my back, and I cried out as the pressure of the table on my bottom pushed the plug deeper. His head bent, and he kissed and sucked on my breast, not soothing me at all, just making me wiggle and writhe and *feel* that plug ten times as much as I had while on my tummy. My back arched and my eyes squeezed shut, then Hunter's lips were gone and replaced with a sudden stab of heat that bit around my tit.

I howled as the nipple clamps' sweet little teeth dug into my tender flesh. But the pain was a welcome twin to the ache in my ass, and I caught my breath a moment later, the room clearing from the haze in my head, Hunter and Nireas both hovering over me.

"Your turn," Hunter said to Nireas.

"Please," I gasped, arching again, now grinding onto the plug, needing the duller ache of its intrusion to soften the burn on my nipple.

Nireas groped at my breast with one hand, pushed damp strands of hair off my face with another, and smiled gently down on me. "You really are incredible. There's no act on stage that could match the marvel that is being here with you, touching you, watching every little drop of sweat roll down your skin, and hearing all the smallest sounds you make."

His thumb and forefinger plumped my nipple again as he had in the study, flicking, flicking, flicking, waiting until I'd stopped bracing myself. He bent as Hunter had, gave my breast a wet, licking kiss and a deep suckle, and then snuck the clamp into place just as he flicked gently at the other.

"Bastard!" I snarled, but the word was a lie, the pain divine, and Nireas only chuckled.

"Withes," Hunter called to the far door. "Bring in the last course."

"Course?" I breathed, gasping for air, staring between the two men, craning my neck to watch as the gargoyle butler appeared with a large cut crystal bowl in his hands.

"I chose the flavor especially to complement your own," Hunter said, nodding to the surface of the table at my side.

The gargoyle didn't even look at me as he set the bowl down, and it was almost strange to be on display but not admired. Nice too. I was not an actress here. There was no audience. Any witnesses were coincidental. I was only for my masters to enjoy.

And enjoy me they would. I was dessert.

My lips parted as Hunter drew a large spoon out of the bowl, with a small scoop of what looked like ice cream or sorbet cradled in silver. My belly jumped as he lowered the spoon to my skin, his smile wicked.

"You're our dish tonight, little one. Every bit as much a part of the tasting experience as you are to serve as the plate."

I squealed as the icy scoop dropped to the center of my stomach and immediately began to melt. I moaned as Hunter spread my legs wide to either side and drew his chair up to the table again. His tongue was a fiery contrast to the melting dessert as he licked it directly off my flesh, sucking and kissing and lapping me clean, even biting me slightly.

My sex was pulsing, pleading for touch, and hot tears trickled out of my eyes. Not from pain. Only need, and also gratitude. This was obscene and absurd and spectacular, and absolutely unlike anything Hunter would've asked of me a month ago.

I whined as Hunter finished licking the dessert off me and immediately moved to licking my pussy clean of arousal. His hands reached up, petting and groping my breasts gently, avoiding the clamps but jostling them all the same, the throb ringing down to my cunt. I bucked shamelessly into his mouth, relieved when he purred his approval. His tongue was long and thick, sliding in and out of my core, nose nuzzling at my clit, and I came with the pounding pain of his playful touches batting at the nipple clamps, heady sensation echoing through me like an avalanche.

Hunter groaned into my sex, continued thrusting his tongue until I was limp, and pulled away, wiping his chin and face clean and licking every one of his fingers. "Exceptional. Gourmet, I'd say." He stood and offered his chair to Nireas.

"Oh god," I whispered, realizing their intention. The crystal bowl was still quite full. They would each have a turn.

Nireas took a small scoop and pressed the edge of the spoon to the inside of my knee, the liquid melting in rivulets down my calf and thigh. "I've always had a sweet tooth," he said, watching me gasp before bending his head and attending to his dessert.

❧

I SCREAMED AND HOWLED, the cries raspy and mingling with Ronan's ravenous noises as he sucked and licked and fucked me with his tongue like it might satisfy the bonfire of arousal Jude had built up in him but refused to ignite with a final match. He was almost cruel with his hungry lips and teeth and tongue, except cruelty hadn't been what made me orgasm for a second time. With him. I'd lost count overall.

"Enough," Hunter said.

Ronan let out a string of hoarse curses as Jude dragged his seat out of reach.

"Enough?" I repeated.

"Are you tired, little one?" Hunter asked.

Something cool and soft brushed up my chest, and for a moment, I thought it must be the silver spoon again, Hunter returning for a third helping, but no, this was fabric, not metal. Oh, he was tidying me up.

"Hazel," Hunter prompted, reaching for my face, making me focus on his as he loomed over me. "Enough for tonight?"

Enough for tonight? Did he mean...?

"But you haven't fucked me yet," I said, pouting.

Someone else laughed, and Hunter's lips twitched. "No, we haven't. We don't have to if you're—"

"Master, I haven't let you pinch and stretch and lick me to within an inch of my sanity just so you can *not* give me your cock," I said, frowning, flapping my arms at my side to remind them of the mess they'd made of me.

Hunter laughed now too. "Very well. First, we'll take these off."

He was gentle, careful, massaging and soothing, but that didn't stop me from biting a yelp behind clenched teeth as he unclamped first one nipple and then the other. God, it was so much worse when they came *off*. I was already arching into Hunter's hands, as if I could help him soothe the stabbing burn in my breasts, when I found myself suddenly and unapologetically fucked.

Or rather, stuffed with Hunter's cock.

"Oh!" My back bowed further, hair dragging over the woven table runner.

Hunter drew slowly out, plunging in again and making me slide atop the dining table as he sank in to the hilt.

"There now," Hunter murmured, his nose grazing my throat. "There now, little one, it's all right."

All right? It was more than all right. My cunt was swollen from pleasure, my breasts were being stabbed by shocks of dull pain, and Hunter was already panting, thrusting, fucking me with a natural finesse he'd learned in our time together, grinding the beads at the base of his cock against my clit with every stroke.

"I'm going to come again," I gasped, reaching for him as I started to flutter, my cunt pounding with a heavy pulse of pleasure that echoed like a drum in my ears. "Oh, Hunter, how is this even..."

How was it possible to feel so much, to take so much, to want *more?*

"Our pretty pet, our little nymph," Hunter groaned, snapping his hips into mine.

A pair of hands stroked up my calf as Nireas observed us from around the corner of the table. Jude was whispering filth into Ronan's ear, petting lightly at his wings, as the imp tried and failed to fuck the empty air.

And then Hunter stopped moving, his hands pinning me down by my breasts, his head back, shirt opened, and pants slung low. Beautiful. Untidy. Not at all a gentleman. I smiled up at him and he sighed, shrugging off his shirt and then gathering me up into his arms.

"I ought to have moved us upstairs, but I couldn't wait," Hunter said, which was a relief to hear. I was glad not to be the only one driven insensible by lust.

He lifted me off the table, and I thought at first he meant to carry me upstairs like this, mostly undressed and with me stuffed by his cock. Instead, he simply turned and lay down where I'd just been, draping me over his chest.

"There. Now Nireas's patience will bear fruit," Hunter said, kissing my temple.

Nireas's patience? Then there was a teasing press and pull on the plug in my ass, and my eyes widened, a long moan falling from my lips.

"Jude, give her a show, something to distract her while I start," Nireas said.

I wanted to say that there would be no distraction for a cock as big as Nireas's in my ass, but then he was pumping the plug at my opening and Jude was dropping to his knees and taking the head of Ronan's cock between his lips, and Hunter had started to move again. I wasn't distracted. I was inundated, overwhelmed, consumed.

"Such a good girl, a perfect nymph. Reddy was a fool to tell you to keep that a secret, as if you weren't a perfect design for a monster's needs," Nireas said. I braced myself against Hunter's chest, worked myself between the plug and his cock, needing friction.

"So pretty, so soft," Ronan whined, bucking up into Jude's lips. Jude retreated, turning his head to smile at me.

"You were all fools. I saw her clearly right away," Jude murmured. "Perfection and sin and a pair of bow lips to match."

"Oh, please," I whined, not sure if I was begging for more pretty words, more sweetness, or for them to stop before my heart drummed its way right out of my chest. "Please. Please, I *need*."

"Yes, pretty little one," Hunter rasped. "Your need is dripping down over my cock, soaking me. Your sweet little cunt is sucking my cock so well, begging."

I moaned and shuddered, a quieter, smaller orgasm rushing through me, and Hunter groaned and gritted his teeth and held still as I rode the wave. I sagged at the end, and Nireas grunted as the plug pulled free.

"Don't make her wait," Hunter hissed and then corrected himself. "Don't make *me* wait."

"No more waiting," Nireas said, solemn and tender, and two hands stroked down my sides as another pair adjusted my hips.

I buried my face into Hunter's chest as Nireas pressed to my hole. His tip was hot and silky and slick. And also broad as hell, bigger than the plug had been. Hunter and Nireas petted me and murmured soothing, meaningless words as he filled me. It was agonizing, burning, but the pain was as satisfying to me as any orgasm might be. My body could, *would*, accept the cock. I was made for this, made to pleasure and be pleased. I breathed through the stretch, clenched and relaxed, and when Nireas's chest finally touched my back, it was him who was breathless.

"Fuck. Hazel, I—I..." He didn't know what, so instead he flexed, both Hunter and I groaning.

They were gentle with me, Nireas alternating long strokes in my ass with Hunter's deep grind of his pelvis against my clit. When I lost track of my own breath, too consumed by the churning storm of pressure and stretch and heat, Nireas paused, hips pressed to my ass, and ran his fingertips up and down my back as if he were playing a familiar piece of music. Hunter kissed me, tongue soothing and stroking against my own, and I softened between them, breathing in the pattern of the rise and fall of Hunter's chest and Nireas's stroking touch.

I didn't notice the slow contraction of my own muscles, or the way I started to flutter and squeeze on their cocks. I was lost, my attention split to tiny fractions in too many directions. What I did notice was Nireas's hands tightening around my hips, his compromised rhythm with Hunter breaking, Hunter's groan vibrating against my sweat-slicked breasts.

Pleasure was white noise in comparison with the little details of my lovers, the swell of Nireas's cock growing just a bit thicker, stretching me just a bit more. Hunter bucking gently up to try and press closer, tongue fucking deeper in my mouth as he growled.

"Hazel, nymph, you're killing me," Nireas gasped out, and then released a long groan as his stomach draped over my back and he splashed hot and deep in my ass.

Hunter followed quickly as I shook, sucking on his tongue, gushing on his cock. The heat and breadth of them around me was like a cocoon of safety, made up of familiar flesh and scents, and I had eight hands stroking my sides and limbs as we settled, two pairs of lips kissing my cheeks and shoulders and throat. I was sinking toward sleep when a snarl and a sob drew me out of my reverie, my head turning to rest my cheek on Hunter's warm chest.

Ronan's muscles were shaking with tension, his wrists pulling hard at the straps that held him to the seat, little flames biting at the leather. Nireas pushed up on wobbling arms, kissing my temple, and we both held our breath as he dragged himself carefully out of me. He was barely out when he slipped a finger into my hole, plugging me and soothing my tired muscle at the same time.

"If we tease Ronan any further, he won't be in a fit state to touch her," Jude said, sitting on the floor at Ronan's side, his pants open and cock hard.

"I'd never hurt her," Ronan muttered, but he thrashed in his seat again slightly, still fighting to get free.

Hunter stifled a groan as he sat up, holding my limp form on his lap, petting and teasing me with the measured scratch of his claws.

"If you tease him any further, he'll burst before I can enjoy him in all his wildness," I said, smiling at Ronan.

Hunter leaned back, pushing hair out of my face and looking me over once more.

"I'm fine," I said, my blink heavy with satiated lethargy. "Let me have you all tonight, master. Even the naughty pet."

Ronan moaned, head falling back on his shoulder as Hunter nodded down to Jude on the floor, who scrambled up eagerly, shedding his clothes. Jude's touch was cool as he wrapped around my back, shadows slithering over my arms like strips of silk, calming my fevered and flushed skin. I gasped as Hunter lifted me off his cock, and Jude eagerly took his place from behind, the pair of them maneuvering me onto Jude's lap. Jude pulled my arms up and back to reach around his neck, and he sat down at the edge of the table, putting me on display directly in front of Ronan's starving gaze. His hands reached down to my waist, working me up and down on his cock.

"Fuck, god, so fucking wet, love," Jude hissed. "Christ, Ronan, you don't know how good she feels."

"I know exactly how good she feels," Ronan growled, pulling at his restraints, bracing against the floor and arching his hips in my direction, as if he might be able to reach from those scant two feet away. His black wings were stretching out behind him, and I smiled, knowing that with just a few beats he might be able to propel himself closer.

"Don't make him wait. I want you both," I murmured, rolling myself on Jude's cock. "I want more." I turned my head to gaze at Hunter, who was back in the throne of his chair, observing us all with a smile. "Let him fuck me, master."

"I'll be so good," Ronan rasped, but he couldn't tear his eyes off where I bounced lightly on Jude's length, Hunter's cum sliding out of me.

Jude's breath was rough in my ear, hand sliding up from my waist to caress my breasts, pinch my tender nipples between two fingers.

"You can take them both?" Hunter asked me. "Like this?"

Could I fit two cocks in my cunt at once? My grin was lazy, already drunk with good sex. "Absolutely."

Not Nireas and Hunter, perhaps, but Jude and Ronan together would be a rewarding challenge. And that was all the reassurance Hunter required. He nodded to Nireas, who barely managed to pull the strap out from the buckle before Ronan was able to wrench his wrist free, red fingers shaking as he twisted to do the same for the other hand.

I expected Ronan to launch at me, to thrust inside with that same sudden urgency Hunter had used. But my imp stood, shook his wings, and stepped forward once. The tip of his swollen, angry cock kissed at my belly button, left a drip of molten arousal on my skin. He bent forward, reaching those trembling hands for my face, and drew me close for a kiss. It was all biting teeth and growls, soothed after by his scorching tongue, and I reached out with one arm to stroke his chest, finding his muscles straining like tightly coiled springs.

"Such a good pet," I whispered, sliding my hand up his dewy chest and linking my fingers into the loop on his collar.

"Fuck. Your pet. I'm your pet," Ronan laughed, the words rough and husky.

"Yes," I agreed. I was Hunter's, but Ronan was absolutely mine. Jude could share us, be shared by us. It was all starting to mix together in lovely combinations that ensured I would never be bored or unsatisfied.

"You know what I want, nut," Ronan breathed out.

I nodded and leaned back, Jude nuzzling at my cheek,

lowering us down to our backs. Ronan moaned at the sight of us, at the junction of where Jude was fitted inside of me. He pulled Jude's heels up to the edge of the table, my legs draped over his thighs, and it spread me wider, fitted our half-fae lover deeper inside of me. And then Ronan was holding his cock to my opening, stroking himself up to swirl over my clit, his eyes fluttering shut and mouth open on a silent cry.

"Fuck us, Ro," I murmured.

"Mmm, want to feel the pair of you together," Jude called to him.

Ronan bent, mouth falling to my breasts, suckling sweetly at the same moment he notched himself inside of me. Jude howled and I gasped as Ronan started with short, careful thrusts, working me up to fit him, adjusting Jude's seat in my cunt, distracting me with pleading kisses on my breasts.

Jude was cursing, hips rocking, rubbing himself against Ronan, and the pair of them began to race, clumsy and eager. Ronan's hand found mine on his collar, clutching me as he buried himself in deep thrusts. Jude pulled my other hand back to his lips, kissing and licking at my palm as he whined and fucked me.

"Pretty," Nireas remarked.

"Exceptional," Hunter agreed.

And then it was only Ronan and Jude and me, whimpers and cries and twisting muscles, tumbling drums of sensation, the press and push and rub at every nerve inside of me. Ronan's free hand hitched my thigh higher, pulling me closer, and Jude slid fingers between us to rub at my clit.

It was a series of explosions set off. First my own, snapping out of my body and into thick blooms of ecstasy, flowers of pleasure bursting in the sweaty, damp heat of summer. Jude followed, bowing and lifting us both up and into Ronan's fucking, our release splashing against our desperate, unraveled imp. Ronan's wings beat as he roared and came, clutching my hand and thigh, rising up onto his hooves and stiffening. He started to buck after the first burst inside of me, moaning and leaning forward.

"Too soon," he gasped. "Too soon, I want more."

I found his kiss on my lips, freed my hands to stroke his face and calm him. He could have more if he wanted, although I wasn't sure I could do more than wrap myself around him and hold on, but he relaxed and drooped heavily onto me, still thrusting softly inside of me, slowing to a stop and sighing out an endless breath. I fluttered around them both and Jude hissed, hips kicking and making Ronan grunt and push up.

"She needs rest," Hunter said.

Ronan kissed my throat before sliding away, lifting me from on top of Jude. I had all the strength of a wet blanket.

"Put her down in front of me."

I shivered as Ronan rested me on the table in front of Hunter's seat, supporting me with an arm around my back. Hunter's bright gaze studied me, eyes tracing over every inch of flushed skin, every rumpled, sweaty strand of hair. Then he leaned in. I held my breath as he moved closer and closer, head bowing down, gentle hands spreading my legs. He stopped when his face was just an inch from my sex, stare flicking up to meet mine as he inhaled, long and deep. His eyes shut, and I shivered at the slow smile on his beautiful lips.

"Perfect," he said, voice low and breath breezing against my tender flesh. His eyes opened again, met mine. "You're ours, little one."

I nodded dutifully, ignored the aroused pulse in my core. "Yours," I said. I reached out to Hunter's face, lifted it to mine and pressed a kiss on his lips. "Gratefully." I turned to Ronan, and he met my kiss with the same welcomingly weary expression on his face that I was sure I wore. "Delightedly." I twisted and Jude was there, waiting, smiling, kissing me on my forehead. "Devotedly."

Nireas reached into the tangle of us, lifting me into his arms, cradling me to his chest. "Finally," he finished for me, mouth soft on mine. "Time for bed, nymph."

I went slack and relaxed in his hold, the others following close behind as he carried me through the house and up the stairs.

42.

ALLIES ARRIVE

"**D**o you think this Birsha bastard has given up?" Alexa asked, her tone wistful as she wiped an oiled cloth over a well-worn wooden paddle.

I was glaring at a suspicious residue on the riding crop—someone hadn't done proper clean up after their act as we were supposed to—when she spoke, and my answer came out unconsciously.

"Not a chance."

"But no other girls have—"

"No other girls have gone missing because there's only the six of us, and we all know better than to put ourselves in danger," Evie said, arching an eyebrow briefly at me.

I raised my hands. "I've behaved. Recently."

"I think Reddy made Birsha up," Isabella spat out, scrubbing roughly at the laundry in the bucket between her knees.

"Made him up?" Christine murmured.

We were down under the trap doors, where all the props were stored and near the vampires' resting place, taking care of a few basic chores while over our heads, Hugh plotted out a new scene with a female guest act. She was a beautiful lamia—her top half an exquisite human form and bottom half a long snake-like form, with amethyst purple scales and a soft pink underbelly. Isabella had been bitter enough the week before, when Hugh had enjoyed his scenes with audience members a little too much, but she was *livid* now.

"Don't be absurd," I muttered, grabbing a cloth and working the crop clean.

"I say Reddy just doesn't want to admit to us that some of those beasts get a little too eager with us girls. Brutes. Just like men, but with claws and horns and—"

Evie dropped her own work and marched over to Isabella, slapping a hand roughly over the younger woman's running mouth, bending down to stare hard into her pretty blue eyes. "Hush. Before one of them hears you."

My eyes widened at the pair. "Reddy isn't lying to you. And Birsha hasn't given up, but he just got trounced by our allies, monsters determined to protect women like us, whether we're their lovers or not. So we're lucky right now, but we're not safe. And those beasts aren't all brutes, not unless you ask them to be. Just like we're not all skittish, prudish women who judge a man's worth on having a pretty *human* face or deep pockets." I was a little breathless by the end of my speech and grateful for the dim lighting down in this basement, so my flushed cheeks might not be so obvious.

"That's lovely," Alexa said, smiling up at me. "Here, here!"

Isabella growled and tossed the wet wad of clothing back into the water, jumping up from the crate she sat on and storming out of the room.

Evie stared between the pair of us and sighed. "I'm not finishing the laundry for her."

I put the crop aside, moving to the crate. "I'll do it. But I'm not apologizing to her."

"She isn't prudish, and she isn't after Hugh for his money, you know, because he doesn't have any," Christine said softly, glancing at me out of the corner of her eye. "It's just that she's jealous, of course."

"I'll never go back to fucking human men after Leon and Samson," Alexa said with a shrug. "Perhaps it's the same for Hugh? What's a normal human girl got to offer when you could fuck a woman with an enormous scaled tail for a lower body?"

We all stared blankly back at her until her lips twitched. "Joking."

I snorted and relaxed, about to dunk my arms into the water, when a pair of footsteps stormed over our heads and down the stairs behind me.

"Something's happened," Evie said, sitting up.

And before anyone else could answer, the door banged open. Frank appeared, shaggy black hair wild around his head, face just barely lit from the hall behind him, and lovely brown eyes bright. He was an exceptionally handsome man when not in his werebear form, and I recalled that Isabella had chased him for a bit when she'd first arrived. That must've fizzled away with her discomfort with monstrous forms.

"She's here. She's back," Frank gasped out.

"Who?" I asked, rising up, a little too eager to leave the laundry behind. It *was* Isabella's job.

"The girl," Frank said, waving massive hands. "You know. The one. The one with the fancy scientist man who turned into the—"

Evie squealed. "She's here? Now?"

"The girl," as Frank referred to her, was infamous in our theater. She'd attended a performance almost a year ago with a vampire and another gentleman, and they'd put her on stage for our final act, where she'd been strapped into some bizarre stand, electrocuted, tortured with a vibration machine, and then had very determinedly and enthusiastically fucked a giant beast of a man on the stage for all to see. She'd put the audience into an absolute frenzy, and our backstage had been packed to the brim with writhing fucking bodies, all in search of her.

I'd wondered if she was part nymph, like me.

"Here. Now. With a whole pack of monsters. She asked for Reddy."

"Who?" Christine asked as Alexa, Evie, and I scrambled toward the door.

Had she come here for a job? As a guest act? *Was* she human?

Evie and I laughed, shoving each other through the narrow doorway and out into the hall. I tripped and bounced across the hall into a wall, attracting the attention of the small gathering at Reddy's office door.

I recognized one of the men right away, the delicate and handsome gentleman who transformed into a terrifying giant, as he turned and blinked at my clumsy arrival. At his side was a pale man with ice blue eyes and black hair, who I would've sworn was a vampire if it weren't the middle of the afternoon. Behind the group, flickering in and out of sight, was a cheerful and burly looking redheaded man with a thick beard, standing next to a white marble enchanted statue with gray veins running through. Halfway in the door was a beautiful and bronze man in an elegant white linen suit, his dark and slightly feline slanted eyes glancing briefly in my direction. Finally, at his side, was the Girl.

She was petite, especially when surrounded by her pack of men, with pink, almost sunburned cheeks and a thick head of dark curls, nearly black. She was dressed in rich, draping cloth-ing, not at all suited to London fashion but somehow incredibly stylish. All five of the men surrounding her regularly touched her, not with intention, but in absent and familiar ways.

"Nix? That you crashing around?" Reddy asked, sticking his head farther out the door to glare at me.

I blushed as the six newcomers turned to stare at me. "I'm fine, just tripped," I said unnecessarily.

"Come with us to the dining room. We won't all fit in my office," Reddy said, waving his hand at me and then speaking to the others. "Nix has a few mutual friends looking into matters as well. She'll be able to pass anything relevant on."

My eyes widened. So the girl wasn't here for work at the theater. She was here about Birsha. The men moved fluidly around her, following Mr. Reddy, but she turned and waited for my approach, holding out a hand.

"Esther Reed."

"Hazel Nix," I answered, shaking her offered hand.

She looked human, although very pretty, and as one of the men called to her, she turned her head, revealing a perfectly rounded and normal ear. *So just a spectacularly enthusiastic woman when it came to fucking monsters, not a nymph*, I thought. I was sure Reddy would make her an offer of a job before she left.

"Your employer said you had a run-in with the killer," Esther said. I nodded, joining her on the way to the canteen. Her voice surprised me. I'd been expecting something more polished and refined, but her accent was sweet and common, not so different from the ones I'd grown up with. "I had a close call with a water wraith Birsha sent to Rooksgrave Manor."

The name struck like a match in my mind, recalling all of Hunter's explanations. "You're the young woman Hunter told me about. The one who injured Birsha?"

"Just a little stabbing," Esther said, shrugging a shoulder, eyes drifting up in thought. "Hunter... Oh! Mary's Hunter?"

I stiffened and nearly growled at the mention of the other woman. "*My* Hunter," I blurted out, and then flushed. "But I suppose..."

Esther waved her hand at me and beamed. "Oh, I am happy to hear that! He seemed like a lovely orc to me, but I had my hands quite full...literally," she added in a snickering laugh as we stepped into the canteen and her men rose eagerly from their chairs to greet her. "I still do."

❦

BY THE TIME Asterion and Hunter arrived, as well as the monsters who worked at the theater who were volunteering their help, I'd been introduced to all of Esther's gentlemen and found myself in a kind of kinship with the young woman. She was the other person Magdalena Mortimer had mentioned, with a heart large enough to love so many monsters. And they were obviously devoted to her.

She was younger, brighter, and she'd been swept off her feet by her lovers with ease, according to her own admission. In comparison, I felt as though I had quite a few years of wear and tear on my heart, but as Nireas pulled me into his arms on his lap, and Ronan took my free hand in his, and Hunter absently brushed a hand over the crown of my head, I knew that whatever harm those years had done to me would be eased and smoothed away soon. I was well cared for.

Loved, probably, I realized as Nireas kissed the lobe of my ear and the handsome sphinx Amon cleared his throat, standing from the table where his unique little family was gathered together. I didn't have time to worry over the revelation at the moment.

"Jude should be here," I whispered, adding privately, *and Constantine*.

"We'll have to fill him in, but I think he wants to give his notice at work soon," Ronan answered, and I nodded.

The room hushed as Amon stared at each of us in turn. We'd never had a sphinx at the theater, and this one seemed a bit haughty and imperious, at least until he turned and offered Esther a smile I was sure was made of actual sunlight.

"You should tell them, my star," he said, not bothering to raise his voice, certain no one would dare interrupt them.

Esther's cheeks blushed, and she accepted his offered hand, rising but then holding him to her side. "Last spring, when Birsha attacked Rooksgrave Manor, he ate a vampire's heart while sitting right in front of me. He was very comfortable with the act, knew exactly what he could do in order to keep the vampire alive and feeling the sensation of being devoured."

I shivered and snuggled deeper into Nireas's arms, glad Alexa wasn't in the room to overhear this. She'd worry horribly for Leon's sake if she knew.

"Obviously, a vampire's blood is the key to creating another vampire, but Birsha *isn't* a vampire, and eating their organs isn't quite the same. Still, Jonathon—Dr. Underwood—decided to test some subtle experiments," Esther explained, gesturing to the tidy gentleman gazing back at her. "To be honest, I don't really understand all of it, but we think Birsha may have discovered a method of stealing the powers and gifts of monsters.

"Just a couple months ago, we took a trip to visit..." Esther looked to Amon for guidance, who nodded. "To visit Lilith. And we were able to bargain for information that led us to the ruins of Birsha's palace near the Dead Sea. There wasn't much left, but we found a temple underground, all but buried. The evidence was there. Birsha has and likely still is killing monsters, eating their organs, or whatever parts of you all that hold your strength or your magic or—"

"It's all scientific," Dr. Underwood cut in.

"Maybe to you," Esther answered, teasing. "And if you want it to sound scientific, you'd better stand up and tell it yourself."

There were a few chuckles, and the doctor's cheeks were

flushed as he rose, his fingers slyly pinching Esther through her skirt as she squeaked and stole his seat. "Vampire blood has certain chemical properties, just as my own does—much by my own accidental design. I haven't discerned what the key is for every species, and I admit there are some gifts I cannot offer explanation for, but there's enough information available, and I do have some—"

"Jonathon," the vampire murmured.

Dr. Underwood cleared his throat, blushing even darker. "Right. We found the remains of at least one vampire, demon, naga, and what we think must've been an oracle in the temple. They'd been preserved. The vampire's heart had been cut out, the demon's horns pulled out from the root, the naga's spinal cord, and the oracle's eyes. We, or rather I, assume these are the elements he used, consumed, to ensure his survival at the fall of Gomorrah."

Asterion rose up slightly from his own seat at the table to my left. "There are whispers, even in the Seven Veils and Birsha's own circles, of monsters going missing. Most assume these are individuals who cross him, but perhaps it's even more sinister than vengeance."

"I can't say for certain, given the nature of the act, but I suspect Birsha is still continuing to consume monsters' organs. Either to accumulate abilities, to balance the combinations, or simply for his own sadistic enjoyment," Dr. Underwood said. "Either way, it's knowledge that would certainly turn the tide of support against Birsha. Even those who currently prefer to sit the conflicts out would take issue with his actions."

"Then that's exactly what they should find out," Reddy said, words dark as he stepped forward from the corner of the room. "And I have just the idea for how the rumor can start to spread."

43.

PANTOMIME

"Cut!" Mr. Reddy cried out for what was surely the hundred and nineteenth time that evening.

I sighed, scooting back from Ronan's grinning face and sitting on his chest, drawing out an *oof*. Upstage, at the throne, Alexa and Evie groaned, dropping their massive feather fans to the floor again.

"Isabella, you're being tortured, you're not meant to be torturing the audience in the process," Mr. Reddy barked.

"I thought it'd be easier here than Drury Lane," Evie muttered, leaning back against the makeshift throne that Hugh was seated on. "More fucking, less dropping a scene and starting over dozens of times."

I stretched out on the rug next to Ronan, prepared for a long lecture from Reddy to offer me a break from the scene. Evie was right, in a way. Scenes at the theater were usually short and with one easy point to make: sex. This was different. Reddy was trying to create a pantomime version of Birsha's origins and crimes against humans and monsters alike. There were costume changes, blocking, props, and dozens of cues for everyone. It took up all of the third act and was the most ambitious production I'd ever seen at the Company of Fiends.

It was a clear and loud condemnation of Birsha. It would create whispers, conversation, all of which would spread quickly once our audience walked out of our doors. Rumors our allies would be feeding and adding more information to. I just worried it would be a slow poison against Birsha's reputation in the monster community. Constantine was still missing, or hidden away in Birsha's collection, and I was impatient, missing and worrying over my demon.

"If we're supposedly in such danger from this Birsha, why are we intentionally doing an act that will surely make him more determined than ever to punish us?" Isabella hollered back at Mr. Reddy, rising from the floor and setting her hands on her hips.

"Girlie, if you don't listen and do your job properly—" Reddy snarled.

"You'll what? Have Goliath torture me for real?" Isabella shouted.

"Iz, stop," Evie snapped as Goliath reared back, a wounded look on his gentle face.

"Or will you have me chased down in some alley and killed like Beth and Margaret?!" Isabella finished at a crescendo, and the appropriate silence answered her.

Our guests, Esther and her clan, and the lamia, Valentina, all gaped up at the human girl in horror. Mr. Reddy's jaw dropped and his eyes widened at that statement, openly gobsmacked by the idea that he might've been directly responsible for the girls' deaths.

"How dare you?" Myra gasped, rising from her seat and resting her hand over Mr. Reddy's shoulder. "You know better. You do!"

"All I know is that I wish I'd never walked through your horrible doors," Isabella said, eyes glassy with tears, chin high and jutting out.

Silence fell over us like a stage curtain. I wished Isabella had never walked through our doors too, because now she was the reason Goliath was hunched in on himself and Frank was flushed with shame. She'd been hurt, I supposed. It was no excuse to throw that damage back at the monsters around her now.

Mr. Reddy's lips pursed, and his gaze narrowed. "I'm going to offer this, and I don't mean it as a threat, but do you want me to call the man and have your memory erased and send you out of here? If you've had enough of the company I won't try and keep you, but you can't leave us all at risk."

All eyes turned in Isabella's direction, her cheeks flushing red with anger and embarrassment. Only one girl had chosen to leave the theater in all the time I'd been here, but she had done it quietly and with no hard feelings I'd heard of.

"Maybe we ought to take a break," Myra whispered to Reddy.

But Isabella ignored her, round toward upstage, turning that bright blue stare onto one person only. Hugh, sitting on the gold throne, acting as our Birsha. His hands tightened on the arms of the chair as she faced him, his expression pale and hard.

"Is that what you want?" Isabella asked him. "For me to leave? To forget you?"

Hugh's brow crumpled, and he rose but didn't cross to her. "Bella, no, of course not. I love you."

Her bottom lip wobbled and her head whipped back and forth. "You don't."

"I *do*. But I love this theater too. I love the acts and the lights and the audience and—"

"The monsters. The ones you fuck," Isabella spat. "You love me, but not as much as you love fucking monsters."

Hugh's lips tightened and his eyes narrowed. "I love you. But I think you want me to *make* you happy, more than you want to be happy with me. I love you, but no, I never wanted to leave the theater for you. If I'd known from the beginning that was what you wanted, I would've..." His head shook in refusal, shoulders dropping with a sigh.

Isabella turned away from him again, cold nobility surrounding her as she stared down to Mr. Reddy in the front row. "I need a few minutes."

He sighed heavily, but Isabella didn't wait for her permission, marching herself and all her wounded dignity to stage right and around the back to the downstairs.

"Someone should follow her," I whispered to Ronan, who nodded.

"Take ten minutes, everyone," Mr. Reddy called out.

The stage was a flurry of activity, Christine running after Isabella, monsters slipping into the wings, Hugh falling back into the throne with a weary resignation painted over his face. Evie rose and perched on the arm of the chair, speaking to him in a low voice.

"Reddy should've given that hire a little more thought," Ronan muttered.

"It wasn't quite his fault. Isabella came to the theater on the arm of a vampire. He left that night without her," I said, stretching my back and then rising up from the rug, offering my hand out for Ronan. "Myra convinced Reddy to take Isabella on rather than have her memories of the night stolen. Monsters can be careless with girls' hearts, every bit as much as we can with theirs."

Ronan stood, tugging on my hand and pulling me into his chest. His head dipped, lips landing on my nose. "I'll watch your heart if you watch mine, nut."

"He'll have help."

I twisted to smile back at Nireas as he approached us. "Deal."

Nireas's lower arms looped around my waist, two more hands resting on my shoulders, and his chin settling on the crown of my head. Ronan's thumbs stroked over the back of my hands and my eyes fell shut, sinking into the comfort of them.

"What would you think if I asked Reddy not to partner me with anyone else?"

I blinked, staring back at Ronan in the wake of his quiet question. "Anyone else...but me?"

His smile tilted, and he nodded.

"Would he... Do you think..." I swallowed and reminded myself that this wasn't about Reddy. Ronan just wanted to know how I would feel. "I'd like that. Very much."

"Yeah?" Ronan asked, brightening.

I nodded, grinning back at him. "I wish I could get away with asking the same."

"You could, if you wanted," Nireas said immediately. "Between Ronan and me, Constantine when we free him, and visits from Hunter and Jude, you'd have more than enough of us for scenes."

I bit my lip. Reddy had always used me with the guest acts who were too challenging for human girls—centaurs, trolls, a very notable tentacle monster. I wasn't sure he'd be thrilled to give up that advantage.

He doesn't have to be thrilled. It's my choice, I realized, releasing a deep breath. "That sounds nice. I won't bring it up now—Isabella's caused enough of a stir—but I think that's what I want."

"Then that's how it will be," Nireas said, kissing the top of my head. Mr. I-Own-Fifty-One-Percent-of-the-Company had spoken, apparently.

"Good, I have enough other men to be jealous of," Ronan said, gaze sparking with mischief.

I arched an eyebrow. "Oh, and should I be jealous of Jude or Con and Antin?"

Ronan stepped forward until I was pressed firmly between my giant and my imp, his words purring softly to me. "Oh, Hazelnut, I wish you would."

I snorted, turning my cheek to him as he leaned in for a kiss. Nireas pushed my hair aside, nipping at my throat, and I made a soft and insincere sound of protest, trying to calm my own arousal as we stood on the stage in our little cluster, the rest of the company milling around us.

My giddy mood quickly burst as Christine returned to the stage in a running panic, breath panting and face pale.

"I tried to stop her, but she took off. She ran out alone!"

Damnit, Isabella, I thought and then shook myself. I'd done the same when my scene with Nireas had unsettled me, and Isabella's discomfort had been made much more public than mine.

"We have to go after her," Goliath said, which was sweet, considering the way Isabella had treated him.

"We do," Mr. Reddy said, a weary huff passing out his lips. "Nireas, you stay here with the girls. I'll check the alley, see if our guards are on her trail."

"Eston went to follow her," Christine said in a small voice.

"Eston?" Ronan echoed, frowning. "Eston doesn't give a shit about Isabella."

Christine gaped back at him. "Maybe he just...wanted to help? I—I don't know—" Her bottom lip trembled and I sighed, pushing Nireas and Ronan back just as Christine burst into tears.

The stage was chaos, everyone running in opposite directions, shouting the news to others. And in the middle of it all,

Hugh sat on that half-painted, chintzy gold throne made of cobbled parts, staring into empty air with slack terror.

"The gargoyle's not at his post," Johnny murmured to Mr. Reddy at my left. "He must've followed them right away."

"Good, then she's not alone, no matter what," Reddy answered. "Give a task to the unknowns, keep them here, we don't need any more unaccounted for."

Unknowns? I wondered as I crossed the stage. Oh. The monsters who we couldn't be certain of yet. The ones without alibis, without alliance.

I knelt in front of Hugh, and his eyes landed on mine, still unseeing. "We're prepared. She'll be fine."

"I should've pulled her aside. She's just been wanting attention," Hugh murmured. "Affection. Someone to care more about her than themselves."

"Come on, help us organize—" Before I could finish the sentence, the doors to the theater banged open.

"Now what?" Reddy growled.

"Hazel!" Ronan barked.

I was already standing again, turning to face the shadow at the back of the seats. The breeze traveling to stage was sweet and caramelized but tinged with a dangerous metallic edge, familiar and incomplete and brutal all at once. The shadow moving closer was the same, a lone figure, curling horns drooping low, the body hunched.

"Constantine," I breathed, darting forward just as the figure reached the light spilling over from the stage.

It wasn't Constantine. Not all of him.

Antin stumbled forward alone, ruby skin glistening, breath labored and ragged, and it took me a moment to realize he wasn't sweating but *bleeding*, his blood a perfect match for his flesh.

"Antin!" I shouted, running for the stairs to meet him. "What's happened, where's Con?"

"Someone get that bastard—"

"Shut it. He's hurt and he's ours," Ronan snarled back to whoever had started to complain.

Antin fell to his knees just as I reached him, and I wrapped my arms around him, pulling him to my chest without thinking, pressing my face to his head between his horns. I moaned and shivered, but the pleasure racing through me was pale in comparison to what he usually offered. He was hurt, weakened, or maybe he was too far away from—

"Where's Con?" I whispered, ignoring the gentle tingling waves of sweetness rolling through my muscles, stroking my hands over the demon's bare back.

"They forced me here. I tried to fight it, but—"

"Hush," I said, finding his face with my hands, lifting it up and leaning down to press a kiss to the center of his long brow. His skin made my lips throb. "Who forced you here?"

"Birsha and—" Antin's mouth opened, his jaw worked, but no sound came out and his whole body trembled against me.

"The warlock," I said, and Antin released a heavy breath, sagging into me.

"They have Con, they're trying to cut us apart. But they sent me here as bait, Hazel, you can't—"

"I can and I will. I've told you. I'll fight for you. They sent you here because they knew I would come after them, chase down Con. And they'll get what they ask for and more," I said, glancing over my shoulder and searching for Nireas and Ronan. They were right behind me, Nireas's jaw clenching and Ronan's shoulders straightening. Not arguing with me, thank god.

The theater was growing quiet around us and Antin's head tilted back, almost as if he had the eyes to gaze up at me. "I can't feel him. It might already be over."

"It's not," I said, my voice hard even as my hand soothed over his cheek, fingertips bloodied. If Birsha and his horrible warlock had succeeded, then I'd lost two lovers in the process, or at the very least Constantine when he was whole. "It's not over. If they want me to come and save him, they won't have finished it yet," I said.

"She's right. Birsha will want her to see the pair of you in pain," Esther Reed said, rising from the audience, flanked by her lovers, her arm wrapped tightly around Auguste, the daywalking vampire. "He'll want her to hope she might be able to save you, if only so he can enjoy destroying that hope." She grimaced in apology at me, but the warning only made me more determined than ever.

"He knows the truth about me," I said. I'd all but heard Birsha say as much. "He knows I'll present a challenge."

"I'm sorry. I'm sorry. I fought every step here," Antin rasped.

"It's all right, Antin," I said, stroking down the back of his head, the warm thrill rushing through my blood simply background noise to my racing thoughts. "It only means he's underestimated me."

I turned to face the stage, where the company was gathering, all the familiar faces, old and new, who made up my friends—my family in our strange way—staring back at me. "Ronan, fly and find Hunter and Jude. Bring them and anyone else you can think of here. We need Asterion too. We're taking the battle to Birsha's door. *Tonight*."

44.

ARROGANT MONSTERS

I scowled as I watched Goliath, Leon, Conall, and a few other unfamiliar faces leave the theater. A heavy arm slid over my shoulders, and I leaned into Nireas's side as he hunched to whisper at me.

"You can't expect them all to put Constantine before Isabella," he murmured.

I pursed my lips but didn't argue. I'd barely managed my authoritative declaration of war on Birsha before I was promptly beaten down by arguments. Isabella was a member of the company, and in spite of her parting insults, we owed her our loyalty. On the other hand, there was no love lost between the rest of the company and any piece of my Gemini demon, bleeding or otherwise.

I turned to glare into the shadowy wing of the stage where Asterion, Hunter, Mr. Reddy, and Amon were questioning Antin. At least he was cleaned up, bandaged, and dressed.

"I want to go to Con," I said, too many times to count now.

A pair of shadows spiraled over the floor of the stage as Jude and Ronan flew down from Ronan's loft, a familiar stack of books in their arms. The texts they'd been reading with Constantine, researching the hold the warlock had over my demon.

"We're wasting time." I tried to take a step towards the wings to argue with the men, but Nireas's arm tightened around my shoulders, holding me to him.

"I will go after Con myself if I have to, nymph, for you. But give it just a little more time. We're more likely to be successful if we have a plan," Nireas said, glancing around the theater and then back to me. "And plenty of friends to help us."

I tore my eyes from Antin—his head bowed low and shoulders drooping, cornered by other monsters—to glance around at the crowd gathered. Esther Reed and her men were huddled together, speaking in whispers. The rest of the company mingled in the seats in front of the stage with a group of monsters Hunter and Asterion had brought with them, collective gazes glancing in my direction and then skirting away again. Were they embarrassed or guilty, unable to meet my eyes because they'd already decided to refuse to help Constantine?

Or were they afraid?

Afraid of the unknown, of what Birsha might be capable of? Or of what he would take from them if they fought against him?

And as Mr. Reddy stepped onto the stage, his eyes flicking between the floor and mine, his throat clearing softly, I knew what his answer would be.

I refused to hear it.

"You're a coward," I said.

Mr. Reddy sighed and turned his palms out at his sides. "Listen, Nix."

"No. I won't. You waited too long to tell us what was going on. You *allowed* Birsha to plant Constantine in the company, you kept your suspicions a secret from us. You kept Birsha's interest in the theater a secret, never warned any of us what kind of man or monster he was. Constantine is *enslaved*, but it isn't *your* problem," I said, and I glared at the faces in the audience too.

I stepped forward, shrugging off Nireas's arm, my hands clenched into fists at my side and a fire burning in my chest. "Why do you all keep waiting for Birsha to attack you first? To hurt someone you love? To hurt you?"

"He has allies—" a man in the audience started.

"So do we!" I cried out, waving an arm around the room. "Or are you only allies as long as it doesn't require you to risk your own neck?"

Over Mr. Reddy's shoulder, Hunter's lamplight gaze was

glowing on me, his lips softly curved. That was pride glowing on his face, and it straightened my back and lifted my chin.

"I think the real problem is that you monsters are arrogant," I said. "Not one of you believes Birsha will reach *you*. So you turn your back on each other. On the women you supposedly covet. On his actions. You've allowed him to go on this way, and you'll continue to allow it if you decide not to do anything tonight. Not to stand up for Constantine, or for this theater, or even for yourselves."

"That's quite enough," Amon said, his voice cool but his eyes snagged on Esther as she stepped forward.

"I happen to agree with her, my love," Esther said, arching an eyebrow.

And just like that, the elegant sphinx sealed his lips and rolled his eyes to the heavens.

"So do I," a smooth voice called from the theater entrance.

The crowd turned in the direction of a small arrival party of men and women. At the front was a tall and shockingly handsome man with smooth black hair, gently curving ridged horns, and a pair of opaque black glasses covering his eyes.

"Marius," Asterion greeted, stepping forward to the edge of the stage. "I didn't think Mortimer would be able to convince you to come."

"She didn't. I had already volunteered," the man answered.

"That's a basilisk," Nireas whispered in my ear. "They're incredibly dangerous. And rare. One look at his eyes would kill you."

"That's even more surprising," Asterion said to Marius, but the minotaur was smiling.

The obscured stare turned in my direction, and even with the basilisk's eyes covered, I shivered. His power was obvious and eerie, and it reminded me of the first time I'd met Constantine. But he walked smoothly up the steps to the stage as if being slightly blinded didn't affect him, and I dropped my own stare to the floor, just in case those glasses slipped.

"Birsha made an enemy of me. And I agree with the girl— we've been meeting him with a weak defense for too long. It's time to remind him that we are the monsters he ought to fear, not the other way around."

I smiled to myself, and Hunter rounded Mr. Reddy and Asterion, Antin leaning on his arm and led to our small circle. "Dangerous is good. I like him," I whispered to my lovers.

Marius approached the stage, reaching a dark glove into his coat and pulling out a small white envelope. "Mortimer did send me with message for you," he said.

I hurried forward, my eyes remaining fixed to that card rather than risk catching his eye, and the stage waited in silence as I opened the note. Hope overflowed in my chest like the sudden pop of a champagne bottle as I read the elegantly scrawled words.

Sir Gabriel Anson. Bastard, I thought. *I'll find you.*

"Magdalena's found Constantine's warlock, and he's at the Seven Veils," I said, lifting my head to glare at those monsters who'd been resisting my urging. "Just as we'd guessed. *Now* will you act?"

A few gazes ducked away from mine, but some looked thoughtful at last.

"We needn't involve everyone," Dr. Underwood said slowly. "Mr. Tanner would be eager to take a fight to Birsha."

"I'm handy in a pinch," a cheeky voice announced from what appeared to be thin air.

I sighed at the sudden turn, my shoulders drooping with relief.

"Mutiny from my own house," Amon muttered, rubbing a furred hand over his face. He turned and smiled at Esther. "I suppose I'll go to make sure they don't get themselves killed."

"Thank you, my love," Esther cooed with exaggerated sweetness.

I returned to the cluster of my own men, licking my lips, wondering how much I might have to beg. "Hunter," I started, prepared for resistance.

Hunter huffed and leaned forward, kissing my brow. "I already told the others I would go myself and search for Con. But you made a very good speech, little warrior," he said, smiling.

I blew out a breath, echoes of volunteers now rising readily around us. I wasn't sure if it was due to the basilisk and his news, or Amon, or that a minority had turned into a majority, or simply if no monster wanted to be called a coward, but now everyone in the theater seemed plenty eager to go chase down Birsha.

Asterion cleared his throat and raised his hands. "The young lady has made her point. And for what it's worth, I agree with her too. But Birsha is practically a ghost, and while we know he can be injured, physically weakened, we don't know for certain yet how to kill him. But I have an idea for how to hurt him in another way, one that would give me great satisfaction.

"We should attack the Seven Veils," Asterion said. "Take away Birsha's foothold in London. Destroy his house as he's been trying to do here at the theater and Star Manor."

I frowned, head tipping. "But surely all the humans there—"

Asterion shook his head before I could finish. "You mistake me, Miss Nix. I don't want to harm the innocents. I want to free them and then tear that building apart, one brick at a time."

I glanced at Antin, whose breathing was slightly ragged, and reached out for his hand. The pleasure was weaker than before, just a little soft warmth, and I was afraid of what that might mean for Con or their connection.

Asterion continued, "The house is surrounded by a park. It's enchanted, of course, but it doesn't require an invitation. Just the right intention. And—"

"Did you say a park?" I asked, blinking.

Asterion's nostrils flared in irritation at the interruption, but he nodded.

"What kind of park?" I asked.

"Hazel," Jude whispered. "It's not safe."

"Large. Wooded," Asterion said with a shrug. "Fairly dense, very private."

"How close are the trees to the house?" I asked.

Asterion frowned. "It... Not far. Why do you ask?"

I bit my lip, an idea forming in my head, but one that made me feel as though I was standing on a stage with a spotlight glaring so brightly down at me, I was blind to the edge and might go toppling off without warning. Mr. Reddy shifted behind Asterion, catching my eye, and he nodded once at me.

"I'm coming too," I said.

Hunter's brow furrowed at that.

"Sweet creature, *no*," Antin said immediately.

"Nut—" Ronan started.

"I'm coming. I know how we can bring the house down, and you'll need me to do it," I said.

"Miss Nix, it will take more than a human girl to bait Birsha into vulnerability," Amon said.

"Not *much* more," Esther whispered, and her sphinx growled softly back.

"You misunderstand. I don't intend on playing bait. Because I'm not human," I said, my voice trembling.

A few gasps rose up from the audience, where the company members who knew me watched from the seats. Asterion had already heard this news, and he stepped eagerly forward.

"You have a plan?" he asked, large dark eyes narrowing to slits.

I licked my lips and offered the truth. "I have an *idea*."

Asterion opened his mouth, probably to object, but Dr. Underwood spoke first. "I find ideas are usually the best beginnings to plans. And I believe we should be mindful of the urgency," he added, nodding his head at Antin, who was leaning heavily into Hunter and me.

Asterion snorted with irritation, reaching up and tugging on one of his broad horns. "Fine. Let's hear it."

❦

JUDE HELD my hand in his, fingers locked together, as Asterion's carriage rolled to a stop near the end of the long drive. We'd been holding our breath, focusing on Asterion's coaching intentions, the urge to fulfill harsh desires and violent cravings. I found it somewhat easy, as I had distinctly violent cravings when it came to destroying this house.

Outside the frosted window, the lights of the building ahead of us glowed red, winking and pulsing like fragile heartbeats. Asterion stepped down from the carriage with one of the new arrivals, an intimidating and heavily scarred werewolf named

Byron, at his side. I moved to exit out the door after them, blocked from view of the house by the mass of the carriage, but Jude held my hand fast in his.

"Hazel, love, are you sure about this?" Jude whispered.

The others were already in the woods, waiting for the sounds of chaos that would rise from the house as I did my work.

"Mostly," I said, twisting to face Jude and offering him a feeble smile. "I think I can do it. I *will* do it."

Jude smiled back, but it was equally unconvincing. "It's not that I don't think you can convince the trees to help, I just..." He leaned closer and lowered his voice to a whisper, the sound of boots impatiently shuffling over gravel urging us from outside of the carriage. "Will you make it back out?"

Jude's eyes were pale, the corners creased with worry, his brow wrinkled too. Jude was the only one who'd seen me in the woods, although I'd told them all about the rosemary pot that had broken in my kitchen the night of my attack. My being able to communicate with the trees, to beg them to do my bidding, wasn't our only option tonight. The monsters could all charge the building, break down the doors and battle Birsha's guards.

My plan just happened to have better odds of our side making it out alive.

But I'd told Jude how it had felt to lose myself in old roots, to hide in the network of trees in Asterion's woods. He was right to be worried.

"I will," I said, nodding my head firmly. Jude's eyes narrowed at me. "I will. I'll be fine. It's the safest place for me."

His lips pursed. I'd used that argument with Hunter and the others, and it'd done a fair job of convincing them all that I could come help.

"This is bigger than hide and seek," Jude pressed.

"I know, but it's also much more important," I whispered, reaching for Jude's shoulders, leaning in and kissing him. "I will be fine. In the woods, it was you who called me out again. I want Con back. I want...I want all of us together, more than anything." I breathed the words out, too fragile to speak openly. "So I *will* make it out. I have very good reason to."

Jude sighed, grazing his lips against mine again.

"Miss Nix," Asterion prompted gently from outside of the carriage.

"I want that too, but it only works if we have you, Hazel," Jude murmured with another firm kiss, dragging it to my cheek and jaw.

We both breathed in deeply before pulling away, and Jude slid past me, stepping down from the carriage and escorting me out.

"Have a look," Asterion said, gesturing around the carriage toward the house.

We were still far enough away to comfortably study without worrying about being seen. The house was tall and built of dark stone, with spindly turrets piercing the sky and torches burning eerie green fire from the broad front steps. Two great rowan trees grew closest on either side of the house, their branches extending toward stained glass windows.

"What do you think?" Asterion asked.

There was a ring of oaks around the property too, and I closed my eyes, reached out to the trees, and felt them answer, a gloomy and sorrowful warning passing to me. *Don't enter, child, don't come closer.*

I called back to them, studied them through a foggy distance, the whole property repeating the same refrain of caution.

"The roots are already close to the basement level," I said, opening my eyes. "The trees don't like the house. I think they'll help, but there is a sort of...poisonous flavor in the ground."

The werewolf nodded, grunting, as Asterion stared down at me. "You can tell so much from here?" Asterion asked.

I shrugged. "It's easier when I'm somewhere farther from so many buildings and people. Breaking the foundation won't be hard, coaxing roots up to the first level isn't a great stretch, but I'm not sure how much I can push before it's dangerous for those inside."

"Leave that to us," Asterion said. "If you can convince roots to break stone and shatter doorframes, that's more than enough."

"The imp is in the sky," Byron said, looking up into the shadows of the trees around us, his dark hair falling back from his face and revealing the riotous tangle of old wounds on the sides of his face and throat.

Asterion nodded. "Ronan and Jude will watch over you. You'll be able to find your way back out?"

"Yes," I said, although it was mostly a guess, and Jude must've known as much. He didn't give me away, setting a hand on my shoulder and squeezing me gently.

"Then I will see you on the other side of victory, Miss Nix," Asterion said with a gentlemanly bow I didn't know how to answer.

Jude pulled me into the shadows of trees as the minotaur and werewolf marched toward the house. "How close do you need to be?"

I bit my lip and searched the woods, pointing toward the outer circle of oaks, where a few younger trees were growing under the shadow of the oldest circle. They were less cautious and more curious than the others, and I had a feeling they would help me rally the woods to my cause.

Jude wrapped a cool shadow around us that dimmed the outside world and pulled me along by a steady grip on my hand. The house had a soft murmur of noise from inside, eerie music and a thrum of conversation, and we'd nearly reached our destination when the broad front doors opened to greet the approaching figures of Asterion and Byron. A sharp scream spilled out of the building and into the quiet woods. An owl answered from its perch, swooping through branches and arching in front of the house, talons stretched toward the red glass windows.

I shivered, and Jude and I held ourselves frozen behind one of the slender oaks, waiting for the doors to shut and the cry for help to break into silence again.

"Do you think Con—" Jude started, but I cut him off with a shake of my head.

"No. Birsha has him trapped somewhere," I whispered. Con wouldn't be in a parlor torturing some helpless girl. Not while Antin was withering and bleeding. They weren't two opposing forces bound together in one man. They were a perfect balance, a measured union.

And they were mine.

We stopped on the left side of the house, close enough to see shadows moving by the windows, hands pressed and sliding over the glass in the upper stories.

"We may not be alone in these woods," Jude said.

I nodded, aware of the same sense of being observed. I twisted, wrapped my arms around his shoulders, and our hearts pounded through our chests together as we held one another, the muted moans of the house mingling with the rustle of branches.

"Stay safe and hidden," I breathed in Jude's ear.

He nodded. "And you do the same. Be careful when you come back out of the trees and...Hazel—" He leaned back and met my eyes, his stare glowing in our shroud of shadows. "*Come back.*"

I kissed him roughly, pressing all my nerves and worry into the bite of my lips around his. His fingers dug into my back, holding me to his chest, but the bark of the tree scratched gently at my shoulders, welcoming me. I leaned into the trunk, thought of Constantine, of Margaret and Beth, and allowed myself to vanish.

Jude groaned, his eyes opening and glaring back at me as I slid backward into the young oak tree. "Be careful," he hissed.

And then my world was still and dark, none of the bright lines of life threaded through like before. This wood knew the danger it was in, the danger of the house, and it sat quietly. The oak was eager to keep me, protect me from the threat nearby.

Stay where you are safe, sister.

I sank into the darkness, answering gently, finding the roads of roots at the ends of my toes. *Help me make these woods safe again. Let's remove the house, let all the innocents inside escape.*

We're trying, the oak answered. *But it's many years of work, and we've lost numbers along the way.*

There was anger in the words, and memories of the woods being richer, fuller, before trees were torn out, their roots corrupted by intentional poison. But I found the network of hidden life, sliding along their path into the heavy rich earth, all the tendrils reaching for the house, reaching for the heavy black stone buried into the ground. The trees wanted the house gone, Birsha gone.

Let me help you, I said, and offered them my own anger, my fear, my energy. It blazed in me like the glare of sunlight reflected over mirrors, washed through my veins like a rainstorm, and it fed the earth I was nestled in. The ground rumbled around me, and I found myself rushing downward, down into the branching foot of the trees, growing thinner with the roots, but stronger too, extending fine tendrils toward the rock.

There were bodies buried in this earth—Birsha's victims, no doubt, monsters and humans—and I begged their forgiveness as the roots of the woods bound around the lost souls and stole new strength from their bodies.

We've missed the company of wild children, the oaks said, tangling roots together, tying me up in the net of them. *You bring us life.*

Help me crack the house apart. I will come back and visit you, I promised.

Some of the trees were slower to respond, more reluctant to grow involved, like the pair of rowans closer to the house who'd been fed with magic. But the rest urged them along, whatever contribution I offered tempting the rowans to our side.

I met the black stone of the basement with a physical thud that created an all-over nausea, some of the friendly roots recoiling.

Please, I begged, even as I wanted to retreat too. Con was inside. He needed me. Antin needed me. And the rest of the monsters were nearby, waiting, waiting for the house to fall, waiting to prove to Birsha that he didn't own them or control them or make them surrender in fear.

Here, wild sister, here is a crack, a young maple called.

I tumbled through their knotted trails, dizzy and twisting in every direction, before finding the opening. Stone bore down on me from every side, pressure and pain. But it was nothing compared to my time with Con. This was only like holding my breath at the bottom of a pool, waiting to see how long before I had to swim to the surface again. I burned and cramped, and the trees gently wormed through rock, carrying me along.

We broke through, and the flavor was damp and metallic, like blood. I found myself spilling down to a craggy floor, and it took me a moment to remember my own body, my knees on the ground, my palms pressed to cool stone. I patted and groped at myself, rediscovering my form, surprised that all the parts seemed to still be in the right place, if not slightly tangled in the tender fingertips of the trees. They slid away from me reluctantly.

Be safe, they whispered.

Do the work you've craved, I encouraged.

I was alone in a hallway full of shadows, with just one candle burning in a gold sconce. The stone around me trembled, and the hinge of a door ahead and to my right squeaked with resistance.

"Don't stop," I whispered, and then repeated it in my thoughts. *Don't stop. Find the seams, the locks, and crumble them.* I closed my eyes and sighed a breath of relief as I tugged, calling for the trees, and they answered back, close and eager.

I groped at the wall and pulled myself to standing. I was in a basement corridor, with a long passage of doorways along the right. Roots were twisting eagerly through the edge of the floor and a few fragile cracks in the stone on my left, and there was a persistent snarl bleeding through the door that had started to protest.

There was also a whiff of harsh cinnamon that conjured memories of Con's grip on my jaw, his silver eyes blazing down at me as he rubbed the tip of his cock along my tongue. I chased the scent to the end of the hall, aware of the shuffling steps and growls slipping out from under the doors on my right. This wasn't a safe place for me, and I'd promised Jude and the others that I would do this one act of breaking the house up with the help of the trees, and then return. But Con was here, I was certain of it.

I needed to hurry.

The last door was cracked open, and the cinnamon was blended with that same sticky corrosive odor that had corrupted Antin's sweeter scent. Blood.

I pushed the door open with my shoulder, and I caught my breath at the sight before me.

Con was spread out over the floor, naked, stained in glistening blue blood, surrounded by white painted symbols that formed a circle. His chest was rising and falling slowly, the motion shallow, and one of his legs was twisted in the wrong direction at the knee.

"Con," I murmured.

We were alone, and his head jerked up, silver stare wild on me as I ran to his side. His head shook, and there was blood running down from his brow into one eye. I landed heavily on my knees, and the impact of stone under me was more painful than the gentle shock that bit at my palm as I cupped his face.

He huffed and strained beneath me as I bent, kissing his brow and cheekbone. His frustration vibrated through his muscles, and he sat up, trying to shake me off.

"It's not just me," I said. "We're here to take down Birsha. And to rescue you. It's all right," I said.

Con's brow furrowed, eyes wide.

"I don't care about the warlock," I breathed, wrapping a tense arm around his bare shoulders to pull him upright. "We'll sort it out later. You're coming with me."

But I looked into his eyes and knew, saw it reflected there.

We weren't alone. Of course we weren't. This was meant to be a trap for me after all.

The figure stepped out of the shadows behind me, now illuminated in Con's silver eyes.

"Is it Birsha?" I mouthed to Con.

He shook his head once.

"They gave you away from the beginning, simply by how hard they fought to not speak of you," the warlock said, announcing his arrival in a silky, sly tone that made me cringe.

I twisted on the floor, holding onto Con, shielding him from the man's gaze.

The warlock was tall, handsome in a plain sort of way, broad-shouldered and square-chested with thick, golden-blond locks of hair swept back. I don't know why, but I'd imagined him as elderly or thin or with dark hair, anything but this. Here was a young, strapping gentleman, so very human.

But those blue eyes were cruel, and his smirk made me want to launch myself at him, claw him with my fingernails.

He stepped closer, and I drew in a sharp breath at the quick movement. The air around the warlock was stale, dusty, and smelling slightly of rot.

Oh. No, he wasn't young at all, I realized. Just feeding off Constantine to appear so.

"Over a century together, and not once had this demon ever fought me with such stunning insistence," the warlock said.

Con's hand was on my waist, holding me to his chest, and I didn't know if it was because *he* wanted me close, or if the warlock had a plan for me and Con would be forced to play his part.

"You know, I think the fool might be in love with you," the man said.

I covered the back of Con's hand with mine, stroked the smooth skin there, ignored the flare of pain that echoed up the bones of my arm.

The warlock huffed and rolled his neck on his shoulders, an uncomfortable melody of cracks and snaps sounding. Behind him, at the far exterior wall of the room, thin roots slithered through stone.

"You're very dull," the warlock moaned, cracking his hands in front of him next, the sound horrifyingly loud. Was this man really a bundle of tinder ready to go up in a blaze underneath all that sorcery? "I was hoping we might have some fun before I have the demon strangle you to death."

Under my palm, fine threads of an eager rowan tree tickled my skin.

"I'm going to kill you," I said softly.

The warlock snorted and nodded at Con. "He won't let you."

I brushed my other hand over Con's again, holding the warlock's gaze. "Lie down, darling."

The warlock smirked as Con lay down on the floor again at my order, arms and legs extended. "You'll have to do better than that, little halfling," the warlock hissed. "He does *my* bidding. Con—"

Now, I begged the trees. *Trap him, but don't hurt him, please.*

And before the warlock could get another word out, dark roots burst forth from the ground, tangling around Con's blue body like corrupted veins.

"Wha—?!"

I launched myself at the warlock, tackling him to the floor. This...this I did not have a plan for. I hadn't even expected to find Con. And the walls were groaning, growls and howls rising from the other cells, the sounds drifting through the open door. Jude and Ronan would be panicking for me.

The warlock managed to roll us, my back hitting the floor and breath *whooshing* out of me. Con's leg strained for freedom out of the corner of my eye. There was a candlestick on the floor, just out of reach, and I stretched, grunting as the warlock's heavy forearm landed on my throat, stealing all my breath. My fingers clutched around warm brass, and the candle went toppling to the floor, sputtering out against the stone. I struck with the makeshift weapon, and the warlock bellowed as I hit him over the head, but he only shook himself, pressing harder against my throat.

Beside us, Con fought the roots, snaps sounding and whimpers of pain echoing in my head to match as my demon strained against his binding, tearing one arm free. Would he come to my aid or the warlock's?

Help, I gasped, striking hard against the man's head again. This time his weight lessened as he jerked away, swaying slightly. I couldn't catch my breath, couldn't quite see clearly, but I swung again, knocking him to his back. The illusion of him wavered, and what was there was a withered figure, those blue eyes fogged with magic.

We're hungry, the trees hinted, wicked vined voices in my head.

Yes, I offered eagerly. *Yes, take him.*

They did so with vigor, roots bursting from the floor again, tangling the bewildered figure of the warlock, twisting around him. He growled, illusion restored, and bursts of small flame ate at the roots that tried to manacle him to the floor. One thick root burrowed up directly through his thigh as he screamed, but with a wave of his free hand, it withered.

I was hurting Con. Hurting the roots that tried to help me.

They tore at the warlock's clothes, strangled his throat and limbs, but he punished each one with flame and rot. I tried to scramble up to my feet when Con reached me, yanked on my ankle, and dropped me to my knees between them. And as I fell, a flicker of gold caught my eye.

A bright medallion on a thin chain, peeking through the torn collar of the warlocks's shirt. Con dragged me back an inch, and I clawed my way forward again, kicking back at him, crying out in pain and apology. I ignored the warlock's purpling face, ignored the flames and the cries of the roots, and stared at that mark of gold.

A talisman. A talisman forms the tie.

I glanced at Con, and his eyes flicked on that little round of gold, silver round and wide, desperate. He reached for me, still under his master's bidding, but I scrambled forward. I reached through the fire, around the rot, and wrapped my fist around that bright, hot coin. Scorching fists took hold of my wrist, a howl of fire singing loose strands of my face, but the talisman was in my possession now.

I pulled the chain from the summoner's neck with a brutal yank and fell back as the little flames became a roaring blaze, licking up my ankles toward my thin skirt.

Free Con, please, free him!

The warlock was rising up from the floor, looming over me, but so too was my demon. I flinched as Con lunged, tackling the man down, but I couldn't deny the swell of pride at the sound of the warlock's agonized screams.

I stamped the flames out, soothed my hands over the dry and withered roots. Con's back was broad and whole, and by the howls and the writhing motion of the body under him, I knew his power was restored. The roots had broken through the marks of the circle that bound him, and I was holding the talisman.

Constantine was free. Con was free and—

I stood and stared down at the pair. Con was torturing his former master, long blue fingers around the warlock's throat, his other hand scratching over bared skin. The warlock's face was dark with struggle, eyes rolling back, but Con was toying with him, pulling away and returning. I had no sympathy for the warlock, but the sounds coming from the hall were restless. We needed to leave.

I braced myself, stepped forward and pressed my hand to Con's back, crying out and then swallowing the pain down. It was familiar. Beloved.

"That's for me," I forced out. "Con. Stop. Stop. Your gifts are for me."

Con pulled his hands away, twisting to stare up at me, brow furrowed but eyes wide, almost innocent.

Is he ours now? the roots asked.

Yes! Yes, please, I answered, my head muddled and my arm numb, still touching Con.

"We have to leave. Save your gifts for me," I said.

Lively roots burst from the floor, and Con's head turned, blinking at the sight, but then he stood. The warlock managed one weak effort to rise before eager ropes of life tightened around his throat, squeezing and twisting until they drew out a horrifying internal crack.

The gold medallion was hot in my hand, electric pain running like a current up my other arm, and the man on the floor was revealed in full, a rapidly disintegrating husk of age and the corrosive influence of dark magic. Con pulled away from my touch and I gasped, staring at him as he stepped over the warlock, staring down, reassuring himself of the man's death.

I'd barely caught my breath when Con turned and snapped me up in his arms, my scream at the sudden vivid shock, equal parts desperate and delighted. He pressed his face to my bared throat and then rubbed me against his groin, where he was growing hard.

"Not here," I gasped out, my chest tight and struggling for air. Con growled and shook, a set of claws scratching over my ass. I wanted to laugh, but it was impossible in this strained state, torment coursing through me. Still, it was nice to know he was happy to see me.

The walls around us shook, and I recalled my point. "The house is about to come down. We have to get out."

In the hallway, metal groaned and a dangerous, high-pitched rending sounded.

Con set me back on my feet, pushing me toward the wall. A shadow blurred over the hallway's stone, and a snarl echoed nearer. Shit. Something or someone had gotten out, and I didn't know if they were friend or foe. Con twisted and pointed me toward the roots crumbling the stone wall at my back.

"What about you?" I asked.

He reached for my hand, brought it up to his face, and I whimpered as he nuzzled my palm, holding my gaze with his. A claw scratched over my pulse, a wretched slicing sensation as a gesture of reassurance.

He would make it out. Especially if he didn't have me to worry about.

"Take this," I said, holding the talisman out on its chain.

But his head shook, hand retreating, and he turned away. Which meant the talisman was in my care, at least for now. I wrapped the chain around my palm as an enormous, glistening, twisted beast of a creature extended one vast, taloned foot in front of the cell door.

Con's knees bent, his shoulders flexing, spreading himself out like a shield in front of me. *He will have an easier time making it out once I'm gone*, I told myself.

"I'll see you outside."

He nodded without looking back, and I stumbled back into the roots, their thin hands reaching for me eagerly.

45.

HUNGRY TREES

The roots were wild, vibrant with rage, tangling together through the walls and floorboards, making a new structure of the building they'd corrupted. They fed on the dead Birsha had left behind, the magic of the warlock I'd offered up to them, and the wards seamed into the very walls.

I was flying through the house, following their path, tripping and toppling along in their urgency and entirely lost in the maze.

When the roots burst through a wall, I found myself stepping down into the center of chaos, the battle waging around me, monsters grappling together, furniture torn apart. A young woman with a long blonde braid streaked by me, her thin white strips of a dress ragged, her dark eyes wild and panicked.

Wait, I called, but I forgot to speak out loud, and a root reached out to her, wrapping around her ankle and tripping her to the floor. She cried out as she landed on the floor, and a brilliant gold demon ran for her, his hands coated in blood, his hungry expression promising violence.

No!

The roots released her and dove for him instead, and she scrambled up and ran from the room before I could call to her.

A familiar broad pair of horns appeared in the doorway.

"Asterion!" I cried out.

He glanced at me, and his bronze cheeks were stained with blood. "Run!" The word was a clap of thunder as the minotaur grabbed the golden demon by the collar.

A clawed hand snagged my wrist, and I turned to find a

ravenous feathered face looming closer. I fell backwards into the roots, and the monster snarled as I escaped.

Were we winning or losing? I wondered, wishing I'd spotted Hunter and Nireas in the melee, reassuring myself they were safe. But they wouldn't forgive me if I got myself hurt or killed in the process of searching for them, and Jude and Ronan would be wild with worry by now.

Take me outside, I pleaded with the roots. They answered in a rushing motion, sweeping me out through cracked floorboards and a shattered window, sliding me safely back into the earth, where it was crowded and quiet.

I settled in the safety of the roots, swimming through their pathways back to the large and patient bodies of the trees.

Thank you, wild sister.

Thank you, I answered, rising up in the dark hollow of an oak, resting in the silence for a moment, afraid of what I might hear or see when I stepped outside.

I pulled myself free slowly, the cries of struggle, howls of war, and screams of freedom at my back. But they were distant sounds. The trees had carried me far from the battle, and as I stepped out onto cool grass, I looked back and realized that I was on the opposite side of the estate as I'd been before. I had to find Jude and Ronan, but it would involve moving through the woods while a war of monsters was taking place.

There were shadows churning, a soft gasp and cry rushing past me, more victims escaping the house, but no friendly calls or familiar voices.

I have the trees, I reminded myself, moving forward, pointing myself in the direction of the chaos and the drive, toward where I'd left Jude. The woods answered with a distracted encouragement. They were busy with the work I'd set for them, but they were here. I knew my way back into their shelter if I needed them.

A rush of wings passed over my head as I took shelter under an old oak, and I debated calling out. Was that Ronan flying over me, or an enemy, or even simply an owl? I waited for the sound to pass and then ran forward, nearing the drive.

A scuffle of snarls and growls hissed through the shadows on my right, and I flinched in the opposite direction, drifting farther from the house to avoid notice. I was dashing across the gravel drive, ignoring the bite of stone under the soles of my feet —my shoes were lost somewhere in the house or underground— when a figure stepped out of the cover of a tree.

Moonlight struck him, his blue and opal horns catching the light, and for a moment my heart stuttered in relief at the familiarity. And then Eston leapt forward, wrapping his arms around me and clapping a hand over my mouth. Barbs dug into my hips and shoulders, and my eyes widened up at the demon, a familiar clogging and sickly perfume filling my lungs.

He'd vanished after Isabella ran, and I recalled Mr. Reddy's confusion at the fact. Recalled the padded, pillowed sensation of my attacker in my home, like a figure trying to hide recognizable features—small horns that had rutted against me on stage. Recalled Eston's bitter words about Beth's memorial, my own harsh words to him the night before my home was broken into, his wary surprise at my apology the next day.

He stared back at me, vivid blue eyes glowing in the dark, a perfect understanding passing between us. I knew. He knew.

Here was the killer we'd been searching for, under our noses the whole time. A member of the company, just as I'd sworn would be impossible.

"Why?" I asked, choking on the disguising scent he wore, the word mumbled against his hot palm.

"Money," Eston whispered, glancing up at the house behind me. "A place here, where I can do as I like instead of doing as I'm ordered by that *halfling* bastard. I don't want to be tamed and humiliated on a stage. I'm *better* than that. Better than you and fucking Reddy and all the others." He grinned down at me, his fanged smile glinting as he shook his head. "What are you doing here, Hazel?"

Because Eston hadn't heard my confession at the theater, and he still thought I was just a human girl.

"Con," I said into Eston's palm, allowing the fragrance to make tears spill out of my eyes, as if I were helpless, afraid. "I came for Con. Where's Isabella?"

"In there," Eston said, glaring at the house. "I brought her for Birsha, but the old coward *ran* from London sometime last night."

I blinked at that news. Birsha wasn't in the house? Was that good or bad?

"What am I going to do with you if I can't sell you to him?" Eston murmured, thinking out loud. "I suppose you'll have to go the way of Beth and Marge."

I struggled in his hold, the only appropriate response to the threat of death, kicking at his ankles and hoping it kept him distracted.

He frowned then and stared down at me again. "Why haven't you screamed yet? They always screamed."

"Hazel!" A voice—Jude's—shouted behind us.

Eston stiffened, eyes widening, and his arms constricting around me, jostling me. His hand slipped from my mouth as he reached for my throat.

"Tear him apart," I said, not shouting but speaking calmly, echoing the thought in my mind.

"Nix!" Mr. Reddy called, but both he and Jude were too far away.

Eston's mouth opened, sharp fingers and claws on my throat, but then he looked down. Tree roots bound his ankles, crawled up his legs, strangled his thighs. He grunted, and his hand tightened briefly on my throat, my vision shadowing.

I was patient. And the trees were hungry.

Eston snarled, thrashed, shook me a little by the throat, but then a root snapped up like a rearing viper and grabbed the arm that held me captive, yanking it down to his side. I stumbled backward, freed, gasping, and fell promptly to my ass, blinking up at Eston.

"Hazel!" Hunter roared, somewhere behind me.

"Here!" I called, my voice just above that of a croak.

"What—Help!" Eston cried out as a thick root twisted and squeezed around his waist. He grunted and bent over, doubled in half, as the root around his arm forced him toward the ground. "Help! Hazel! Stop this. Stop this!"

"You were just a bit of stage dressing, Eston," I said,

watching the ground churn, crawling backward slowly. "Nothing important."

Eston's face was dark, whipping up to glare at me. "You little human *cunt*. I'll make you—" But the following words were eaten as a muddy root drove itself into Eston's mouth, down his throat, brilliant blue eyes bugging wide.

"You should've known your place," I whispered, shock wiping away feeling.

A pair of legs skidded and slid onto the ground, and my view of Eston's panic and fear, his understanding of imminent death, were blocked from my gaze by the beautiful sight of Jude, pale and worried, his hands sweeping in soothing brushes over my body.

"Fuck, you've been gone for ages. Are you all right?" Jude gasped out.

There was a gruesome squelch from behind Jude, and I flinched at last. *Stop*, I thought to the roots, but it was too late. I'd offered Eston up to them, wanted to watch him tortured the way he'd surely done to Beth and Margaret. And they'd worked hard tonight, earned their feast.

"Bring her away from there," Hunter ordered.

A pair of red hoofed feet landed on the gravel out of the corner of my eye. Jude drew me into his chest, his hand on the back of my head carefully tucking my face into his chest as he lifted me from the ground. Ronan's wings surrounded us, muffling the hungry, violent sounds of the roots.

"This way, toward the house, almost everyone is out now," Ronan said. His cheek nuzzled the back of my head. "Are you all right, nut?"

"I'm fine. I'm okay. I got lost in the roots on my way out. I found Con. Are you both—Is everyone okay?"

I twisted in Jude's arms, studying the pair, finding Jude scuffed but unharmed and Ronan safe. I craned my neck to see around Ronan's wings, searching for a glimpse of Hunter, but my gaze remained shielded until they'd carried me a satisfying distance away. Ronan stepped back, and I gasped at the sight before me.

Someone had tried to start a fire in the house, no doubt to

burn away the trees, but it was already smoking, a spray of water catching light as it poured out the window. Still, the small blaze and the remaining flickering lamps inside offered enough light to reveal the squirming, strangling life of the roots as they burrowed and twisted and shattered through stone. The walls were alive, writhing, and the roof was crumbling. The rowan trees had arched their branches into the top stories, tangling together in their effort to tear the house apart.

A crowd was gathered outside, figures struggling in monsters' arms—humans who hadn't realized they were being held by rescuers, not new captives. My heart ached for them, but my eyes didn't stop searching.

"Where's Nireas?" I whispered, pushing around Ronan's side. I released a tiny sob at the sudden sight of my orc standing proudly before me, his cheek cut and bleeding.

Hunter gathered me up in his arms, and I sucked in a breath of his summer flavor, kissing his throat. "Thank you," I whispered into Hunter's skin, but the words were for the woods. My men were safe. Or at least...

As quickly as relief came at seeing one of them, the determination to reassure myself that Nireas and Constantine were safe as well struck hard.

"Wait, little one," Hunter said, catching my wrist in a gentle grip, tightening his hand and tugging me closer as I tried to pull away. "Nireas is coming. Are you hurt?"

I shook my head, although in truth, my throat was burning and my left ribs ached from my tussle with the warlock.

"Antin? And Con? Where are—Oh!"

My hands flew over my mouth as an enormous figure appeared, backlit by the pulsing red glow of the house's now crooked maw, six arms spread wide to hold open the front doors before they could crumble in. Bowed bodies ducked under Nireas's arms, the final exodus a mix of young women and monsters.

Hunter released me and I ran forward just as Nireas leapt from the front steps, his heavy, dark tail draped limply over one arm. And behind him followed Constantine.

My knees tried to falter as I ran, and I ignored their weakness and the claw of stone under my feet.

"We left a few bodies inside," Asterion called out to Hunter. "No one we want to recover."

I ignored him, the sobs and screams, the gentle growls, and ran toward my men. I reached Nireas first, flying up into his arms with a jump, eagerly wrapping myself around him. His arms surrounded me, banding around my hips and thighs and back, squeezing me to his chest.

"Are you hurt?" we asked in unison.

"The killer was Eston," I said.

"I was starting to suspect as much," Nireas murmured in my ear, turning his head and kissing my lobe.

He was already turning as I started to wrestle myself free, and he stepped to the side, setting me down gently in the grass, directly in front of Constantine.

My demon had an arm wrapped around his own waist, one horn chipped at the end. But he was whole. Free. His eyes caught moonlight and reflected it back at me, and his arms opened at his side, body hunched into his wound. I stepped forward once, clasped my hands around his warm jaw, and drew him down into a kiss.

He tasted of blood. When he clutched me to his chest, arms tight around my ribs, his wound was hot and wet, seeping through my dress to mirror the spot on my side. Briefly, two arms became four, and I moaned into a pair of sweet lips as I shuddered and seized with agony and ecstasy, and then Con and Antin were one again and I was climbing higher into Constantine's grip, our tongues tangled and hearts hammering together.

Behind Constantine, the house roared, beams and brick snapping. Familiar voices approached us, but no one interrupted. Constantine's lips were patient, his kisses slow and deep, and he trembled against me. I petted his face, stroked his neck and shoulders, rubbed my cheek to his as our mouths finally slid apart.

Don't leave me again, I thought, but then a last gasping flicker of firelight caught on the gold still wrapped around my palm, the chain biting into my flesh, and I pulled away.

"This is yours," I said, holding the round talisman between us.

"Mine," Constantine said, blinking down at the mark. "Mine, and yet I can't touch it. Sir Gabriel Anson found it in his travels." Constantine's eyes widened, and his arms tightened roughly around my waist. "Sir Gabriel Anson. Sir Gabriel Anson summoned me."

"And now he's dead," I said, watching the understanding wash over Constantine in a kind of horrified joy.

"After a century," he whispered, gaze distant. "He's dead. And I'm..."

"I can't keep this," I said, although my fingers closed over the talisman protectively. "I don't want to be your next jailer. I don't want to possess you. Not like that at least."

Constantine's head tipped, gaze focusing on me once more, lips curving ever so slightly. "Then don't learn to summon a demon. That is the tool, but it does nothing unless you do." Constantine set me on my feet, still pressed comfortably to his chest. We were surrounded by the others, safely sheltered from any prying eyes. Constantine's hands slid between us, wrapping themselves around my fist. "Keep my talisman. Keep it safe, and I remain free."

My fist tightened firmly around the gold. I would cut open my own chest and tuck the coin inside if it would work. Constantine leaned forward, and my eyes fell shut as his lips pressed to my forehead, warm and soft, a charged touch.

"Thank you, sweet creature," he whispered into my skin.

"It's coming down!" someone shouted.

"We should move away," Nireas said.

I was bundled between their larger frames and shuffled back on the damp grass, into the shadow of the broad old oaks.

The black stone was knotted in roots, the building pulled in on itself. The fire had sputtered out, strangled by new green life, and the red lamps had shattered. The screams and sobs were quiet now, the whole audience rapt to the destruction before us, cast in silver moonlight.

"Hazel, this is... You did this," Ronan whispered in terrified awe. His hand reached out, cupped my shoulder gently, a balm to my own minor alarm.

Thank you, wild sister, the trees called, a sigh of relief in their collective voices.

"The woods wanted the house gone," I said. And Birsha had embedded the ground with the magic of his kills. I'd given the signal, the initial push, but he'd left the fuel for his house's destruction surrounding the property. "But Eston said Birsha left last night. He wasn't here."

"He ran when he realized Miss Reed and her companions had returned to London," Hunter said, a slight smirk on his lips. "He's shown his own cowardly hand now. And you've given him more reason than ever to fear young women and monsters."

The house was growing quiet now, the rubble cracking and bubbling like stew in a pot. The woods would erase all evidence by morning.

"Then he should be terrified of me. I am both," I said, lifting my chin in pride.

46.

CARRY ON

I woke, buried under greedy limbs, surrounded by hot skin and soft bedding, and glared up at the ceiling. Had I always slept like the dead? How were these men always managing to transport me about and slide me into bed without my noticing?

Perhaps you're just having an especially exhausting spring, my mind suggested.

I closed my eyes again. I was in Hunter's bed, cluttered with lovers, and Constantine was—

I sat up, mismatched arms sliding off my chest. I was dressed only in my shift, a bloodstain turned brown on my side. And on either side of me, two men dozed.

I frowned. Only four other bodies were on the mattress. And poor Nireas barely fit. We needed to find a different bed. But none of the four were Constantine. Hunter woke as I started to slide out from under the sheets, his hand stroking my back. He had new scars from the battle, but they were healing already, just as my own bruises and cuts were.

"I'll come back to bed," I whispered, bending to kiss his brow. "Just want to know where my demon slipped off to."

Hunter grunted and nodded, his eyelids heavy. "He has a great adjustment ahead of him."

I licked my lips, staring back at Hunter as I considered that. It was true. Constantine had been entrapped by the warlock —*Sir Gabriel Anson*, he'd repeated, the name like a curse on his tongue—for a century. I slid off the end of the bed and winced at my tender feet, still healing from the gravel, then found Hunter's robe, wrapping it around myself. I needed a bath and a fresh shift, and another day's worth of sleep, considering my sore muscles and my vague recollection of the sunrise's glow turning the wreckage of the Seven Veils rosy as we finally turned away.

But I needed to see Constantine more. Just to reassure myself he was here, still safe. The talisman was tied around my neck by a thin ribbon. It would need a chain, preferably today, and it would be remaining on my person from now on, a promise to keep the demon safe from any further influence.

I tiptoed out of the bedroom, glanced into the rooms I passed, but I found Constantine quickly. He was at the front windows of Hunter's receiving room, staring out to the busy street of Mayfair, watching traffic and passersby. He was fully dressed, and the sight of him caused an immediate pang in my chest, almost as if Con had grazed his finger over my breast. He wore his own ragged and stained pair of trousers and what I was fairly certain was Nireas's large white dress shirt, a collection of cuffs stuffed into the sleeves of one of Hunter's velvet dinner jackets. Wrapped around his neck and shoulders was one of my hand-knit shawls.

"You're leaving," I said, standing at the top of the stairs, my breath catching unevenly in my chest.

He turned slowly, eyes reluctantly dragged from the world outside, rising up to meet mine. "Can you understand why?"

Not a refusal. I wanted to fall down onto this step and weep, but his question rang in my head. Of course I could. He'd been held captive, made into Birsha's toy, tortured and commanded. He hadn't been permitted to live under his own willpower for decades.

I knew a little—a tiny fraction—of what that felt like. My father's death had been a sorrowful liberation, but an escape all the same, terrifying and exciting. And I'd never known a life before him, so it'd all been new. Constantine had been aware this past century of what was robbed from him.

Still, the words squeezed their way out of my lips. "Would I be such a terrible cage?"

"Come here."

Constantine reached up toward the stairs, but he didn't move from the window. I wanted to refuse, to run back to the shelter of the others. Constantine was leaving. *Guest acts always leave. Whether I fell in love with them or not. Why should he be any different?*

They were bitter, petty, self-indulgent thoughts. I walked slowly down the stairs, the tile cold and comforting under my sore feet as I crossed to him. Tears cut at my eyes as Constantine pulled me into his chest, arms wrapped firmly around me.

"You will never be a cage, sweet creature," he whispered, his breath cascading over my hair. "You were the key that set me free. I'll return to you."

I winced into the soft wool of my own shawl. *They never return.*

"I'll keep the talisman safe, no matter what—you know that, right? You don't have to come back," I said, although the words were like knives on their way up my throat.

Constantine was quiet for a moment, holding me, and I wondered if I'd just guaranteed he would remain absent from my life.

I fell in love with you. Somewhere between the stage and your dressing room. Somewhere between sex and you staring at me like I'm a puzzle, I thought. I couldn't tell him. I didn't want to burden him with my own feelings, as if they might be a weight to drag him back to me or hold him in place, a new set of bars.

"I would like to return. If you'll all have me," he said, that languid voice so careful in its choice of words.

I nodded, rubbing my head against his chest and releasing a warbling sigh. "We will. When you're ready."

Please be ready soon.

Constantine leaned back, lifted my face gently up to stare back at him. And there was that look, the one where he frowned at me and tipped his head and my heart decided to beat just a hint faster. The danger of being *seen*, possibly even understood.

"I don't understand why you saved me," he said. "I don't understand why you let me touch you, *want* me to touch you. I don't understand why the others would help, would want to share you with me."

"You deserve your freedom," I said, shrugging. *And I love you.*

"I enjoy hurting you."

I smiled a little at that. "I enjoy being hurt, Constantine." I wet my lips, stroked his back through Nireas's stolen shirt. "It will hurt me more to watch you walk out that door than any touch from Con ever could."

Constantine's frown deepened, and a flash of blue rushed over his cheeks.

"I'm not saying you shouldn't leave. I just... There's a difference between action and sensation, is all. You've never hurt me with your actions," I said.

Constantine's head dipped and I rose to my toes, meeting that soft and curious kiss with a gentle whimper.

Don't leave me.

"I'll hurt you when I leave?" he asked, still frowning, brow furrowed.

I nodded, trying to keep my voice calm, even. "The pain will pass when you return."

I reached up and smoothed my fingers over the lines of his face, making it as impassive and cool as it was when I'd first met him. I pressed another quick kiss to his lips, offered him a weak and limping smile.

"You'll come back," I said, more for my own sake, forcing my hands to not clench around him.

"I will," he answered, the plain nature of the words a surprising comfort. He was certain of the fact, even if I wasn't.

I took the kiss he offered and clung to his shoulders—not too tightly, even when I wanted to strangle him to me. And in spite of Constantine's claims of leaving, we remained in the embrace through the chiming hour mark of the grandfather clock, lips grazing, tongues caressing, simply breathing one another in for long stretches of minutes.

Please don't leave me. I love you, my mind chanted. But the words felt like a bribe or a leash. So I pressed the meaning from my mouth to his without the structure of the letters. Spelled out affection with my hands running up and down his back, my need described in the press of my hips to his.

My back was to the wall when Constantine finally stepped away, our hands sliding together, palms kissing briefly. I watched

him walk to the door, then lift one of Hunter's hats to his head
—one that disguised his horns and the tone of his skin, but
didn't transform him into a comical little man—and met grey
eyes where there should've been gleaming silver. The door
opened, silent, and sunlight washed over my demon, blurred by
gathering tears. I didn't know if he looked back at me, or only
out at the street, but I watched his hazy figure pause at the
threshold, the cry and bustle of London spilling into the still
hall.

"Take care, sweet creature."

"Constan—" His name was whispered, broken by a gasping
sob, and then shuttered by the click of the door closing behind
him, the hall dark and quiet again. I swallowed the cry in my
throat and squeezed my eyes shut, fisting my hands at my sides. I
would not chase him, drag him back, beg him to stay.

He said he would return.

And I was not alone.

With a huff of breath and a swipe of my hands over my
cheeks, I marched up the stairs, back to the bedroom where my
lovers had spread out to fill the space I'd left. Constantine
leaving was the pain of heartbreak, yes, but this sight was the
blessing of another four hearts beating true and steady in my
chest.

I shed Hunter's robe, then the soiled shift, and found Ronan
watching me with a sleepy smile.

"Hello, nut."

The bite of sorrow, the honeyed lick of affection, married
together in my chest.

"I love you," I said, picking up another shift, slipping it on
over my head.

Ronan sat up abruptly, eyes blinking and growing wide. "You
what?"

"I love you," I repeated, frowning at him. Hunter had twisted
on the bed, confused and sleepy and beautifully mussed. "I love
you too. Is it okay to say it down a line like this, or is that rude?"

"What the fuck do I care, just keep saying it," Ronan said as
the others stirred awake.

Hunter frowned. "Little one, have you been crying?"

"I love you," I repeated to Ronan. "You persistent, darling, irksome, delicious man."

"You *have* been crying," Ronan said, scooting to the edge of the bed, now scowling.

"And I love you," I said to Hunter. "You dreadfully noble, exceptionally wild, marvelously deviant warrior."

Hunter relaxed, even as my throat grew tight.

Jude's eyebrows were raised expectantly, his lips twitching and brow creasing as I set my hands on my hips. "I love you, and I barely understand it because it feels like you're part of me, like someone cut us out of one cloth. And I barely know how to love myself most days, but loving you is exceptionally easy and somehow making it a bit easier to extend that—"

"Hazel, love, yes. Yes to every word of that. I love you, now come *here*," Jude pleaded.

Nireas's eyes were wide, his face pale, and I knew with a simple glance that he was bracing himself to be left out.

"And I've loved you for eight years, you *bastard*, for making me wait so long and then making it so horribly simple to forgive you!"

Ronan jumped up from the bed, scooping me into his arms as they all scrambled to meet us at the end of the bed.

"Hazel, what's happened?" Hunter asked.

"I love you, too," Nireas said, stroking my hips and shoulders and ankles with all six of his hands as they found a way to cradle me between the four of them. "I'll keep it very easy to continue to forgive me, I promise. I'll make it absolutely worth the eight years."

"Nut, what's wrong?"

"Can't you just say it back?" I whined.

"I love you!" all four of them shouted quickly.

"Where's Constantine?" Jude asked, lowering his voice to soothe me, his hand finding mine and drawing my knuckles to his lips, thumb stroking over my skin.

I tried to take a breath, but my chest was too tight, and I closed my eyes to their stares. "Please don't ever leave me," I whispered.

Hunter didn't hesitate. "Never, my love."

I sighed, sank into the mass of them, rode the gentle jostle of their bodies as they scooted us back to the head of the bed, keeping me tangled in their embrace.

"We'll never leave you," Hunter said, his claws dragging through my hair. "Never."

❧

FOR THE FIRST time in over eight years—maybe ever; I hadn't asked Nireas—The Company of Fiends canceled a show.

"Well, our rehearsals were ruined by all the hubbub, weren't they?" Mr. Reddy grouched, but the man had dark circles under his eyes and he was holding Myra close on his lap.

"We'll be back on tomorrow," I said, patting Mr. Reddy on his shoulder as I crossed to sit with Nireas and Ronan on the organ bench.

Jude and Hunter were in the wings behind us, holding a quiet discussion with Asterion, Marius the basilisk, Esther Reed, and her gentlemen.

"What's going to happen to all those poor people you brought with you?" Myra asked Reddy. "They're so frightened. The girls have them tucked away in the canteen, but they're absolutely terrified of the monsters. They can't stay here."

Asterion rose from the seats, clearing his throat and giving Myra a small bow that drew a blush out on her cheek. "I'll be offering up my own home for their use. Their refuge. We'll have to find a few capable humans who can take care of the house and of their needs."

"I'd offer my own services, but I think we must leave soon. See if we can't find what route Birsha has taken in his escape," Dr. Underwood said.

"The only woman you're treating for hysteria is me," Esther muttered.

"His house in Paris was extensive, well-established," Auguste said, smirking as Underwood blushed. "At the very least, he would pass through France. We'll start there and work our way out."

"I could help at the house," Myra offered, her voice small.

"Don't be absurd," Reddy barked, and she straightened to glare at him. "What would the company do without you? You've made the pixies dependent. Woman, you've made *me* dependent. I can't spare you!"

I hid my smile against Ronan's shoulder, squeezing one of Nireas's hand in mine as Myra's cheeks went pink. She grasped Reddy's face in two hands and pulled him close for a noisy kiss, Reddy scowling at her for a moment before his eyes fell shut and his arms wrapped around her. The couple settled, Myra resting her head on Reddy's shoulder, and he resumed his glaring at everyone else.

"And don't ask about my girls. They can help out if they like, but the theater won't have shows without them," Reddy said to Asterion as their party from the wings broke up.

Jude and Hunter appeared at the organ, sitting at the edge of the stage and leaning back into our tangle of legs.

Asterion puffed and considered Reddy for a moment of thought. "Perhaps Mortimer might be able to—"

"I can help."

I had to lean forward to stare back into the wings of the stage to see her. Isabella walked out slowly. Her cheek was bruised, her throat too—Eston's work, no doubt—and she looked tired and frightened and nervous, but her shoulders were straight.

"I'd like to help them," she said, her voice a little ragged. "And I...I was never very good here, anyway. I know I can't leave this world. And maybe one day, I won't mind that. But in the meantime, I'd like to help those people. I *can* help them, if you let me."

"Good girl, lovey," Myra murmured.

Asterion offered Isabella a bow, just as he had for Myra, although his eyes were slightly narrowed. He hadn't witnessed the scene here the night before, but perhaps he had his own suspicions about the young woman.

"I offer my gratitude," he said simply.

Ronan cleared his throat, gathering their attention. "Is that it, then? Do we believe Birsha's gone into hiding and that'll be the end of our trouble?" he asked.

"No," Marius said immediately. "You never turn your back on an enemy like Birsha."

Asterion nodded. "Until we know for certain Birsha is dead, we remain vigilant, we guard the vulnerable, and we rightfully blacken his reputation to others."

"And we hunt him," Conall growled, crossing to stand with Asterion. "We don't cease until we've caught and killed him."

I reached for Hunter's hand, finding it already rising back to meet mine. Jude leaned between Ronan's and my thighs. Nireas's arms wove over my back with Ronan's arm, and I managed a moment of peace, even in the wake of Conall's dark words.

Whatever role I took now, company girl or ferocious monster, I did so with these men at my side.

47.

ENCORE

"It's getting better," Isabella said, bustling by me, her arms loaded with baskets of groceries. "At least for most of them."

I glanced up at the balcony, where a young woman watched us from a shadowy doorway. Nireas and Ronan waited outside in the carriage when I made my visits to Grace House, the refuge in the woods Asterion had gifted to the humans we'd recovered after the destruction of the Seven Veils.

Grace House was gifted, protected, and provided for by monsters, but none were welcome within its walls.

"How many are still missing?" Evie whispered.

Isabella sighed, her eyes counting the contents of the basket. I liked this new version of the young woman. She had dozens to care for here at Grace House, and any prejudice she'd held against monsters seemed to have vanished or was managed well under the terms of the house. She and a few women sent by Magdalena Mortimer kept a kind of boarding house, nurturing and comforting those lives tormented by Birsha and his clients. It kept the monster's secrets safe, yes, but gave the humans peace too.

"Asterion thinks another half-dozen at least," Isabella said. "A few of the residents say it's more, but they also aren't...aren't positive how many Birsha killed before he left."

I winced at the news. I knew from Hunter that Asterion had been searching the streets of London for weeks and had managed to catch more than a few girls huddling in doorways at night or turning nervous tricks in alleyways. Jude had also been checking with hospitals and asylums for word of any potential escapees.

"Everyone says that no matter what, as long as they aren't with Birsha, they're better off," Isabella murmured. Her shoulders squared, and she patted the basket we'd brought her. "Thank you for this. The fruit looks beautiful. We've been having some cooking lessons when we're up to it. Perhaps it's time for a pie."

"We'll leave you to it," I said, glancing up at the balcony again. I liked to visit Grace House, but I could tell I made the humans here almost as nervous as the monsters did. Some had seen me that night at the Seven Veils. Others just knew I consorted with monsters.

It'd been just over a month now since we'd attacked Birsha's house, and there was still no sign of retribution from the man. Esther Reed had sent word that they'd caught his trail on their way to France, but lost it again in Paris. As far as any of us knew, our victory would only be a temporary reprieve. It didn't stop me from feeling a little smug that it'd lasted so long already.

Evie and I made our goodbyes to Isabella and stepped out into the balmy night together. London was warming up in summer, and with that came an unfortunate odor. I wrinkled my nose, and Ronan grinned at me through the glass of the carriage as Goliath waited for Evie at the bottom of the steps, hidden in his human disguise.

"I think I might talk him into staying with me tonight," Evie mused, wearing a sly smile as she walked down the steps of Grace House toward the yeti.

"That'd be...what...the third time this month?" I teased.

"Fifth," Evie said.

My eyebrows raised. Evie and Goliath both had a long history of sampling all the company might have to offer them. It would be a surprise to see them settle together...but perhaps they might continue their sampling as a joint effort. Or maybe they'd just found each other as the right flavors.

"Will you be at rehearsal tomorrow?" Evie asked.

"I think I'll stay home, actually. Jude should be done at the precinct at last," I said.

"Ooh, celebrations *are* in order then," Evie said, grinning. We stopped on the last step and she leaned in, kissing my cheek. "Night then, Haze."

"Night."

Ronan opened the carriage door for me, pulling me inside and onto his lap, Nireas rolling his eyes across from us.

"How are they?" Ronan asked.

"Same as usual, I think, but Isabella seems satisfied," I said.

"Good for her," Nireas murmured, leaning forward and picking my heels up off the floor to rest in his lap. "Now, let's get home before Withes starts to fret about dinner."

I smiled, leaning back as my eyes fell shut. It had been harder than I'd expected to say goodbye to my flat in Stepney Green, so much so that Hunter had almost insisted I keep it. But as I'd locked the door for the final time last week, there'd been relief too. I'd kept my promise to my father for his entire life, stayed with him, cared for him. I didn't need to keep that vow to my own death too. It was time to move on.

"It's been a month," I murmured, mostly to myself.

"No sign of the bastard yet," Ronan said. I flinched at the words, reaching toward my throat before dropping my hand, and Ronan's arms tightened around my waist. "Oh, nut. I'm sorry. You know I didn't mean—"

"I know," I said quickly, nodding.

Ronan had been thinking of Birsha, not Constantine. Not that there'd been any sign of the Gemini either. Not even a whisper, from what Conall had shared over dinner last week. Constantine was free and...vanished. Even to monsters.

A whole month. *Only* a month. My head could never decide which interpretation hurt more. That he'd managed to stay away so long, or that he might very well continue on that way for months and even years more.

I stroked the back of Ronan's hands where they rested over my waist, and in spite of the brief ache of missing Constantine, I was reminded of one simple fact.

"I'm very happy," I said softly, opening my eyes as I smiled at Nireas.

"We know," Nireas said, smiling back.

Ronan kissed my temple, and we rested in quiet all the way back to Mayfair.

"AND HAVE you found an office for your new venture?" Hunter asked Jude over dessert.

Jude shook his head, his cheeks flushed from the whiskey we'd all shared in the library before dinner, and the wine drained from his glass.

"Not yet, although Asterion tells me Picadilly might be a good neighborhood."

Hunter hummed and nodded. "High monster population there. Easy traffic."

"But I think I'd like to take a little time first. Just a couple weeks, if that isn't trespassing on your generosity too much," Jude said.

Hunter huffed, brow furrowing and mouth curving down, and I hid my grin around the rim of my wine glass.

"My generosity?" Hunter asked.

Jude blushed again and glanced around the table. "You know. You've welcomed us all into your home and—"

"Our home."

"—and I'd like to be able to contribute. I don't take you for granted, Hunter," Jude said, stumbling over the words slightly.

It was Hunter's turn to blush, his spoon stabbing at his empty bowl. "You—we're a family," he grumbled.

"So long as you don't mind," Jude said, grinning.

Hunter shifted in his chair. "I don't."

"You're all very cute," I said.

Hunter's cheeks darkened another shade further, but he relaxed at last. At least until Ronan spoke.

"I told you," he said to Jude. "Hunter is Daddy."

I choked on my bite of sorbet, and Nireas hid his grin behind one hand, patting me gently on the back with another.

"I am not—" Hunter blustered.

"He's the head of our family," Nireas said before Ronan could embarrass Hunter any further.

I looked up from my bowl just in time to see Ronan's lips twitching, no doubt with wicked arguments. I shook my head once as he opened his mouth, eyes glittering, but we were all saved by the sudden ringing of the doorbell.

I rose from my chair, eager for the interruption, and all four men followed.

"Withes will answer," Hunter said.

"Yes, but I want to know who it is. Only exciting visitors come at dinnertime," I said.

Hunter crossed to beat me to the doorway of the dining room, the others crowding at our back.

"At this rate, we might as well answer it," Ronan hissed as we waited together for the butler to reach the door.

Withes did so with heavy steps, dark wings at his back, his usual solemn expression in place. I'd managed to crack a smile on his lips once or twice, mostly by asking after the egg he and his wife were waiting on to hatch—only three more years left, and Withes was fairly certain their child would be a girl. He was eager to try for another in the next decade. Gargoyles were a very patient race, apparently.

I was not, and I slid under Hunter's arm, walking down the hall as Withes opened the door. I couldn't hear our visitor from the hall, but Withes bowed to him and stepped back, allowing them entrance. Probably Conall or Asterion.

Except those weren't Asterion's curling horns, and that wasn't Conall's shawl wrapped around those familiar shoulders.

It was mine.

"Constantine," I gasped, freezing in the hall.

The door closed, and Constantine's head turned as he lifted his hat, those molten silver eyes finding me immediately. He stepped forward, paused, and then marched swiftly in my direction.

This was not the demon who had left me a month ago. There were no stiff movements, no awkward hunch and shift to his shoulders. He was free, and he was practically charging at me.

And I realized with one brief, stunned blink that I wasn't surprised to see him. I'd *known* he would return. He had promised as much, and even though every experience of my life up until quite recently had proven otherwise, I'd known he would come back to me.

I ran for him, even though it was barely a few feet of distance, and the collision stole my breath from my lungs. The sensations struck me in a wave of relief; spice and sticky sugar, his tall, hard body, those long arms snatching me off my feet to press my breasts to his broad chest. His mouth met mine, our eyes still open, pools of starlight glaring down at me, and I wanted to laugh but he felt too good. Determined, tender, and fierce. His clutch around me was almost brutal, like he was trying to fuse us together the way Con and Antin did.

And as if he'd read my mind, they appeared, Antin's mouth on my throat making me liquid in Con's arms. Con's brow touched mine, and I let out a garbled cry as I came, a sudden, rude *boom* of sensation rocking through my body, my hands limp and core clenching on nothing.

They melded back together, and Constantine soothed my shudders with light kisses along my jaw.

"I told you I didn't understand," Constantine whispered, setting me down on my toes, still holding me upright, finding my gaze. So direct, and somehow calmer too. "I do now. I love you, Hazel Nix. I love your courage and your fear. I love your openness and all your secrets. I love your selfish heart and your generous mind. I love that you saved me and then let me leave, even though it was a useless endeavor."

"It wasn't useless," I murmured, my palms pressed to his chest, aware of the rough and uneven drum of his heartbeat under my touch. It wasn't useless if it gave Constantine this new confidence or all these perfect words to say.

He smiled, and it made me gasp. I'd forgotten how beautiful he really was, what that smile could do to my knees. "It *was* useless. All I thought about was you—the puzzle I couldn't rest until I'd solved. And then it was only worse, because I suddenly understood why a woman so good, so beautiful, so eager to be pleasured, would go to so much trouble to save me, free me."

"I love you," I said, voice cracking.

"Yes," Constantine said, grinning, dazzling me. "That's what I realized. Thank you for giving me time to discover it on my own."

A small whine rose up in my throat, and Constantine stifled it with another kiss, clasping me to his chest. His mouth was patient and hungry over mine, suckling on my lips, pressing and breathing with me. He pulled away, nose stroking against mine.

"I love your pleasure and your pain, sweet creature," Constantine murmured. "Just as you love mine."

"Yes," I said, trying to climb back into his arms, lifting my chin and pleading for another kiss. "I need them. Need you. Always come back to me."

Constantine stood straight, and I growled because his mouth was now out of reach. His thumb stroked my cheek. "How about I won't leave again without you?" He looked over my shoulder and smiled at the others, dipping his head in greeting. "Without any of you."

"Welcome home, Constantine," Hunter said.

I sighed, turning and beaming back at my orc in gratitude.

"Are you hungry? We just finished dinner," Ronan said.

Constantine shook his head slowly, eyes falling slowly back to me. "Only for one thing."

I shivered at his stare, that feral glare so familiar—Con's need for contact, connection. I'd thought he'd wanted to hurt me the first time I saw him. I knew better now. He'd wanted desperately to bring pleasure, had thought it impossible.

Not with me.

"We'll give you some time together then. She's missed you," Nireas said.

"No," Constantine said, smiling down at me.

"No?" I asked, glaring back at him.

He looked up to the others. "All of us together. Our nymph deserves her feast. Don't you, sweet creature?" he asked, stroking fingers over my pulse, that heavy, vibrant touch calling forth an eager pulse from my core.

"Together," I said, nodding. Because he wasn't leaving again. I didn't need a private reunion. I needed my men, needed my entire family together at once.

"I'll get the harnesses," Jude said.

&

HOT SLICK SPLASHED against my chest as I moaned, squirming on Hunter's cock buried deep in my ass. Nireas's fingers stroked over my breasts, drummed over my clit, curled and plunged in my cunt, playing me like a piece of music. Perhaps I was one.

The sun was coming up, and I'd had no more than a handful of minutes for rest in the night. Constantine *loved* the harness. He'd used Hunter's leash for me on my back, pulling me onto Con's cock as I slurped over Antin's length, guzzling down arousal as I gushed and screamed for them.

And now Con had Ronan held up by the collar, the pair of them kneeling on either side of me, Con stroking his foreskin over the head of Ronan's cock, the imp howling in giddy pain. Antin stroked Ronan's back, ruby red foreskin wrapped around Jude's length, keeping the ravaged fae up by a one-handed grip on my leather harness. It looked pretty on Jude. Jude looked even better, face flushed and skin slick with sweat, in what I thought must've been his dozenth orgasm, a thick pool of cum spilled onto my belly.

That's so creative, I thought, my own body somewhat numb aside from the occasional thrill at Nireas's fingers. I blinked and tipped my head, watching Con thrust three fingers into Jude's slack mouth, Jude's eyes growing wide and alert again as he screamed and bit down.

Hunter's tusks rubbed at my throat, his bucking beneath me growing uneven.

"Make her come, Nireas," Hunter growled. "One last time."

Ronan had pulled away from Con, who was jerking himself to his finish over my breasts, and twisted to wrap his lips around Antin's nipple. The pair of them and Jude came together one last time, and I giggled at the profane mess they made on me, on each other. Filthy and scorching. Hunter or Nireas would bathe me later, always so gentle after they'd put me through my paces in bed.

Jude had barely fallen backwards into the mattress when Nireas spread my thighs wide, plunging deep where his fingers had been, his thumb rubbing determinedly on my clit. I howled and arched, thrust myself into the stuffed sensation. So complete, so full, so utterly and devotedly destroyed by these men.

"So good! So good, yes," I gasped.

Con and Antin settled on either side of me, bending their heads to suck on my nipples, perfectly in contrast, driving me mad. My arms wrapped up to clutch them closer, a sob of relief and a scream of pleasure blending together.

Hunter growled, barely moving as Nireas fucked me, rough and hard, grunting above me, seeking his own finish with a rare selfish quality I loved to watch. But I was too busy falling apart. I would enjoy the view another time. For now, I gave myself over to the storm rushing through me.

"Yes! Yes, fuck! I love you," I cried out, and then babbled nonsense as I crashed into the rapture, stretched and filled and shivering at the heady rush of heat and electric pleasure racing through my muscles and veins.

Con and Antin untangled my hands from their horns, pulling away with final kisses. Hunter growled in my ear as Nireas slammed deep, stilled, and together they burst inside of me.

They'd barely finished, and I was still stiff with my release when I spoke. "No more. No more. I'm dead."

Ronan huffed and rolled over at my side as Constantine unified and stretched next to him. "Finally. I thought you'd never quit."

Nireas moaned, collapsing against me, and then stiffened, letting out a soft sound of disgust. "You know you can't challenge her like that," he muttered, rolling to the side, making Ronan scoot away or be crushed.

"Please always challenge her like that," Hunter mumbled, turning and spooning my back, nuzzling my throat as he softened in my ass.

I caught my breath, nestled between them, Jude unapologetically wrapping an arm over Hunter to clasp my hand. I hummed, blinked at the ceiling, and then stretched up briefly just to count them. All five. All five, here with me. For good this time. And in a bed that took up the majority of the room to fit us all properly.

Constantine blinked sleepily at me, smiling, his arm resting over Ronan, cupping the dark cock between red thighs, looking outrageously content and only a little confused. He was still accepting us all for what we were—not his owners or jailers, but friends and lovers now, his family. It would take time, but he was here, just as he'd promised.

"I need a bath," I murmured.

Hunter hummed, a heavy, sleepy sound, and Nireas kissed my cheek. "My turn," he said, gathering me carefully into his arms.

"Can I join you?" Constantine asked.

Nireas nodded. "She gets very slippery in the bath. Doesn't do a lick of work for herself," he teased.

I snorted, staring down at the tangle of men we'd left on the bed, all glossy with sweat, a little stained with their own releases. So satisfied.

Not a lick of work indeed, I thought, fiercely proud of their exhaustion.

"Oh!" I cried out, stiffening in Nireas's arms as the idea struck me.

"What's wrong?" Constantine asked, jumping up.

"Nothing! I just realized what a good juggling act that would make for the company," I said, grinning.

Ronan blinked one bleary eye open. "What? All eight hours of fucking?"

I laughed as Nireas carried me toward the bathroom. "Just the last half hour will do, if you're up for it."

Ronan grumbled and muttered something about "insatiable nymph appetites," rolling over in the bed and promptly starting to snore.

"Reddy doesn't deserve a mind as wicked as yours," Nireas said.

"Nor do we," Constantine said.

"Too bad. You lot are stuck with me now," I said, a riotous joy bubbling in my chest at the truth of the words.

"And lucky as kings for it, nymph," Nireas whispered in my ear. "We won't forget it."

I know, I thought, soft and content in four arms, in a pretty house in Mayfair, and in the hearts of my lovers. *I won't forget my luck either*.

EPILOGUE

"Stars above, look at that," Ronan breathed out.

I pursed my lips and wiggled my nose, trying to inch the blindfold over my eyes upwards. "I *can't*."

Nireas chuckled, hands cupped around my hips, elbows, and shoulders, guiding me gently forward over the crunch of fine pebbles. I rolled my neck on my shoulders, and Nireas's fingers at my elbow trailed down to my wrists, helping me stretch in place.

We'd been traveling by carriage for the better part of three days, visiting monster acquaintances in the evenings to rest our heads, but I was sore and eager to see our destination at last. I sucked in a deep breath, and my eyes widened behind the mask.

"Oh!" I gasped as my head connected with the wildness that surrounded us, the ancient woods so close at hand, the warm flavors of earth and life sweetened on my tongue. I tried to reach for the cloth covering my eyes, but Nireas stopped me.

"Wait, little one," Hunter warned.

"It's worth it, love," Jude said.

We shuffled along together, the chuff of horses at my ear briefly before we reached some unknown stopping point. A great creak and groan of heavily burdened hinges sounded ahead of me. I jumped as hands reached for the blindfold's tie, Hunter's summer scent blending in with our surroundings.

A soft kiss pressed to my forehead, and then I was blinking against the glare of daylight, squinting to study the mass of shadow I'd been placed in front of. My lips parted slowly as my vision cleared.

"My god, it's a *mansion*," I breathed, gaping.

"It's...a country house," Hunter said.

I let out a panicked cackle of laughter at the thought of this *behemoth* of a building being referred to as either *country* or *house*. Constantine stood in the open doorway, smiling back at me, beckoning me inside.

Nireas nudged me forward, and I shook my head.

"You don't like it?" Hunter asked, face falling immediately.

"What? No, I—Give me a moment to *look*," I said, laughing and reaching out to squeeze Hunter's hands.

The *country house* was a massive, dressed stone building, with peaked gable roofs and brightly painted bay windows. Dozens and dozens of windows glimmered in the sunlight, and more roofs and hints of wings rose up behind, with a square tower and a battlement like something that ought to sit on a castle. I caught a glimpse of a beautifully carved dark wood banister through the open doors, and then my gaze snapped in an entirely new direction to a little thatched roof outbuilding. There was so much to look at!

Hunter was rattling off information, and I caught the thread only at the very end. "...and over a dozen bedrooms, so we'll have plenty of room to entertain."

"Dozen?" I cried.

"Come and see for yourself, sweet creature," Constantine called, laughing.

"Asterion and his lot will come to visit. Esther too, when she and her men can manage the trip," Jude said.

"This is madness," I said.

"You don't like it," Hunter repeated.

I laughed again and hurried forward, wrapping my arm around my orc's and tugging him along in my tide. "Quit telling me I don't like it! I'm just *shocked*, Hunter. It's incredible. It's overwhelming, but in a good way."

Hunter huffed, but his shoulders straightened and his steps joined mine in their urgency to explore.

"It's a long way from London," Nireas noted as we stepped inside, pausing together in a cluster as our eyes adjusted.

"Reddy has more than enough new acts," I said, drifting forward on my own to gape up the stairs. Lord, there were so many stairs. And every intricately carved bit of wood gleamed with polish. "We could cut back to one weekend a month. Would your business be able to spare you?" I asked Hunter.

He nodded, watching me with bright eyes as I explored. "I am disentangling myself from some of the businesses. It's time for my gentleman persona to seek retirement, after all. We can keep the Mayfair house, it's well-protected, but it might be best to find a new base for us together."

I nodded, licking my lips and stepping slowly into the next room, my breath still in my chest. This was as much a museum as it was a home. The floors were striped in two shades of wood, the ceilings bearing detailed crown molding and the ornamentation of wooden blooms on every panel. The walls were papered in a deep emerald shade sprinkled with jewel-toned birds. And this wasn't even a sitting room or a dining room, just an antechamber to pass through on the way to somewhere more significant.

Sunlight shone through dappled glass windows, and I closed my eyes as I stepped into their rays. Behind me, my men waited.

"It's so quiet here," I murmured, smiling. "Peaceful."

"We're overdue for a bit of peace," Ronan said, and I nodded.

I opened my eyes again, marveled at another gloriously decorated, incredibly lavish room through a broad doorway. Over a dozen bedrooms around here somewhere, and probably more for hosting to be explored. But really, the rooms weren't what called to me.

I turned slowly and smiled at Hunter. "You know what I want to see most?" I asked.

"The bed?" Ronan asked.

"The stage?" Jude suggested.

I blinked. "There's a stage?!"

"Private performances," Nireas said, waggling his eyebrows.

Constantine turned and smiled at Hunter. "Show her."

Hunter nodded and sighed. "I do, little one. Follow me."

It was as good a way to take a tour of the house as any, our slow procession through a fully stocked library, a bright and airy dining room, a darkly feminine sitting room. There were gaps in the interior, places for us to fill the space with our own touches and belongings, and even rooms I could imagine redecorating as the lady of the house, but the estate came more than well provided for as it was.

None of it mattered—or no, it mattered *less* than our destination.

My eyes were wide, lips parted, as we reached an amply furnished study that looked over the back of the estate and its wild gardens. And the *woods*.

"Oh, *Hunter*," I whispered as he opened the broad doors to the stone patio.

"Fifty acres, little one," Hunter said gently.

Fifty acres in the Forest of Dean. A house with rooms to host friends. The loves of my life at my side.

The trees sang with birdsong and patient greetings, warm words of welcome. I walked out over the stone patio with blind eyes, the world blurring behind tears.

"She likes it," Ronan chuckled.

"I *love* it. Oh, it's—" I pressed my lips together, blinked my eyes clear, afraid to say the word, as if this home might be snatched out of my grasp before I had the chance to claim it.

"Ours," Hunter said, and I spun to face him. He was nervous, which was rare for Hunter now, but I remembered the old signs, his eyes narrowed and shoulders rising. "It's ours. I can sell it again if you've any objections, but I thought we might lose our chance if I didn't—"

"Perfect! Hunter, it's *perfect*," I said, throwing myself into his chest, pressing kisses into his beard, against the tusk at the corner of his mouth. "I love you. This is perfect. *Thank you*."

Hunter's rambles went silent, and he wrapped his arms around me.

"Oh, but what does everyone else think?" I asked, remembering that I was one of six.

Nireas laughed at the question, and Jude shook his head at me.

"It's perfect," Constantine said with a nod, not that any of them were likely to object now.

Good, I decided, selfishly pleased and equally assured that they didn't mind.

"When can we move in?" I asked, turning in Hunter's arms, leaning back against his chest.

"It's ours now. Withes and the others will do their best for us tonight, and we'll find enough staff for the house with no trouble," Hunter said. "As long as you are happy, this is our home now."

Happy. I snorted. I was happy with a kiss on the cheek, let alone a *country house* in the Forest of Dean.

With fifty acres.

Fifty acres of woods.

"Look at her. We'll be lucky to get her back inside by dinnertime," Nireas said.

My lips curved, and a wonderful idea brewed. This was our homecoming. Why not celebrate it? "You'll have to catch me," I said.

"Catch you?" Constantine repeated.

Hunter understood, his arms loosening and allowing me to slip free. I kicked my slippers off on the stone and ran down the stairs into the tidy, brief lawn of grass.

"Catch me," I said again, grinning over my shoulder, arching an eyebrow in invitation. "Hunt me, gentlemen. Winner may have his prize."

"Quick, don't give her a head start," Jude warned.

But it was too late. I was running, laughing, bolting into the trees already. A growl sounded behind me, and my heart raced as I darted through the woods. My home now. My home with my men.

"Hurry and catch me," I called to them, laughing.

Hurry and hide me, I whispered to the trees.

I reached for the buttons of my blouse. I would leave it and my skirt behind in the woods and lose the rest in the trees as my men gave chase, hunting the nymph they loved, their monstrous girl.

The End

AFTERWORD

Dear Reader,

Are you in need of more monsters and their lady loves? Curious about men like Asterion and Conall, or what happened to some of those people who escaped the Seven Veils? Don't worry, there's one more book in the main Tempting Monsters series left!! If you want to stay in touch and be the first to read teasers and learn about the characters of the upcoming Sanctuary with Kings, Tempting Monsters Book Three, I highly recommend joining my Facebook group Kathryn's Moongazers!

Speaking of curious monsters, were you intrigued by Marius the Basilisk? Get to know both him and his lady love in **The Basilisk of Star Manor**, a Tempting Monsters novella — now available in the upcoming Wolves and Warriors anthology!

Much love in the meantime,
Kathryn Moon

SERIES IN PROGRESS

Sweet Pea Mysteries

The Baker's Guide To Risky Rituals

The Knitter's Guide to Banishing Boyfriends

Tempting Monsters

A Lady of Rooksgrave Manor

The Company of Fiends

ACKNOWLEDGMENTS

Thank you to:

Jodie-Leigh, my incredible cover designer and delightful enabler.

Jess Whetsel my keen-eyed and word-wise editor. Meghan Leigh Daigle, my precise proofreader.

The BetaQueens: Desiree, Helen, Jami, Jess, Kathryn, Ash, and crunch time hero Mallorie!

The Cinnamons who I fell in love with while listening to Alex's lovely Scottish accent giggle through Rooksgrave!

My amazing Moongazers who cheer on each and every kinky and playful step. TikTokers who found Rooksgrave and made it blow up well beyond a success I even knew how to imagine!

My writing pack, made up of the most amazing women a girl could be lucky enough to know and get to talk to regularly!

And finally, my amazing family and close friends who cheer for me so hard their arms must be super tired from waving the pompoms like that. I'm incredibly lucky to share my life and my work with so many amazing people, and just like Hazel, I intend not to forget it!

ABOUT THE AUTHOR

USA Today Best Selling Author Kathryn Moon, is a country mouse who started dictating stories to her mother at an early age. The fascination with building new worlds and discovering the lives of the characters who grew in her head never faltered, and she graduated college with a fiction writing degree. She loves writing women who are strong in their vulnerability, romances that are as affectionate as they are challenging, and worlds that a reader sinks into and never wants to leave. When her hands aren't busy typing they're probably knitting sweaters or crimping pie crust in Ohio. She definitely believes in magic.

You can reach her on Facebook and at ohkathrynmoon@ gmail.com or you can sign up for her newsletter!